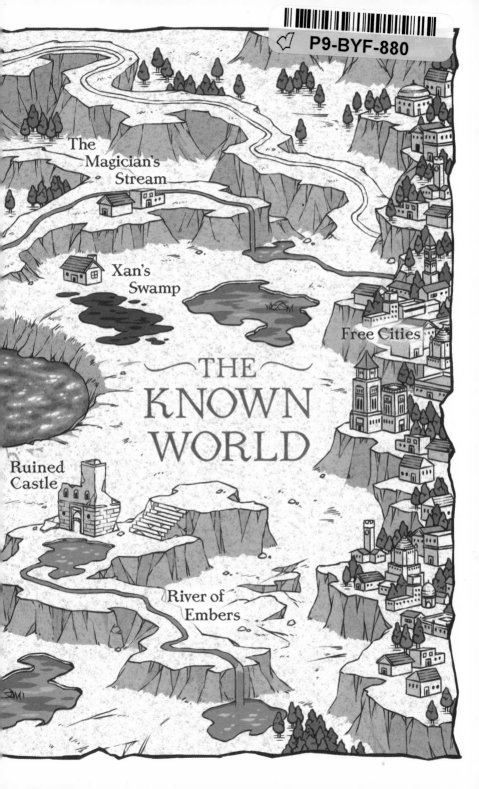

The
Magician's
Stream

Xan's
Swamp

THE
KNOWN
WORLD

Free Cities

Ruined
Castle

River of
Embers

# The Girl Who Drank the Moon

Kelly Barnhill

ALGONQUIN YOUNG READERS • 2019

*For Ted,*
*with love.*

∽

Published by
Algonquin Young Readers
an imprint of Algonquin Books of Chapel Hill
Post Office Box 2225
Chapel Hill, North Carolina 27515-2225

a division of
Workman Publishing
225 Varick Street
New York, New York 10014

First gift edition, Algonquin Young Readers, October 2019.
Originally published in hardcover by Algonquin Young Readers in August 2016.
Printed in the United States of America.
Published simultaneously in Canada by Thomas Allen & Son Limited.
Design by Carla Weise.
The short story "In Which a Lost Girl Discovers Bees"
originally appeared on EW.com in July 2016.

LIBRARY OF CONGRESS CATALOGING-IN-PUBLICATION DATA
Names: Barnhill, Kelly Regan, author.
Title: The girl who drank the moon / Kelly Barnhill.
Description: First edition. | Chapel Hill, North Carolina :
Algonquin Young Readers, 2016. | "Published simultaneously in Canada by
Thomas Allen & Son Limited"—Title page verso. | Audience: 4 to 6. | Summary:
"An epic fantasy about a young girl raised by a witch, a swamp monster, and
a Perfectly Tiny Dragon, who must unlock the powerful magic buried
deep inside her"—Provided by publisher.
Identifiers: LCCN 2016006542 | ISBN 9781616205676
Subjects: LCSH: Witches—Juvenile fiction. | Magic—Juvenile fiction. |
Friendship in children—Juvenile fiction. | CYAC: Witches—Fiction. | Magic—
Fiction. | Friendship—Fiction. | Fantasy. | LCGFT: Fantasy fiction.
Classification: LCC PZ7.B26663 Gi 2016 | DDC [Fic]—dc23
LC record available at http://lccn.loc.gov/2016006542

ISBN 978-1-61620-997-1 (gift edition)

10 9 8 7 6 5 4 3 2 1
First Gift Edition

# 1

## In Which a Story Is Told

Yes.

There is a witch in the woods. There has always been a witch.

Will you stop your fidgeting for once? My stars! I have never seen such a fidgety child.

No, sweetheart, I have not seen her. No one has. Not for ages. We've taken steps so that we will never see her.

Terrible steps.

Don't make me say it. You already know, anyway.

Oh, I don't know, darling. No one knows why she wants children. We don't know why she insists that it must always be the very youngest among us. It's not as though we could just ask her. She hasn't been seen. We make sure that she will not be seen.

Of course she exists. What a question! Look at the woods! So dangerous! Poisonous smoke and sinkholes and boiling geysers and terrible dangers every which way. Do you think it is so by accident? Rubbish! It was the Witch, and if we don't do as she says, what will become of us?

You really need me to explain it?

I'd rather not.

Oh, hush now, don't cry. It's not as though the Council of Elders is coming for you, now is it. You're far too old.

From our family?

Yes, dearest. Ever so long ago. Before you were born. He was a beautiful boy.

Now finish your supper and see to your chores. We'll all be up early tomorrow. The Day of Sacrifice waits for no one, and we must all be present to thank the child who will save us for one more year.

Your brother? How could I fight for him? If I had, the Witch would have killed us all and then where would we be? Sacrifice one or sacrifice all. That is the way of the world. We couldn't change it if we tried.

Enough questions. Off with you. Fool child.

# 2

## In Which an Unfortunate Woman Goes Quite Mad

Grand Elder Gherland took his time that morning. The Day of Sacrifice only came once a year, after all, and he liked to look his best during the sober procession to the cursed house, and during the somber retreat. He encouraged the other Elders to do the same. It was important to give the populace a show.

He carefully dabbed rouge on his sagging cheeks and lined his eyes with thick streaks of kohl. He checked his teeth in the mirror, ensuring they were free of debris or goop. He loved that mirror. It was the only one in the Protectorate. Nothing gave Gherland more pleasure than the possession of a thing that was unique unto him. He liked being *special*.

The Grand Elder had ever so many possessions that were unique in the Protectorate. It was one of the perks of the job.

The Protectorate—called the Cattail Kingdom by some and the City of Sorrows by others—was sandwiched between a treacherous forest on one side and an enormous bog on the other. Most people in the Protectorate drew their livelihoods from the Bog. There was a future in bogwalking, mothers told their children. Not much of a future, you understand, but it was better than nothing. The Bog was full of Zirin shoots in the spring and Zirin flowers in the summer and Zirin bulbs in the fall—in addition to a wide array of medicinal and borderline magical plants that could be harvested, prepared, treated, and sold to the Traders from the other side of the forest, who in turn transported the fruits of the Bog to the Free Cities, far away. The forest itself was terribly dangerous, and navigable only by the Road.

And the Elders owned the Road.

Which is to say that Grand Elder Gherland owned the Road, and the other Elders had their cut. The Elders owned the Bog, too. And the orchards. And the houses. And the market squares. Even the garden plots.

This was why the families of the Protectorate made their shoes out of reeds. This was why, in lean times, they fed their children the thick, rich broth of the Bog, hoping that the Bog would make them strong.

This was why the Elders and their families grew big and strong and rosy-cheeked on beef and butter and beer.

The door knocked.

"Enter," Grand Elder Gherland mumbled as he adjusted the drape of his robe.

It was Antain. His nephew. An Elder-in-Training, but only because Gherland, in a moment of weakness, had promised the ridiculous boy's more ridiculous mother. But that was unkind. Antain was a nice enough young man, nearly thirteen. He was a hard worker and a quick study. He was good with numbers and clever with his hands and could build a comfortable bench for a tired Elder as quick as breathing. And, despite himself, Gherland had developed an inexplicable, and growing, fondness for the boy.

But.

Antain had big ideas. Grand notions. And *questions*. Gherland furrowed his brow. Antain was—how could he put it? *Overly keen.* If this kept up, he'd have to be dealt with, blood or no. The thought of it weighed upon Gherland's heart, like a stone.

"UNCLE GHERLAND!" Antain nearly bowled his uncle over with his insufferable enthusiasm.

"Calm yourself, boy!" the Elder snapped. "This is a solemn occasion!"

The boy calmed visibly, his eager, doglike face tilted toward the ground. Gherland resisted the urge to pat him gently on the head. "I have been sent," Antain continued in a mostly soft voice, "to tell you that the other Elders are ready. And all the populace waits along the route. Everyone is accounted for."

"Each one? There are no shirkers?"

"After last year, I doubt there ever will be again," Antain said with a shudder.

"Pity." Gherland checked his mirror again, touching up his rouge. He rather enjoyed teaching the occasional lesson to the citizens of the Protectorate. It clarified things. He tapped the sagging folds under his chin and frowned. "Well, Nephew," he said with an artful swish of his robes, one that had taken him over a decade to perfect. "Let us be off. That baby isn't going to sacrifice itself, after all." And he flowed into the street with Antain stumbling at his heels.

✤

Normally, the Day of Sacrifice came and went with all the pomp and gravity that it ought. The children were given over without protest. Their numb families mourned in silence, with pots of stew and nourishing foods heaped into their kitchens, while the comforting arms of neighbors circled around them to ease their bereavement.

Normally, no one broke the rules.

But not this time.

Grand Elder Gherland pressed his lips into a frown. He could hear the mother's howling before the procession turned onto the final street. The citizens began to shift uncomfortably where they stood.

When they arrived at the family's house, an astonishing sight met the Council of Elders. A man with a scratched-up face and a swollen lower lip and bloody bald spots across his skull where his hair had been torn out in clumps met them at the door. He tried to smile, but his tongue went instinctively to the gap where a tooth had just recently been. He sucked in his lips and attempted to bow instead.

"I am sorry, sirs," said the man—the father, presumably. "I don't know what has gotten into her. It's like she's gone mad."

From the rafters above them, a woman screeched and howled as the Elders entered the house. Her shiny black hair flew about her head like a nest of long, writhing snakes. She hissed and spat like a cornered animal. She clung to the ceiling beams with one arm and one leg, while holding a baby tightly against her breast with the other arm.

"GET OUT!" she screamed. "You *cannot* have her. I spit on your faces and curse your names. Leave my home at once, or I shall tear out your eyes and throw them to the crows!"

The Elders stared at her, openmouthed. They couldn't *believe* it. No one fought for a doomed child. It simply wasn't *done*.

(Antain alone began to cry. He did his best to hide it from the adults in the room.)

Gherland, thinking fast, affixed a kindly expression on his

craggy face. He turned his palms toward the mother to show her that he meant no harm. He gritted his teeth behind his smile. All this kindness was nearly killing him.

"We are not taking her at all, my poor, misguided girl," Gherland said in his most patient voice. "The Witch is taking her. We are simply doing as we're told."

The mother made a guttural sound, deep in her chest, like an angry bear.

Gherland laid his hand on the shoulder of the perplexed husband and gave a gentle squeeze. "It appears, my good fellow, that you are right: your wife has gone mad." He did his best to cover his rage with a façade of concern. "A rare case, of course, but not without precedent. We must respond with compassion. She needs care, not blame."

"LIAR," the woman spat. The child began to cry, and the woman climbed even higher, putting each foot on parallel rafters and bracing her back against the slope of the roof, trying to position herself in such a way that she could remain out of reach while she nursed the baby. The child calmed instantly. "If you take her," she said with a growl, "I will find her. I will find her and take her back. You see if I won't."

"And face the Witch?" Gherland laughed. "All on your own? Oh, you pathetic, lost soul." His voice was honey, but his face was a glowing ember. "Grief has made you lose your senses. The shock has shattered your poor mind. No matter. We shall heal you, dear, as best we can. Guards!"

He snapped his fingers, and armed guards poured into the room. They were a special unit, provided as always by the Sisters of the Star. They wore bows and arrows slung across their backs and short, sharp swords sheathed at their belts. Their long braided hair looped around their waists, where it was cinched tight—a testament to their years of contemplation and combat training at the top of the Tower. Their faces were implacable as stones, and the Elders, despite their power and stature, edged away from them. The Sisters were a frightening force. Not to be trifled with.

"Remove the child from the lunatic's clutches and escort the poor dear to the Tower," Gherland ordered. He glared at the mother in the rafters, who had gone suddenly very pale. "The Sisters of the Star know what to do with broken minds, my dear. I'm sure it hardly hurts at all."

The Guard was efficient, calm, and utterly ruthless. The mother didn't stand a chance. Within moments, she was bound, hobbled, and carried away. Her howls echoed through the silent town, ending suddenly when the Tower's great wooden doors slammed shut, locking her inside.

The baby, on the other hand, once transferred into the arms of the Grand Elder, whimpered briefly and then turned her attention to the sagging face in front of her, all wobbles and creases and folds. She had a solemn look to her—calm, skeptical, and intense, making it difficult for Gherland to look away. She had black curls and black eyes. Luminous skin, like polished amber. In the center of her forehead, she had a birth-mark in the shape of a crescent moon. The mother had a similar mark. Common lore insisted that such people were special. Gherland disliked lore, as a general rule, and he certainly disliked it when citizens of the Protectorate got it in their heads to think themselves better than they were. He deepened his frown and leaned in close, wrinkling his brow. The baby stuck out her tongue.

*Horrible child,* Gherland thought.

"Gentlemen," he said with all the ceremony he could muster, "it is time." The baby chose this particular moment to let loose a large, warm, wet stain across the front of Gherland's robes. He pretended not to notice, but inwardly he fumed.

She had done it on purpose. He was sure of it. What a revolting baby.

The procession was, as usual, somber, slow, and insufferably plodding. Gherland felt he might go mad with impatience. Once the Protectorate's gates closed behind them, though, and the citizens returned with their melancholy broods of children to their drab little homes, the Elders quickened their pace.

"But why are we running, Uncle?" Antain asked.

"Hush, boy!" Gherland hissed. "And keep up!"

No one liked being in the forest, away from the Road. Not even the Elders. Not even Gherland. The area just outside the Protectorate walls was safe enough. In theory. But everyone knew someone who had accidentally wandered too far. And fell into a sinkhole. Or stepped in a mud pot, boiling off most of their skin. Or wandered into a swale where the air was bad, and never returned. The forest was dangerous.

They followed a winding trail to the small hollow surrounded by five ancient trees, known as the Witch's Handmaidens. Or six. *Didn't it used to be five?* Gherland glared at the trees, counted them again, and shook his head. There were six. No matter. The forest was just getting to him. Those trees were almost as old as the world, after all.

The space inside of the ring of trees was mossy and soft, and the Elders laid the child upon it, doing their best not to look at her. They had turned their backs on the baby and started to hurry away when their youngest member cleared his throat.

"So. We just leave her here?" Antain asked. "That's how it's done?"

"Yes, Nephew," Gherland said. "That is how it's done." He felt a sudden wave of fatigue settling on his shoulders like an ox's yoke. He felt his spine start to sag.

Antain pinched his neck—a nervous habit that he couldn't break. "Shouldn't we wait for the Witch to arrive?"

The other Elders fell into an uncomfortable silence.

"Come again?" Elder Raspin, the most decrepit of the Elders, asked.

"Well, surely . . ." Antain's voice trailed off. "Surely we must wait for the Witch," he said quietly. "What would become of us if wild animals came first and carried her off?"

The other Elders stared at the Grand Elder, their lips tight.

"Fortunately, Nephew," he said quickly, leading the boy away, "that has never been a problem."

"But—" Antain said, pinching his neck again, so hard he left a mark.

"But nothing," Gherland said, a firm hand on the boy's back, striding quickly down the well-trodden path.

And, one by one, the Elders filed out, leaving the baby behind.

They left knowing—all but Antain—that it was not a matter of *if* the child were eaten by animals, but rather that she surely *would be.*

They left her knowing that there surely *wasn't* a witch. There never *had* been a witch. There were only a dangerous forest and a single road and a thin grip on a life that the Elders had enjoyed for generations. The Witch—that is, the belief in her—made for a frightened people, a subdued people, a compliant people, who lived their lives in a saddened haze, the clouds of their grief numbing their senses and dampening their minds. It was terribly convenient for the Elders' unencumbered rule. Unpleasant, too, of course, but that couldn't be helped.

They heard the child whimper as they tramped through the trees, but the whimpering soon gave way to the swamp sighs and birdsong and the woody creaking of trees through-out the forest. And each Elder felt as sure as sure could be that the child wouldn't live to see the morning, and that they would never hear her, never see her, never think of her again.

They thought she was gone forever.

They were wrong, of course.

# 3

# In Which a Witch Accidentally Enmagics an Infant

At the center of the forest was a small swamp—bubbly, sulfury, and noxious, fed and warmed by an underground, restlessly sleeping volcano and covered with a slick of slime whose color ranged from poison green to lightning blue to blood red, depending on the time of year. On this day—so close to the Day of Sacrifice in the Protectorate, or Star Child Day everywhere else—the green was just beginning to inch its way toward blue.

At the edge of the swamp, standing right on the fringe of flowering reeds growing out of the muck, a very old woman leaned on a gnarled staff. She was short and squat and a bit bulbous about the belly. Her crinkly gray hair had been pulled back into a thick, braided knot, with leaves and flowers growing out of the thin gaps between the twisted plaits. Her face, despite its cloud of annoyance, maintained a brightness in those aged eyes and a hint of a smile in that flat, wide mouth. From certain angles, she looked a bit like a large, good-tempered toad.

Her name was Xan. And she was the Witch.

"Do you think you can hide from me, you ridiculous monster?" she bellowed at the swamp. "It isn't as though I don't know where you are. Resurface *this minute* and apologize." She pressed her expression into something closely resembling a scowl. *"Or I will make you."* Though she had no real power over the monster himself—he was far too old—she certainly had the power to make that swamp cough him up as if he were nothing more than a glob of phlegm in the back of the throat. She could do it with just a flick of her left hand and a jiggle of her right knee.

She attempted to scowl again.

"I MEAN IT," she hollered.

The thick water bubbled and swirled, and the large head of the swamp monster slurped out of the bluish-green. He blinked one wide eye, and then the other, before rolling both toward the sky.

"Don't you roll your eyes at me, young man," the old woman huffed.

"Witch," the monster murmured, his mouth still half-submerged in the thick waters of the swamp. "I am many centuries older than you." His wide lips blew a bubble in the algae slick. *Millennia, really,* he thought. *But who's counting?*

"I don't believe I like your tone." Xan puckered her wrinkled lips into a tight rosette in the middle of her face.

The monster cleared his throat. "As the Poet famously said, dear lady: '*I don't give a rat's*—'"

"GLERK!" the Witch shouted, aghast. "Language!"

"Apologies," Glerk said mildly, though he really didn't mean it. He eased both sets of arms onto the muck at the shore, pressing each seven-fingered hand into the shine of the mud. With a grunt, he heaved himself onto the grass. *This used to be easier,* he thought. Though, for the life of him, he couldn't remember when.

"Fyrian is over there by the vents, crying his eyes out, poor thing," Xan fumed. Glerk sighed deeply. Xan thrust her staff onto the ground, sending a spray of sparks from the tip, surprising them both. She glared at the swamp monster. "And you are just *being mean.*" She shook her head. "He's only a baby, after all."

"My dear Xan," Glerk said, feeling a rumble deep in his chest, which he hoped sounded imposing and dramatic, and not like someone who was simply coming down with a cold. "He is *also* older than you are. And it is high time—"

"Oh, you know what I mean. And anyway, I promised his mother."

"For five hundred years, give or take a decade or two, that

dragonling has persisted in these delusions—fed and perpet-
uated by you, my dear. How is this helping him? He is not a
Simply Enormous Dragon. At this point, there is no indication
that he ever will be. There is no shame at all in being a Perfectly Tiny Dragon. Size isn't everything, you know. His is an
ancient and honorable species, filled with some of the greatest
thinkers of the Seven Ages. He has much to be proud of."

"His mother was very clear—" Xan began, but the monster interrupted her.

"In any case, the time is long past that he know his heritage
and his place in the world. I've gone along with this fiction for
far longer than I should have. But now . . ." Glerk pressed his
four arms to the ground and eased his massive bottom under
the curve of his spine, letting his heavy tail curl around the
whole of him like a great, glistening snail's shell. He let the
paunch of his belly sag over his folded legs. "I don't know, my
dear. Something has shifted." A cloud passed over his damp
face, but Xan shook her head.

"Here we go again," she scoffed.

"As the Poet says, 'Oh ever changéd Earth—'"

"Hang the Poet. Go apologize. Do it right now. He looks
up to you." Xan glanced at the sky. "I must fly, my dear. I'm
already late. *Please.* I am counting on you."

Glerk lumbered toward the Witch, who laid her hand on
his great cheek. Though he was able to walk upright, he often
preferred to move on all sixes—or all sevens, with the use of

his tail as an occasional limb, or all fives, if he happened to be using one of his hands to pluck a particularly fragrant flower and bring it to his nose, or to collect rocks, or to play a haunting tune on a hand-carved flute. He pressed his massive forehead to Xan's tiny brow.

"Please be careful," he said, his voice thick. "I have been beset of late by troubling dreams. I worry about you when you are gone." Xan raised her eyebrows, and Glerk leaned his face away with a low grumble. "Fine," he said. "I will perpetuate the fiction for our friend Fyrian. 'The path to Truth is in the dreaming heart,' the Poet tells us."

"That's the spirit!" Xan said. She clucked her tongue and blew the monster a kiss. And she vaulted up and forward on her staff's fulcrum, sprinting away into the green.

Despite the odd beliefs of the people of the Protectorate, the forest was not cursed at all, nor was it magical in any way. But it was dangerous. The volcano beneath the forest—low-sloped and impossibly wide—was a tricky thing. It grumbled as it slept, while heating geysers till they burst and restlessly worrying at fissures until they grew so deep that no one could find the bottom. It boiled streams and cooked mud and sent waterfalls disappearing into deep pits, only to reappear miles away. There were vents that spewed foul odors and vents that spewed ash and vents that seemed to spew nothing at all—until a person's lips and fingernails turned blue from bad air, and the whole world started to spin.

The only truly safe passage across the forest for an ordinary person was the Road, which was situated on a naturally raised seam of rock that had smoothed over time. The Road didn't alter or shift; it never grumbled. Unfortunately, it was owned and operated by a gang of thugs and bullies from the Protectorate. Xan never took the Road. She couldn't abide thugs. Or bullies. And anyway, they charged too much. Or they did, last time she checked. It had been years since she had gone near it—many centuries now. She made her own way instead, using a combination of magic and know-how and common sense.

Her treks across the forest weren't easy by any means. But they were necessary. A child was waiting for her, just outside the Protectorate. A child whose very life depended on her arrival—and she needed to get there in time.

For as long as Xan could remember, every year at about the same time, a mother from the Protectorate left her baby in the forest, presumably to die. Xan had no idea why. Nor did she judge. But she wasn't going to let the poor little thing perish, either. And so, every year, she traveled to that circle of sycamores and gathered the abandoned infant in her arms, carrying the child to the other side of the forest, to one of the Free Cities on the other side of the Road. These were happy places. And they loved children.

At the curve of the trail, the walls of the Protectorate came into view. Xan's quick steps slowed to a plod. The Protectorate itself was a dismal place—bad air, bad water, sorrow settling over the roofs of its houses like a cloud. She felt a yoke of sadness settle onto her own bones.

"Just get the baby and go," Xan reminded herself, as she did every year.

Over time, Xan had started making certain preparations— a blanket woven of the softest lamb's wool to wrap the child and keep it warm, a stack of cloths to freshen a wet bottom, a bottle or two of goat's milk to fill an empty tummy. When the goat's milk ran out (as it invariably did—the trek was long, and milk is heavy), Xan did what any sensible witch would do: once it was dark enough to see the stars, she reached up one hand and gathered starlight in her fingers, like the silken threads of spiders' webs, and fed it to the child. Starlight, as every witch knows, is a marvelous food for a growing infant. Starlight collection takes a certain knack and talent (magic, for starters), but children eat it with gusto. They grow fat and sated and *shining*.

It didn't take long for the Free Cities to treat the yearly arrival of the Witch as something of a holiday. The children she brought with her, their skin and eyes bright with starlight, were seen as a blessing. Xan took her time selecting the proper family for each child, making sure their characters and inclinations and senses of humor were a good match for the little life that she had cared for over the course of such a long journey.

And the Star Children, as they were called, grew from happy infants to kind adolescents to gracious adults. They were accomplished, generous of spirit, and successful. When they died of old age, they died rich.

When Xan arrived at the grove, there was no baby to be seen, but it was still early. And she was tired. She went to one of the craggy trees and leaned against it, taking in the loamy scent of its bark through the soft beak of her nose.

"A little sleep might do me good," she said out loud. And it was true, too. The journey she'd been on was long and taxing, and the journey she was about to begin was longer. And more taxing. Best to dig in and rest awhile. And so, as she often did when she wanted some peace and quiet away from home, the Witch Xan transformed herself into a tree—a craggy thing of leaf and lichen and deep-grooved bark, similar in shape and texture to the other ancient sycamores standing guard over the small grove. And as a tree she slept.

She didn't hear the procession.

She didn't hear the protestations of Antain or the embarrassed silence of the Council or the gruff pontifications of Grand Elder Gherland.

She didn't even hear the baby when it cooed. Or when it whimpered. Or when it cried.

But when the child opened its throat into a full-fledged wail, Xan woke up with a start.

"Oh my precious stars!" she said in her craggy, barky, leafy voice, for she had not yet un-transformed. "I did not see you lying there!"

The baby was not impressed. She continued to kick and flail and howl and weep. Her face was ruddy and rageful and her tiny hands curled into fists. The birthmark on her forehead darkened dangerously.

"Just give us a second, my darling. Auntie Xan is going as fast as she is able."

And she was. Transformation is a tricky business, even for one as skilled as Xan. Her branches began to wind back into her spine, one by one, while the folds of bark were devoured, bit by bit, by the folds of her wrinkles.

Xan leaned on her staff and rolled back her shoulders a few times to release the kinks in her neck—one side and then the other. She looked down at the child, who had quieted some, and was now staring at the Witch in the same way that she had stared at the Grand Elder—with a calm, probing, unsettling gaze. It was the sort of gaze that reached into the tight strings of the soul and plucked, like the strings of a harp. It nearly took the Witch's breath away.

"Bottle," Xan said, trying to ignore the harmonics ringing in her bones. "You need a bottle." And she searched her many pockets to find a bottle of goat's milk, ready and waiting for a hungry belly.

With a flick of her ankle, Xan allowed a mushroom to

enlarge itself enough to make a fine stool to sit upon. She let the child's warm weight rest against the soft lump of her mid-section and waited. The crescent moon on the child's forehead dimmed to a pleasant shade of pink, and her dark curls framed her darker eyes. Her face shone like a jewel. She was calm and content with the milk, but her gaze still bored into Xan—like tree roots hooking into the ground. Xan grunted.

"Well," she said. "There's no use looking at me like that. I can't bring you back to where you were. That's all gone now, so you might as well forget about it. Oh hush now," for the child began to whimper. "Don't cry. You'll love the place where we are going. Once I decide which city to bring you to. They are all perfectly nice. And you'll love your new family, too. I'll see to that."

But just saying so made an ache in Xan's old heart. And she was, all at once, unaccountably sad. The child pulled away from the bottle and gave Xan a curious expression. The Witch shrugged.

"Well, don't ask me," she said. "I have no idea why you were left in the middle of the woods. I don't know why people do half the things they do, and I shake my head at the other half. But I am certainly not going to leave you here on the ground to feed some common stoat. You've got better things ahead of you, precious child."

The word *precious* caught strangely in Xan's throat. She couldn't understand it. She cleared the debris from her old lungs and gave the girl a smile. She leaned toward the baby's face and pressed her lips against the child's brow. She always gave the babies a kiss. At least, she was pretty sure she did. The child's scalp smelled like bread dough and clabbering milk. Xan closed her eyes, only for a moment, and shook her head. "Come now," she said, her voice thick. "Let's go see the world, shall we?"

And, wrapping the baby securely in a sling, Xan marched into the woods, whistling as she walked.

And she would have gone straight to the Free Cities. She certainly intended to.

But there was a waterfall that the baby would like. And there was a rocky outcropping with a particularly fine view. And she noticed herself wanting to tell the baby stories. And sing her songs. And as she told and as she sang, Xan's step grew slower and slower and slower. Xan blamed the onset of old age and the crick in her back and the fussiness of the child, but none of those things was true.

Xan found herself stopping again and again just to take yet another opportunity to unsling the baby and stare into those deep, black eyes.

Each day, Xan's path wandered farther afield. It looped, doubled back, and wiggled. Her traverse through the forest, normally almost as straight as the Road itself, was a twisty, windy mess. At night, once the goat's milk was exhausted, Xan gathered the gossamer threads of starlight on her fingers, and the child ate gratefully. And each mouthful of starlight deepened the darkness in the child's gaze. Whole universes burned in those eyes—galaxies upon galaxies.

After the tenth night, the journey that usually only took three and a half days was less than a quarter done. The waxing moon rose earlier each night, though Xan did not pay it much mind. She reached up and gathered her starlight and didn't heed the moon.

There is magic in starlight, of course. This is well known. But because the light travels such a long distance, the magic in it is fragile and diffused, stretched into the most delicate of threads. There is enough magic in starlight to content a baby and fill its belly, and in large enough quantities, starlight can awaken the best in that baby's heart and soul and mind. It is enough to *bless*, but not to *enmagic*.

Moonlight, however. That is a different story.

Moonlight *is* magic. Ask anyone you like.

Xan couldn't take her eyes off the baby's eyes. Suns and stars and meteors. The dust of nebulae. Big bangs and black holes and endless, endless Space. The moon rose, big and fat and shining.

Xan reached up. She didn't look at the sky. She didn't notice the moon.

*(Did she notice how heavy the light felt on her fingers? Did she notice how sticky it was? How sweet?)*

She waved her fingers above her head. She pulled her hand down when she couldn't hold it up anymore.

*(Did she notice the weight of magic swinging from her wrist? She told herself she didn't. She said it over and over and over until it felt true.)*

And the baby ate. And ate. And ate. And suddenly she shuddered and buckled in Xan's arms. And she cried out—once. And very loud. And then she gave a contented sigh, falling instantly asleep, pressing herself into the softness of the Witch's belly.

Xan looked up at the sky, feeling the light of the moon falling across her face. "Oh dear me," she whispered. The moon had grown full without her noticing. And powerfully magic. One sip would have done it, and the baby had had—*well*. More than one sip.

Greedy little thing.

In any case, the facts of the matter were as clear as the moon sitting brightly on the tops of the trees. The child had become *enmagicked*. There was no doubt about it. And now things were more complicated than they had been before.

Xan settled herself cross-legged on the ground and laid the sleeping child in the crook of her knee. There would be no waking her. Not for hours. Xan ran her fingers through the girl's black curls. Even now, she could feel the magic pulsing under her skin, each filament insinuating itself between cells, through tissues, filling up her bones. In time, she'd become unstable—not forever, of course. But Xan remembered enough from the magicians who raised her long ago that rearing a magic baby is no easy matter. Her teachers were quick to tell her as much. And her Keeper, Zosimos, mentioned it endlessly. "Infusing magic into a child is akin to putting a sword in the hand of a toddler—so much power and so little sense. Can't you see how you age me so, girl?" he had said, over and over.

And it was true. Magical children were dangerous. She certainly couldn't leave the child with just anyone.

"Well, my love," she said. "Aren't you more troublesome by half?"

The baby breathed deeply through her nose. A tiny smile quivered in the center of her rosebud mouth. Xan felt her heart leap within her, and she cuddled the baby close.

"Luna," she said. "Your name will be Luna. And I will be your grandmother. And we will be a family."

And just by saying so, Xan knew it was true. The words hummed in the air between them, stronger than any magic.

She stood, slid the baby back into the sling, and began the long journey toward home, wondering how on earth she'd explain it to Glerk.

# 4

## In Which It Was Just a Dream

*You ask too many questions.*

*No one knows what the Witch does with the children she takes. No one asks this. We can't ask it—don't you see? It hurts too much.*

*Fine. She eats them. Are you happy?*

*No. That's not what I think.*

*My mother told me she ate their souls, and that their soulless bodies have wandered the earth ever since. Unable to live. Unable to die. Blank-eyed and blank-faced and aimless walking. I don't think that's true. We would have seen them, don't you think? We would at least have seen one wander by. After all these years.*

*My grandmother told me she keeps them as slaves. That they live in the catacombs under her great castle in the forest and* operate her fell machines and stir her great cauldrons and do her bidding from morning till night. But I don't think that's true, either. Surely, if it was, at least one of them would have escaped. In all these years, surely one person would have found a way out and come home. So, no. I don't think they are enslaved.

Really, I don't think anything at all. There is nothing at all to think.

Sometimes. I have this dream. About your brother. He would be eighteen now. No. Nineteen. I have this dream that he has dark hair and luminous skin and stars in his eyes. I dream that when he smiles, it shines for miles around. Last night I dreamed that he waited next to a tree for a girl to walk by. And he called her name, and held her hand, and his heart pounded when he kissed her.

What? No. I'm not crying. Why would I cry? Silly thing.

Anyway. It was just a dream.

# 5

## In Which a Swamp Monster Accidentally Falls in Love

Glerk did not approve, and said so the first day the baby arrived.

And he said so again, on the next day.

And the next.

And the next.

Xan refused to listen.

"Babies, babies, babies," sang Fyrian. He was utterly delighted. The tiny dragon perched on the branch extending over the door of Xan's tree home, opening his multicolored wings as wide as he could and arching his long neck toward the sky. His voice was loud, warbled, and atrociously off-key. Glerk covered his ears. "Babies, babies, babies, BABIES!" Fyrian continued. "Oh, how I love babies!" He had never met a baby before, at least not that he could remember, but that did not stop the dragon from loving them all to bits.

From morning till night, Fyrian sang and Xan fussed, and no one, Glerk felt, would listen to reason. By the end of the second week, their entire habitation had been transformed: diapers and baby clothes and bonnets hung on newly strung clotheslines to dry; freshly blown glass bottles dried on recently constructed racks next to a brand-new washing station; a new goat had been procured (Glerk had no idea how), and Xan had separate milk jugs for drinking and cheese making and butter churning; and, quite suddenly, the floor became thoroughly strewn with toys. More than once, Glerk's foot had come down hard on a cruel-cornered wooden rattle, sending him howling with pain. He found himself shushed and needled out of the room, lest he wake the baby, or frighten the baby, or bore the baby to death with poetry.

By the end of the third week, he'd had quite enough.

"Xan," he said. "I must insist that you do not fall in love with that baby."

The old woman snorted, but she did not answer.

Glerk scowled. "Indeed. I forbid it."

The Witch laughed out loud. The baby laughed with her. They were a mutual admiration society of two, and Glerk could not bear it.

"Luna!" Fyrian sang, flying in through the open door. He

flitted about the room like a tone-deaf songbird. "Luna, Luna, Luna, LUNA!"

"No more singing," Glerk snapped.

"You don't have to listen to him, Fyrian, dear," Xan said. "Singing is good for babies. Everyone knows that." The baby kicked and cooed. Fyrian settled on Xan's shoulder and hummed tunelessly. An improvement, to be sure, but not much.

Glerk grunted in frustration. "Do you know what the Poet says about Witches raising children?" he asked.

"I cannot think what any poet might say about babies or Witches, but I have no doubt that it is marvelously insightful." She looked around. "Glerk, could you please hand me that bottle?"

Xan sat cross-legged on the rough plank floor, and the baby lay in the hollow of her skirts.

Glerk moved closer, leaned his head near the baby, and gave her a skeptical expression. The baby had her fist in her mouth, leaking drool through the fingers. She waved her other hand at the monster. Her pink lips spread outward into a wide smile around her wet knuckles.

*She is doing that on purpose,* he thought as he tried to force his own smile away from his wide, damp jaws. *She is being adorable as some sort of hideous ruse, to spite me. What a mean baby!*

Luna gave a giggly squeal and kicked her tiny feet. Her eyes caught the swamp monster's eyes, and they sparkled like stars.

*Do not fall in love with that baby,* he ordered himself. He tried to be stern.

Glerk cleared his throat.

"The *Poet,*" he said with emphasis, and narrowed his eyes on the baby, "says *nothing* about Witches and babies."

"Well then," Xan said, touching her nose to the baby's nose and making her laugh. She did it again. And again. "I suppose we don't have to worry, then. *Oh no we don't!*" Her voice went high and singsong, and Glerk rolled his tremendous eyes.

"My dear Xan, you are missing the point."

"And you are missing this babyhood with all your huffing and puffing. The child is here to stay, and that is that. Human babies are only tiny for an instant—their growing up is as swift as the beat of a hummingbird's wing. Enjoy it, Glerk! Enjoy it, or get out." She didn't look at him when she said this, but Glerk could feel a cold prickliness emanating from the Witch's shoulder, and it nearly broke his heart.

"Well," Fyrian said. He was perched on Xan's shoulder, watching the baby kick and coo with interest. "I like her."

He wasn't allowed to get too close. This, Xan explained, was for both of their safeties. The baby, full to bursting with magic, was a bit like a sleeping volcano—internal energy and heat and power can build over time, and erupt without warning. Xan and Glerk were both mostly immune to the volatilities of magic (Xan because of her arts and Glerk because he was older than magic and didn't truck with its foolishness) and had less to worry about, but Fyrian was delicate. Also, Fyrian was prone to the hiccups. And his hiccups were usually on fire.

"Don't get too close, Fyrian, dear. Stay behind Auntie Xan."

Fyrian hid behind the crinkly curtain of the old woman's hair, staring at the baby with a combination of fear and jealousy and longing. "I want to *play* with her," he whined.

"You will," Xan said soothingly, as she positioned the baby to take her bottle. "I just want to make sure that the two of you don't hurt one another."

"I *never* would," Fyrian gasped. Then he sniffed. "I think I'm allergic to the baby," he said.

"You're not allergic to the baby," Glerk groaned, just as Fyrian sneezed a bright plume of fire onto the back of Xan's head. She didn't even flinch. With a wink of her eye, the fire transformed to steam, which lifted several spit-up stains that she had not bothered to clean yet from her shoulders.

"Bless you, dear," Xan said. "Glerk, why don't you take our Fyrian for a walk."

"I dislike walks," Glerk said, but took Fyrian anyway. Or Glerk walked, and Fyrian fluttered behind, from side to side and forward and back, like a troublesome, overlarge butterfly. Primarily, Fyrian decided to occupy himself in the collection of flowers for the baby, a process hindered by his occasional hiccups and sneezes, each with its requisite dollops of flame, and each reducing his flowers to ashes. But he hardly noticed. Instead, Fyrian was a fountain of questions.

"Will the baby grow up to be a giant like you and Xan?" he asked. "There must be more giants, then. In the wider world, I mean. The world past *here*. How I long to see the world beyond *here*, Glerk. I want to see all the giants in all the world and all the creatures who are bigger than I!"

Fyrian's delusions continued unabated, despite Glerk's protestations. Though he was about the same size as a dove, Fyrian continued to believe he was larger than the typical human habitation, and that he needed to be kept far away from humanity, lest he be accidentally seen and start a worldwide panic.

"When the time is right, my son," his massive mother had told him in the moments before she plunged herself into the erupting volcano, leaving this world forever, "you will know your purpose. You are, and will be, a giant upon this fair earth. Never forget it."

Her meaning, Fyrian felt, was clear. He was Simply Enormous. There was no doubt about it. Fyrian reminded himself of it every single day.

And for five hundred years, Glerk continued to fume.

"The child will grow as children do, I expect," Glerk said evasively. And when Fyrian persisted, Glerk pretended to take a nap in the calla lily bog and kept his eyes closed until he actually slept.

✤

Raising a baby—magical or not—is not without its challenges: the inconsolable crying, the near-constant runny noses, the obsession with putting very small objects into a drooling mouth.

And the *noise.*

"Can you please magic her quiet?" Fyrian had begged, once the novelty of a baby in the family had worn off. Xan refused, of course.

"Magic should never be used to influence the will of another person, Fyrian," Xan told him over and over. "How could I do the thing that I must instruct her to *never* do, once she knows how to understand? That's hypocrisy, is what."

Even when Luna was content, she still was not quiet. She hummed; she gurgled; she babbled; she screeched; she guffawed; she snorted; she yelled. She was a waterfall of sound, pouring, pouring, pouring. And she never stopped. She even babbled in her sleep.

Glerk made a sling for Luna that hung from all four of his shoulders as he walked on all sixes. He took to pacing with the baby from the swamp, past the workshop, past the castle ruin, and back again, reciting poetry as he did so.

He did not intend to love the baby.

And yet.

"'*From grain of sand,*'" recited the monster.

*"'Births light*
*births space*
*births infinite time,*
*and to grain of sand*
*do all things return.'"*

It was one of his favorites. The baby gazed as he walked, studying his protruding eyeballs, his conical ears, his thick lips on wide jaws. She examined each wart, each divot, each slimy lump on his large, flat face, a look of wonder in her eyes. She reached up one finger and stuck it curiously into a nostril. Glerk sneezed, and the child laughed.

"Glerk," the baby said, though it was probably a hiccup or a burp. Glerk didn't care. She said his name. She *said* it. His heart nearly burst in his chest.

Xan, for her part, did her best not to say, *I told you so.* She mostly succeeded.

☼

In that first year, both Xan and Glerk watched the baby for any sign of magical eruption. Though they could both see the oceans of magic thrumming just under the child's skin (and they could feel it, too, each time they carried that girl in their arms), it remained inside her—a surging, unbroken wave.

At night, moonlight and starlight bent toward the baby, flooding her cradle. Xan covered the windows with heavy curtains, but she would find them thrown open, and the child drinking moonlight in her sleep.

"The moon," Xan told herself. "It is full of tricks."

But a whisper of worry remained. The magic continued to silently surge.

In the second year, the magic inside Luna increased, nearly doubling in density and strength. Glerk could feel it. Xan could feel it, too. Still it did not erupt.

*Magical babies are dangerous babies*, Glerk tried to remind himself, day after day. When he wasn't cradling Luna. Or singing to Luna. Or whispering poetry into her ear as she slept. After a while, even the thrum of magic under her skin began to seem ordinary. She was an energetic child. A curious child. A naughty child. And that was enough to deal with on its own.

The moonlight continued to bend toward the baby. Xan decided to stop worrying about it.

In the third year, the magic doubled again. Xan and Glerk hardly noticed. Instead they had their hands full with a child who explored and rummaged and scribbled on books and threw eggs at the goats and once tried to fly off a fence, only to end up with two skinned knees and a chipped tooth. She climbed trees and tried to catch birds and sometimes played tricks on Fyrian, making him cry.

"Poetry will help," Glerk said. "The study of language ennobles the rowdiest beast."

"Science will organize that brain of hers," Xan said. "How can a child be naughty when she is studying the stars?"

"I shall teach her math," Fyrian said. "She will not be able to play a trick on me if she is too busy counting to one million."

And so, Luna's education began.

"*In every breeze exhales the promise of spring,*" Glerk whispered as Luna napped during the winter.

"*Each sleeping tree*
*dreams green dreams;*
*the barren mountain*
*wakes in blossom.*'"

Wave after wave of magic surged silently under her skin. They did not crash to the shore. Not *yet*.

# 6

## In Which Antain Gets Himself in Trouble

During Antain's first five years as an Elder-in-Training, he did his best to convince himself that his job would one day get easier. He was wrong. It didn't.

The Elders barked orders at him during Council meetings and community functions and after-hours discussions. They berated him when they ran into him on the street. Or when they sat in his mother's dining room for yet another sumptuous (though uncomfortable) supper. They admonished him when he followed in their wake during surprise inspections.

Antain hung in the background, his eyebrows knit together into a perplexed knot.

It seemed that no matter what Antain did, the Elders erupted into purple-faced rage and sputtering incoherence.

"Antain!" the Elders barked. "Stand up straight!"

"Antain! What have you done with the proclamations?"

"Antain! Wipe that ridiculous look off your face!"

"Antain! How could you have forgotten the snacks?"

"Antain! What on earth have you spilled all over your robes?"

Antain, it seemed, could not do anything right.

His home life wasn't any better.

"How can you possibly still be an Elder-in-Training?" his mother fumed night after night at supper. Sometimes, she'd let her spoon come crashing down to the table, making the servants jump. "My brother promised me that you would be an Elder by now. He *promised*."

And she would seethe and grumble until Antain's youngest brother, Wyn, began to cry. Antain was the oldest of six brothers—a small family, by Protectorate standards—and ever since his father died, his mother wanted nothing else but to make sure that each of her sons achieved the very best that the Protectorate had to offer.

Because didn't she, after all, *deserve* the very best, when it came to sons?

"Uncle tells me that things take time, Mother," Antain said quietly. He pulled his toddler brother onto his lap and began rocking until the child calmed. He pulled a wooden toy that he had carved himself from his pocket—a little crow with spiral eyes and a clever rattle inside its belly. The boy was delighted, and instantly shoved it into his mouth.

"Your uncle can boil his head," she fumed. "We *deserve* that honor. I mean *you* deserve it, my dear son."

Antain wasn't so sure.

He excused himself from the table, mumbling something about having work to do for the Council, but really he only planned on sneaking into the kitchen to help the kitchen staff. And then into the gardens to help the gardeners in the last of the daylight hours. And then he went into the shed to carve wood. Antain loved woodworking—the stability of the material, the delicate beauty of the grain, the comforting smell of sawdust and oil. There were few things in his life that he loved more. He carved and worked deep into the night, trying his best not to think about his life. The next Day of Sacrifice was approaching, after all. And Antain would need yet another excuse to make himself scarce.

The next morning, Antain donned his freshly laundered robe and headed into the Council Hall well before dawn. Every day, his first task of the morning was to read through the citizen complaints and requests that had been scrawled with bits of chalk on the large slate wall, and deem which ones were worth attention and which should simply be washed down and erased.

("But what if they *all* are important, Uncle?" Antain had asked the Grand Elder once.

"They can't possibly be. In any case, by denying access, we give our people a gift. They learn to accept their lot in life. They learn that any action is inconsequential. Their days remain, as they should be, cloudy. There is no greater gift than that. Now. Where is my Zirin tea?")

Next, Antain was to air out the room, then post the day's agendas, then fluff the cushions for the Elders' bony bottoms, then spray the entrance room with some kind of perfume concocted in the laboratories of the Sisters of the Star—designed, apparently, to make people feel wobbly-kneed and tongue-tied and frightened and grateful, all at once—and then he was to stand in the room as the servants arrived, giving each one an imperious expression as they entered the building, before hanging up his robes in the closet and going to school.

("But what if I don't know how to make an imperious expression, Uncle?" the boy asked again and again.

"Practice, Nephew. Continue to practice.")

Antain walked slowly toward the schoolhouse, enjoying the temporary glimmers of sun overhead. It would be cloudy in an hour. It was always cloudy in the Protectorate. Fog clung to the city walls and cobbled streets like tenacious moss. Not many people were out and about that early in the morning. *Pity,* thought Antain. *They are missing the sunlight.* He lifted his face and felt that momentary rush of hope and promise.

He let his eyes drift toward the Tower—its black, devil-ishly complicated stonework mimicking the whorls of gal-axies and the trajectories of stars; its small, round windows winking outward like eyes. That mother—the one who went mad—was still in there. Locked up. The madwoman. For five years now she had convalesced in confinement, but she still had not healed. In Antain's mind's eye, he could see that wild face, those black eyes, that birthmark on her forehead—livid and red. The way she kicked and climbed and shrieked and fought. He couldn't forget it.

And he couldn't forgive himself.

Antain shut his eyes tight and tried to force the image away.

*Why must this go on?* His heart continued to ache. *There must be another way.*

As usual, he was the first one to arrive at school. Even the teacher wasn't there. He sat on the stoop and took out his jour-nal. He was done with his schoolwork—not that it mattered. His teacher insisted on calling him "Elder Antain" in a breathy fawning voice, even though he wasn't an elder yet, and gave him top marks no matter what kind of work he did. He could likely turn in blank pages and still get top marks. Antain still worked hard in spite of that. His teacher, he knew, was just hoping for special treatment later. In his journal, he had sev-eral sketches of a project of his own design—a clever cabinet to house and neatly organize garden tools, situated on wheels so that it could be pulled easily by a small goat—a gift intended for the head gardener, who was always kind.

A shadow fell across his work.

"Nephew," the Grand Elder said.

Antain's head went up like a shot.

"Uncle!" he said, scrambling to his feet, accidentally dropping his papers, scattering them across the ground. He hurriedly gathered them back up into his arms. Grand Elder Gherland rolled his eyes.

"Come, Nephew," the Grand Elder said with a swish of his robes, motioning for the boy to follow him. "You and I must talk."

"But what about school?"

"There is no need to be in school in the first place. The purpose of this structure is to house and amuse those who have no futures until they are old enough to work for the benefit of the Protectorate. People of your stature have tutors, and why you have refused such a basic thing is beyond comprehension. Your mother prattles on about it endlessly. In any case, you will not be missed."

This was true. He would not be missed. Every day in class, Antain sat in the back and worked quietly. He rarely asked questions. He rarely spoke. Especially now, since the one person whom he wouldn't have minded speaking to—and even better, if she spoke back to him in return—had left school entirely. She had joined the novitiate at the Sisters of the Star. Her name was Ethyne, and though Antain had never exchanged three words in succession with her, still he missed her desperately, and now only went to school day after day on the wild hope that she would change her mind and come back.

It had been a year. No one ever left the Sisters of the Star. It wasn't *done*. Yet, Antain continued to wait. And hope.

He followed his uncle at a run.

The other Elders still had not arrived at the Council Hall, and likely would not until noon or later. Gherland told Antain to sit.

The Grand Elder stared at Antain for a long time. Antain couldn't get the Tower out of his mind. Or the madwoman. Or the baby left in the forest, whimpering piteously as they walked away. *And oh, how that mother screamed. And oh, how she fought. And oh, what have we become?*

It pierced Antain every day, a great needle in his soul.

"Nephew," the Grand Elder said at last. He folded his hands and brought them to his mouth. He sighed deeply. Antain realized that his uncle's face was pale. "The Day of Sacrifice approaches."

"I know, Uncle," Antain said. His voice was thin. "Five days. It —" He sighed. "It waits for no one."

"You were not there last year. You were not standing with the other Elders. An infection in your foot, as I recall?"

Antain tilted his gaze to the ground. "Yes, Uncle. I had a fever, too."

"And it resolved itself the next day?"

"Bog be praised," he said weakly. "It was a miracle."

"And the year before," Gherland said. "It was pneumonia, was it?"

Antain nodded. He knew where this was going.

"And before that. A fire in the shed? Is that right? Good thing no one was injured. And there you were. All by yourself. Fighting the fire."

"Everyone else was along the route," Antain said. "No shirkers. So I was alone."

"Indeed." Grand Elder Gherland gave Antain a narrowed look. "Young man," he said. "Who on earth do you think you're fooling?"

A silence fell between them.

Antain remembered the little black curls, framing those wide black eyes. He remembered the sounds the baby made when they left her in the forest. He remembered the thud of the Tower doors when they locked the madwoman inside. He shivered.

"Uncle—" Antain began, but Gherland waved him off.

"Listen, Nephew. It was against my better judgment to offer you this position. I did so not because of the incessant needling of my sister, but because of the great love I had, and have, for your dear father, may he rest easily. He wanted to make sure your path was assured before he passed away, and I could not deny him. And having you here"—the hard lines of

Gherland's face softened a bit—"has been an antidote to my own sadness. And I appreciate it. You are a good boy, Antain. Your father would be proud."

Antain found himself relaxing. But only for a moment. With a broad sweep of robes, the Grand Elder rose to his feet.

"But," he said, his voice reverberating strangely in the small room. "My affection for you only goes so far."

There was, in his voice, a brittle edge. His eyes were wide. Strained. Even a bit wet. *Is my uncle worried about me?* Antain wondered. *Surely not,* he thought.

"Young man," his uncle continued. "This cannot go on. The other Elders are muttering. They . . ." He paused. His voice caught in his throat. His cheeks were flushed. "They aren't happy. My protection over you extends far, my dear, dear boy. But it is not infinite."

*Why would I need to be protected?* Antain wondered as he stared at his uncle's strained face.

The Grand Elder closed his eyes and calmed his ragged breathing. He motioned for the boy to stand. His face resumed its imperious expression. "Come, Nephew. It's time for you to return to school. We shall expect you, as usual, at mid-afternoon. I do hope you are able to make at least one person grovel today. It would put to rest so many misgivings among the other Elders. Promise me you'll try, Antain. Please."

Antain shuffled toward the door, the Grand Elder gliding just behind. The older man lifted his hand to rest on the boy's shoulder and let it hover just above for a moment, before thinking better of it and letting it drift back down.

"I'll try harder, Uncle," Antain said as he walked out the door. "I promise I will."

"See that you do," the Grand Elder said in a hoarse whisper.

✻

Five days later, as the Robes swept through the town toward the cursed house, Antain was home, sick to his stomach, vomiting his lunch. Or so he said. The other Elders grumbled during the entire procession. They grumbled as they retrieved the child from its pliant parents. They grumbled as they hurried toward the sycamore grove.

"The boy will have to be dealt with," the Elders muttered. And each one knew exactly what that meant.

*Oh, Antain my boy, my boy, oh Antain my boy!* Gherland thought as they walked, tendrils of worry curling around his heart, cinching into a hard, tight knot. *What have you done, you foolish child? What have you done?*

# 7

## In Which a Magical Child Is More Trouble by Half

When Luna was five years old, her magic had doubled itself five times, but it remained inside her, fused to her bones and muscles and blood. Indeed, it was inside every cell. Inert, unused—all potential and no force.

"It can't go on like this," Glerk fussed. "The more magic she gathers, the more magic will spill out." He made funny faces at the girl in spite of himself. Luna giggled like mad. "You mark my words," he said, vainly trying to be serious.

"You don't know that," Xan said. "Maybe it will never come out. Maybe things will never be difficult."

Despite her tireless work finding homes for abandoned babies, Xan had a deep loathing for difficult things. And sorrowful things. And unpleasant things. She preferred not to think of them, if she could help it. She sat with the girl, blowing bubbles—lovely, lurid, mostly magical things, with pretty colors swirling on their surfaces. The girl chased and caught each bubble on her fingers, and set each of them surrounding daisy blossoms or butterflies or the leaves of trees. She even climbed inside a particularly large bubble and floated just over the tips of the grass.

"There is so much beauty, Glerk," Xan said. "How can you possibly think about anything else?"

Glerk shook his head.

"How long can this last, Xan?" Glerk said. The Witch refused to answer.

Later, he held the girl and sang her to sleep. He could feel the heft of the magic in his arms. He could feel the pulse and undulation of those great waves of magic, surging inside the child, never finding their way to shore.

The Witch told him he was imagining things.

She insisted that they focus their energies on raising a little girl who was, by nature, a tangle of mischief and motion and curiosity. Each day, Luna's ability to break rules in new and creative ways was an astonishment to all who knew her. She tried to ride the goats, tried to roll boulders down the mountain and into the side of the barn (*for decoration*, she explained), tried to teach the chickens to fly, and once almost drowned in the swamp. (Glerk saved her. Thank goodness.) She gave ale to

the geese to see if it made them walk funny (it did) and put pep-
percorns in the goat's feed to see if it would make them jump
(they didn't jump; they just destroyed the fence). Every day she
goaded Fyrian into making atrocious choices or she played
tricks on the poor dragon, making him cry. She climbed, hid,
built, broke, wrote on the walls, and spoiled dresses when they
had only just been finished. Her hair ratted, her nose smudged,
and she left handprints wherever she went.

"What will happen when her magic comes?" Glerk asked
again and again. "What will she be like then?"

Xan tried not to think about it.

❈

Xan visited the Free Cities twice a year, once with Luna and
once without. She did not explain to the child the purpose for
her solo visit—nor did she tell her about the sad town on the
other side of the forest, or of the babies left in that small clearing, presumably to die. She'd have to tell the girl eventually,
of course. One day, Xan told herself. Not now. It was too sad.
And Luna was too little to understand.

When Luna was five, she traveled once again to one of the
farthest of the Free Cities—a town called Obsidian. And Xan
found herself fussing at a child who would not sit quietly. Not
for anything.

"Young lady, will you please remove yourself from this
house at once, and go find a friend to play with?"

"Grandmama, look! It's a hat." And she reached into the

bowl and pulled out the lump of rising bread dough and put it on her head. "It's a hat, Grandmama! The prettiest hat."

"It is not a hat," Xan said. "It is a lump of dough." She was in the middle of a complex bit of magic. The schoolmistress lay on the kitchen table, deep in sleep, and Xan kept both palms on the sides of the young woman's face, concentrating hard. The schoolmistress had been suffering from terrible headaches that were, Xan discovered, the result of a growth in the center of her brain. Xan could remove it with magic, bit by bit, but it was tricky work. And dangerous. Work for a clever witch, and none was more clever than Xan.

Still. The work was difficult—more difficult than she felt it should have been. And taxing. Everything was taxing lately. Xan blamed old age. Her magic emptied so quickly these days. And took so long to refill. And she was so tired.

"Young man," Xan said to the schoolmistress's son—a nice boy, fifteen, probably, whose skin seemed to glow. One of the Star Children. "Will you please take this troublesome child outside and play with her so I may focus on healing your mother without killing her by mistake?" The boy turned pale. "I'm only kidding, of course. Your mother is safe with me." Xan hoped that was true.

Luna slid her hand into the boy's hand, her black eyes shining like jewels. "Let's play," she said, and the boy grinned back. He loved Luna, just like everyone else did. They ran, laughing, out the door and disappeared into the woods out back.

Later, when the growth had been dispatched and the brain healed and the schoolmistress was sleeping comfortably, Xan felt she could finally relax. Her eye fell on the bowl on the counter. The bowl with the rising bread dough.

But there was no bread dough in the bowl at all. Instead, there was a hat—wide-brimmed and intricately detailed. It was the prettiest hat Xan had ever seen.

"Oh dear," Xan whispered, picking up the hat and noticing the magic laced within it. Blue. With a shimmer of silver at the edges. Luna's magic. "Oh dear, oh dear."

Over the next two days, Xan did her best to conclude her work in the Free Cities as quickly as she could. Luna was no help at all. She ran circles around the other children, racing and playing and jumping over fences. She dared groups of children to climb to the tops of trees with her. Or into barn lofts. Or onto the ridgepoles of neighborhood roofs. They followed her higher and higher, but they couldn't follow her all the way. She seemed to float above the branches. She pirouetted on the tip of a birch leaf.

"Come down this instant, young lady," the Witch hollered.

The little girl laughed. She flitted toward the ground, leaping from leaf to leaf, guiding the other children safely behind her. Xan could see the tendrils of magic fluttering behind her like ribbons. Blue and silver, silver and blue. They billowed and swelled and spiraled in the air. They left their etchings on the ground. Xan took off after the child at a run, cleaning up as she did so.

A donkey became a toy.

A house became a bird.

A barn was suddenly made of gingerbread and spun sugar.

*She has no idea what she is doing,* Xan thought. The magic poured out of the girl. Xan had never seen so much in all her life. *She could so easily hurt herself,* Xan fussed. *Or someone else. Or everyone in town.* Xan tore down the road, her old bones groaning, undoing spell after spell, before she caught up to the wayward girl.

"Nap time," the Witch said, brandishing both palms, and Luna collapsed onto the ground. She had *never* interfered in the will of another. *Never.* Years ago—almost five hundred— she made a promise to her guardian, Zosimos, that she never would. But now . . . *What have I done?* Xan asked herself. She thought she might be sick.

The other children stared. Luna snored. She left a puddle of drool on the ground.

"Is she all right?" one boy asked.

Xan picked Luna up, feeling the weight of the child's face on her shoulder and pressing her wrinkled cheek against the little girl's hair.

"She's fine, dear," she said. "She's just sleepy. She is so sleepy. And I do believe you have chores to do." Xan carried

Luna to the guesthouse of the mayor, where they happened to be staying.

Luna slept deeply. Her breathing was slow and even. The crescent moon birthmark on her forehead glowed a bit. A pink moon. Xan smoothed the child's black hair away from her face, winding her fingers in the shining curls.

"What have I been missing?" she asked herself out loud. There was something she wasn't seeing—something important. She didn't think about her childhood if she could help it. It was too sad. And sorrow was dangerous—though she couldn't quite remember why.

Memory was a slippery thing—slick moss on an unstable slope—and it was ever so easy to lose one's footing and fall. And anyway, five hundred years was an awful lot to remember. But now, her memories came tumbling toward her—a kindly old man, a decrepit castle, a clutch of scholars with their faces buried in books, a mournful mother dragon saying good-bye. And something else, too. Something scary. Xan tried to pluck the memories as they tumbled by, but they were like bright pebbles in an avalanche: they flashed briefly in the light, and then they were gone.

There was something she was *supposed* to remember. She was sure of it. If she could only remember what.

# 8

## In Which a Story Contains
## a Hint of Truth

*A story? Fine. I will tell you a story. But you won't like it. And it will make you cry.*

*Once upon a time, there were good wizards and good witches, and they lived in a castle in the center of the wood.*

*Well, of course the forest wasn't dangerous in those days. We know who is responsible for cursing the forest. It is the same person who steals our children and poisons the water. In those days, the Protectorate was prosperous and wise. No one needed the Road to cross the forest. The forest was a friend to all. And anyone could walk to the Enchanters' Castle for remedies or advice or general gossip.*

But one day, an evil Witch rode across the sky on the back of a dragon. She wore black boots and a black hat and a dress the color of blood. She howled her rage to the sky.

Yes, child. This is a true story. What other kinds of stories are there?

As she flew on her cursed dragon, the land rumbled and split. The rivers boiled and the mud bubbled and entire lakes turned into steam. The Bog—our beloved Bog—became toxic and rank, and people died because they could not get air. The land under the castle swelled—it rose and rose and rose, and great plumes of smoke and ash came billowing from its center.

"It's the end of the world," people cried. And it might have been, if one good man had not dared to stand up to the Witch.

One of the good wizards from the castle—no one remembers his name—saw the Witch on her fearsome dragon as they flew across the broken land. He knew what the Witch was trying to do: she wanted to pull the fire from the bulge of the earth and spread it across the land, like a cloth over a table. She wanted to cover us all in ash and fire and smoke.

Well, of course that's what she wanted. No one knows why. How could we? She is a witch. She needs no rhyme and no reason, neither.

Of course this is a true story. Haven't you been listening?

And so the brave little wizard—ignoring his own great peril—ran into the smoke and flame. He leaped into the air and pulled the Witch from the back of her dragon. He threw the dragon into the flaming hole in the earth, stopping it up like a cork in a bottle.

But he didn't kill the Witch. The Witch killed him instead.

This is why it doesn't pay to be brave. Bravery makes nothing, protects nothing, results in nothing. It only makes you dead. And this is why we don't stand up to the Witch. Because even a powerful old wizard was no match for her.

I already told you this story is true. I only tell true stories. Now. Off with you, and don't let me catch you shirking on your chores. I might send you to the Witch and have her deal with you.

# 9

# In Which Several
# Things Go Wrong

The journey home was a disaster.

"Grandmama!" Luna cried. "A bird!" And a tree stump became a very large, very pink, and very perplexed-looking bird, who sat sprawled on the ground, wings akimbo, as if shocked by its own existence.

Which, Xan reasoned, the poor thing probably *was*. She transformed it back into a stump the moment the child wasn't looking. Even from that great distance, she could sense its relief.

"Grandmama!" Luna shrieked, running up ahead. "Cake!" And the stream up ahead suddenly ceased. The water vanished and became a long river of cake.

"Yummy!" Luna cried, grabbing cake by the handful, smearing multicolored icing across her face.

Xan hooked her arm around the girl's waist, vaulted over the cake-stream with her staff, and shooed Luna forward along the winding path up the slope of the mountain, undoing the accidental spell over her shoulder.

"Grandmama! Butterflies!"

"Grandmama! A pony!"

"Grandmama! Berries!"

Spell after spell erupted from Luna's fingers and toes, from her ears and eyes. Her magic skittered and pulsed. It was all Xan could do to keep up.

At night, after falling into an exhausted heap, Xan dreamed of Zosimos the wizard—dead now these five hundred years. In her dream, he was explaining something—something important—but his voice was obscured by the rumble of the volcano. She could only focus on his face as it wrinkled and withered in front of her eyes, his skin collapsing like the petals of a lily drooping at the end of the day.

❊

When they arrived back at their home nestled beneath the peaks and craters of the sleeping volcano and wrapped in the lush smell of the swamp, Glerk stood at his full height, waiting for them.

"Xan," he said, as Fyrian danced and spun in the air,

screeching a newly created song about his love for everyone that he knew. "It seems our girl has become more complicated." He had seen the strands of magic skittering this way and that and launching in long threads over the tops of the trees. He knew even at that great distance that he wasn't seeing Xan's magic, which was green and soft and tenacious, the color and texture of lichen clinging to the lee of the oaks. No, this was blue and silver, silver and blue. Luna's magic.

Xan waved him off. "You don't know the half of it," she said, as Luna went running to the swamp to gather the irises into her arms and drink in the scent. As Luna ran, each footstep blossomed with iridescent flowers. When she waded into the swamp, the reeds twisted themselves into a boat, and she climbed aboard, floating across the deep red of the algae coating the water. Fyrian settled himself at the prow. He didn't seem to notice that anything was amiss.

Xan curled her arm across Glerk's back and leaned against him. She was more tired than she'd ever been in her life.

"This is going to take some work," she said.

Then, leaning heavily on her staff, Xan made her way to the workshop to prepare to teach Luna.

It was, as it turned out, an impossible task.

Xan had been ten years old when she was enmagicked. Until then, she had been alone and frightened. The sorcerers who studied her weren't exactly kind. One in particular seemed to hunger for sorrow. When Zosimos rescued her and bound her to his allegiance and care, she was so grateful that she was ready to follow any rule in the world.

Not so with Luna. She was only five. And remarkably bull-headed. "Sit still, precious," Xan said over and over and over as she tried to get the girl to direct her magic at a single candle. "We need to look inside the flame in order to understand the—*Young lady. No flying in the classroom.*"

"I am a crow, Grandmama," Luna cried. Which wasn't entirely true. She had simply grown black wings and proceeded to flap about the room. "Caw, caw, caw!" she cried.

Xan snatched the child out of the air and undid the transformation. Such a simple spell, but it knocked Xan to her knees. Her hands shook and her vision clouded over.

*What is happening to me?* Xan asked herself. She had no idea.

Luna didn't notice. She transformed a book into a dove and enlivened her pencils and quills so that they stood on their own and performed a complicated dance on the desk.

"Luna, *stop*," Xan said, putting a simple blocking spell on the girl. Which should have been easy. And should have lasted at least an hour or two. But the spell ripped from Xan's belly, making her gasp, and then didn't even work. Luna broke through the block without a second thought. Xan collapsed onto a chair.

"Go outside and play, darling," the old woman said, her body shaking all over. "But don't touch anything, and don't hurt anything, and *no magic.*"

"What's magic, Grandmama?" Luna asked as she raced out the door. There were trees to climb and boats to build. And Xan was fairly certain she saw the child talking to a crane.

Each day, the magic became more unruly. Luna bumped tables with her elbows and accidentally transformed them to water. She transformed her bedclothes to swans while she slept (they made an awful mess). She made stones pop like bubbles. Her skin became so hot it gave Xan blisters, or so cold that she made a frostbitten imprint of her body on Glerk's chest when she gave him a hug. And once she made one of Fyrian's wings disappear in mid-flight, causing him to fall. Luna skipped away, utterly unaware of what she had done.

Xan tried encasing Luna in a protective bubble, telling her it was a fun game they were playing, just to keep all that surging power contained. She cast bubbles around Fyrian, and bubbles around the goats and bubbles around each chicken and a very large bubble around the house, lest she accidentally allow their home to burst into flames. And the bubbles held—they were strongly magic, after all—until they didn't.

"Make more, Grandmama!" Luna cried, running in circles on the stones, each of her footprints erupting in green plants and lurid flowers. "More bubbles!"

Xan had never been so exhausted in her life.

"Take Fyrian to the south crater," Xan told Glerk, after a

week of backbreaking labor and little sleep. She had dark circles under her eyes. Her skin was as pale as paper.

Glerk shook his massive head. "I can't leave you like this, Xan," he said as Luna made a cricket grow to the size of a goat. She gave it a lump of sugar that had appeared in her hand and climbed aboard its back for a ride. Glerk shook his head. "How could I possibly?"

"I need to keep the both of you safe," Xan said.

The swamp monster shrugged. "Magic has nothing on me," he said. "I've been around for far longer than it has."

Xan wrinkled her brow. "Perhaps. But I don't know. She has . . . *so much*. And she has no idea what she's doing." Her bones felt thin and brittle, and her breath rattled in her chest. She did her best to hide this from Glerk.

❊

Xan followed Luna from place to place, undoing spell after spell. The wings were removed from the goats. The eggs were untransformed from muffins. The tree house stopped floating. Luna was both amazed and delighted. She spent her days laughing and sighing and pointing with wonder. She danced about, and where she danced, fountains erupted from the ground.

Meanwhile, Xan grew weaker and weaker.

Finally Glerk couldn't stand it anymore. Leaving Fyrian at the crater's edge, he galumphed down to his beloved swamp.

After a quick dip in the murky waters, he made his way toward Luna, who was standing by herself in the yard.

"Glerk!" she called. "I'm so happy to see you! You are as cute as a bunny."

And, just like that, Glerk was a bunny. A fluffy, white, pink-eyed bunny with a puff for a tail. He had long white lashes and fluted ears, and his nose quivered in the center of his face.

Instantly, Luna began to cry.

Xan came running out of the house and tried to make out what the sobbing girl had told her. By the time she began to look for Glerk, he was gone. He had hopped away, having no idea who he was, or what he was. He had been enrabbited. It took hours to find him.

Xan sat the girl down. Luna stared at her.

"Grandmama, you look different."

And it was true. Her hands were gnarled and spotted. Her skin hung on her arms. She could feel her face folding over itself and growing older by the moment. And in that moment, sitting in the sun with Luna and the rabbit-that-once-was-Glerk shivering between them, Xan could feel it—the magic in her bending toward Luna, just as the moonlight had bent toward the girl when she was still a baby. And as the magic flowed from Xan to Luna, the old woman grew older and older and older.

"Luna," Xan said, stroking the ears of the bunny, "do you know who this is?"

"It's Glerk," Luna said, pulling the rabbit onto her lap and cuddling it affectionately.

Xan nodded. "How do you know it is Glerk?"

Luna shrugged. "I saw Glerk. And then he was a bunny."

"Ah," Xan said. "Why do you think he became a bunny?"

Luna smiled. "Because bunnies are wonderful. And he wanted to make me happy. Clever Glerk!"

Xan paused. "But *how,* Luna? How did he become a bunny?" She held her breath. The day was warm, and the air was wet and sweet. The only sounds were the gentle gurgling of the swamp. The birds in the forest quieted down, as if to listen.

Luna frowned. "I don't know. He just did."

Xan folded her knotty hands together and pressed them to her mouth. "I see," she said. She focused on the magic stores deep within her body, and noticed sadly how depleted they were. She could fill them up, of course, with both starlight and moonlight, and any other magic that she could find lying around, but something told her it would only be a temporary solution.

She looked at Luna, and pressed her lips to the child's forehead. "Sleep, my darling. Your grandmama needs to learn some things. Sleep, sleep, *sleep, sleep, sleep.*"

And the girl slept. Xan nearly collapsed from the effort of it. But there wasn't time for that. She turned her attention to Glerk, analyzing the structure of the spell that had enrabbited him, undoing it bit by bit.

"Why do I want a carrot?" Glerk asked. The Witch explained the situation. Glerk was not amused.

"Don't even start with me," Xan snapped.

"There's nothing to say," Glerk said. "We both love her. She is family. But what now?"

Xan pulled herself to her feet, her joints creaking and cracking like rusty gears.

"I hate to do this, but it's for all our sakes. She is a danger to herself. She is a danger to all of us. She has *no idea* what she's doing, and I don't know how to teach her. Not now. Not when she's so young and impulsive and . . . *Luna-ish*."

Xan stood, rolled her shoulders, and braced herself. She made a bubble and hardened the bubble into a cocoon around the girl—adding bright threads winding around and around.

"She can't breathe!" Glerk said, suddenly alarmed.

"She doesn't need to," Xan said. "She is in stasis. And the cocoon holds her magic inside." She closed her eyes. "Zosimos used to do this. To me. When I was a child. Probably for the same reason."

Glerk's face clouded over. He sat heavily on the ground, curling his thick tail around him like a cushion. "I remember. All at once." He shook his head. "Why had I forgotten?"

Xan pushed her wrinkled lips to one side. "Sorrow is dangerous. Or, at least, it was. I can't remember why, now. I think we both became accustomed to not remembering things. We just let things get . . . foggy."

Glerk guessed it was something more than that, but he let the matter drop.

"Fyrian will be coming down after a bit, I expect," Xan said. "He can't stand being alone for too long. I don't think it matters, but don't let him touch Luna, just in case."

Glerk reached out and laid his great hand on Xan's shoulder. "But where are *you* going?"

"To the old castle," Xan said.

"But . . ." Glerk stared at her. "There's nothing there. Just a few old stones."

"I know," Xan said. "I just need to stand there. In that place. Where I last saw Zosimos, and Fyrian's mother, and the rest of them. I need to remember things. Even if it makes me sad."

Leaning heavily on her staff, Xan began hobbling away.

"I need to remember a lot of things," she muttered to herself. "Everything. Right now."

# 10

## In Which a Witch Finds a Door, and a Memory, Too

Xan turned her back on the swamp and followed the trail up the slope, toward the crater where the volcano had opened its face to the sky so long ago. The trail had been fashioned with large, flat rocks, inlaid into the ground, and fitted so close to one another that the seam between them could hardly let in a piece of paper.

It had been years since Xan last walked this trail. Centuries, really. She shivered. Everything looked so different. And yet . . . *not*.

There had been a circle of stones in the courtyard of the castle, once upon a time. They had surrounded the central, older Tower like sentinels, and the castle had wrapped around the whole of it like a snake eating its tail. But the Tower was gone now (though Xan had no idea where) and the castle was rubble, and the stones had been toppled by the volcano, or swallowed up by the earthquake, or crumbled by fire and water and time. Now there was only one, and it was difficult to find. Tall grasses surrounded it like a thick curtain, and ivy clung to its face. Xan spent well over half a day just trying to find it, and once she did, it was a full hour of hard labor just to dislodge the lattice of persistent ivy.

When she got down to the stone itself, she was disappointed. There were words carved into the flat of the stone. A simple message on each side. Zosimos himself had carved it, long ago. He had carved it for her, when she was still a child.

"Don't forget," it said on one side of the stone.

"I mean it," it said on the other.

*Don't forget what?*

*You mean what, Zosimos?*

She wasn't sure. Despite the spottiness of her memories, one thing she *did* remember was his tendency toward the obscure. And his assumption that because vague words and insinuations were clear enough for him, they must be perfectly comprehensible to all.

And after all these years, Xan remembered how *annoying* she had found it then.

"Confound that man," she said.

She approached the stone and leaned her forehead against

the deeply carved words, as if the stone might be Zosimos himself.

"Oh, Zosimos," she said, feeling a surge of emotion that she hadn't felt in nearly five centuries. "I'm sorry. I've forgotten. I didn't mean to, but—"

The surge of magic hit her like a falling boulder, knocking her backward. She landed with a thud on her creaking hips. She stared at the stone, openmouthed.

*The stone is enmagicked!* she thought to herself. *Of course!*

And she looked up at the stone just as a seam appeared down the middle and the two sides swung inward, like great stone doors.

*Not* like *stone doors,* Xan thought. *They* are *stone doors.*

The shape of the stone still stood like a doorway against the blue sky, but the entrance itself opened into a very dim corridor where a set of stone steps disappeared into the dark.

And in a flash, Xan remembered that day. She was thirteen years old and terribly impressed with her own witchy cleverness. And her teacher—once so strong and powerful—was fading by the day.

"Be careful of your sorrow," he had said. He was so old then. Impossibly old. He was all angles and bones and papery skin, like a cricket. "Your sorrow is dangerous. Don't forget that *she* is still about." And so Xan had swallowed her sorrow. And her memories, too. She buried both so deep that she would never find them. Or so she thought.

But now she remembered the castle—*she remembered!* Its crumbly strangeness. Its nonsensical corridors. And the people who lived in the castle—not just the wizards and scholars, but the cooks and scribes and assistants as well. She remembered how they scattered into the forest when the volcano erupted. She remembered how she put protective spells on each of them—well, each of them but *one*—and prayed to the stars that each spell would hold as they ran. She remembered how Zosimos hid the castle within each stone in the circle. Each stone was a door. "Same castle, different doors. Don't forget. I mean it."

"I won't forget," she said at thirteen.

"You will surely forget, Xan. Have you not met yourself?" He was so old then. How did he get so old? He had practically withered to dust. "But not to worry. I have built that into the spell. Now if you don't mind, my dear. I have treasured knowing you, and lamented knowing you, and found myself laughing in spite of myself each day we were together. But that is all past now, and you and I must part. I have many thousands of people to protect from that blasted volcano, and I do hope you'll make sure they are ever so thankful, won't you dear?" He shook his head sadly. "What am I saying? Of course you won't." And he and the Simply Enormous Dragon disappeared into the smoke and plunged themselves into the heart of the mountain, stopping the eruption, forcing the volcano into a restless sleep.

And both were gone forever.

Xan never did anything to protect his memory, or to explain what he had done.

Indeed, within a year, she could barely remember him. It never occurred to her to find it strange—the part of her that *would* have found it strange was on the other side of the curtain. Lost in the fog.

She peered into the gloom of the hidden castle. Her old bones ached, and her mind raced.

Why had her memories hidden themselves from her? And why had Zosimos hidden the castle?

She didn't know, but she was certain where she would find the answer. She knocked her staff against the ground three times, until it produced enough light to illuminate the dark. And she walked into the stone.

# 11

## In Which a Witch Comes to a Decision

Xan gathered books by the armload and carried them from the ruined castle to her workshop. Books and maps and papers and journals. Diagrams. Recipes. Artwork. For nine days she neither slept nor ate. Luna remained in her cocoon, pinned in place. Pinned in time, too. She didn't breathe. She didn't think. She was simply paused. Every time Glerk looked at her, he felt a sharp stab in his heart. He wondered if it would leave a mark.

He needn't have wondered. It surely did.

"You cannot come in," Xan told him through the locked door. "I must focus." And then he heard her muttering inside.

Night after night, Glerk peered into the windows of

the workshop, watching as Xan lit her candles and scanned through hundreds of open books and documents, taking notes on a scroll that grew longer and longer by the hour, muttering all the while. She shook her head. She whispered spells into lead boxes, quickly slamming the door shut the moment the spell was uttered and sitting on the lid to hold it in. Afterward, she'd cautiously open the box and peek inside, inhaling deeply as she did so, through her nose.

"Cinnamon," she'd say. "And salt. Too much wind in the spell." And she'd write that down.

Or: "Methane. No good. She'll accidentally fly away. Plus she'll be flammable. Even more than usual."

Or: "Is that sulfur? Great heavens. What are you trying to do, woman? Kill the poor child?" She crossed several things off her list.

"Has Auntie Xan gone mad?" Fyrian asked.

"No, my friend," Glerk told him. "But she has found herself in deeper water than she expected. She is not accustomed to not knowing exactly what to do. And it is frightening to her. As the Poet says,

'The Fool, when removed
from solid ground, leaps—
From mountaintop,
to burning star,
to black, black space.

*The scholar,*
*when bereft of scroll,*
*of quill,*
*of heavy tome,*
*Falls.*
*And cannot be found.'"*

"Is that a real poem?" Fyrian asked.

"Of course it is a real poem," Glerk said.

"But who made it, Glerk?"

Glerk closed his eyes. "The Poet. The Bog. The World. And me. They are all the same thing, you know."

But he wouldn't explain what he meant.

❄

Finally, Xan threw the doors of the workshop wide open, a look of grim satisfaction on her face. "You see," she explained to a very skeptical Glerk as she drew a large chalk circle on the ground, leaving a gap open to pass through. She drew thirteen evenly spaced marks along the circumference of the circle and used them to map out the points of a thirteen-pointed star. "In the end, all we are doing is setting a clock. Each day ticks by like the perfect whirring of a well-tuned gear, you see?"

Glerk shook his head. He did not see.

Xan marked out the time along the almost-complete circle—a neat and orderly progression. "It's a thirteen-year cycle. That's all the spell will allow. And less than that in our case, I'm afraid—the whole mechanism synchronizes to her own biology. Not much I can do about that. She's already five, so the clock will set itself to five, and will go off when she reaches thirteen."

Glerk squinted. None of this made any sense to him. Of course, magic itself always felt like nonsense to the swamp monster. Magic was not mentioned in the song that built the world, but rather had arrived in the world much later, in the light from the stars and moon. Magic, to him, always felt like an interloper, an uninvited guest. Glerk much preferred poetry.

"I'll be using the same principle as the protective cocoon that she sleeps in. All that magic is kept inside. But in this case, it will be inside *her*. Right at the front of her brain, behind the center of her forehead. I can keep it contained and *tiny*. A grain of sand. All that power in a grain of sand. Can you imagine?"

Glerk said nothing. He gazed down at the child in his arms. She didn't move.

"It won't—" he began. His voice was thick. He cleared his throat and started again. "It won't . . . *ruin* things, will it? I think I rather like her brain. I would like to see it unharmed."

"Oh, piffle," Xan admonished. "Her brain will be perfectly fine. At least I'm more than fairly sure it will be fine."

"*Xan!*"

"Oh, I'm only kidding! Of course she will be fine. This will simply buy us some time to make sure she has the good sense to know what to do with her magic once it is unleashed. She needs to be educated. She needs to know the contents of those books, there. She needs to understand the movements of the stars and the origins of the universe and the requirements of kindness. She needs to know mathematics and poetry. She must ask questions. She must seek to understand. She must understand the laws of cause and effect and unintended consequences. She must learn compassion and curiosity and awe. All of these things. We have to instruct her, Glerk. All three of us. It is a great responsibility."

The air in the room became suddenly heavy. Xan grunted as she pushed the chalk through the last edges of the thirteen-pointed star. Even Glerk, who normally wouldn't be affected, found himself both sweaty and nauseous.

"And what about you?" Glerk said. "Will the siphoning of *your* magic stop?"

Xan shrugged. "It will slow, I expect." She pressed her lips together. "Little bit by bit by bit. And then she will turn thirteen and it will flow out all at once. No more magic. I will be an empty vessel with nothing left to keep these old bones moving. And then I'll be gone." Xan's voice was quiet and smooth, like the surface of the swamp—and lovely, as the swamp is lovely. Glerk felt an ache in his chest. Xan attempted to smile. "Still, if I had my druthers, it's better to leave her orphaned *after* I can teach her a thing or two. Get her raised up properly. Prepare her. And I'd rather go all at once instead of wasting away like poor Zosimos."

"Death is always sudden," Glerk said. His eyes had begun to itch. "Even when it isn't." He wanted to clasp Xan in his third and fourth arms, but he knew the Witch wouldn't stand for it, so he held Luna a little bit closer instead, as Xan began to unwind the magical cocoon. The little girl smacked her lips together a few times and cuddled in close to his damp chest, warming him through. Her black hair shone like the night sky. She slept deeply. Glerk looked at the shape on the ground. There was still an open walkway for him to pass through with the girl. Once Luna was in place and Glerk was safely outside the chalk rim, Xan would complete the circle, and the spell would begin.

He hesitated.

"You're sure, Xan?" he said. "Are you very, very sure?"

"Yes. Assuming I've done this right, the seed of magic will open on her thirteenth birthday. We don't know the exact day, of course, but we can make our guesses. That's when her magic will come. And that's when I will go. It's enough. I've already outlasted any reasonable allotment of life on this earth. And I'm ever so curious to know what comes next. Come. Let's begin."

And the air smelled of milk and sweat and baking bread. Then sharp spice and skinned knees and damp hair. Then working muscles and soapy skin and clear mountain pools. And something else, too. A dark, strange, earthy smell.

And Luna cried out, just once.

And Glerk felt a crack in his heart, as thin as a pencil line. He pressed his four hands to his chest, trying to keep it from breaking in half.

# 12

## In Which a Child Learns About the Bog

No, child. The Witch does not live in the Bog. What a thing to say! All good things come from the Bog. Where else would we gather our Zirin stalks and our Zirin flowers and our Zirin bulbs? Where else would I gather the water spinach and muck-eating fish for your dinner or the duck eggs and frog spawn for your breakfast? If it weren't for the Bog your parents would have no work at all, and you would starve.

Besides, if the Witch lived in the Bog, I would have seen her.

Well, no. Of course I haven't seen the whole Bog. No one has. The Bog covers half the world, and the forest covers the other half. Everyone knows that.

But if the Witch was in the Bog, I would have seen the waters ripple with her cursed footsteps. I would have heard the reeds whisper her name. If the Witch was in the Bog, it would cough her out, the way a dying man coughs out his life.

Besides, the Bog loves us. It has always loved us. It is from the Bog that the world was made. Each mountain, each tree, each rock and animal and skittering insect. Even the wind was dreamed by the Bog.

Oh, of course you know this story. Everyone knows this story.

Fine. I will tell it if you must hear it one more time.

In the beginning, there was only Bog, and Bog, and Bog. There were no people. There were no fish. There were no birds or beasts or mountains or forest or sky.

The Bog was everything, and everything was the Bog.

The muck of the Bog ran from one edge of reality to the other. It curved and warbled through time. There were no words; there was no learning; there was no music or poetry or thought. There were just the sigh of the Bog and the quake of the Bog and the endless rustle of the reeds.

But the Bog was lonely. It wanted eyes with which to see the world. It wanted a strong back with which to carry itself from place to place. It wanted legs to walk and hands to touch and a mouth that could sing.

And so the Bog created a Body: a great Beast that walked out of the Bog on its own strong, boggy legs. The Beast was the Bog, and the Bog was the Beast. The Beast loved the Bog and the Bog loved the Beast, just as a person loves the image of himself in a quiet pond of water, and looks upon it with tenderness. The Beast's chest was full of warm and life-giving compassion. He felt the shine of love radiating outward. And the Beast wanted words to explain how he felt.

And so there were words.

And the Beast wanted those words to fit together just so, to explain his meaning. He opened his mouth and a poem came out.

"Round and yellow, yellow and round," the Beast said, and the sun was born, hanging just overhead.

"Blue and white and black and gray and a burst of color at dawn," the Beast said. And the sky was born.

"The creak of wood and the softness of moss and the rustle and whisper of green and green and green," the Beast sang. And there were forests.

Everything you see, everything you know, was called into being by the Bog. The Bog loves us and we love it.

The Witch in the Bog? Please. I've never heard anything so ridiculous in all my life.

# 13

## In Which Antain
## Pays a Visit

The Sisters of the Star always had an apprentice—always a young boy. Well, he wasn't much of an apprentice— more of a serving boy, really. They hired him when he was nine and kept him on until he was dispatched with a single note.

Every boy received the same note. Every single time.

"We had high hopes," it always said, "but this one has disappointed us."

Some boys served only a week or two. Antain knew of one from school who had only stayed a single day. Most were sent packing at the age of twelve—right when they had begun to get comfortable. Once they became aware of how much learning there was to be had in the libraries of the Tower and they became hungry for it, they were sent away.

Antain had been twelve when he received his note—one day after he had been granted (after years of asking) the privilege of the library. It was a crushing blow.

The Sisters of the Star lived in the Tower, a massive structure that unsettled the eye and confounded the mind. The Tower stood in the very center of the Protectorate—it cast its shadow everywhere.

The Sisters kept their pantries and auxiliary libraries and armories in the seemingly endless floors belowground. Rooms were set aside for bookbinding and herb mixing and broadsword training and hand-to-hand combat practice. The Sisters were skilled in all known languages, astronomy, the art of poisons, dance, metallurgy, martial arts, decoupage, and the finer points of assassinry. Aboveground were the Sisters' simple quarters (three to a room), spaces for meeting and reflection, impenetrable prison cells, a torture chamber, and a celestial observatory. Each was connected within an intricate framework of oddly-angled corridors and intersecting staircases that wound from the belly of the building to its deepest depths to the crown of its sky-viewer and back again. If anyone was foolish enough to enter without permission, he might wander for days without finding an exit.

During his years in the Tower, Antain could hear the Sisters' grunts in the practice rooms, and he could hear the occasional weeping from the prison rooms and torture chamber, and he could hear the Sisters engaged in heated discussions about the science of stars and the alchemical makeup of Zirin bulbs or the meaning of a particularly controversial poem. He could hear the Sisters singing as they pounded flour or boiled down herbs or sharpened their knives. He learned how to take dictation, clean a privy, set a table, serve an excellent luncheon, and master the fine art of bread-slicing. He learned the requirements for an excellent pot of tea and the finer points of sandwich-making and how to stand very still in the corner of a room and listen to a conversation, memorizing every detail, without ever letting the speakers notice that you are present. The Sisters often praised him during his time in the Tower, complimenting his penmanship or his swiftness or his polite demeanor. But it wasn't enough. Not really. The more he learned, the more he knew what more there *was to learn*. There were deep pools of knowledge in the dusty volumes quietly shelved in the libraries, and Antain thirsted for all of them. But he wasn't allowed to drink. He worked hard. He did his best. He tried not to think about the books.

Still, one day he returned to his room and found his bags already packed. The Sisters pinned a note to his shirt and sent him home to his mother. "We had high hopes," the note said. "But this one has disappointed us."

He never got over it.

Now as an Elder-in-Training he was supposed to be at

the Council Hall, preparing for the day's hearings, but he just couldn't. After making excuses, yet again, about missing the Day of Sacrifice, Antain had noticed a distinct difference in his rapport with the Elders. An increased muttering. A proliferation of side-eyed glances. And, worst of all, his uncle refused to even look at him.

He hadn't set foot in the Tower since his apprenticeship days, but Antain felt that it was high time to visit the Sisters, who had been, for him, a sort of short-term family—albeit odd, standoffish, and, admittedly, murderous. Still. Family is family, he told himself as he walked up to the old oak door and knocked.

(There was another reason, of course. But Antain could hardly even admit it to himself. And it was making him twitch.)

His little brother answered. Rook. He had, as usual, a runny nose, and his hair was much longer than it had been when Antain saw it last—over a year ago now.

"Are you here to take me home?" Rook said, his voice a mixture of hope and shame. "Have I disappointed them, too?"

"It's nice to see you, Rook," Antain said, rubbing his little brother's head as though he were a mostly-well-behaved dog. "But no. You've only been here a year. You've got plenty of time to disappoint them. Is Sister Ignatia here? I'd like to speak to her."

Rook shuddered, and Antain didn't blame him. Sister Ignatia was a formidable woman. And terrifying. But Antain had always gotten on with her, and she always seemed fond of him.

The other Sisters made sure that he knew how rare this was. Rook showed his older brother to the study of the Head Sister, but Antain could have made it there blindfolded. He knew every step, every stony divot in the ancient walls, every creaky floorboard. He still, after all these years, had dreams of being back in the Tower.

"Antain!" Sister Ignatia said from her desk. She was, from the look of it, translating texts having to do with botany. Sister Ignatia's life's greatest passion was for botany. Her office was filled with plants of all description—most coming from the more obscure sections of the forest or the swamp, but some coming from all around the world, via specialized dealers in the cities at the other end of the Road.

"Why, my dear boy," Sister Ignatia said as she got up from her desk and walked across the heavily perfumed room to take Antain's face in her wiry, strong hands. She patted him gently on each cheek, but it still stung. "You are many times more handsome today than you were when we sent you home."

"Thank you, Sister," Antain said, feeling a familiar stab of shame just thinking of that awful day when he left the Tower with a note.

"Sit, please." She looked out toward the door and shouted in a very loud voice. "BOY!" she called to Rook. "BOY, ARE YOU LISTENING TO ME?"

"Yes, Sister Ignatia," Rook squeaked, flinging himself through the doorway at a run and tripping on the threshold.

Sister Ignatia was not amused. "We will require lavender tea and Zirin blossom cookies." She gave the boy a stormy look, and he ran away as though a tiger was after him.

Sister Ignatia sighed. "Your brother lacks your skills, I'm afraid," she said. "It is a pity. We had such high hopes." She motioned for Antain to sit on one of the chairs—it was covered with a spiky sort of vine, but Antain sat on it anyway, trying to ignore the prickles in his legs. Sister Ignatia sat opposite him and leaned in, searching his face.

"Tell me, dear, are you married yet?"

"No, ma'am," Antain said, blushing. "I'm a bit young, yet."

Sister Ignatia clucked her tongue. "But you are sweet on someone. I can tell. You can hide nothing from me, dear boy. Don't even try." Antain tried not to think about the girl from his school. Ethyne. She was somewhere in this tower. But she was lost to him, and there was nothing he could do about it.

"My duties with the Council don't leave me much time," he said evasively. Which was true.

"Of course, of course," she said with a wave of her hand. "The Council." It seemed to Antain that she said the word with a little bit of a sneer in her voice. But then she sneezed a little, and he assumed he must have imagined it.

"I have only been an Elder-in-Training for five years now, but I am already learning . . ." He paused. "Ever so much," he finished in a hollow voice.

*The baby on the ground.*

*The woman screaming from the rafters.*

No matter how hard he tried, he still couldn't get those images out of his mind. Or the Council's response to his questions. Why must they treat his inquiries with such disdain? Antain had no idea.

Sister Ignatia tipped her head to one side and gave him a searching look. "To be frank, my dear, dear boy, I was stunned that you made the decision to join that particular body, and I confess I assumed that it was not your decision at all, but your . . . lovely mother's." She puckered her lips unpleasantly, as though tasting something sour.

And this was true. It was entirely true. Joining the Council was not Antain's choice at all. He would have preferred to be a carpenter. Indeed, he told his mother as much—often, and at length—not that she listened.

"Carpentry," Sister Ignatia continued, not noticing the shock on Antain's face that she had, apparently, read his mind, "would have been my guess. You were always thusly inclined."

"You—"

She smiled with slitted eyes. "Oh, I know quite a bit, young man." She flared her nostrils and blinked. "You'd be amazed."

Rook stumbled in with the tea and the cookies, and managed to both spill the tea and dump the cookies on his brother's lap. Sister Ignatia gave him a look as sharp as a blade, and he ran out of the room in a panicked rush, as though he was already bleeding.

"Now," Sister Ignatia said, taking a sip of her tea through her smile. "What can I do for you?"

"Well," Antain said, despite the mouthful of cookie. "I just wanted to pay a visit. Because I hadn't for a long time. You know. To catch up. See how you are."

*The baby on the ground.*

*The screaming mother.*

*And oh, god, what if something got to it before the Witch? What would happen to us then?*

*And oh, my stars, why must this continue? Why is there no one to stop it?*

Sister Ignatia smiled. "Liar," she said, and Antain hung his head. She gave his knee an affectionate squeeze. "Don't be ashamed, poor thing," she soothed. "You're not the only one who wishes to gawk and gape at our resident caged animal. I am considering charging admission."

"Oh," Antain protested. "No, I—"

She waved him off. "No need. I completely understand. She is a rare bird. And a bit of a puzzle. A fountain of sorrow." She gave a bit of a sigh, and the corners of her lips quivered, like the very tip of a snake's tongue. Antain wrinkled his brow.

"Can she be cured?" he asked.

Sister Ignatia laughed. "Oh, sweet Antain! There is no cure for sorrow." Her lips unfurled into a wide smile, as though this was most excellent news.

"Surely, though," Antain persisted. "It can't last forever.

So many of our people have lost their children. And not everyone's sorrow is like this."

She pressed her lips together. "No. No, it is not. Her sorrow is amplified by madness. Or her madness stems from her sorrow. Or perhaps it is something else entirely. This makes her an interesting study. I do appreciate her presence in our dear Tower. We are making good use of the knowledge we are gaining from the observation of her mind. Knowledge, after all, is a precious commodity." Antain noticed that the Head Sister's cheeks were a bit rosier than they had been the last time he was in the Tower. "But honestly, dear boy, while this old lady appreciates the attention of such a handsome young man, you don't need to stand on ceremony with me. You're to be a full member of the Council one day, dear. You need only ask the boy at the door and he has to show you to any prisoner you wish to see. That's the law." There was ice in her eyes. But only for a moment. She gave Antain a warm smile. "Come, my little Elderling."

She stood and walked to the door without making a sound. Antain followed her, his boots clomping heavily on the floorboards.

Though the prison cells were only one floor above them, it took four staircases to get there. Antain peeked hopefully from room to room, on the off chance that he might catch sight of Ethyne, the girl from school. He saw many members of the novitiate, but he didn't see her. He tried not to feel disappointed.

The stairs swung left and right and pulled down into a tight spiral into the edge of the central room of the prison floor. The central room was a circular, windowless space, with three Sisters sitting in chairs at the very middle with their backs facing one another in a tight triangle, each with a crossbow resting across her lap.

Sister Ignatia gave an imperious glance at the nearest Sister. She flicked her chin toward one of the doors.

"Let him in to see number five. He'll knock when he's ready to leave. Mind you don't accidentally shoot him."

And then with a smile, she returned her gaze to Antain and embraced him.

"Well, I'm off," she said brightly, and she went back up the spiral stair as the closest Sister rose and unlocked the door marked "5."

She met Antain's eyes and she shrugged.

"She won't do much for you. We had to give her special potions to keep her calm. And we had to cut off her pretty hair, because she kept trying to pull it out." She looked him up and down. "You haven't got any paper on you, have you?"

Antain wrinkled his brow. "Paper? No. Why?"

The Sister pressed her lips into a thin line. "She's not permitted to have paper," she said.

"Why not?"

The Sister's face became a blank. As expressionless as a hand in a glove. "You'll see," she said.

And she opened the door.

The cell was a riot of paper. The prisoner had folded and torn and twisted and fringed paper into thousands and thousands of paper birds, of all shapes and sizes. There were paper swans in the corner, paper herons on the chair, and tiny paper hummingbirds suspended from the ceiling. Paper ducks; paper robins; paper swallows; paper doves.

Antain's first instinct was to be scandalized. Paper was expensive. Enormously expensive. There were paper makers in the town who made fine sheaves of writing stock from a combination of wood pulp and cattails and wild flax and Zirin flowers, but most of that was sold to the traders, who took it to the other side of the forest. Whenever anyone in the Protectorate wrote anything down, it was only after much thought and consideration and planning.

And here was this lunatic. *Wasting it.* Antain could hardly contain his shock.

And yet.

The birds were incredibly intricate and detailed. They crowded the floor; they heaped on the bed; they peeked out of the two small drawers of the nightstand. And they were, he couldn't deny it, *beautiful.* They were *so beautiful.* Antain pressed his hand on his heart.

"Oh, my," he whispered.

The prisoner lay on the bed, fast asleep, but she stirred at the sound of his voice. Very slowly, she stretched. Very slowly, she pulled her elbows under her body and inched her way to a small incline.

Antain hardly recognized her. That beautiful black hair was gone, shaved to the skin, and so were the fire in her eyes and the flush of her cheeks. Her lips were flat and drooping, as though they were too heavy to hold up, and her cheeks were sallow and dull. Even the crescent moon birthmark on her forehead was a shadow of its former self—like a smudge of ashes on her brow. Her small, clever hands were covered with tiny cuts—*Paper, probably,* Antain thought—and dark smudges of ink stained each fingertip.

Her eyes slid from one end of him to the other, up, down, and sideways, never finding purchase. She couldn't pin him down.

"Do I know you?" she said slowly.

"No, ma'am," Antain said.

"You look"—she swallowed—"familiar." Each word seemed to be drawn from a very deep well.

Antain looked around. There was also a small table with more paper, but this was drawn on. Strange, intricate maps with words he didn't understand and markings he did not know. And all of them with the same phrase written in the bottom right corner: "She is here; she is here; she is here."

*Who is here?* Antain wondered.

"Ma'am, I am a member of the Council. Well, a provisional member. An Elder-in-Training."

"Ah," she said, and she slumped back down onto the bed, staring blankly at the ceiling. "You. I remember you. Have you come to ridicule me, too?"

She closed her eyes and laughed.

Antain stepped backward. He felt a shiver at the sound of her laugh, as though someone was slowly pouring a tin of cold water down his back. He looked up at the paper birds hanging from the ceiling. Strange, but all of them were suspended from what looked like strands of long, black, wavy hair. And even stranger: they were all facing him. Had they been facing him before?

Antain's palms began to sweat.

"You should tell your uncle," she said very, very slowly, laying each word next to the one before, like a long, straight line of heavy, round stones, "that he was wrong. She is *here*. And she is *terrible*."

*She is here*, the map said.

*She is here.*

*She is here.*

*She is here.*

But what did it mean?

"Who is where?" Antain asked, in spite of himself. Why was he talking to her? *One can't*, he reminded himself, *reason with the mad. It can't be done.* The paper birds rustled overhead. *It must be the wind*, Antain thought.

"The child he took? My child?" She gave a hollow laugh.

"She didn't die. Your uncle thinks she is dead. *Your uncle is wrong.*"

"Why would he think she is dead? No one knows what the Witch does with the children." He shivered again. There was a shivery, rustling sound to his left, like the flapping of a paper wing. He turned but nothing moved. He heard it again at his right. Again. Nothing.

"All I know is this," the mother said as she pulled herself unsteadily to her feet. The paper birds began to lift and swirl.

*It is just the wind,* Antain told himself.

"I know where she is."

*I am imagining things.*

"I know what you people have done."

*Something is crawling down my neck. My god. It's a hummingbird. And—OUCH!*

A paper raven swooped across the room, slicing its wing across Antain's cheek, cutting it open, letting him bleed.

Antain was too amazed to cry out.

"But it doesn't matter. Because the reckoning is coming. It's coming. It's coming. And it is nearly here."

She closed her eyes and swayed. She was clearly mad. Indeed, her madness hung about her like a cloud, and Antain knew he had to get away, lest he become infected by it. He pounded on the door, but it didn't make any sound. "LET ME OUT," he shouted to the Sisters, but his voice seemed to die the moment it fell from his mouth. He could feel his words thud on the ground at his feet. Was he catching madness? Could such a thing happen? The paper birds shuffled and shirred and gathered. They lifted in great waves.

"PLEASE!" he shouted as a paper swallow went for his eyes and two paper swans bit his feet. He kicked and swatted, but they kept coming.

"You seem like a nice boy," the mother said. "Choose a different profession. That's my advice." She crawled back into bed.

Antain pounded on the door again. Again his pounding was silent.

The birds squawked and keened and screeched. They sharpened their paper wings like knives. They massed in great murmurations—swelling and contracting and swelling again. They reared up for the attack. Antain covered his face with his hands.

And then they were upon him.

# 14

## In Which There Are Consequences

When Luna woke, she felt different. She didn't know why. She lay in her bed for a long time, listening to the singing of the birds. She didn't understand a thing they were saying. She shook her head. Why would she understand them in the first place? They were only birds. She pressed her hands to her face. She listened to the birds again.

"No one can talk to birds," she said out loud. And it was true. So why did it feel like it wasn't? A brightly colored finch landed on the windowsill and sang so sweetly, Luna thought her heart would break. Indeed, it *was* breaking a little, even now. She brought her hands to her eyes and realized that she was crying, though she had no idea why.

"Silly," she said out loud, noticing a little waver and rattle in her voice. "Silly Luna." She was the silliest girl. Everyone said so.

She looked around. Fyrian was curled up at the foot of her bed. That was regular. He loved sleeping on her bed, though her grandmother often forbade it. Luna never knew why.

At least she *thought* she didn't know why. But it felt, deep inside herself, that maybe once upon a time she *did*. But she couldn't remember when.

Her grandmother was asleep in her own bed on the other side of the room. And her swamp monster was sprawled out on the floor, snoring prodigiously.

*That* is *strange,* Luna thought. She couldn't remember a single other time when Glerk had slept on the floor. Or inside. Or un-submerged in the swamp. Luna shook her head. She squinched up her shoulders to her ears—first one side, and then the other. The world pressed on her strangely, like a coat that no longer fit. Also, she had a terrible pain in her head, deep inside. She hit her forehead a few times with the heel of her hand, but it didn't help.

Luna slid out of bed and slid out of her nightgown and slipped on a dress with deep pockets sewn all over, because it is how she asked her grandmother to make it. She gently laid the sleeping Fyrian into one of the pockets, careful not to wake him up. Her bed was attached to the ceiling with ropes and pulleys to make room in the small house during the day, but Luna was still too small to be able to hoist it up on her own. She left it as it was and went outside.

It was early, and the morning sun had not yet made it over the lip of the ridge. The mountain was cool and damp and alive. Three of the volcanic craters had thin ribbons of smoke lazily curling from their insides and meandering toward the sky. Luna walked slowly toward the edge of the swamp. She looked down at her bare feet sinking slightly into the mossy ground, leaving footsteps. No flowers grew out of the places where she stepped.

But that was a silly thing to think, wasn't it? Why would something grow out of her footsteps? "Silly, silly," she said out loud. And then she felt her head go fuzzy. She sat down on the ground and stared at the ridge, thinking nothing at all.

✣

Xan found Luna sitting by herself outside, staring at the sky. Which was odd. Normally the girl woke in a whirlwind, rousting awake all who were near. Not so today.

*Well,* Xan thought. *Everything's different now.* She shook her head. *Not everything,* she decided. Despite the bound-up magic curled inside her, safe and sound for now, she was still the same girl. She was still *Luna.* They simply didn't have to worry about her magic erupting all over the place. Now she could learn in peace. And today they were going to get started.

"Good morning, precious," Xan said, letting her hand slide

along the curve of the girl's skull, winding her fingers in the long black curls. Luna didn't say anything. She seemed to be in a bit of a trance. Xan tried not to worry about it.

"Good morning, Auntie Xan," Fyrian said, peeking out of the pocket and yawning, stretching his small arms out as wide as they would go. He looked around, squinting. "Why am I outside?"

Luna returned to the world with a start. She looked at her grandmother and smiled. "Grandmama!" she said, scrambling to her feet. "I feel like I haven't seen you for days and days."

"Well, that's because—" Fyrian began, but Xan interrupted.

"Hush, child," she said.

"But Auntie Xan," Fyrian continued excitedly, "I just wanted to explain that—"

"Enough prattling, you silly dragon. Off with you. Go find your monster."

Xan pulled Luna to her feet and hurried her away.

"But where are we going, Grandmama?" Luna asked.

"To the workshop, darling," Xan said, shooting Fyrian a sharp look. "Go help Glerk with breakfast."

"Okay, Auntie Xan. I just want to tell Luna this one—"

"Now, Fyrian," she snapped, and she ushered Luna quickly away.

☼

Luna loved her grandmother's workshop, and had already been taught the basics of mechanics—levers and wedges and pulleys and gears. Even at that young age, Luna possessed a mechanical mind, and was able to construct little machines that whirred and ticked. She loved finding bits of wood that she could smooth and connect and fashion into something else.

For now, Xan had pushed all of Luna's projects into a corner and divided the whole workshop into sections, each with its own sets of bookshelves and tool shelves and materials shelves. There was a section for inventing and a section for building and one for scientific study and one for botany and one for the study of magic. On the floor she had made numerous chalk drawings.

"What happened here, Grandmama?" Luna asked.

"Nothing, dear," Xan said. But then she thought better of it. "Well, actually, many things, but there are more important items to attend to first." She sat down on the floor, across from the girl, and gathered her magic into her hand, letting it float just above her fingers like a bright, shining ball.

"You see, dearest," she explained, "the magic flows through me, from earth to sky, but it collects in me as well. Inside me. Like static electricity. It crackles and hums in my bones. When I need a little extra light, I rub my hands together like so, and let the light spin between my palms, until it is enough to float wherever I need it to float. You've seen me do this before, hundreds of times, but I have never explained it. Isn't it pretty, my darling?"

But Luna did not see. Her eyes were blank. Her face was

blank. She looked as though her soul had gone dormant, like a tree in winter. Xan gasped.

"Luna?" she said. "Are you well? Are you hungry? *Luna?*" There was nothing. Blank eyes. Blank face. A Luna-shaped hole in the universe. Xan felt a rush of panic bloom in her chest.

And, as though the blankness had never happened at all, the light returned to the child's eyes. "Grandmama, may I have something sweet?" she said.

"What?" Xan said, her panic increasing in spite of the light's return to the child's eyes. She looked closer.

Luna shook her head as though to dislodge water from her ears. "Sweet," she said slowly. "I would like something sweet." She crinkled her eyebrows together. "Please," she added. And the Witch obliged, reaching into her pocket and pulling out a handful of dried berries. The child chewed them thoughtfully. She looked around.

"Why are we here, Grandmama?"

"We've been here this whole time," Xan said. She searched the child's face with her eyes. *What was going on?*

"But why though?" Luna looked around. "Weren't we just outside?" She pressed her lips together. "I don't . . ." she began, trailing off. "I don't remember . . ."

"I wanted to give you your first lesson, darling." A cloud passed over Luna's face, and Xan paused. She put her hand on the girl's cheek. The waves of magic were gone. If she concentrated very hard, she could feel the gravitational pull of that dense nugget of power, smooth and hard and sealed off like a nut. Or an egg.

She decided to try again. "Luna, my love. Do you know what magic is?"

And once again, Luna's eyes went blank. She didn't move. She barely breathed. It was as if the *stuff* of Luna—light, motion, intelligence—had simply vanished.

Xan waited again. This time it took even longer for the light to return and for Luna to regain herself. The girl looked at her grandmother with a curious expression. She looked to her right and she looked to her left. She frowned.

"When did we get here, Grandmama?" she asked. "Did I fall asleep?"

Xan pulled herself to her feet and started pacing the room. She paused at the invention table, surveying its gears and wires and wood and glass and books with intricate diagrams and instructions. She picked up a small gear in one hand and a small spring—so sharp at the ends it made a point of blood bloom on her thumb—in the other. She looked back at Luna and pictured the mechanism inside that girl—rhythmically ticking its way toward her thirteenth birthday, as even and inexorable as a well-tuned clock.

Or, at least, that was how the spell was *supposed* to work. Nothing in Xan's construction of the spell had indicated this kind of . . . *blankness*. Had she done it wrong?

She decided to try another tactic.

"Grandmama, what are you doing?" Luna asked.

"Nothing, darling," Xan said as she bustled over to the magic table and assembled a scrying glass—wood from the earth, glass made from a melted meteorite, a splash of water, and a single hole in the center to let the air in. It was one of her better efforts. Luna didn't seem to even see it. Her gaze slid from one side to the other. Xan set it up between them and looked at the girl through the gap.

"I would like to tell you a story, Luna," the old woman said.

"I love stories." Luna smiled.

"Once upon a time there was a witch who found a baby in the woods," Xan said. Through the scrying glass, she watched her dusty words fly into the ears of the child. She watched the words separate inside the skull—*baby* lingered and flitted from the memory centers to the imaginative structures to the places where the brain enjoys playing with pleasing-sounding words. *Baby, baby, b-b-bab-b-b-eeee,* over and over and over again. Luna's eyes began to darken.

"Once upon a time," Xan said, "when you were very, very small, I took you outside to see the stars."

"We always go outside to see the stars," Luna said. "Every night."

"Yes, yes," Xan said. "Pay attention. One night, long ago, as we looked at the stars, I gathered starlight on my fingertips, and fed it to you like honey from the comb."

And Luna's eyes went blank. She shook her head as though

clearing away cobwebs. "Honey," she said slowly, as though the word itself was a great burden.

Xan was undeterred. "And then," she pressed. "One night, Grandmama did not notice the rising moon, hanging low and fat in the sky. And she reached up to gather starlight, and gave you moonlight by mistake. And this is how you became en-magicked, my darling. This is where your magic comes from. You drank deeply from the moon, and now the moon is full within you."

It was as though it was not Luna sitting on the floor, but a picture of Luna instead. She did not blink. Her face was as still as stone. Xan waved her hand in front of the girl's face, and nothing happened. Nothing at all.

"Oh, dear," Xan said. "Oh dear, oh dear, oh dear."

Xan scooped the girl into her arms and ran out the door, sobbing, looking for Glerk.

It took most of the afternoon for the child to regain herself.

"Well," Glerk said. "This is a bit of a pickle."

"It's nothing of the kind," Xan snapped. "I'm sure it's temporary," she added, as though her words alone could make it true.

But it wasn't temporary. This was the consequence of Xan's spell: the child was now unable to learn about magic. She couldn't hear it, couldn't speak it, couldn't even know the word. Every time she heard anything to do with magic, her consciousness and her spark and her very soul seemed to simply disappear. And whether the knowledge was being sucked into the kernel in Luna's brain, or whether it was flying away entirely, Xan did not know.

"What will we do when she comes of age?" Glerk asked. "How will you teach her then?" *Because you will surely die then,* Glerk thought but did not say. *Her magic will open, and yours will pour away, and you, my dear, darling five-hundred-year-old Xan, will no longer have magic in you to keep you alive.* He felt the cracks in his heart grow deeper.

"Maybe she won't grow," Xan said desperately. "Maybe she will stay like this forever, and I will never have to say good-bye to her. Maybe I mislaid the spell, and her magic will never come out. Maybe she was never magic to begin with."

"You know that isn't true," Glerk said.

"It might be true," Xan countered. "You don't know." She paused before she spoke again. "The alternative is too sorrow-ful to contemplate."

"Xan—" Glerk began.

"Sorrow is dangerous," she snapped. And she left in a huff.

They had this conversation again and again, with no reso-lution. Eventually, Xan refused to discuss it at all.

*The child was never magic,* Xan started telling herself. And indeed, the more Xan told herself that it *might* be true, the more she was able to convince herself that it *was* true. And if Luna ever was magic, all that power was now neatly stoppered up and wouldn't be a problem. Perhaps it was stuck forever.

Perhaps Luna was now a regular girl. *A regular girl.* Xan said it again and again and again. She said it so many times that it *must* be true. It's exactly what she told people in the Free Cities when they asked. *A regular girl,* she said. She also told them Luna was allergic to magic. *Hives,* she said. *Seizures. Itchy eyes. Stomach upset.* She asked everyone to never mention magic near the girl.

And so, no one did. Xan's advice was always followed to the letter.

In the meantime, there was a whole world for Luna to learn—science, mathematics, poetry, philosophy, art. Surely that would be enough. Surely she would grow as a girl grows, and Xan would continue as she was—still-magic, slow-to-age, deathless Xan. Surely, Xan would never have to say good-bye.

"This can't go on," Glerk said, over and over. "Luna needs to know what's inside her. She needs to know how magic works. She needs to know what death is. She needs to be *prepared.*"

"I'm sure I have no idea what you are talking about," Xan said. "She's just a regular girl. Even if she wasn't before, she certainly is now. My own magic is replenished—and I hardly ever use it in any case. There is no need to upset her. Why would we speak of impending loss? Why would we introduce her to that kind of sorrow? It's dangerous, Glerk. Remember?"

Glerk wrinkled his brow. "Why do we think that?" he asked.

Xan shook her head. "I have no idea." And she didn't. She knew, once, but the memory had vanished.

It was easier to forget.

And so Luna grew.

And she didn't know about the starlight or the moonlight or the tight knot behind her forehead. And she didn't remember about the enrabbiting of Glerk or the flowers in her footsteps or the power that was, even now, clicking through its gears, pulsing, pulsing, pulsing inexorably toward its end point. She didn't know about the hard, tight seed of magic readying to crack open inside her.

She had absolutely no idea.

# 15

## In Which Antain Tells a Lie

The scars from the paper birds never healed. Not properly, anyway.

"They were just paper," Antain's mother wailed. "How is it possible that they cut so deep?"

It wasn't just the cuts. The infections after the cuts were far worse. Not to mention the considerable loss of blood. Antain had lain on the floor for a long time while the madwoman attempted to stop his bleeding with paper—and not very well. The medicines the Sisters gave her made her woozy and weak. She drifted in and out of consciousness. When the guards finally came in to check on him, both he and the madwoman lay in a puddle of so much blood, it took them a moment to find out who, exactly, it belonged to.

"And why," his mother fumed, "did they not come for you when you cried out? Why did they abandon you?"

No one knew the answer to that one. The Sisters claimed they had no idea. They hadn't heard him. And later, one look at the whiteness of their faces and their bloodshot eyes led everyone to believe that it was true.

People whispered that Antain had cut himself.

People whispered that his story of the paper birds was just a fantasy. After all, no one found any birds. Just bloody wads of paper on the ground. And, anyway, who had ever heard of an attacking paper bird?

People whispered that a boy like *that* had no business being an Elder-in-Training. And on that point, Antain couldn't have agreed more. By the time his wounds were healed, he had announced to the Council that he was resigning. Effective immediately. Freed from school, from the Council, and from the constant needling of his mother, Antain became a carpenter. And he was very good at it.

The Council, owing to its members' profound discomfort whenever they had to look at the deep scars covering the poor boy's face—not to mention his mother's insistence—had given the boy a tidy sum of money with which he was able to secure rare woods and fine tools from the traders who did their business via the Road. (And oh! Those scars! And oh! How handsome he used to be! And oh! That lost potential. Such a pity it was. What a great and terrible pity.)

Antain got to work.

Very quickly, as word of his skill and artistry spread on both ends of the Road, Antain made a good enough living to keep his mother and brothers happy and content. He built a separate home for himself—smaller, simpler, and infinitely more humble, but comfortable all the same.

Still. His mother did not approve of his departure from the Council, and told him as much. His brother Rook didn't understand, either, though his disapproval came much later, after he had been dismissed from the Tower and returned home in shame. (Rook's note, unlike his brother's, did not contain the preface, "We had high hopes," and instead simply said, "This one has disappointed us." Their mother blamed Antain.)

Antain hardly noticed. He spent his days away from everyone else—working with wood and metal and oil. The itch of sawdust. The slip of the grain under the fingers. The making of something beautiful and whole and *real* was all he cared about. Months passed. Years. Still his mother fussed at him.

"What kind of person leaves the Council?" she howled one day after she had insisted that he accompany her to the Market. She needled and complained as she perused the different stalls, with their various selections of medicinal and beautifying flowers, as well as Zirin honey and Zirin jam and dried Zirin petals, which could be reconstituted with milk and slathered over the face to prevent wrinkles. Not everyone could afford to shop in the Market; most people bartered with their neighbors to keep their cupboards slightly less bare. And even those who could manage a visit to the Market could not afford the heaps of goods that Antain's mother piled into her basket. Being the only sister of the Grand Elder had its advantages.

She narrowed her eyes at the dried Zirin petals. She gave the woman standing in the stall a hard look. "How long ago were these harvested? And don't you dare lie to me!" The flower woman turned pale.

"I cannot say, madam," she mumbled.

Antain's mother gave her an imperious look. "If you cannot say, then I shall not pay." And she moved on to the next stall.

Antain did not comment, and instead let his gaze drift upward to the Tower, running his fingers over the deep gouges and gorges and troughs that marred his face, following the rivers of scars like a map.

"Well," his mother said as she browsed through bolts of cloth that had been brought from the other end of the Road, "we can only hope that when this ridiculous carpentry enterprise winds itself toward its inevitable end, your Honorable Uncle will take you back—if not as a Council member, then at least as a member of his staff. And then, one day, your little brother's staff. At least *he* has the good sense to listen to his mother!"

Antain nodded and grunted and said nothing. He found himself wandering toward the paper vendor's stall. He hardly ever touched paper anymore. Not if he could help it. Still.

These Zirin papers were lovely. He let his fingers drift across the reams and let his mind drift to the rustly sounds of paper wings flying across the face of the mountain and disappearing from sight.

⁕

Antain's mother was wrong about his coming failure, though. The carpentry shop remained a success—not only among the small, moneyed enclave of the Protectorate and the famously tightfisted Traders Association. His carvings and furniture and clever constructions were in high demand on the other side of the Road, as well. Every month the traders arrived with a list of orders, and every month, Antain had to turn some of them away, explaining kindly that he was only one person with two hands, and his time was naturally limited.

On hearing such refusals, the traders offered Antain more and more money for his handiwork.

And as Antain honed his skills and as his eye became clear and cunning and as his designs became more and more clever, so too did his renown increase. Within five years, his name was known in towns he had never heard of, let alone thought to visit. Mayors of far-off places requested the honor of his company. Antain considered it; of course he did. He had never left the Protectorate. He didn't know anyone who *had*, though his family could certainly afford to. But even the thought of doing anything but work and sleep, the occasional book read by the fire, was more than he could manage. Sometimes it felt to him that the world was heavy, that the air, thick with sorrow, draped over his mind and body and vision, like a fog.

Still. Knowing that his handiwork found good homes satisfied Antain to the core. It felt good to be *good* at something. And when he slept, he was mostly content.

His mother now insisted that she always knew her son would be a great success, and how fortunate, she said again and again, he had been to escape a life of drudgery with those doddering old bores on the Council, and how much better it was to follow your talents and bliss and whatnot, and hadn't she always said so.

"Yes, mother," Antain said, suppressing a smile. "You truly always said so."

And in this way, the years passed: a lonely workshop; solid, beautiful things; customers who praised his work but winced at the sight of his face. It wasn't a bad life, actually.

✿

Antain's mother stood in the doorway of the workshop late one morning, her nostrils wrinkling from the sawdust and the sharp smell of Zirin hip oil, which gave the wood its particular sheen. Antain had just finished the final carved details on the headboard of a cradle—a sky full of bright stars. This was not the first time he had made such a cradle, and it was not the first time he had heard the term *Star Child,* though he did not know what it meant. The people on the other end of the Road were strange. Everyone knew it, though no one had met any.

"You should get an apprentice," his mother said, eyeing the room. The workshop was well organized, well appointed, and comfortable. Well, comfortable for some people. Antain, for example, was extremely comfortable there.

"I do not want an apprentice," Antain said as he rubbed oil into the curve of the wood. The grain shone like gold.

"You would do better business with an extra pair of hands. Your brothers—"

"Are dunces with wood," Antain replied mildly. And it was true.

"Well," his mother huffed. "Just think if you—"

"I am doing fine as it is," Antain said. And that was also true.

"Well then," his mother said. She shifted her weight from side to side. She adjusted the drape of her cloak. She had more cloaks herself than most extended families had among them. "What about your *life*, son? Here you are building cradles for other women's grandchildren, and not my own. How am I supposed to bear the continuing shame of your un-Councilment without a beautiful grandchild to dandle upon my blessed knee?"

His mother's voice cracked. There was a time, Antain knew, when he might have been able to stroll through the Market with a girl on his arm. But he had been so shy then, he never dared. In retrospect, Antain knew that it likely wouldn't have been hard, had he tried. He had seen the sketches and portraits that his mother commissioned back then and knew that, once upon a time, he had been handsome.

No matter. He was good at his work and he loved it. Did he really need anything more?

"I'm sure Rook will marry one day, Mother. And Wynn. And the rest of them. Do not fret. I will make each of my brothers a bureau and a marriage bed and a cradle when the time is right. You'll have grandchildren hanging from the rafters in no time."

*The mother in the rafters. The child in her arms. And oh! The screaming.* Antain shut his eyes tightly and forced the image away.

"I have been talking with some other mothers. They have set a keen eye on the life you've built here. They are interested in introducing you to their daughters. Not their prettiest daughters, you understand, but daughters nonetheless."

Antain sighed, stood, and washed his hands.

"Mother, thank you, but no." He walked across the room and leaned over to kiss his mother on the cheek. He saw how she flinched when his ruined face got too close. He did his best not to let it hurt.

"But, Antain—"

"And now, I must be going."

"But where are you going?"

"I have several errands to attend to." This was a lie. With each lie he told, the next became easier. "I shall be at your house in two days' time for dinner. I haven't forgotten." This was also a lie. He had no intention of eating in his family's house, and was perfecting several excuses to remove himself from the vicinity at the last moment.

"Perhaps I should come with you," she said. "Keep you company." She loved him, in her way. Antain knew that.

"It's best if I go alone," Antain said. And he tied his cloak around his shoulders and walked away, leaving his mother behind in the shadows.

Antain kept to the lesser-used alleys and lanes throughout the Protectorate. Though the day was fair, he pulled his hood well over his forehead to keep his face in shadow. Antain had noticed long ago that his hiding himself made people more comfortable and minimized the staring. Sometimes small children would shyly ask to touch his scars. If their families were nearby, the child would invariably be shooed away by a mortified parent, and the interaction would be over. If not, though, Antain would soberly sit on his haunches and look the child in the eye. If the child did not bolt, he would remove his hood and say, "Go ahead."

"Does it hurt?" the child would ask.

"Not today," Antain always said. Another lie. His scars always hurt. Not as much as they did on that first day, or even the first week. But they hurt all the same—the dull ache of something lost.

The touch of those small fingers on his face—tracing the

furrows and ridges of the scars—made Antain's heart constrict, just a little. "Thank you," Antain would say. And he meant it. Every time.

"Thank you," the child always replied. And the two would part ways—the child returning to his family, and Antain leaving alone.

His wanderings brought him, as they always did whether he liked it or not, to the base of the Tower. His home, for a short, wondrous time in his youth. And the place where his life changed forever. He shoved his hands in his pockets and tilted his face to the sky.

"Why," said a voice. "If it isn't Antain. Back to visit us at last!" The voice was pleasant enough, though there was, Antain realized, a bit of a growl, buried so deeply in the voice that it was difficult to hear.

"Hello, Sister Ignatia," he said, bowing low. "I am surprised to see you out of your study. Can it be that your wondrous curiosities have finally loosened their grip?"

It was the first time they had exchanged words face-to-face since he was injured, years now. Their correspondence had consisted of terse notes, hers likely penned by one of the other sisters and signed by Sister Ignatia. She had never bothered to check on him—not once—since he was injured. He tasted something bitter in his mouth. He swallowed it down to keep himself from grimacing.

"Oh, no," she said airily. "Curiosity is the curse of the

Clever. Or perhaps cleverness is the curse of the Curious. In any case, I am never lacking for either, I'm afraid, which does keep me rather busy. But I do find that tending my herb garden gives me some amount of comfort—" She held up her hand. "Mind you don't touch any leaves. Or flowers. And maybe not the dirt, either. Not without gloves. Many of these herbs are deadly poisonous. Aren't they pretty?"

"Quite," Antain said. But he wasn't thinking much about the herbs.

"And what brings you here?" Sister Ignatia said, narrowing her eyes as Antain's gaze drifted back up to the window where the madwoman lived.

Antain sighed. He looked back at Sister Ignatia. Garden dirt caked her work gloves. Sweat and sunshine slicked her face. She had a sated look about her, as if she had just eaten the most wonderful meal in the world and was now quite full. But she couldn't have. She had been working outside. Antain cleared his throat.

"I wanted to tell you in person that I would not be able to build you the desk you requested for another six months, or perhaps a year," Antain said. This was a lie. The design was fairly simple, and the wood required was easily obtainable from the managed forest on the western side of the Protectorate.

"Nonsense," Sister Ignatia said. "Surely you can make some rearrangements. The Sisters are practically family."

Antain shook his head, let his eyes drift back to the

window. He had not really seen the madwoman—not up close anyway—since the bird attack. But he saw her every night in his dreams. Sometimes she was in the rafters. Sometimes she was in her cell. Sometimes she was riding the backs of a flock of paper birds and vanishing into the night.

He gave Sister Ignatia half a smile. "Family?" he said. "Madam, I believe you have met my family."

Sister Ignatia pretended to wave the comment away, but she pressed her lips together, suppressing a grin.

Antain glanced back at the window. The madwoman stood at the narrow window. Her body was little more than a shadow. He saw her hand reach through the bars, and a bird flutter near, nestling in her palm. The bird was made of paper. He could hear the dry rustle of its wings from where he stood.

Antain shivered.

"What are you looking at?" Sister Ignatia said.

"Nothing," Antain lied. "I see nothing."

"My dear boy. Is there something the matter?"

He looked at the ground. "Good luck with the garden."

"Before you go, Antain. Why don't you do us a favor, since we cannot entice you to apply your clever hands to the making of beautiful things, no matter how many times we ask?"

"Madam, I—"

"You there!" Sister Ignatia called. Her voice instantly took on a much harsher tone. "Have you finished packing, girl?"

"Yes, Sister," came a voice inside the garden shed—a clear,

bright voice, like a bell. Antain felt his heart ring. *That voice*, he thought. *I remember that voice.* He hadn't heard it since they were in school, all those years ago.

"Excellent." She turned to Antain, her words honeyed once again. "We have a novice who has opted not to apply herself to an elevated life of study and contemplation, and has decided to reenter the larger world. Foolish thing."

Antain was shocked. "But," he faltered. "That *never* happens!"

"Indeed. It never does. And it will not ever again. I must have been deluded when she first came to us, wanting to enter our Order. I shall be more discerning next time."

A young woman emerged from the garden shed. She wore a plain shift dress that likely fit her when she first entered the Tower, shortly after her thirteenth birthday, but she had grown taller, and it barely covered her knees. She wore a pair of men's boots, patched and worn and lopsided, that she must have borrowed from one of the groundskeepers. She smiled, and even her freckles seemed to shine.

"Hello, Antain," Ethyne said gently. "It has been a long time."

Antain felt the world tilt under his feet.

Ethyne turned to Sister Ignatia. "We knew one another at school."

"She never talked to me," Antain said in a hoarse whisper, tilting his face to the ground. His scars burned. "No girls did."

Her eyes glittered and her mouth unfurled into a smile. "Is that so? I remember differently." She *looked at him*. At his scars. She looked *right at him*. And she didn't look away. And she didn't flinch. Even his mother flinched. *His own mother.*

"Well," he said. "To be fair. I didn't talk to any girls. I still don't, really. You should hear my mother go on about it."

Ethyne laughed. Antain thought he might faint.

"Will you please help our little disappointment carry her things? Her brothers have gotten themselves ill and her parents are dead. I would like all evidence of this fiasco removed as quickly as possible."

If any of this bothered Ethyne, she did not show it. "Thank you, Sister, for everything," she said, her voice as smooth and sweet as cream. "I am ever so much more than I was when I walked in through that door."

"And ever so much *less* than you could have been," Sister Ignatia snapped. "The youth!" She threw up her hands. "If we cannot bear them, how can they possibly bear themselves?" She turned to Antain. "You will help, won't you? The girl doesn't have the decency to show even the tiniest modicum of sorrow for her actions." The Head Sister's eyes went black for a moment, as though she was terribly hungry. She squinted and frowned, and the blackness vanished. Perhaps Antain had imagined it. "I cannot tolerate another second in her company."

"Of course, Sister," he whispered. Antain swallowed.

There seemed to be sand in his mouth. He did his best to recover himself. "I am ever at your service. Always."

Sister Ignatia turned and stalked away, muttering as she went.

"I would rethink that stance, if I were you," Ethyne muttered to Antain. He turned, and she gave him another broad smile. "Thank you for helping me. You always were the kindest boy I ever knew. Come. Let's get out of here as quickly as possible. After all these years, the Sisters still give me the shivers."

She laid her hand on Antain's arm and led him to her bundles in the garden shed. Her fingers were calloused and her hands were strong. And Antain felt something flutter in his chest—a shiver at first, and then a powerful lift and beat, like the wings of a bird, flying high over the forest, and skimming the top of the sky.

# 16

## In Which There Is Ever
## So Much Paper

The madwoman in the Tower could not remember her own name.

She could remember no one's name.

What was a name, anyway? You can't hold it. You can't smell it. You can't rock it to sleep. You can't whisper your love to it over and over and over again. There once was a name that she treasured above all others. But it had flown away, like a bird. And she could not coax it back.

There were so many things that flew away. Names. Memories. Her own knowledge of herself. There was a time, she knew, that she was smart. Capable. Kind. Loving and loved. There was a time when her feet fit neatly on the curve of the earth and her thoughts stacked evenly—one on top of the other—in the cupboards of her mind. But her feet had not felt the earth in ever so long, and her thoughts had been replaced by whirlwinds and storms that swept all her cupboards bare. Possibly forever.

She could remember only the touch of paper. She was hungry for paper. At night she dreamed of the dry smoothness of the sheaf, the painful bite of the edge. She dreamed of the slip of ink into the deepening white. She dreamed of paper birds and paper stars and paper skies. She dreamed of a paper moon hovering over paper cities and paper forests and paper people. A world of paper. A universe of paper. She dreamed of oceans of ink and forests of quills and an endless bog of words. She dreamed of all of it in abundance.

She didn't only dream of paper; she had it, too. No one knew how. Every day the Sisters of the Star entered her room and cleared away the maps that she had drawn and the words that she had written without ever bothering to read them. They tutted and scolded and swept it all away. But every day, she found herself once again awash in paper and quills and ink. She had all that she needed.

A map. She drew a map. She could see it as plain as day. *She is here*, she wrote. *She is here, she is here, she is here.*

"Who is here?" the young man asked, over and over again. First, his face was young, and fine, and clear. Then, it was red, and angry, and bleeding. Eventually, the cuts from the paper birds healed, and became scars—first purple, then pink, then white. They made a map. The madwoman wondered if he could see it. Or if he understood what it meant. She wondered if anyone could—or if such things were intelligible to her alone. Was she alone mad, or had the world gone mad with her? She was in no position to say. She wanted to pin him down and write "She is here" right where his cheekbone met his earlobe. She wanted to make him understand.

*Who is here?* she could feel him wondering as he stared at the Tower from the ground.

*Don't you see?* she wanted to shout back. But she didn't. Her words were jumbled. She didn't know if anything that came out of her mouth made any sense.

Each day, she released paper birds out the window. Sometimes one. Sometimes ten. Each one had a map in its heart.

*She is here,* in the heart of a robin.

*She is here,* in the heart of a crane.

*She is here, she is here, she is here,* in the hearts of a falcon and a kingfisher and a swan.

Her birds didn't go very far. Not at first. She watched from her window as people reached down and picked them up from the ground nearby. She watched the people gaze up at the Tower. She watched them shake their heads. She heard them sigh, "The poor, poor thing," and clutch their loved ones a little more closely, as though madness was contagious. And maybe they were right. Maybe it was.

No one looked at the words or the maps. They just crumpled the paper—probably to pulp it and make it new paper. The madwoman couldn't blame them. Paper was expensive. Or it was for most people. She got it easily enough. She just reached through the gaps of the world, pulling out leaf after leaf. Each leaf was a map. Each leaf was a bird. Each leaf she launched into the sky.

She sat on the floor of her cell. Her fingers found paper. Her fingers found quill and ink. She didn't ask how. She just drew the map. Sometimes she drew the map as she slept. The young man was coming closer. She could feel his footsteps. Soon he would stop a good ways away and stare up, a question mark curling over his heart. She watched him grow from youth to artisan to business owner to a man in love. Still, the same question.

She folded the paper into the shape of a hawk. She let it rest on her hand for a moment. Watched it begin to shiver and itch. She let it launch itself into the sky.

She stared out the window. The paper bird had been lamed. She had rushed too quickly, and didn't fold it properly. The poor thing would not survive. It landed on the ground, struggling mightily, right in front of the young man with scars on his face. He paused. He stepped on the bird's neck with his foot. Compassion or revenge? Sometimes the two were the same.

The madwoman pressed her hand to her mouth, the touch

of her fingers as light as paper. She tried to see his face, but he was in shadow. Not that it mattered. She knew his face as well as she knew her own. She could follow the curve of each scar with her fingers in the dark. She watched him pause, unfold the bird, and stare at the drawings she had done. She watched his eyes lift to the Tower, and then arc slowly across the sky and land on the forest. And then look at the map once again.

She pressed her hand to her chest and felt her sorrow—the merciless density of it, like a black hole in her heart, swallowing the light. Perhaps it had always been so. Her life in the Tower felt infinite. Sometimes she felt she had been imprisoned since the beginning of the world.

And in one profound, sudden flash, she felt it transform.

*Hope,* her heart said.

*Hope,* the sky said.

*Hope,* said the bird in the young man's hand and the look in his eye.

*Hope and light and motion,* her soul whispered. *Hope and formation and fusion. Hope and heat and accretion. The miracle of gravity. The miracle of transformation. Each precious thing is destroyed and each precious thing is saved. Hope, hope, hope.*

Her sorrow was gone. Only hope remained. She felt it radiate outward, filling the Tower, the town, the whole world.

And, in that moment, she heard the Head Sister cry out in pain.

# 17

## In Which There Is a Crack
## in the Nut

Luna thought she was ordinary. She thought she was loved.
She was half right.

She was a girl of five; and later, she was seven; and later she
was, incredibly, eleven.

It was a fine thing indeed, Luna thought, being eleven.
She loved the symmetry of it, and the lack of symmetry. Eleven
was a number that was visually even, but functionally not—it
*looked* one way and *behaved* in quite another. Just like most
eleven-year-olds, or so she assumed. Her association with
other children was always limited to her grandmother's visits to the Free Cities, and only the visits on which Luna was

permitted to come. Sometimes, her grandmother went without her. And every year, Luna found it more and more enraging.

She was eleven, after all. She was both even and odd. She was ready to be many things at once—child, grown-up, poet, engineer, botanist, dragon. The list went on. That she was barred from *some* journeys and not *others* was increasingly galling. And she said so. Often. And loudly.

When her grandmother was away, Luna spent most of her time in the workshop. It was filled with books about metals and rocks and water, books about flowers and mosses and edible plants, books about animal biology and animal behavior and animal husbandry, books about the theories and principles of mechanics. But Luna's favorite books were the ones about astronomy—the moon, especially. She loved the moon so much, she wanted to wrap her arms around it and sing to it. She wanted to gather every morsel of moonlight into a great bowl and drink it dry. She had a hungry mind, an itchy curiosity, and a knack for drawing, building, and fashioning.

Her fingers had a mind of their own. "Do you see, Glerk?" she said, showing off her mechanical cricket, made of polished wood and glass eyes and tiny metal legs attached to springs. It hopped; it skittered; it reached; it grabbed. It could even sing. Right now, Luna set it just so, and the cricket began to turn the pages of a book. Glerk wrinkled his great, damp nose.

"It turns pages," she says. "Of a book. Has there ever been a cleverer cricket?"

"But it's just turning the pages willy-nilly," he said. "It isn't as though it is *reading* the book. And even if it was, it wouldn't be reading at the same time as you. How would it know when to approach the page and turn it?" He was just needling her, of course. In truth, he was very impressed. But as he had told her a thousand times, he couldn't possibly be impressed at *every* impressive thing that she ever did. He might find that his heart had swelled beyond its capacity and sent him out of the world entirely.

Luna stamped her foot. "Of course it can't *read*. It turns the page when *I* tell it to turn the page." She folded her arms across her chest and gave her swamp monster what she hoped was a hard look.

"I think you are both right," Fyrian said, trying to make peace. "I love foolish things. And clever things. I love all the things."

"*Hush, Fyrian,*" both girl and swamp monster said as one.

"It takes longer to position your cricket to turn the page than it does to actually turn the page on your own. Why not simply turn the page?" Glerk worried that he had already taken the joke too far. He picked up Luna in his four arms and positioned her at the top of his top right shoulder. She rolled her eyes and climbed back down.

"Because then there wouldn't be a *cricket*." Luna's chest felt prickly. Her whole body felt prickly. She had been prickly all day. "Where is Grandmama?" she asked.

"You know where she is," Glerk said. "She will be back next week."

"I dislike next week. I wish she was back *today*."

"The Poet tells us that impatience belongs to small things—fleas, tadpoles, and fruit flies. You, my love, are ever so much more than a fruit fly."

"I dislike the Poet as well. He can boil his head."

These words cut Glerk to his core. He pressed his four hands to his heart and fell down heavily upon his great bottom, curling his tail around his body in a protective gesture. "What a thing to say."

"I mostly mean it," Luna said.

Fyrian fluttered from girl to monster and monster to girl. He did not know where to land.

"Come, Fyrian," Luna said, opening one of her side pockets. "You can take a nap, and I will walk us up to the ridge to see if we can see my grandmother on her journey. We can see terribly far from up there."

"You won't be able to see her yet. Not for days." Glerk looked closely at the girl. There was something . . . *off* today. He couldn't put his finger on it.

"You never know," Luna said, turning on her heel and walking up the trail.

"'*Patience has no wing*,'" Glerk recited as she walked.

*"'Patience does not run*
*Nor blow, nor skitter, nor falter.*
*Patience is the swell of the ocean;*
*Patience is the sigh of the mountain;*
*Patience is the shirr of the Bog;*
*Patience is the chorus of stars,*
*Infinitely singing.'"*

"I am not listening to you!" Luna called without turning around. But she was. Glerk could tell.

☼

By the time Luna reached the bottom of the slope, Fyrian was already asleep. That dragon could sleep anywhere and anytime. He was an expert sleeper. Luna reached into her pocket and gave his head a gentle tap. He didn't wake up.

"Dragons!" Luna muttered. This was the given answer to many of her questions, though it didn't always make very much sense. When Luna was little, Fyrian was older than she—that was obvious. He taught her to count, to add and subtract, and to multiply and divide. He taught her how to make numbers into something larger than themselves, applying them to larger concepts about motion and force, space and time, curves and circles and tightened springs.

But now, it was different. Fyrian seemed younger and younger every day. Sometimes, it seemed to Luna that he was going backward in time while she stood still, but other times it seemed that the opposite was true: it was Fyrian who was standing still while Luna raced forward. She wondered why this was.

*Dragons!* Glerk would explain.

*Dragons!* Xan would agree. They both shrugged. Dragons, it was decided. What can one do?

Which never actually answered anything. At least Fyrian never attempted to deflect or obfuscate Luna's many questions. Firstly because he had no idea what *obfuscate* meant. And secondly because he rarely knew any answers. Unless they pertained to mathematics. Then he was a fountain of answers. For everything else, he was just *Fyrian,* and that was enough.

Luna reached the top of the ridge before noon. She curled her fingers over her eyes and tried to look out as far as she could. She had never been this high before. She was amazed Glerk had let her go.

The Cities lay on the other side of the forest, down the slow, southern slope of the mountain, where the land became stable and flat. Where the earth no longer was trying to kill you. Beyond that, Luna knew, were farms and more forests and more mountains, and eventually an ocean. But Luna had never been that far. On the other side of her mountain—to the north—there was nothing but forest, and beyond that was a bog that covered half the world.

Glerk told her that the world was born out of that bog.

"How?" Luna had asked a thousand times.

"A poem," Glerk sometimes said.

"A song," he said at other times. And then, instead of explaining further, he told her she'd understand some day.

Glerk, Luna decided, was horrible. Everyone was horrible. And most horrible was the pain in her head that had been getting worse all day. She sat down on the ground and closed her eyes. In the darkness behind her eyelids, she could see a blue color with a shimmer of silver at the edges, along with something else entirely. A hard, dense something, like a nut.

And what's more, the *something* seemed to be pulsing—as though it contained intricate clockwork. *Click, click, click.*

*Each* click *brings me closer to the close,* Luna thought. She shook her head. Why would she think that? She had no idea.

*The close of what?* she wondered. But there was no answer.

And all of a sudden, she had an image in her head of a house with hand-stitched quilts draped on the chairs and art on the walls and colorful jars arranged on shelves in bright, tempting rows. And a woman with black hair and a crescent moon birthmark on her forehead. And a man's voice crooning, *Do you see your mama? Do you, my darling?* And that word in her mind, echoing from one side of her skull to the other, *Mama, mama, mama,* over and over and over again, like the cry of a faraway bird.

"Luna?" Fyrian said. "Why are you crying?"

"I'm not crying," Luna said, wiping her tears away. "And anyway, I just miss my grandmama, that's all."

And that was true. She did miss her. No amount of standing and staring was going to change the amount of time that it takes to walk from the Free Cities to their home at the top of the sleeping volcano. That was certain. But the house and the quilts and the woman with the black hair—Luna had seen them before. But she didn't know where.

She looked down toward the swamp and the barn and the workshop and the tree house, with its round windows peering out from the sides of the massive tree trunk like astonished, unblinking eyes. *There was another house. And another family. Before this house. And this family.* She knew it in her bones.

"Luna, what is wrong?" Fyrian asked, a note of anguish in his voice.

"Nothing, Fyrian," Luna said, curling her hands around his midsection and pulling him close. She kissed the top of his head. "Nothing at all. I'm just thinking about how much I love my family."

It was the first lie she ever told. Even though her words were true.

# 18

## In Which a Witch Is Discovered

Xan couldn't remember the last time she had traveled so slowly. Her magic had been dwindling for years, but there was no denying that it was happening more quickly now. Now the magic seemed to have thinned into a tiny trickle dripping through a narrow channel in her porous bones. Her vision dimmed; her hearing blurred; her hip pained her (and her left foot and her lower back and her shoulders and her wrists and, weirdly, her nose). And her condition was only about to get worse. Soon, she would be holding Luna's hand for the last time, touching her face for the last time—speaking her words of love in the hoarsest of whispers. It was almost too much to bear.

In truth, Xan was not afraid to die. Why should she be?

She had helped ease the pain of hundreds and thousands of people in preparation for that journey into the unknown. She had seen enough times in the faces of those in their final moments, a sudden look of surprise—and a wild, mad joy. Xan felt confident that she had nothing to fear. Still. It was the *before* that gave her pause. The months leading her toward the end she knew would be far from dignified. When she was able to call up memories of Zosimos (still difficult, despite her best efforts), they were of his grimace, his shudder, his alarming thinness. She remembered the pain he had been in. And she did not relish following in his footsteps.

*It is for Luna,* she told herself. *Everything, everything is for Luna.* And it was true. She loved that girl with every ache in her back; she loved her with every hacking cough; she loved her with every rheumatic sigh; she loved her with every crack in her joints. There was nothing she would not endure for that girl.

And she needed to tell her. Of course she did.

*Soon,* she told herself. *Not yet.*

✿

The Protectorate sat at the bottom of a long, gentle slope, right before the slope opened up into the vast Zirin Bog. Xan climbed up a rocky outcropping to catch a view of the town before her final descent.

There was something about that town. The way its many sorrows lingered in the air, as persistent as fog. Standing far above the sorrow cloud, Xan, in her clearheadedness, chastised herself.

"Old fool," she muttered. "How many people have you helped? How many wounds have you healed and hearts have you soothed? How many souls have you guided on their way? And yet, here are these poor people—men and women and children—that you have refused to help. What do you have to say for yourself, you silly woman?"

She had nothing to say for herself.

And she still didn't know why.

She only knew that the closer she got, the more desperate she felt to leave.

She shook her head, brushed the gravel and leaves from her skirts, and continued down the slope toward the town. As she walked, she had a memory. She could remember her room in the old castle—her favorite room, with the two dragons carved in stone on either side of the fireplace, and a broken ceiling, open to the sky, but magicked to keep the rain away. And she could remember climbing into her makeshift bed and clutching her hands to her heart, praying to the stars that she might have a night free from bad dreams. She never did. And she could remember weeping into her mattress—great gushes of tears. And she could remember a voice at the other side of the door. A quiet, dry, scratchy voice, whispering, *More. More. More.*

Xan pulled her cloak tightly around her arms. She did not like being cold. She also did not like remembering things. She shook her head to clear away the thoughts and marched down the slope. Into the cloud.

✿

The madwoman in the Tower saw the Witch hobbling through the trees. She was far away—ever so far, but the madwoman's eyes could see around the world if she let them.

Had she known how to do this before she went mad? Perhaps she had. Perhaps she simply did not notice. She had been a devoted daughter once. And then a girl in love. And then an expectant mother, counting the days until her baby came. And then everything had gone wrong.

The madwoman discovered that it was possible for her to *know* things. Impossible things. The world, she knew in her madness, was littered with shiny bits and precious pieces. A man might drop a coin on the ground and never find it again, but a crow will find it in a flash. Knowledge, in its essence, was a glittering jewel—and the madwoman was a crow. She pressed, reached, picked, and gathered. She knew *so many things*. She knew where the Witch lived, for example. She could walk there blindfolded if she could just get out of the Tower for long enough. She knew where the Witch took the children. She knew what those towns were like.

"How is our patient doing this morning?" the Head Sister said to her at the dawning of each day. "How much sorrow presses on her poor, poor soul?" She was hungry. The madwoman could feel it.

—143

*None*, the madwoman could have said if she felt like speaking. But she didn't.

For years, the madwoman's sorrows had fed the Head Sister. For years she felt the predatory pounce. (*Sorrow Eater*, the madwoman discovered herself knowing. It was not a term that she had ever learned. She found it the way she found anything that was useful—she reached through the gaps of the world and worried it out.) For years she lay silently in her cell while the Head Sister gorged herself on sorrow.

And then one day, there was no sorrow to be had. The madwoman learned to lock it away, seal it off with something else. Hope. And more and more, Sister Ignatia went away hungry.

"Clever," the Sister said, her mouth a thin, grim line. "You have locked me out. For now."

*You have locked me in*, the madwoman thought, a tiny spark of hope igniting in her soul. *For now.*

The madwoman pressed her face to the thick bars in her thin window. The Witch had left the outcropping and was, right now, limping toward the town walls, just as the Council was carrying the latest baby to the gates.

No mother wailed. No father screamed. They did not fight for their doomed child. They watched numbly as the infant was carried into the horrors of the forest, believing it would keep those horrors away. They set their faces and stared at fear.

*Fools,* the madwoman wanted to tell them. *You are looking the wrong way.*

The madwoman folded a map into the shape of a falcon. There were things that she could make happen—things that she could not explain. This was true before they came for her baby, before the Tower—one measure of wheat would become two; fabric worn thin as paper would become thick and luxurious in her hands. But slowly, during her long years in the Tower, her gifts had become sharp and clear. She found bits and pieces of magic in the gaps of the world and squirreled them away.

The madwoman took aim. The Witch was heading for the clearing. The Elders were headed for the clearing. And the falcon would fly directly to where the baby was. She knew it in her bones.

✺

Grand Elder Gherland was, it was true, getting on in years. The potions he received every week from the Sisters of the Star helped, but these days they seemed to help *less* than usual. And it annoyed him.

And the business with the babies annoyed him, too—not the *concept* of it, really, nor the *results.* He simply did not enjoy touching babies. They were loud, boorish, and, frankly, *selfish.*

Plus, they stank. The one he held now certainly did.

Gravitas was all fine and good, and it was important to maintain appearances, but—Gherland shifted the baby from one arm to the other—he was getting too old for this sort of thing.

He missed Antain. He knew he was being silly. It was better this way, with the boy gone. Executions are a messy business, after all. Especially when family is involved. Still. As much as Antain's irrational resistance to the Day of Sacrifice had irritated Gherland to no end, he felt they had lost something when Antain resigned, though he couldn't say exactly what. The Council felt empty with Antain gone. He told himself that he just wanted someone else to hold the wriggling brat, but Gherland knew there was more to the feeling than that.

The people along the walkway bowed their heads as the Council walked by, which was all fine and good. The baby wriggled and squirmed. It spat up on Gherland's robes. Gherland sighed deeply. He would not make a scene. He owed it to his people to take these discomforts in stride.

It was difficult—no one would ever know *how* difficult—to be this beloved and honorable and selfless. And as the Council swept through the final causeway, Gherland made sure to congratulate himself for his kind, humanitarian nature.

The baby's wails devolved into self-indulgent hiccups.

"*Ingrate*," muttered Gherland.

❄

Antain made sure he was seen on the road as the Council walked by. He made brief eye contact with his uncle

Gherland—*Awful man,* he thought with a shudder—and then slipped out behind the crowd and hooked through the gate when no one was looking. Once under the cover of the trees, he headed toward the clearing at a run.

Ethyne was still standing on the side of the road. She had a basket ready for the grieving family. She was an angel, a treasure, and was now, incredibly, Antain's wife—and had been since a month after she left the Tower. And they loved one another desperately. And they wanted a family. But.

*The woman in the rafters.*

*The cry of the baby.*

*The cloud of sorrow hanging over the Protectorate like a fog.*

Antain had watched that horror unfold and had done nothing. He had stood by as baby after baby was taken and left in the forest. *We couldn't stop it if we tried,* he had told himself. It's what everyone told themselves. It's what Antain had always believed.

But Antain had also believed that he would spend his life alone, and lonely. And then love proved him wrong. And now the world was brighter than it was before. If that belief could be proved wrong, could not others be as well?

*What if we are wrong about the Witch? What if we are wrong about the sacrifice?* Antain wondered. The question itself was revolutionary. And astonishing. *What would happen if we tried?*

Why had the thought never occurred to him before?

Wouldn't it be better, he thought, to bring a child into a world that was good and fair and kind?

Had anyone ever tried to talk to the Witch? How did they *know* she could not be reasoned with? Anyone that old, after all, had to have a little bit of wisdom. It only made sense.

Love made him giddy. Love made him brave. Love made foggy questions clearer. And Antain needed answers.

He rushed past the ancient sycamore trees and hid himself in the bushes, waiting for the old men to leave.

It was there he found the paper falcon, hanging like an ornament in the yew bush. He grabbed it and held it close to his heart.

❋

By the time Xan reached the clearing, she was already late. She could hear that baby fussing from half a league away.

"Auntie Xan is coming, dearest!" she called out. "Please don't fret!"

She couldn't believe it. After all these years, she had never been late. *Never.* The poor little thing. She closed her eyes tight and tried to send a flood of magic into her legs to give them a little more speed. Alas, it was more like a puddle than a flood, but it did help a bit. Using her cane to spring her forward, Xan sprinted through the green.

"Oh, thank goodness!" she breathed when she saw the baby—red-faced and enraged, but alive and unharmed. "I was so worried about you, I—"

And then a man stepped between her and the child.

"STOP!" he cried. He had a heavily scarred face and a weapon in his hands.

The puddle of magic, compounded now with fear and surprise and worry for the child that was on the other side of this dangerous stranger, enlarged suddenly into a tidal wave. It thrummed through Xan's bones, lighting her muscles and tissues and skin. Even her hair sizzled with magic.

"OUT OF MY WAY," Xan shouted, her voice rumbling through the rocks. She could feel her magic rush from the center of the earth, through her feet and out the top of her head on its way to the sky, back and forth and back and forth, like massive waves pushing and pulling at the shore. She reached out and grabbed the man with both hands. He cried out as a surge hit him square in the solar plexus, knocking his breath clear away. Xan flung him aside as easily as if he was a rag doll. She transformed herself into an astonishingly large hawk, descended on the child, gripped the swaddling clothes in her talons, and lifted the baby into the sky.

Xan couldn't stay that way—she just didn't have enough magic—but she and the child could stay airborne over at least the next two ridges. Then she would give food and comfort, assuming she didn't collapse first. The child opened its throat and wailed.

✵

The madwoman in the Tower watched the Witch transform. She felt nothing as she watched the old nose harden into a beak. She felt nothing as she saw the feathers erupt from her pores, as her arms widened and her body shortened and the old woman screamed in power and pain.

The madwoman remembered the weight of an infant in her arms. The smell of the scalp. The joyful kick of a brand-new pair of legs. The astonished waving of tiny hands.

She remembered bracing her back against the roof.

She remembered her feet on the rafters. She remembered wanting to fly.

"Birds," she murmured as the Witch took flight. "Birds, birds, birds."

There is no time in the Tower. There is only loss.

*For now,* she thought.

She watched the young man—the one with the scars on his face. Pity about the scars. She hadn't meant to do it. But he was a kind boy—clever, curious, and good of heart. His kindness was his dearest currency. His scars, she knew, had kept the silly girls away. He deserved someone extraordinary to love him.

She watched him stare at the paper falcon. She watched him carefully unfold each tight crease and flatten the paper on a stone. The paper had no map. Instead it had words.

*Don't forget,* it said on one side.

*I mean it,* said the other.

And in her soul, the madwoman felt a thousand birds—birds of paper, birds of feathers, birds of hearts and minds and flesh—leap into the sky and soar over the dreaming trees.

# 19

## In Which There Is a Journey to the Town of Agony

For the people who loved Luna, time passed in a blur. Luna, however, worried that she might never be twelve. Each day felt like a heavy stone to be hoisted to the top of a very tall mountain.

In the meantime, each day increased her knowledge. Each day caused the world to simultaneously expand and contract; the more Luna *knew*, the more she became frustrated by what she did *not* yet know. She was a quick study and quick-fingered and quick-footed and sometimes quick-tempered. She cared for the goats and cared for the chickens and cared for her grandmother and her dragon and her swamp monster. She knew how to coax milk and gather eggs and bake bread and fashion inventions and build contraptions and grow plants and press cheese and simmer a stew to nourish the mind and the soul. She knew how to keep the house tidy (though she didn't like that job much) and how to stitch birds onto the hem of a dress to make it delightful.

She was a bright child, an accomplished child, a child who loved and was loved.

*And yet.*

There was something missing. A gap in her knowledge. A gap in her life. Luna could *feel* it. She hoped that turning twelve would solve this—build a bridge across the gap. It didn't.

Instead, once she finally did turn twelve, Luna noticed that several changes had begun to occur—not all of them pleasant. She was, for the first time, taller than her grandmother. She was more distractible. Impatient. Peevish. She snapped at her grandmother. She snapped at her swamp monster. She even snapped at her dragon, who was as close to her heart as a twin brother. She apologized to all of them, of course, but the *fact of it happening* was itself an irritation. Why was everyone vexing her so? Luna wondered.

And another thing. While Luna had always believed that she had read every single book in the workshop, she began to realize that there were several more that she had never read at all. She knew what they looked like. She knew where they sat on the shelf. But try as she might, she could not picture their titles, nor remember a single clue as to their contents.

And what's more, she found that she could not even read the words on the spines of certain volumes. She should have been able to read them. The words were not foreign and the letters hooked into one another in ways that ought to have made perfect sense.

And yet.

Every time she tried to look at the spines, her eyes would slide from one side to the other, as though they were not made of leather and ink, but of glass slicked with oil. It did not happen when she looked at the spine *The Lives of a Star* and it did not happen when she looked at the beloved copy of *Mechanica*. But other books, they were as slippery as marbles in butter. And what's more, whenever she reached for one of them, she would find herself unaccountably lost in a memory or a dream. She would find herself going cross-eyed and fuzzy-headed, whispering poetry or making up a story. Sometimes she would regain her senses minutes or hours or half a day later, shaking her head to un-addle her brains, and wondering what on earth she had been doing, or for how long.

She didn't tell anyone about these spells. Not her grandmother. Not Glerk. Certainly not Fyrian. She didn't want to worry any of them. These changes were too embarrassing. Too *strange*. And so she kept it secret. Even still, they sometimes gave her strange looks. Or odd answers to her questions, as if they already knew something was wrong with her. And that *wrongness* clung to her, like a headache that she couldn't shake.

Another thing that happened after Luna turned twelve: she began to draw. All the time. She drew both mindlessly and mindfully. She drew faces, places, and minute details of plants and animals—a stamen here, a paw there, the rotted-out tooth of an aged goat. She drew star maps and maps of the Free Cities and maps of places that existed only in her imagination. She drew a tower with unsettling stonework and intersecting corridors and stairways crowding its insides, looming over a town drenched in fog. She drew a woman with long, black hair. And a man in robes.

It was all her grandmother could do to keep her in paper and quills. Fyrian and Glerk took to making her pencils from charcoal and stiff reeds. She could never get enough.

☼

Later that year, Luna and her grandmother walked to the Free Cities again. Her grandmother was always in high demand. She checked in on the pregnant women and gave advice to the midwives and healers and apothecaries. And while Luna loved visiting the towns on the other side of the forest, this time the journey also vexed her.

Her grandmother—as stable as a boulder all of Luna's life—was starting to weaken. Luna's increasing worry for her grandmother's health pricked at her skin, like a dress made of thorns.

Xan had been limping the whole way. And it was getting worse. "Grandmama," Luna said, watching her grandmother wince with each step. "Why are you still walking? You should be sitting. I think you should sit down right now. Oh, look. A log. For sitting on."

"Oh, tosh," her grandmother said, leaning heavily on her staff and wincing again. "The more I sit, the longer the journey will take us."

"The more you walk, the more pain you'll be in," Luna countered.

Every morning, it seemed, Xan had a new ache or a new pain. A cloudiness in the eye or a droop to a shoulder. Luna was beside herself.

"Do you want me to sit on your feet, Grandmama?" she asked Xan. "Do you want me to tell you a story or sing you a song?"

"What has gotten into you, child?" Luna's grandmother sighed.

"Maybe you should eat something. Or drink something. Maybe you should have some tea. Would you like me to make you tea? Perhaps you should sit down. For tea."

"I'm perfectly fine. I have made this trip more times than I can count, and I have never had any trouble. You are making a fuss over nothing." But Luna knew something was changing in her grandmother. There was a tremor in her voice and a tremble in her hands. And she was so thin! Luna's grandmother used to be bulbous and squat—all soft hugs and squishy cuddles. Now she was fragile and delicate and light—dry grasses wrapped in crumbling paper that might fall apart in a gust of wind.

✷

When they arrived in the town called Agony, Luna ran ahead to the widow woman's house, just at the border.

"My grandmother's not well," Luna told the widow woman. "Don't tell her I said so."

And the widow woman sent her almost-grown-up son (a Star Child, like so many others), who ran to the healer, who ran to the apothecary, who ran to the mayor, who alerted the League of Ladies, who alerted the Gentlemen's Association and the Clockmakers Alliance and the Quilters and the Tinkers and the town school. By the time Xan hobbled into the widow woman's garden, half the town was already there, setting up tables and tents, with legions upon legions of busybodies preparing themselves to fuss over the old woman.

"Foolishness," Xan sniffed, though she lowered herself gratefully into the chair that a young woman placed right next to the herb garden for her.

"We thought it best," the widow woman said.

"*I* thought it best," corrected Luna, and what seemed like a thousand hands caressed her cheeks and the top of her head

—157

and her shoulders. "Such a good girl," the townspeople murmured. "We knew she would be the best of best girls, and the best of best children, and one day the best of best women. We do so love being right."

This attention wasn't unusual. Whenever Luna visited the Free Cities, she found herself warmly received and fawned over. She didn't know why the townspeople loved her so, or why they seemed to hang on her every word, but she enjoyed their admiration.

They remarked at her fine eyes, dark and glittering as the night sky, her black hair shot with gold, the birthmark on her forehead in the shape of a crescent moon. They remarked on her intelligent fingers and her strong arms and her fast legs. They praised her for her precise way of speaking and her clever gestures when she danced and her lovely singing voice.

"She sounds like magic," the town matrons sighed, and then Xan shot them a poisonous look, at which they started mumbling about the weather.

That word made Luna frown. In that moment, she knew she must have heard it before—she *must* have. But a moment later, the word flew out of her mind, like a hummingbird. And then it was gone. Just a blank space was left where the word had been, like a fleeting thought at the edge of a dream.

Luna sat among a collection of Star Children—all different ages—one infant, some toddlers, and moving upward to the oldest, who was an impressively old man.

("Why are they called Star Children?" Luna had asked possibly thousands of times.

"I'm sure I don't know what you are talking about," Xan answered vaguely.

And then she changed the subject. And then Luna forgot. Every time.

Only lately, she could remember herself forgetting.)

The Star Children were discussing their earliest memories. It was a thing they did often—seeing which one could get as close as possible to the moment when Old Xan brought them to their families and marked them as beloved. Since no one could actually remember such a thing—they had been far too young—they went as deep into their memories as they could to find the earliest image among them.

"I can remember a tooth—how it became wiggly and fell out. Everything before that is a bit of a blur, I'm afraid," said the older Star Child gentleman.

"I can remember a song that my mother used to sing. But she still sings it, so perhaps it isn't a memory after all," said a girl.

"I remember a goat. A goat with a crinkly mane," said a boy.

"Are you sure that wasn't just Old Xan?" a girl asked him, giggling. She was one of the younger Star Children.

"Oh," the boy said. "Perhaps you are right."

Luna wrinkled her brow. There were images lurking in the

back of her mind. Were they memories or dreams? Or memories of dreams of memories? Or perhaps she had made them up. How was she supposed to know?

She cleared her throat.

"There was an old man," she said, "with dark robes that made a swishing sound like the wind, and he had a wobbly neck and a nose like a vulture, and he didn't like me very much."

The Star Children cocked their heads.

"Really?" one of the boys said. "Are you sure?" They stared at her intently, curling their lips between their teeth and biting down.

Xan waved her left hand dismissively while her cheeks began to flush from pink to scarlet.

"Don't listen to her." Xan rolled her eyes. "She has no idea what she's talking about. There was no such man. We see lots of silly things when we dream."

Luna closed her eyes.

"And there was a woman who lived on the ceiling whose hair waved like the branches of the sycamore trees in a storm."

"Impossible," her grandmother scoffed. "You don't know anyone that I didn't meet first. I was there for your whole life." She gazed at Luna with a narrowed eye.

"And a boy who smelled like sawdust. Why would he smell like sawdust?"

"Lots of people smell like sawdust," her grandmother said. "Woodcutters, carpenters, the lady who carves spoons. I could go on and on."

This was true, of course, and Luna had to shake her head. The memory was old, and faraway, but at the same time, *clear.* Luna didn't have very many memories that were as tenacious as this one—her memory, typically, was a slippery thing, and difficult to pin down—and so she hung on to it. This image *meant* something. She was *sure* of it.

Her grandmother, now that she thought about it, never spoke of memories. Not ever.

❊

The next day, after sleeping in the guest room of the widow woman, Xan walked through the town, checking on the pregnant women, advising them on their work level and food choices, listening to their bellies.

Luna tagged along. "So you may learn something useful," her grandmother said. Her words stung, no mistake.

"I'm useful," Luna said, tripping on the cobblestones as they hurried to the first patient's house on the other edge of town.

The woman's pregnancy was so far along, she looked as though she might burst at any second. She greeted both grandmother and grandchild with a serene exhaustion. "I'd get up," she said, "but I fear I may fall over." Luna kissed the lady on the cheek, as was customary, and quickly touched the mound of belly, feeling the child leap inside. Suddenly she had a lump in her throat.

"Why don't I make some tea?" she said briskly, turning her face away.

*I had a mother once,* Luna thought. *I must have.* She frowned. And surely, she must have asked about it, too, but she couldn't seem to remember doing so.

Luna made a list of what she knew in her head.

*Sorrow is dangerous.*

*Memories are slippery.*

*My grandmother does not always tell the truth.*

*And neither do I.*

These thoughts swirled in Luna's mind as she swirled the tea leaves in the boiling water.

"Can the girl rest her hands on my belly for a little bit?" the woman asked. "Or perhaps she could sing to the child. I would appreciate her blessing—living as she does in the presence of magic."

Luna did not know why the woman would want her blessing—or even what a blessing *was*. And that last word . . . it sounded familiar. But Luna couldn't remember. And just like that, she could barely remember the word at all—and was only aware of a pulsing sensation in her skull, like the ticking of a clock. In any case, Luna's grandmother hastily shooed her out the door, and then her thinking went fuzzy, and then she was back inside pouring tea from the pot. But the tea had gone cold. How long had she been outside? She hit the side of her head a few times with the heel of her hand to un-addle her brains. Nothing seemed to help.

At the next house, Luna arranged the herbs for the mother's care in order of usefulness. She rearranged the furniture to better accommodate the growing belly of the expectant lady, and rearranged the kitchen supplies so she wouldn't have to reach as far.

"Well, look at you," the mother said. "So helpful!"

"Thank you," Luna said bashfully.

"And smart as a whip," she added.

"Of course she is," Xan agreed. "She's mine, isn't she?"

Luna felt a rush of cold. Once again, that memory of waving black hair, and strong hands and the smell of milk and thyme and black pepper, and a woman's voice screaming, *She's mine, she's mine, she's mine.*

The image was so clear, so present and immediate, that Luna felt her breath catch and her heart pound. The pregnant woman didn't notice. Xan didn't notice. Luna could feel the screaming woman's voice in her ears. She could feel that black hair in her fingertips. She lifted her gaze to the rafters, but no one was there.

The rest of their visit passed without incident, and Luna and Xan made the long journey home. They did not speak of the memory of the man in the robes. Or of any other kind of memory. They did not speak of sorrow or worries or black-haired women on ceilings.

And the things that they did *not* speak of began to out-weigh the things that they *did*. Each secret, each unspoken thing was round and hard and heavy and cold, like a stone hung around the necks of both grandmother and girl.

Their backs bent under the weight of secrets.

# 20

## In Which Luna Tells a Story

*Listen, you ridiculous dragon. Stop wiggling this minute, or I will not tell you a story ever again in my life.*

*You're still wiggling.*

*Yes, cuddling is fine. You may cuddle.*

*Once upon a time, there was a girl who had no memory.*

*Once upon a time there was a dragon who never grew up.*

*Once upon a time there was a grandmother who didn't tell the truth.*

*Once upon a time there was a swamp monster who was older than the world and who loved the world and loved the people in it but who didn't always know the right thing to say.*

*Once upon a time there was a girl with no memory. Wait. Did I say that already?*

*Once upon a time there was a girl who had no memory of losing her memory.*

*Once upon a time there was a girl who had memories that followed her like shadows. They whispered like ghosts. She could not look them in the eye.*

*Once upon a time there was a man in a robe with a face like a vulture.*

*Once upon a time there was a woman on the ceiling.*

*Once upon a time there was black hair and black eyes and a righteous howl. Once upon a time a woman with hair like snakes said, She is mine, and she meant it. And then they took her away.*

*Once upon a time there was a dark tower that pierced the sky and turned everything gray.*

*Yes. This is all one story. This is my story. I just don't know how it ends.*

*Once upon a time, something terrifying lived in the woods. Or perhaps the woods were terrifying. Or perhaps the whole world is poisoned with wickedness and lies, and it's best to learn that now.*

*No, Fyrian, darling. I don't believe that last bit, either.*

# 21

## In Which Fyrian Makes a Discovery

Luna, Luna, Luna, Luna," Fyrian sang, spinning a pirouette in the air.

Two weeks she had been home. Fyrian remained delighted.

"Luna, Luna, Luna, Luna." He finished his dance with a bit of a flourish, landing on one toe on the center of Luna's palm. He bowed low. Luna smiled in spite of herself. Her grandmother was sick in bed. Still. She had been sick since they returned home.

When it was time for bed, she kissed Glerk good night and went to the house with Fyrian, who wasn't supposed to sleep in Luna's bed, but surely would.

"Good night, Grandmama," Luna said, leaning over her

sleeping grandmother and kissing her papery cheek. "Sweet dreams," she added, noticing a catch in her voice. Xan didn't move. She continued to sleep her openmouthed sleep. Her eyelids didn't even flutter.

And because Xan was in no condition to object, Luna told Fyrian that he could sleep at the foot of her bed, just like old times.

"Oh, joyful joyness!" Fyrian sighed, clutching his front paws to his heart and nearly fainting dead away.

"But, Fyrian, I will kick you out if you snore. You nearly lit my pillow on fire last time."

"I shall never snore," Fyrian promised. "Dragons do not snore. I am sure of it. Or maybe just dragonlings do not snore. You have my word as a Simply Enormous Dragon. We are an old and glorious race, and our word is our bond."

"You are making all that up," Luna said, tying her hair back in a long, black plait and hiding behind a curtain to change into her nightgown.

"Am not," he said huffily. Then he sighed. "Well. I might be. I wish my mother were here sometimes. It would be nice to have another dragon to talk to." His eyes grew wide. "Not that you are not enough, Luna-my-Luna. And Glerk teaches me ever so many things. And Auntie Xan loves me as much as any mother ever could. Still." He sighed and said no more. Instead he somersaulted into Luna's nightgown pocket and curled his hot little body into a tight ball. It was, Luna thought, like putting a stone from the hearth in her pocket—uncomfortably hot, yet comforting all the same.

"You are a riddle, Fyrian," Luna murmured, resting her hand on the curve of the dragon, curling her fingers into the heat. "You are my favorite riddle." Fyrian at least had a memory of his mother. All Luna had were dreams. And she couldn't vouch for their accuracy. True, Fyrian saw his mother die, but at least he *knew*. And what's more, he could love his new family fully, and with no questions.

Luna loved her family. She *loved them*.

But she had questions.

And it was with a head full of questions that she cuddled under her covers and fell asleep.

By the time the crescent moon slid past the windowsill and peeked into the room, Fyrian was snoring. By the time the moon shone fully through the window, he had begun to singe Luna's nightgown. And by the time the curve of the moon touched the opposite window frame, Fyrian's breath made a bright red mark on the side of Luna's hip, leaving a blister there.

She pulled him out of her pocket and set him on the end of the bed.

"Fyrian," she half slurred and half yelled in her half sleep. "Get OUT."

And Fyrian was gone.

Luna looked around.

"Well," she whispered. *Did he fly out the window?* She couldn't tell. "That was fast."

And she pressed her palm against her injury, trying to imagine a bit of ice melting into the burn, taking the pain away. And after a little bit the pain *did* go away, and Luna was asleep.

⚹

Fyrian did not wake up to Luna's shouting. He had that dream again. His mother was trying to tell him something, but she was very far away, and the air was very loud and very smoky, and he couldn't hear her. But he could see her if he squinted—standing with the other magicians from the castle as the walls crumbled around them.

"Mama!" Fyrian called in his dream-voice, but his words were garbled by the smoke. His mother allowed an impossibly old man to climb upon her shining back, and they flew into the volcano. The volcano, rageful and belligerent, bellowed and rumbled and spat, trying to hock them free.

"MAMA!" Fyrian called again, sobbing himself awake.

He was not curled up next to Luna, where he had fallen asleep, nor was he resting in his dragon sack, suspended over the swamp, so he might whisper good night to Glerk over and over and over again. Indeed, Fyrian had no idea where he was. All he knew was that his body felt strange, like a puffed-up lump of bread dough right before it is punched back down. Even his eyes felt puffy.

"What is going on?" Fyrian asked out loud. "Where is Glerk? GLERK! LUNA! AUNTIE XAN!" No one answered. He was alone in the wood.

He must have sleep-flown there, he thought, though he had never sleep-flown before. For some reason he was unable to fly *now*. He flapped his wings, but nothing happened. He beat them so hard that the trees on either side of him bent away and lost their leaves (*Did that always happen? It must,* he decided) and the dirt on the ground swirled up in great whirlwinds as he heaved his wings. His wings felt heavy and his body felt heavy and he could not fly.

"This always happens when I'm tired," Fyrian told himself firmly, even though that wasn't true, either. His wings always worked, just like his eyes always worked and his paws always worked, and he was always able to walk or crawl or peel the skin off ripe guja fruits and climb trees. All of his various bits were in good operating condition. So why weren't his wings working *now*?

His dream had left an ache in his heart. His mother had been a beautiful dragon. Impossibly beautiful. Her eyelids were lined with tiny jewels, each a different color. Her belly was the exact color of a freshly laid egg. When Fyrian closed his eyes he felt as though he could touch each buttery-smooth scale on her hide, each razor-sharp spike. He felt as though he could smell the sweet sulfur on her breath.

How many years had it been? Not that many, surely. He was still just a young dragonling. (Whenever he thought about time, his head hurt.)

"Hello?" he called. "Is anyone home?"

He shook his head. Of course no one was home. This was no one's *home*. He was in the middle of a deep, dark forest where he was not allowed, and he would probably die here, and it was all his own stupid fault, even though he was not entirely sure what he had *done* to make it happen. Sleep-flying, apparently. Though he thought maybe he had made that term up.

"When you feel afraid," his mother had told him, all those years ago, "sing your fears away. Dragons make the most beautiful music in the world. Everyone says so." And though Glerk assured him this was not true, and that dragons, instead, were masters of self-delusion, Fyrian took every opportunity he could to break into song. And it did make him feel better.

"*Here I am,*" he sang loudly, "*In the middle of a terrifying wood. Tra-la-la!*"

Thump, thump, thump, went his heavy feet. Were his feet always this heavy? They must have been.

"*And I am not afraid,*" he continued. "*Not in the tiniest bit. Tra-la-la!*"

It wasn't true. He was terrified.

"Where *am* I?" he asked out loud. As if to answer his question, a figure appeared out of the gloom. A *monster*, Fyrian thought. Not that monsters as such were frightening. Fyrian loved Glerk, and Glerk was a monster. Still, this monster was much taller than Glerk. And in shadow. Fyrian took a step forward. His great paws sank even deeper into the mud. He tried to flap his wings, but they still wouldn't lift him off the ground. The monster didn't move. Fyrian stepped nearer. The trees rustled and moaned, their great branches shifting under the weight of the wind. He squinted.

"Why, you are not a monster at all. You are a chimney. A chimney with no house."

And it was true. A chimney was standing at the side of a clearing. The house, it seemed, had burned away years ago. Fyrian examined the structure. Carved stars decorated the uppermost stones, and soot blackened the hearth. Fyrian peered down into the top of the chimney and faced an angry mother hawk sitting on her frightened nestlings.

"Sorry," he squeaked, as the hawk nipped his nose, making it bleed. He turned away from the chimney. "What a small hawk," he mused. Though it occurred to him that he was away from the land of giants, and everything was of regular size here. Indeed, he had only to stand on his hind legs and stretch his neck in order to look into the chimney.

He looked around. He was standing in a ruined village, among the remains of houses and a central tower and a wall that perhaps was a place of worship. He saw pictures of dragons and a volcano and even a little girl with hair like starlight.

"This is Xan," his mother told him once. "She will take care of you when I'm gone." He had loved Xan from the first moment. She had freckles on her nose and a chipped tooth and her starlight hair was in long braids with ribbons at the end. But that couldn't be right. Xan was an old woman, and he was a young dragon, and he couldn't have possibly known her when she was young, could he have?

Xan had taken him in her arms. Her cheek was smudged with dirt. They had both been sneaking sweets from the castle pantry. "But I don't know how!" she had said. And then she had cried. She sobbed like a little girl.

But she couldn't have been a little girl. Could she?

"You will. You'll learn," Fyrian's mother's gentle, dragony voice said. "I have faith in you."

Fyrian felt a lump in his throat. Two giant tears welled in his eyes and went tumbling to the ground, boiling two patches of moss clear away. How long had it been? Who could tell? Time was a tricky thing—as slippery as mud.

And Xan had warned him to be mindful of sorrow. "Sorrow is dangerous," she told him over and over again, though he couldn't remember if she ever told him why.

The central tower leaned precariously to one side. Several foundation stones on the lee side had crumbled away, allowing Fyrian to crouch low and peer inside. There was something, two somethings, actually—he could see them by the tiny glimmer at the edges. He reached in and pulled them out. Held them in his paws. They were tiny—both fit into the hollow of his palm.

"Boots," he said. Black boots with silver buckles. They were old—they must be. Yet they shone as though they had just been polished. "They look just like those boots from the old castle," he said. "Of course, these can't be the same. They are much too small. The other ones were giant. And they were worn by giants."

The magicians long ago had been studying boots just like these. They had placed the boots on the table and were examining them with tools and special glasses and powders and cloths and other tools. Every day they experimented and observed and took notes. Seven League Boots, they were called. And neither Fyrian nor Xan was allowed to touch them.

"You're too little," the other magicians told Xan when she tried.

Fyrian shook his head. That can't be right. Xan wasn't little then, was she? It couldn't have been that long ago.

Something growled in the wood. Fyrian jumped to his feet. "*I'm not afraid,*" he sang as his knees knocked together and his breath came in short gasps. Soft, padded footsteps drew nearer. There were tigers in the wood, he knew. Or there had been long ago.

"I am a very fierce dragon!" he called, his voice a tiny squeak. The darkness growled again. "Please don't hurt me," the dragonling begged.

And then he remembered. Shortly after his mother disappeared into the volcano, Xan had told him this: "I will take care of you, Fyrian. For always. You're my family, and I am yours. I am putting a spell on you to keep you safe. You must never wander away, but if you do, and if you get scared, just say 'Auntie Xan' three times very quickly, and it will pull you to me as quick as lightning."

"How?" Fyrian had asked.

"A magic rope."

"But I don't see it."

"Just because you don't see something doesn't mean it isn't there. Some of the most wonderful things in the world are invisible. Trusting in invisible things makes them more powerful and wondrous. You'll see."

Fyrian had never tried it.

The growling came closer.

"A-a-auntie Xan Auntie Xan Auntie Xan," Fyrian shouted. He closed his eyes. Opened them. Nothing happened. His panic crawled into his throat.

"Auntie Xan Auntie Xan Auntie Xan!"

Still nothing. The growling came closer. Two yellow eyes glowed in the darkness. A large shape hunched in the gloom.

Fyrian yelped. He tried to fly. His body was too big and his wings were too small. Everything was wrong. Why was everything so wrong? He missed his giants, his Xan and his Glerk and his Luna.

"Luna!" he cried, as the beast began to lunge. "LUNA LUNA LUNA!"

And he felt a pull.

"LUNA-MY-LUNA!" Fyrian screamed.

"Why are you shouting?" Luna asked. She opened her pocket and lifted out Fyrian, who had curled his tiny body into a tight ball.

Fyrian shivered uncontrollably. He was safe. He almost cried in relief. "I was frightened," he said, his teeth caught on a mouthful of nightgown.

"Hmph," the girl grunted. "You were snoring, and then you gave me a burn."

"I did?" Fyrian asked, truly shocked. "Where?"

"Right here," she said. "Wait a minute." She sat up and looked closer. The scorch mark was gone, as was the hole in her nightgown, as was the burn on her hip. "It *was* here," she said slowly.

"I was in a funny place. And there was a monster. And my body didn't work right and I couldn't fly. And I found some boots. And then I was here. I think you saved me." He frowned. "But I don't know how."

Luna shook her head. "How could I have? I think we both were having bad dreams. I am not burned and you have always been safe, so let's go back to sleep."

And the girl and her dragon curled under the covers and were asleep almost instantly. Fyrian did not dream and did not snore, and Luna never moved.

When Luna awoke again, Fyrian was still fast asleep in the crook of her arm. Two thin ribbons of smoke undulated from his nostrils, and his lizard lips were curled in a sleepy grin. *Never*, Luna thought, *has there been a more contented dragon.* She slid her arm from underneath the dragon's head and sat up. Fyrian still did not stir.

"Pssst," she whispered. "Sleepyhead. Wake up, sleepyhead."

Fyrian still did not stir. Luna yawned and stretched and gave Fyrian a light kiss on the tip of his warm little nose. The smoke made Luna sneeze. Fyrian *still* didn't stir. Luna rolled her eyes.

"Lazybones," she chided as she slid out of bed onto the cool floor and hunted for her slippers and her shawl. The day was cool but would soon be fine. A walk would do Luna good. She reached over to the guide ropes to pull her bed up to the ceiling. Fyrian wouldn't mind waking up with her bed put away, and it felt better to start the day with the beds tied up. That's what her grandmother had taught her.

But once the bed was hoisted and secured, Luna noticed something on the ground.

A large pair of boots.

They were black, leather, and even heavier than they looked like they would be. Luna could barely lift them. And they had a strange smell—one that seemed familiar to Luna, somehow, though she could not place it. The soles were thick, and made of a material that she could not immediately identify. Even stranger, they were inscribed with words on each heel.

"Do not wear us," said the left heel.

"Unless you mean it," said the right.

"What on earth?" Luna said out loud. She hoisted one boot up and tried to examine it more closely. But before she could, she had a sudden sharp headache, right in the middle of her forehead. It knocked her to her knees. She pressed the heels of her hands to her skull and pushed inward, as though to keep her head from flying apart.

Fyrian still didn't stir.

She crouched on the floor for some time until the headache abated.

Luna glared at the underside of the bed. "Some watch you are," she scoffed. Pulling herself back to her feet, she went over to the small, wooden trunk under the window, and opened it with her foot. She kept her mementoes in there—toys she used to play with, blankets she used to love, odd-looking rocks, pressed flowers, leather-bound journals densely scrawled with her thoughts and questions and pictures and sketches.

And now, boots. Large, black boots. With strange words and a strange smell that was giving her a headache. Luna shut the lid and sighed with relief. With the trunk's lid closed, her head didn't hurt anymore. In fact, she could barely remember the pain. Now to tell Glerk.

Fyrian continued to snore.

Luna was thirsty. And hungry. And she was worried about her grandmother. And she wanted to see Glerk. And there were chores to be done. The goats needed milking. The eggs needed gathering. And there was something else.

She paused on her way to the berry patch.

She was going to ask about something. Now what was it?

For the life of her, Luna couldn't remember.

# 22

## In Which There Is Another Story

*Surely I told you about the boots already, child.*

*Well then. Of all the hideous devices owned and used by the Witch, the most terrible of all are her Seven League Boots. Now, on their own, the boots are like any bit of magic—neither good nor bad. They only allow the wearer to travel great distances in an instant, doubling the measure of her movements with each successive step.*

*This is what allows her to snatch our children.*

*This is what allows her to wander the world, spreading her malevolence and sorrow. This is what allows her to elude capture. We have no power. Our grief is without remedy.*

*Long ago, you see, before the forest became dangerous, the Witch was just a little thing. An ant, practically. Her powers were* limited. Her knowledge was small. Her ability to work mischief was hardly worth noticing. A child, lost in the wood. That was how powerful she was, really.

But one day, she found a pair of boots.

Anyway, the boots, once they were on her feet, allowed her to go from one side of the world to the other in an instant. And then she was able to find more magic. She stole it from other magicians. She stole it from the ground. She snuck it out of the air and the trees and the blooming fields. They say she even stole it from the moon. And then she cast a spell over all of us—a great cloud of sorrow, covering the world.

Well, of course it covers the world. That's why the world is drab and gray. That's why hope is only for the smallest of children. Best you learn that now.

# 23

## In Which Luna Draws a Map

L una left a note for her grandmother saying that she wanted to go out and collect berries and sketch the sunrise. In all likelihood, her grandmother would still be sleeping when Luna returned—she slept *so much* lately. And though the old woman assured the girl that she had always slept like that and nothing had changed nor would it ever change, Luna knew it was a lie.

*We are both lying to each other,* she thought, a great needle piercing her heart. *And neither of us knows how to stop.* She set her note on the plank table and quietly closed the door.

Luna slung her satchel across her shoulders and slid on her traveling boots and took the long, crooked way across the back of the swamp before following the slanted trail that led between the two smoking cinder cones at the southern side of the crater. The day was warm and sticky, and she realized with creeping horror that she was starting to stink. This sort of thing had been happening a lot lately—bad smells, strange eruptions on her face. Luna felt as though every single thing on her body had suddenly conspired to alter itself—even her voice had turned traitorous.

But that wasn't the worst of it.

There had been . . . other kinds of eruptions, too. Things that she couldn't explain. The first time she'd noticed it, she had tried to jump to get a better look at a bird's nest, and found herself, quite suddenly, on the topmost branch of the tree, hanging on for dear life.

"It must be the wind," she told herself, though the idea was clearly ridiculous. Who had ever heard of a gust of wind propelling a person to the top of a tree? But since Luna really didn't have any other explanation, *It must be the wind* seemed as good as any. She hadn't told her grandmother or her Glerk. She didn't want to worry them. Also, it felt vaguely embarrassing—like perhaps there was something wrong with her.

Besides. It was just the wind.

And then, a month later, when Luna and her grandmother were gathering mushrooms in the forest, Luna had noticed yet again how tired her grandmother was, how thin and how frail and how her breath rattled painfully in and out.

"I'm worried about her," she said out loud when her

grandmother was out of earshot. Luna felt her voice catching in her throat.

"I am, too," a nut-brown squirrel replied. He was sitting on the lowermost branch, peering down, a knowing expression on his pointy face.

It took a full moment for Luna to realize that squirrels are *not supposed to talk*.

It took another moment for her to realize that it wasn't the first time an animal had spoken to her. It had happened before. She was sure of it. She just couldn't remember when.

And later, when she tried to explain to Glerk what had happened, she drew a blank. She couldn't recall the incident for the life of her. She knew *something* had happened. She just didn't know *what*.

*This has happened before*, said the voice in her head.

*This has happened before.*

*This has happened before.*

It was a pulsing certainty, this knowledge, as sure and steady as the gears of a clock.

Luna followed the path as it curled around the first knoll, leaving the swamp behind. An ancient fig tree spread its branches over the path, as if welcoming all who wandered by. A crow stood on the lowest branch. He was a fine fellow, feathers shining like oil. He looked Luna straight in the eye, as though he was waiting for her.

*This has happened before*, she thought.

"Hello," Luna said, fixing her gaze on the crow's bright eye.

"Caw," the crow said. But Luna felt sure he meant "Hello."

And all at once, Luna remembered.

The day before, she had retrieved an egg from the chicken coop. There was only the one egg in all the nests, and she didn't have a basket, so she simply held it in her hand. Before she reached the house, she realized that the shell of the egg was wiggling. And that it was no longer smooth and warm and regular, but sharp and pointy and ticklish. Then it bit her. She let go of the egg with a cry. But it wasn't an egg at all. It was a crow, full-sized, spiraling over her head and alighting on the nearest tree.

"Caw," the crow had said. Or that is what the crow *should have* said. But it didn't.

"Luna," the crow cawed instead. And it didn't fly away. It perched on the lowest branch of Luna's tree house, and followed her wherever she went for the rest of the day. Luna was at a loss.

"Caw," cawed the crow. "Luna, Luna, Luna."

"Hush," Luna scolded. "I'm trying to *think.*"

The crow was black and shiny, as a crow ought to be, but when Luna squinted and looked at it aslant, she saw another color, too. Blue. With a shimmer of silver at the edges. The extra colors vanished when she opened her eyes wide and looked straight on.

"What are you?" Luna asked.

"Caw," said the crow. "I am the most excellent of crows," the crow meant.

"I see. Make sure my grandmother doesn't see you," Luna said. "Or my swamp monster," she added after considering it. "I think you'll upset them."

"Caw," said the crow. "I agree," it meant.

Luna shook her head.

The crow's being did not make sense. Nothing made sense. And yet the crow was *there*. It was sure and clever and *alive*.

*There is a word that explains this,* she thought. *There is a word that explains everything I don't understand. There must be. I just can't remember what it is.*

Luna had instructed the crow to stay out of sight until she could figure things out, and the crow had complied. It truly was an excellent crow.

And now, here it was again. On the lowest branch of the fig tree.

"Caw," the crow should have said. "Luna," it called instead.

"Quiet, you," Luna said. "You might be heard."

"Caw," the crow whispered, abashed.

Luna forgave the crow, of course. As she walked on, distracted, she tripped on a rock, tumbling hard to the ground and falling on her satchel.

"Ouch," her satchel said. "Get off me."

Luna stared at it. At this point, though, nothing surprised her. Even talking satchels.

Then a small, green nose peeked out from under the flap. "Is that you, Luna?" asked the nose.

Luna rolled her eyes. "What are you doing in my bag?" she demanded. She threw open the flap and glared at the shame-faced dragon climbing out.

"You keep going places," he said, without looking her in the eye. "Without me. And it isn't fair. I just wanted to come." Fyrian fluttered upward and hovered at eye level. "I just want to be part of the *group*." He gave her a hopeful, dragonish smile. "Maybe we should go get Glerk. And Auntie Xan. That's a fun group!"

"No," Luna said firmly, and continued her ascent to the top of the ridge. Fyrian fluttered behind.

"Where are we going? Can I help? I'm very helpful. Hey, Luna! Where are we going?"

Luna rolled her eyes and spun on her heel with a snort.

"Caw," the crow said. He didn't say *Luna* this time, but Luna could feel him thinking it. The crow flew up ahead, as though he already knew where they were going.

They followed the trail to the third cinder cone, the one on the far edge of the crater, and climbed to the top.

"Why are we up here?" Fyrian wanted to know.

"Hush," Luna said.

"Why must we hush?" Fyrian asked.

Luna sighed deeply. "I need you to be very, very quiet, Fyrian. So I may concentrate on my drawing."

"I can be quiet," Fyrian chirped, still hovering in front of her face. "I can be so quiet. I can be quieter than worms, and worms are very quiet, unless they are convincing you not to eat them, and then they are less quiet, and very convincing, though I usually still eat them because they are delicious."

"I mean, be quiet right now," Luna said.

"But I am, Luna! I'm the quietest thing that—"

Luna snapped the dragon's jaws shut with her index finger and her thumb and, to keep his feelings from getting hurt, scooped him up with her other arm and cuddled him close.

"I love you so much," she whispered. "Now hush." She gave his green skull an affectionate tap and let him curl into the heat of her hip.

She sat cross-legged on a flat-topped boulder. Scanning the limit of the land before it curved into the rim of the sky, she tried to imagine what sorts of things lay beyond. All she could see was forest. But surely the forest didn't go on forever. When Luna walked with her grandmother in the opposite direction, eventually the trees thinned and gave way to farms, and the farms gave way to towns, which gave way to more farms. Eventually, there were deserts and more forests and mountain ranges and even an ocean, all accessible by large networks of roads that unwound this way and that, like great spools of yarn. Surely, the same must be true in *this* direction. But she couldn't know for sure. She had never traveled this way. Her grandmother wouldn't let her.

She never explained why.

Luna set her journal on her lap and opened it to an empty page. She peered into her satchel, found her sharpest pencil, and held it in her left hand—lightly, as though it was a butterfly and might fly away. She closed her eyes, and tried to make her mind go blank and blue, like a wide, cloudless sky.

"Do I need to close my eyes, too?" Fyrian asked.

"Hush, Fyrian," Luna said.

"Caw," said the crow.

"That crow is mean," Fyrian sniffed.

"He's not mean. He's a crow." Luna sighed. "And yes, Fyrian, dearest. Close your eyes."

Fyrian gave a delighted gurgle and snuggled into the folds of Luna's skirt. He'd be snoring soon. No one could get comfortable quicker than Fyrian.

Luna turned her attention to the point at which the land met the sky. She pictured it as clear as she could in her mind, as though her mind had transformed to paper, and she need only mark upon it, as careful as could be. She breathed deeply, allowing her heart to slow and her soul to loosen its worries and wrinkles and knots. There was a feeling she would get when she did this. A heat in her bones. A crackling in her fingertips. And, strangest of all, an awareness of the odd birthmark on her forehead, as though it was, quite suddenly, shining—bright and clear, like a lamp. And who knows? Maybe it was.

In her mind, Luna could see the horizon's edge. And she saw the lip of the land begin to extend, farther and farther, as though the world was turning toward her, offering its face with a smile.

Without opening her eyes, Luna began to draw. As she sat, she became so calm that she was hardly aware of anything—her own breathing, the heat of Fyrian pressed close to her hip, the way he was beginning to snore, the crush of images coming so thick and fast she could hardly focus on them, until they all passed by in a great, green blur.

"Luna," a voice came from very far away.

"Caw," said another.

"LUNA!" A roar in her ear. She woke with a start.

"WHAT?" she roared back. But then she saw the look on Fyrian's face, and she was ashamed. "How—" she began. She looked around. The sun, only barely warming the world below when they had arrived on the crater, was now straight up above. "How long have we been here?"

*Half the day*, she already knew. *It's noon.*

Fyrian hovered very close to Luna's face, pressing nose to nose—green to freckles. His expression was grave. "Luna," he breathed. "Are you sick?"

"Sick?" Luna scoffed. "Of course not."

"I think you might be sick," he said in a hushed voice. *"Something very strange just happened to your eyeballs."*

"That's ridiculous," Luna said, closing her journal with a snap and tying the leather straps tightly around the soft covers. She slid it into her satchel and stood up. Her legs nearly buckled under her. "My eyes are regular."

"It's not ridiculous at all," Fyrian said, buzzing about from Luna's left ear to her right. "Your eyes are black and sparkly. Usually. But just now they were two pale moons. That isn't regular. Or, I'm pretty sure it isn't regular."

"My eyes were no such thing," Luna said, stumbling forward. She tried to right herself, hanging on to a boulder for balance. But the boulders gave her no assistance—they had, under the touch of her hands, become as light as feathers. One boulder began to float. Luna grunted in frustration.

"And now your legs won't work," Fyrian pointed out, trying to be helpful. "And what is going on with that boulder?"

"Mind your business," Luna said, summoning her strength to leap forward, landing hard on the smooth, granite slope on the eastern side.

"That was a far jump," Fyrian said, staring openmouthed from the place where Luna had been just a moment ago and arcing over to where Luna now was. "You usually can't jump that far. I mean it, Luna. It almost looked like—"

"Caw," said the crow. Or it should have been *Caw*. But to Luna, it sounded more like *Shut your face*. She decided she rather liked the crow.

"Fine," Fyrian sniffed. "Don't listen to me. No one *ever*

listens to me." And he buzzed down the slope in a blur of petulant green.

Luna sighed heavily and trudged toward home. She'd make it up to him. Fyrian always forgave her. Always.

The bright sun cast sharp shadows on the slope as Luna hurried down. She was filthy and sweaty—from the exercise or the blank drawing time? She had no idea, but she stopped by a stream to wash off. The lake inside the crater was too hot to touch, but the streams that flowed out of it, while unpleasant to drink, were cool enough to splash on a muddy face, or to wash the sweat from the back of the neck or under the arms. Luna knelt down and proceeded to make herself more presentable before facing her grandmother and Glerk—both of whom would likely want answers about her absence.

The mountain rumbled. The volcano, she knew, was hiccupping in its sleep. This was normal for volcanoes, Luna knew—they are restless sleepers—and this restlessness was usually not a problem. Unless it was. The volcano seemed more restless than usual lately—getting worse by the day. Her grandmother told her not to worry about it, which just made Luna worry more.

"LUNA!" Glerk's voice echoed off the slope of the crater. It bounced off the sky. Luna shaded her eyes and looked down the slope. Glerk was alone. He waved three of his arms in greeting and Luna waved back. *Grandmama isn't with him,* she realized with a clench in her heart. *She couldn't possibly still be sleeping,* she thought, her worry tying knots in her stomach. *Not this late.* But even at this far distance, she could see a blur of anxiety swirling around Glerk's head like a cloud.

Luna headed back to her house at a run.

Xan was still in bed. Past noon. Sleeping like the dead. Luna woke her up, feeling tears stinging in her eyes. *Is she sick?* Luna wondered.

"My goodness, child," Xan murmured. "Why on earth are you rousting me at this insane hour? Some of us are trying to sleep." And Xan turned onto her side and went back to sleep.

She didn't get up for another hour. She assured Luna this was perfectly normal.

"Of course it is, Grandmama," Luna said, not looking her grandmother in the eye. "Everything is perfectly normal." And grandmother and granddaughter faced one another with thin, brittle smiles. Each lie they told fell from their lips and scattered on the ground, tinkling and glittering like broken glass.

✿

Later that day, when her grandmother announced that she would like to be alone and left for the workshop, Luna pulled her journal from her satchel and paged through it, looking at the drawings she had done while she was dreaming. She always found she did her best work when she had no memory of what she had done. It was annoying, actually.

She had drawn a picture of a stone tower—one that she had drawn before—with high walls and an observatory pointing at the sky. She had drawn a paper bird flying out of the westernmost window. Another thing she had drawn before. She also had drawn a baby surrounded by ancient, gnarled trees. She had drawn the full moon, beaming promises to the earth.

And she had drawn a map. Two of them, actually. On two pages.

Luna flipped back and forth, stared at her handiwork.

Each map was intricate and detailed, showing topography and trails and hidden dangers. A geyser here. A mud pot there. A sinkhole that could swallow a herd of goats and still groan for more.

The first map was a precise rendering of the landscape and trails that led to the Free Cities. Luna could see each landform, each divot in the trail, each stream and clearing and waterfall. She could even see the downed trees from their recent journey.

The other map was another part of the forest altogether. The trail began at her tree house in one corner, and it followed the slope of the mountain as it tumbled toward the north.

Where she had never been.

She had drawn a trail—all twists and turns and clearly identified landmarks. Places to make camp. Which streams had good water, and which needed to be avoided.

There was a circle of trees. And in the center of it, she had written the word "baby."

There was a town behind a high wall.

And in the town, a Tower.

And next to the Tower, the words, "She is here, she is here, she is here."

Very slowly, Luna pulled the notebook close, and pressed these words next to her heart.

# 24

## In Which Antain Presents
## a Solution

Antain stood outside of his uncle's study for nearly an hour before working up the courage to knock. He took several deep breaths, mouthed paragraphs in front of his reflection in the pane of glass, attempted an argument with a spoon. He paced, he sweated, he swore under his breath. He mopped his brow with the cloth that Ethyne had embroidered—his name surrounded by a series of skillful knots. His wife was a magician with a needle and thread. He loved her so much, he thought he'd die of it.

"Hope," she had told him, tracing the many scars on his face tenderly with her small, clever fingers, "is those first tiny buds that form at the very end of winter. How dry they look!

How dead! And how cold they are in our fingers! But not for long. They grow big, then sticky, then swollen, and then the whole world is green."

And it was with the image of his dear wife in his mind—her rosy cheeks, her hair as red as poppies, her belly swollen to bursting under the dress she had made herself—that he finally knocked on the door.

"Ah!" his uncle's voice boomed from inside. "The shuffler has decided to cease his shuffling and announce his presence."

"I'm sorry, Uncle—" Antain stammered.

"ENOUGH WITH YOUR APOLOGIES, BOY," roared Grand Elder Gherland. "Open the door and be done with it!"

The *boy* stung a bit. Antain had not been a boy for several years now. He was a successful artisan, a keen businessman, and a married man, devoted to his wife. *Boy* was a word that no longer fit.

He stumbled into the study and bowed low before his uncle, as he always did. When he stood, he could see his uncle look upon his face and flinch. This was nothing new. Antain's scars continued to shock people. He was used to it.

"Thank you for seeing me, Uncle," he said.

"I don't believe I have a choice, Nephew," Grand Elder Gherland said, rolling his eyes to avoid looking at the young man's face. "Family is family, after all."

Antain suspected that this wasn't entirely true, but he didn't mention it.

"In any case—"

The Grand Elder stood. "In any case nothing, Nephew. I have waited at this desk for close to an eternity, anticipating your arrival, but now the time has come for me to meet with the Council. You do remember the Council, don't you?"

"Oh, yes, Uncle," Antain said, his face suddenly bright. "That is the reason I am here. I wish to address the Council. As a former member. Right now, if I may."

Grand Elder Gherland was taken quite aback. "You . . ." he stammered. "You wish to *what?*" Ordinary citizens did *not* address the Council. It wasn't *done*.

"If that's all right, Uncle."

"I—" the Grand Elder began.

"I know it is a bit unorthodox, Uncle, and I do understand if it puts you in an uncomfortable position. It has been . . . ever so many years since I wore the robes. I would like, at long last, to address the Council and both explain myself and thank them for giving me a place at their table. I never did, and I feel that it is a thing I owe."

This was a lie. Antain swallowed. And smiled.

His uncle seemed to soften. The Grand Elder steepled his fingers together and pressed them to his bulbous lips. He looked Antain square in the eye. "Tradition be damned," he said. "The Council will be ever so pleased to see you."

The Grand Elder rose and embraced his wayward nephew and, beaming, led him into the hall. As they approached the grand foyer of the house, a silent servant opened the door, and both uncle and nephew walked into the waning light.

And Antain felt that tiny, sticky bud of hope bloom suddenly in his chest.

✻

The Council, as Gherland had predicted, seemed more than happy to see Antain, and used his presence to raise their glasses to his celebrated craftsmanship and fine business sense, as well as his prodigious luck to have wedded the kindest and cleverest girl in the Protectorate. They hadn't been invited to the wedding—and wouldn't have come if they had been—but the way they patted his back and rubbed his shoulders, they seemed like a chortling chaw of benevolent uncles. They couldn't be more proud, and they told him so.

"Good lad, good lad." The Councilmen gurgled and grunted and guffawed. They passed around sweets, almost unheard-of in the Protectorate. They poured wine and ale and feasted on cured meats and aged cheeses and crumbly cakes, heavy with butter and cream. Antain pocketed much of what he was given to present later to his beloved wife.

As servants began clearing away the platters and jugs and goblets, Antain cleared his throat. "Gentlemen," he said, as the Council took their seats, "I have come here with an ulterior motive. Forgive me, please. Particularly you, Uncle. I have been, I admit, less than forthcoming in regard to my intentions."

The room went colder and colder. The Council started

giving Antain's scars, which until then they had pretended to ignore, a hard, almost disgusted, look. Antain steeled his courage and persevered. He thought of the baby growing and moving in his wife's swollen belly. He thought of the madwoman in the Tower. Who was to say that he, too, would not go mad, if forced to relinquish his baby—*his baby*—to the Robes? Who was to say that his beloved Ethyne would not? He could scarcely bear to be parted from her for an hour, but the madwoman had been locked in the Tower for years. *Years.* He would surely die.

"Pray," the Grand Elder said, slitting his eyes like a snake, "continue, boy."

Once again, attempting not to allow the *boy* to have its intended sting, Antain went on.

"As you know," he said, trying his best to turn his guts and spine into the hardest and densest of wood. He had no need to destroy. He was here to build. "As you know, my beloved Ethyne is expecting a child—"

"Splendid," the Elders said, brightening as one. "How very, very splendid."

"And," Antain continued, willing his voice not to shake, "our child is to arrive just after the turning of the year. There are no others expected between then and the Day of Sacrifice. Our child—our dear child—will be the youngest in the Protectorate."

And the happy guffaws stopped suddenly, like a smothered flame. Two elders cleared their throats.

"Hard luck," Elder Guinnot said in his thin, reedy voice.

"Indeed," Antain agreed. "But it does not have to be. I believe I have found a way to stop this horror. I believe I know the way to end the tyranny of the Witch forever."

Grand Elder Gherland's face darkened. "Do not trouble yourself with fantasies, boy," he growled. "Surely you do not think—"

"I saw the Witch," Antain said. He had been holding on to this information for ever so long. And now it was bursting inside of him.

"Impossible!" Gherland sputtered. The other Elders stared at the young man with unhinged jaws, like a council of snakes.

"Not at all. I saw her. I followed the procession. I know it wasn't allowed, and I am sorry for it. But I did it anyway. I followed and I waited with the sacrificial child, and *I saw the Witch*."

"You saw nothing of the kind!" Gherland shouted, standing up. There was not a witch. There had never been a witch. The Elders all knew it. They all rose to their feet, accusation in their faces.

"I saw her waiting in the shadows. I saw her hover over the babe, clucking hungrily. I saw the glittering of her wicked eyes. She saw me and transformed herself into a bird. She cried out in pain as she did so. *She cried out in pain*, gentlemen."

"Lunacy," one of the Elders said. "This is lunacy."

"It is not. The Witch exists. Of course she does. We've all

known that. But what we did not know is that she is *aged*. She feels pain. And not only that, we know where she is."

Antain pulled the madwoman's map from the mouth of his satchel. He laid it on the table, tracing a trail with his fingers.

"The forest, of course, is dangerous." The Elders stared at the map, the color draining from their faces. Antain caught his uncle's eye and held it.

*I see what you are doing, boy,* Gherland's gaze seemed to say.

Antain gazed back. *This is how I change the world, Uncle. Watch me.*

Aloud, Antain said, "The Road is the most direct route across the forest, and certainly the safest, given its width and breadth and clarity. However, there are several other routes of safe passage, as well—albeit somewhat convoluted and tricky."

Antain's finger traced around several thermal vents, skirted the deep ridging that shed razor-sharp shards of rock every time the mountain sighed, and found alternative routes past the cliffs or the geysers or the quickmud flats. The forest covered the sides of a very large and very wide mountain, whose deep creases and slow slopes spiraled around a central cratered peak, which was itself surrounded by a flat meadow and a small swamp. At the swamp a gnarled tree had been drawn. On the tree was a carving of a crescent moon.

*She is here,* the map said. *She is here, she is here, she is here.*

"But where did you get this?" wheezed Elder Guinnot.

"It doesn't matter," Antain said. "It is my belief that it is accurate. And I am willing to stake my life upon that belief." Antain rolled up the map and returned it to his satchel. "Which is why I am here, good fathers."

Gherland felt his breath come in great gasps. *What if it was true? What then?*

"I do not know why," he said, gathering his great, vulturous self to his fullest height, "we are troubling ourselves with this—"

Antain did not let him finish.

"Uncle, I know that what I am asking for is a bit out of the ordinary. And perhaps you are right. This may be a fool's errand. But really, I am not asking for very much at all. Only your blessing. I need no tools, no equipment, no supplies. My wife knows of my intentions, and I have her support. On the Day of Sacrifice the Robes will arrive at our house, and she will relinquish our precious child willingly. The whole Protectorate will sorrow as you walk by—a great sea of sorrow. And you will go to those awful trees—those Witch's Handmaidens. And you will lay that little babe on the moss and you will think that you will never lay eyes on that face again." Antain felt his voice crack. He shut his eyes tight and tried to recompose himself. "And perhaps that will be true. Perhaps I will succumb to the perils of the forest, and it will be the Witch who comes to claim my child."

The room was quiet, and cold. The Elders dared not speak. Antain seemed to grow taller than all of them. His face was lit from the inside, like a lantern.

"Or," Antain continued, "perhaps not. Perhaps it will be me waiting in those trees. Perhaps I shall be the one to lift the babe from the circle of sycamores. Perhaps I shall be the one to bring that baby safely home."

Guinnot found his reedy voice. "But . . . but how, boy?"

"It is a simple plan, good father. I shall follow the map. I shall find the Witch." Antain's eyes were two black coals. "And then I shall kill her."

# 25

## In Which Luna Learns
## a New Word

Luna woke in the dark with a searing headache. It originated from a point right behind her forehead no larger than a grain of sand. But she felt whole universes burst behind her vision, making it alternately light, then dark, then light, then dark. She fell out of her bed and clattered onto the floor. Her grandmother snored in the swing bed on the other side of the room, taking in each breath as though it was filtered through a handful of muck.

Luna pressed her hands to her forehead, trying to keep her skull from flying apart. She felt hot, then cold, then hot again. And was it her imagination, or were her hands glowing? Her feet as well.

"What's happening?" she gasped.

"Caw," her crow should have said from his perch at the window. "Luna," he cawed instead.

"I'm fine," she whispered. But she knew she wasn't. She could feel each of her bones as though they were made of light. Her eyes were hot. Her skin was slick and damp. She scrambled to her feet and stumbled out the door, taking in great gulps of night air as she did so.

The waxing moon had just set, and the sky glittered with stars. Without thinking about it, Luna raised her hands to the sky, letting starlight gather on her fingers. One by one, she brought her fingers to her mouth, letting the starlight slide down her throat. Had she done this before? She couldn't remember. In any case, it eased her headache and calmed her mind.

"Caw," said the crow.

"Come," said Luna, and she made her way down the trail.

Luna did not intend to make her way toward the standing stone in the tall grasses. And yet. There she was. Staring at those words, lit now by the stars.

*Don't forget,* the stone said.

"Don't forget what?" she said out loud. She took a step forward and laid her hand on the stone. Despite the hour and despite the damp, the stone was oddly warm. It vibrated and thrummed under her hand. She glared at the words.

"Don't forget *what*?" she said again. The stone swung open like a door.

*No,* she realized. Not *like* a door. It *was* a door. A door hanging in the air. A door that opened into a candlelit stone corridor, with stairs leading down into the gloom.

"How . . ." Luna breathed, but she could not continue.

"Caw," the crow said, though it sounded more like *I don't think you should go down there.*

"Quiet, you," Luna said. And she walked into the stone doorway and down the stairs.

The stairs led to a workshop, with clean, open workstations and sheaves and sheaves of paper. Open books. A journal with a quill resting across the pages with a bright black drop of ink clinging to the sharp tip, as though someone had stopped in the middle of a sentence before thinking better of it and rushing away.

"Hello?" Luna called. "Is anyone here?"

No one answered. No one but the crow.

"Caw," said the crow. Though it sounded more like *For crying out loud, Luna, let's get out of here.*

Luna squinted at the books and papers. They looked as though they were the scribbles of a crazy person—a tangle of loops and smudges and words that meant nothing.

"Why would someone go to all the trouble of making a book full of gibberish?" she wondered.

Luna walked across the circumference of the room, running her hands along the wide table and the smooth counters.

There was no dust anywhere, but no fingerprints, either. The air wasn't stale, but she could detect no scent of any kind of life.

"Hello!" she called again. Her voice didn't echo, nor did it carry. It seemed to simply fall out of her mouth and hit the ground with a soft thump. There was a window, which was strange, because surely she was underground, wasn't she? She had gone down stairs. But even stranger, the view outside was of the middle of the day. And what's more, it was a landscape that Luna didn't recognize. Where the mountain's crater should have been was instead a peak. A mountain peak with smoke pouring from the top, like a kettle set too long to boil.

"Caw," the crow said again.

"There's something wrong with this place," Luna whispered. The hairs on her arms stood at attention, and the small of her back began to sweat. A piece of paper flew from one of the sheaves and landed on her hand.

She could read it. "Don't forget," it said.

"How could I forget when I didn't know to begin with?" she demanded. But who was she asking?

"Caw," said the bird.

"NO ONE TELLS ME ANYTHING!" Luna shouted. But that wasn't true. She knew it wasn't. Sometimes her grandmother told her things, or Glerk told her things, but their words flew from her mind as soon as they were said. Even now

Luna could remember seeing words like tiny bits of torn-up paper lifting from her heart and hovering just before her eyes and then scattering away, as though caught on a wind. *Come back,* her heart called desperately.

She shook her head. "I'm being silly," she said out loud. "That never happened."

Her head hurt. That hidden grain of sand—tiny and infinite all at once, both compact and expanding. She thought her skull might shatter.

Another sheet of paper flew from the sheaf and landed on her hands.

There was no first word in the sentence—or not as it appeared to her. Instead, it looked like a smudge. After that, the sentence was clear: ". . . is the most fundamental—and yet least understood—element of the known universe."

She stared at it.

"What is the most fundamental?" she asked. She held the paper close to her face. "Show yourself!"

And, all at once, the grain of sand behind her forehead began to soften and release—just a bit. She stared at the word, and watched as letters uncurled from the tangle of haze, mouthing each one as they appeared.

"M," she mouthed. "-A-G-I-C." She shook her head. "What on earth is *that?*"

A sound thundered in her ears. Bursts of light flashed behind her eyes. M, A, G, I, C. This word meant something. She was sure it meant something. And what's more, she was sure she had heard the word before—though, for the life of her, she couldn't remember where. Indeed, she could hardly figure out how to pronounce it.

"Mmmmm," she began, her tongue turning to granite in her mouth.

"Caw," the crow encouraged.

"Mmmmm," she said again.

"Caw, caw, caw," the crow squawked joyfully. "Luna, Luna, Luna."

"Mmmmmmagic," Luna coughed out.

# 26

## In Which a Madwoman Learns
## a Skill and Puts It to Use

When the madwoman was a little girl, she drew pictures. Her mother told her stories about the Witch in the woods—stories that she was never sure were true. According to her mother, the Witch ate sorrow, or souls, or volcanoes, or babies, or brave little wizards. According to her mother, the Witch had big black boots that could travel seven leagues in a single step. According to her mother, the Witch rode on the back of a dragon and lived in a tower so tall it pierced the sky.

But the madwoman's mother was dead now. And the Witch was not.

And in the quiet of the Tower, far above the grimy fog of

the town, the madwoman sensed things that she never could have sensed before her years there. And when she sensed things, she drew them. Over and over and over again.

Every day, the Sisters came into her cell unannounced and clucked their tongues at the masses of paper in the room. Folded into birds. Folded into towers. Folded into likenesses of Sister Ignatia, and then stomped upon with the madwoman's bare feet. Covered over with scribbles. And pictures. And maps. Every day, the Sisters hauled paper by the armload out of the cell to be shredded and soaked and re-pulped into new sheets in the binderies in the basement.

*But where had it come from in the first place?* the Sisters asked themselves.

*It's so easy,* the madwoman wanted to tell them. *Just go mad. Madness and magic are linked, after all. Or I think they are. Every day the world shuffles and bends. Every day I find something shiny in the rubble. Shiny paper. Shiny truth. Shiny magic. Shiny, shiny, shiny.* She was, she knew sadly, quite mad. She might never be healed.

One day as she sat on the floor in the middle of her cell, cross-legged, she had chanced upon a handful of feathers left behind by a swallow who had decided to make her nest on the narrow windowsill of the cell, before a falcon had decided to make the swallow a snack. The feathers drifted in through the madwoman's window and onto the floor.

The madwoman watched them land. The feathers landed

on the floor right in front of her. She stared at them—the quill, the shaft, each filament of down. Then she could see the smaller structures—dust and barb and cell. Smaller and smaller went the details of her vision, until she could see each particle, spinning around itself like a tiny galaxy. She was as mad as they come, after all. She shifted the particles across the yawning emptiness between them, this way and that, until a new whole emerged. The feathers were no longer feathers. They were paper.

Dust became paper.

Rain became paper.

Sometimes her supper became paper, too.

And every time, she made a map. *She is here,* she wrote, over and over and over again.

No one read her maps. No one read her words. No one bothers with the words of the mad, after all. They pulped her paper and sold it at the marketplace for a considerable sum.

Once she mastered the art of paper, she found it was ever so easy to transform *other* things as well. Her bed became a boat for a short time. The bars on her windows became ribbons. Her one chair became a measure of silk, which she wrapped around herself like a shawl, just to enjoy the feel of it. And eventually she found that she could transform her*self* as well—though only into very small things, and only for a little while. Her transformations were so exhausting that they sent her to bed for days.

A cricket.

A spider.

An ant.

She had to be careful not to be trodden on. Or swatted.

A waterbug.

A cockroach.

A bee.

She also had to make sure she was back in her cell when the bonds of her atoms felt as though they were ready to burst and fly apart. Over time, she could hold herself in a particular form for slowly increasing durations. She hoped that one day she might be able to hold her form as a bird long enough to find her way to the center of the forest.

Some day.

Not yet.

Instead she became a beetle. Hard. Shiny. She scuttled right under the feet of the crossbow-wielding Sisters and down the stairs. She climbed onto the toes of the timid boy doing the Sisters' daily chores—poor thing. Afraid of his own shadow.

"Boy!" she heard the Head Sister shout from down the hall. "How long must we wait for our tea?"

The boy whimpered, stacked dishes and baked goods onto a tray with a tremendous clatter, and hurried down the hall. It was all the madwoman could do to hang on to the laces of his boot.

"At last," said the Head Sister.

The boy set the tray on the table with a tremendous crash.

"Out!" the Head Sister boomed. "Before you destroy something else."

The madwoman scuttled under the table, grateful for the shadows. Her heart went out to the poor boy as he stumbled out the door, clutching his hands together as though they were burned. The Sister inhaled deeply through her nose. She narrowed her gaze. The madwoman tried to make herself as small as possible.

"Do you smell something?" the Sister asked the man in the chair opposite.

The madwoman knew that man. He was not wearing his robes. Instead he wore a fine shirt of lovely cloth and a long coat of the lightest of wool. His clothes smelled of money. He was more wrinkled than he had been the last time she had seen him. His face was tired and old. The madwoman wondered if she looked similar. It had been so long—so very, very long—since she had last seen her own face.

"I smell nothing, madam," the Grand Elder said. "Except tea and cakes. And your own excellent perfume, of course."

"There is no need to flatter me, young man," she said, even though the Grand Elder was much older than she. Or he looked much older.

Seeing her next to the Grand Elder, the madwoman realized with a start that after all these years, Sister Ignatia had never seemed to age.

The old man cleared his throat. "And this brings us to the reason I am here, my dear lady. I did what you asked, and I learned what I could learn, and the other Elders did the same. And I did my best to dissuade him, but it was no use. Antain still intends to hunt the Witch."

"Did he follow your advice, at least? Did he keep his plans a secret?" There was a sound inside the voice of the Head Sister, the madwoman realized. Grief. She'd know that sound anywhere.

"Alas, no. People know. I don't know who told them—he or his ludicrous wife. He believes the quest to be possible, and it seems that she does, too. And others now believe the same. They all . . . *hope*." He said the word as though it was the bitterest of pills. The Grand Elder shuddered.

The Sister sighed. She stood and paced the room. "You really don't smell that?" The Grand Elder shrugged, and the Sister shook her head. "It doesn't matter. In all likelihood, the forest will kill him. He has never endeavored such a journey. He has no skills. He has no idea what he is doing. And his loss will prevent other, more—*unpleasant*—questions from being raised. However, it is possible that *he may return*. That is what troubles me."

The madwoman leaned as far out of the shadows as she dared. She watched the Sister's movements become more abrupt and chaotic. She watched as a slick of tears glistened right at the bottoms of her eyes.

"It is too risky." She took in a breath to steady herself. "And it doesn't close the door on the question. If he should return finding nothing, it does not mean that there isn't *something* to be found by another citizen so foolhardy as to take to the woods. And if *that* person finds nothing, then perhaps someone *else* will try as well. And soon those reports of *nothing* become *something*. And soon the Protectorate starts getting ideas."

Sister Ignatia was pale, the madwoman noticed. Pale and gaunt. As though she was slowly starving to death.

The Grand Elder was silent for a long moment. He cleared his throat. "I assume, dear lady . . ." His voice trailed off. He was silent again. Then, "I assume that one of your Sisters could. Well. If they could." He swallowed. His voice was weak.

"This isn't easy for either of us. I can see that you have some feeling for the boy. Indeed, your sorrow—" Her voice broke, and the Sister's tongue quickly darted out and disappeared back into her mouth. She closed her eyes as her cheeks flushed. As though she had just tasted the most delicious flavor in the world. "Your sorrow is very real. But it can't be helped. The boy cannot return. And it must be evident to all that it was the Witch who killed him."

The Grand Elder leaned heavily upon the embroidered sofa in the Sister's study. His face was pale and gaunt. He lifted his eyes to the ceiling. Even from her tiny vantage point, the madwoman could see that his eyes were wet.

"Which one?" he asked hoarsely. "Which one will do it?"

"Does it matter?" the Sister asked.

"It does to me."

Sister Ignatia stood and swept over to the window, looking out. She waited for a long moment. Finally she said, "All the Sisters, you understand, are well trained and thorough. It is not . . . *usual* for any of them to be overly upended by the protestations of feeling. Still. They all cared for Antain more than the other Tower boys. If it was anyone else, I'd send any Sister and be done with it. In this case"—she sighed, turned and faced the Grand Elder—"I shall do it."

Gherland flicked his eyes to dislodge the tears and pinned his gaze on the Sister.

"Are you sure?"

"I am. And you may rest assured: I will be quick. His death will be painless. He will not know of my coming. And he will not know what hit him."

# 27

## In Which Luna Learns More than She Wished

The stone walls were impossibly old and impossibly damp. Luna shivered. She stretched her fingers out, then curled them into fists, in and out and in and out, trying to get the blood flowing. Her fingertips felt like ice. She thought she'd never be warm.

The papers swirled around her feet. Whole notebooks skittered up the crumbling walls. Inky words unhooked themselves from the page and crawled around the floor like bugs before making their way back again, chattering all the while. Each book and each paper, as it turned out, had quite a bit to say. They murmured and rambled; they talked over one another; they stepped on each other's voices.

"Hush!" Luna shouted, pressing her hands over her ears.

"Apologies," the papers murmured. They scattered and gathered; they swirled into great whirlwinds; they undulated across the room in waves.

"One at a time," Luna ordered.

"Caw," agreed the crow. "And no foolishness," it meant.

The papers complied.

Magic, the papers asserted, was worthy of study.

It was worthy of knowledge.

And so it was, Luna learned, that a tribe of magicians and witches and poets and scholars—all dedicated to the preservation, continuation, and understanding of magic—established a haven for learning and study in an ancient castle surrounding an even more ancient Tower in the middle of the woods.

Luna learned that one of the scholars—a tall woman with considerable strength (and whose methods sometimes raised eyebrows)—had brought in a ward from the wood. The child was small and sick and hurt. Her parents were dead—or so the woman said, and why would she lie? The child suffered from a broken heart; she wept ceaselessly. She was a fountain of sorrow. The scholars decided that they would fill that child to bursting with magic. That they would infuse her skin, her bones, her blood, even her hair with magic. They wanted to see if they *could*. They wanted to know if it was *possible*. An adult could only use magic, but a child, the theory went, could *become* magic. But the process had never been tested and observed—not scientifically. No one had ever written down findings and drawn conclusions. All known evidence was anecdotal at best. The scholars were hungry for understanding, but some protested that it could kill the child. Others countered that if they hadn't found her in the first place, she would have died anyway. So what was the harm?

But the girl didn't die. Instead, the girl's magic, infused into her very cells, continued to grow. It grew and grew and grew. They could feel it when they touched her. It thrummed under her skin. It filled the gaps in her tissues. It lived in the empty spaces in her atoms. It hummed in harmony with every tiny filament of matter. Her magic was particle, wave, and motion. Probability and possibility. It bent and rippled and folded in on itself. It infused the whole of her.

But one scholar—an elderly wizard by the name of Zosimos—was vehemently opposed to the enmagickment of the child and was even more opposed to the continuing work. He himself had been enmagicked as a young boy, and he knew the consequences of the action—the odd eruptions, the disruptions in thinking, the unpleasant extension of the life span. He heard the child sobbing at night, and he knew what some might do with that sorrow. He knew that not all who lived in the castle were good.

And so he put a stop to it.

He called himself the girl's guardian and bound their destinies together. This, too, had consequences.

Zosimos warned the other scholars about the scheming of their colleague, the Sorrow Eater. Every day, her power increased. Every day, her influence widened. The warnings of old Zosimos fell on deaf ears. The old man wrote her name with a shiver of fear.

(Luna, standing in that room reading the story, surrounded by those papers, shivered, too.)

And the girl grew. And her powers increased. And she was impulsive and sometimes self-centered, as children often are. And she didn't notice when the wizard who loved her— her beloved Zosimos—began slowly withering away. Aging. Weakening. No one noticed. Until it was too late.

"We only hope," the papers whispered in Luna's ear, "that when she meets the Sorrow Eater again, our girl is older, stronger, and more sure of herself. We only hope that, after our sacrifice, she will know what to do."

"But who?" Luna asked them. "Who was the girl? Can I warn her?"

"Oh," the papers said as they quivered in the air. "We thought we told you already. Her name is Xan."

# 28

## In Which Several People
## Go into the Woods

Xan sat by the fireplace, twisting her apron this way and that until it was all in knots.

There was something in the air. She could feel it. And something underground—a buzzing, rumbling, irritated something. She could feel that, too.

Her back hurt. Her hands hurt. Her knees and her hips and her elbows and her ankles and each bone in her swollen feet hurt and hurt and hurt. As each click, each pulse, each second pulled them closer to that point on the gears of Luna's life when every hand pointed toward thirteen, Xan could feel herself thinning, shrinking, fading. She was as light and as fragile as paper.

*Paper,* she thought. *My life is made of paper. Paper birds. Paper maps. Paper books. Paper journals. Paper words and paper thoughts. Everything fades and shreds and crinkles away to nothing.* She could remember Zosimos—dear Zosimos! How close did he seem to her now!—leaning over his stacks of paper with six candles burning brightly around the perimeter of his desk, scratching his knowledge into the rough, clean space.

*My life was written on paper and preserved on paper—all those bloody scholars scratching their notes and their thoughts and their observations. If I had died, they would have inscribed my demise on paper and never shed a tear. And here is Luna, the same as I was. And here am I holding on to the one word that could explain everything, and the girl cannot read it or even hear it.*

It wasn't fair. What the men and women in the castle had done to Xan was not fair. What Xan had done to Luna was not fair. What the citizens of the Protectorate had done to their own babies was not fair. None of it was fair.

Xan stood and looked out the window. Luna had not returned. Perhaps that was for the best. She would leave a note. Some things were easier said on paper, anyway.

Xan had never left so early to retrieve the Protectorate baby. But she couldn't risk being late. Not after last time. And she couldn't risk being seen, either. Transformations were difficult, and she had to contend with the possibility that she might not have the strength to undo this one. More consequences.

Xan fastened her traveling cloak and slid her feet into

a pair of sturdy boots and packed her satchel full of bottles of milk and soft, dry cloths, and a bit of food for herself. She whispered a spell to keep the milk from spoiling and tried to ignore the degree to which the spell drained her energies and spirits.

"Which bird?" she murmured to herself. "Which bird, which bird?" She considered transforming herself into a raven and taking on a bit of its cunning or an eagle and taking on a bit of its fight. An albatross, with its effortless flight, also seemed like a good idea, except a lack of water might impede her ability to take off and land. In the end, she chose the swallow—small, yes, and delicate, but a good flier and a keen eye. She would have to take breaks, and a swallow was small and brown and nearly invisible to predators.

Xan closed her eyes and pressed her feet to the ground and felt the magic flow through her fragile bones. She felt herself become light and small and keen. Bright eyes, agile toes, a sharp, sharp mouth. She shook her wings, felt so deep within herself the need to fly she thought she might die of it, and with a high, sad cry of loneliness and missing Luna, she fluttered into the air and slid over the fringe of trees.

She was as light as paper.

✿

Antain waited for their child to be born before he began his journey. The Day of Sacrifice was weeks away, but there would be no more births in the ensuing time. There were about two dozen pregnant women in the Protectorate, but all of them had only just begun to show their bellies. Their labors were months away, not weeks.

The birth, thankfully, was an easy one. Or Ethyne claimed it was easy. But every time she cried out, Antain felt himself die inside. Birth was loud and messy and frightening, and it felt to Antain as if it took a lifetime or more, though in truth they were only at it for the better part of the morning. The baby came squalling into the world at lunchtime. "A proper gentleman, this one," the midwife said. "Makes his appearance at the most reasonable of hours."

They named him Luken and they marveled at his tiny toes and his delicate hands and the way his eyes fixed upon their faces. They kissed his small, searching, howling mouth.

Antain never felt more sure of what he had to do.

He left the next morning, well before the sun rose, with his wife and child still asleep in the bed. He couldn't bear to say good-bye.

❄

The madwoman stood at her window, her face resting on the bars. She watched the young man slide out of the quiet house. She had been waiting for him to appear for hours. She didn't know how she knew to wait for him—only that she did. The sun had not yet come up, and the stars were sharp and clear as broken glass, spangled across the sky. She saw him slip out of his front door and close it silently behind him. She watched him as he laid his hand on the door, pressing his palm against the wood. For a moment, she thought he might change his mind and go back inside—back to the family that lay asleep in the dark. But he didn't. He closed his eyes tight, heaved a great sigh, and turned on his heel, hurrying down the dark lane toward the place on the town wall where the climb was least steep.

The madwoman blew him a kiss for luck. She watched him pause and shiver as the kiss hit him. Then he continued on his way, his steps noticeably lighter. The madwoman smiled.

There was a life she used to know. There was a world she used to live in, but she could hardly remember it. Her life before was as insubstantial as smoke. She lived, instead, in this world of paper. Paper birds, paper maps, paper people, dust and ink and pulped wood and time.

The young man walked in the shadows, checking this way and that to see if anyone followed him. He had a satchel and a bedroll slung across his back. A cloak that would be too heavy during the day and not nearly warm enough at night. And swinging at his hip, a long, sharp knife.

"You must not go alone," the madwoman whispered. "There are dangers in the wood. There are dangers here that will follow you into the wood. And there is one who is more dangerous than you could possibly imagine."

When she was a little girl, she had heard stories about the Witch. The Witch lived in the woods, she was told, and had a tiger's heart. But the stories were wrong—and what truth they had was twisted and bent. The Witch was here, in the Tower. And while she didn't have a tiger's heart, she would rip you to shreds if given the chance.

The madwoman stared at the window's iron bars until they were no longer iron bars at all, but paper bars. She tore them to shreds. And the stones surrounding the window's opening were no longer stones—just damp clumps of pulp. She scooped them out of the way with her hands.

The paper birds around her murmured and fluttered and squawked. They opened their wings. Their eyes began to brighten and search. They lifted as one into the air, and they streamed through the window, carrying the madwoman on their collective backs, and flowed silently into the sky.

✻

The Sisters discovered the madwoman's escape an hour after dawn. There were accusations and explanations and search parties and forensic explorations and teams of detectives. Heads rolled. The cleanup was a long, nasty job. But quiet, of course. The Sisters couldn't afford to let news of the escape leak into the Protectorate. The last thing they needed was to allow the populace to be getting ideas. Ideas, after all, are dangerous.

Grand Elder Gherland ordered a meeting with Sister Ignatia just before lunch, despite her protestations that today simply was too difficult.

"I don't care two whits about your feminine complications,"

the Grand Elder roared as he marched into her study. The other Sisters scurried away, shooting murderous glances at the Grand Elder, which thankfully he did not notice.

Sister Ignatia felt it best not to mention the escaped prisoner. Instead, she called for tea and cookies and offered hospitality to the fuming Grand Elder.

"Pray, dear Gherland," she said. "Whatever is this about?" She regarded him with hooded, predatory eyes.

"It has happened," Gherland said wearily.

Unconsciously, Sister Ignatia's eyes flicked in the direction of the now-empty cell. "It?" she asked.

"My nephew. He left this morning. His wife and their baby are sheltering at my sister's house."

Sister Ignatia's mind began to race. They couldn't be connected, these two disappearances. They *couldn't*. She would have *known* . . . wouldn't she? There had been, of course, a marked drop in available sorrow from the madwoman. Sister Ignatia hadn't given it much thought. While it was annoying to have to go hungry in one's own home, there was always sorrow aplenty throughout the Protectorate, hanging over the town like a cloud.

Or normally there was. But this blasted *hope* stirred up by Antain was spreading through the town, disrupting the sorrow. Sister Ignatia felt her stomach rumble.

She smiled and rose to her feet. She gently laid her hand on the Grand Elder's arm, giving it a tender squeeze. Her long, sharp nails pierced his robes like a tiger's claws, making him cry out in pain. She smiled and kissed him on both cheeks. "Fear not, my boy," she said. "Leave Antain to me. The forest is filled with dangers." She pulled her hood over her head and strode to the door. "I hear there's a witch in the wood. Did you know?" And she disappeared into the hall.

✳

"No," Luna said. "No, no, no, no, no." She held the note from her grandmother in her hands for only a moment before she tore it to shreds. She didn't even read past the first sentence. "No, no, no, no, no."

"Caw," the crow said, though it sounded more like, "Don't do anything stupid."

Anger buzzed through Luna's body, from the top of her head to the bottoms of her feet. *This is how a tree must feel,* she thought, *as it is hit by lightning.* She glared at the torn-up note, wishing that it would reassemble itself so that she might tear it up again.

(She turned away before she could notice the pieces begin to quiver slightly, inching toward one another.)

Luna gave the crow a defiant look.

"I'm going after her."

"Caw," the crow said, though Luna knew he meant, "That is a very stupid idea. You don't even know where you're going."

"I do, too," Luna said, sticking out her chin and pulling her journal from her satchel. "See?"

"Caw," the crow said. "You made that up," he meant. "I once had a dream that I could breathe underwater like a fish. You don't see me trying *that*, now do you?"

"She's not strong enough," Luna said, feeling her voice start to crack. What if her grandmother became injured in the woods? Or sick? Or lost? What if Luna never saw her again? "I need to help her. I *need her*."

(The bits of paper with the "Dear" and the "Luna" fluttered their edges together, fusing neatly side by side, until no evidence of their separation remained. So too did the shred bearing "By the time you read this" and "there are things I must explain" underneath. And underneath that was, "you are ever so much more than you realize.")

Luna slid her feet into her boots, and packed a rucksack with whatever she could think of that might be useful on a journey. Hard cheese. Dried berries. A blanket. A water flask. A compass with a mirror. Her grandmother's star map. A very sharp knife.

"Caw," the crow said, though it sounded more like, "Aren't you going to tell Glerk and Fyrian?"

"Of course not. They'd just try to stop me."

Luna sighed. (A small, torn scrap of paper scurried its way across the room, as nimble as any mouse. Luna didn't notice. She didn't notice it creeping up her leg and along the back of her cloak. She didn't notice it burrow its way into her pocket.) "No," she said finally. "They'll figure out where I'm going. And anything I say will come out wrong. Everything I say comes out wrong."

"Caw," the crow said. "I don't think that's true."

But it didn't matter what the crow thought. Luna's mind was made up. She tied on her hood and checked the map that she had made. It looked detailed enough. And of course the crow was right, and of course Luna knew how dangerous the woods were. But she knew the way. She was *sure* of it.

"Are you coming with me or what?" she said to the crow as she left her home and slid into the green.

"Caw," the crow said. "To the ends of the earth, my Luna. To the ends of the earth."

❄

"Well," Glerk said, looking at the mess in the house. "This is not good at all."

"Where is Auntie Xan?" Fyrian wailed. He buried his face in a hankie, by turns lighting it on fire and then dousing the flames with his tears. "Why wouldn't she say good-bye?"

"Xan can take care of herself," Glerk said. "It's Luna who worries me."

He said this because it seemed like it must be true. But it wasn't. His worry for Xan had him tied up in knots. *What was she thinking?* Glerk moaned in his thoughts. *And how can I bring her back safe?*

Glerk sat heavily on the floor, his great tail curled around his body, reading over the note that Xan had left for Luna.

"*Dear Luna,*" it said. "*By the time you read this, I will be traveling quickly across the forest.*"

"Quickly? Ah," he murmured. "She has transformed." He shook his head. Glerk knew better than anyone how Xan's magic had drained away. What would happen if she became stuck in her transformation? If she was permanently ensquirrelled or enbirded or endeered? Or, even more troubling, if she could only manage a halfway transformation.

*"Things are changing in you, dearest. Inside and out. I know you can sense it, but you have no words for it. This is my fault. You have no idea who you are, and that is my fault, too. There are things that I kept from you because of circumstance, and things that I kept from you because I didn't want to break your heart. But it doesn't change the facts: you are ever so much more than you realize."*

"What does it say, Glerk?" Fyrian said, buzzing from one side of Glerk's head to the other, like a persistent, and annoying, bumblebee.

"Give us a moment, will you, my friend?" Glerk murmured.

Hearing Glerk use the word "friend" in relation to himself made Fyrian positively giddy with happiness. He trilled his tongue against the roof of his mouth and turned a backflip and a double spin in the air, accidentally knocking his head against the ceiling.

"Of course I'll give you a moment, Glerk, my *friend*," Fyrian said, shrugging off the bump on his skull. "I'll give you all the moments in the world." He fluttered down to the arm-rest of the rocking chair and made himself as prim and still as he possibly could.

Glerk looked closer at the paper—not at the words, but at the paper itself. It had been torn, he could see, and had been knit back together so tightly, most eyes would not have caught the change. Xan would have seen it. Glerk looked even closer, at the threads of the magic—each individual strand. Blue. A shimmer of silver at the edges. There were millions of them. And none of them originated from Xan.

"Luna," he whispered. "Oh, Luna."

It was starting early. Her magic. All that power—the great surging ocean of it—was leaking out. He had no way of know-ing whether the child meant to do it, or even noticed it happen-ing at all. He remembered when Xan was young, how she would make ripe fruit explode in a shower of stars just by standing too closely. She was dangerous then—to herself and to others. As Luna was when she was young. As she likely was now.

*"When you were a baby, I rescued you from a terrible fate. And then I accidentally offered you the moon to*

*drink—and you did drink it, which exposed you to yet*
*another terrible fate. I am sorry. You will live long and*
*you will forget much and the people you love will die and*
*you will keep going. This was my fate. And now it is yours.*
*There is only one reason for it:"*

Glerk knew the reason, of course, but it was not in the
letter. Instead, there was a perfectly torn hole where the word
*magic* had been. He looked around the floor, but he didn't see it
anywhere. This was one of the things he couldn't stand about
magic, generally. Magic was a troublesome thing. Foolish. And
it had a mind of its own.

*"It is the word that could not stick in your mind, but it is*
*the word that defines your life. As it has defined mine. I*
*only hope I will have enough time to explain everything*
*before I leave you again—for the last time. I love you*
*more than I could possibly say.*

                    *Your Loving Grandmother"*

Glerk folded up the letter and slid it under the candlestick.
He looked around the room with a sigh. It was true that Xan's
days were dwindling, and it was true that, in comparison to
his excessively long life, Xan's was no more than a deep breath,
or a swallow, or the blink of an eye. And soon she would be

gone forever. He felt his heart ball up in his throat in a hard, sharp lump.

"Glerk?" Fyrian ventured. He buzzed toward the ancient swamp monster's face, peering into those large, damp eyes. Glerk blinked and stared back. The dragonling, he had to admit, was a sweet little thing. Bighearted. Young. But unnaturally so. And now was the time for him to grow up.

Past time, really.

Glerk pulled himself to his feet and his first set of arms, bending back a bit to ease out the kinks in his spine. He loved his small swamp—of course he did—and he loved his small life here in the crater of the volcano. He had chosen it without regrets. But he loved the wide world, too. There were parts of himself that he had left behind to live with Xan. Glerk could barely remember them. But he knew they were bountiful and life-giving and *vast*. The Bog. The world. All living things. He had forgotten how much he loved it all. His heart leaped within him as he took his first step.

"Come, Fyrian," he said, holding his top left hand out and allowing the dragon to alight on his palm. "We are going on a journey."

"A real journey?" Fyrian said. "You mean, *away from here?*"

"That is the only kind of journey, young fellow. And yes. Away from here. That sort of journey."

"But . . ." Fyrian began. He fluttered away from the hand

and buzzed to the other side of the swamp monster's great head. "What if we get lost?"

"I never get lost," Glerk said. And it was true. Once upon a time, many Ages ago, he traveled around the world more times than he could count. And in the world. And above and below. A poem. A Bog. A deep longing. He could barely remember it now, of course—one of the hazards of so very long a life.

"But . . ." Fyrian began, zooming from one side of Glerk's face to the other and back again. "What if I should frighten people? With my remarkable size. What if they flee in terror?"

Glerk rolled his eyes. "While it is true, my young friend, that your size is—er—*remarkable,* I believe that a simple explanation from me will ease their fears. As you know, I have excellent skills at explaining things."

Fyrian landed on Glerk's back. "This is true," he murmured. "No one explains things better than you, Glerk." And then he threw his small body against the swamp monster's great, damp back and flung his arms wide in an attempt at a hug.

"There is no need for that," Glerk said, and Fyrian drifted back up into the air, hovering over his friend. "Look," Glerk continued. "Do you see? Luna's footprints."

And so they followed her—the ancient swamp monster and the Perfectly Tiny Dragon—into the wood.

And with each footprint, Glerk became increasingly aware that the magic leaking from the young girl's feet was growing.

It seeped, then shined, then pooled on the ground, then spilled from the edges. At this rate, how long would it take for that magic to flow like water, move like streams and rivers and oceans? How long before it flooded the world?

How long, indeed?

# 29

## In Which There Is a Story with a Volcano in It

*It is not an ordinary volcano, you know. It was made thousands and thousands of years ago by a witch.*

*Which witch? Oh, I don't know. Not the Witch we've got, surely. She is old, but she is not that old. Of course I don't know how old she is. No one does. And no one has seen her. I hear she looks like a young girl sometimes and an old woman sometimes and a grown lady other times. It all depends.*

*The volcano has dragons in it. Or it did. Time was that there were dragons all over creation, but now no one has seen them in an Age. Maybe longer.*

*How should I know what happened to them? Maybe the*

Witch got them. Maybe she ate them. She is always hungry, you know. The Witch is, I mean. Let that keep you in your bed at night.

Every time the volcano erupts it is larger, angrier, more ferocious. Time was, it was no bigger than an ant's hill. Then it was the size of a house. Now it's bigger than the forest. And one day, it will envelop the whole world, you see if it won't.

The last time the volcano erupted, it was the Witch that caused it. You don't believe me? Oh, it's as true as you're standing here. In those days the forest was safe. There were no pitfalls or poisonous vents. Nothing burned. And there were villages dotting this way and that through the forest. Villages that collected mushrooms. Villages that traded in honey. Villages that made beautiful sculptures out of clay and hardened them with fire. And they were all connected by trails and small roads that crossed and crisscrossed the forest like a spider's web.

But the Witch. She hates happiness. She hates it all. So she brought her army of dragons into the belly of the mountain.

"Heave!" she shouted at the dragons. And they heaved fire into the heart of the volcano. "Heave!" she shouted again.

And the dragons were afraid. Dragons, if you must know, are wicked creatures—full of violence and duplicity and deceit. Still, the deceit of a dragon was nothing in the face of the wickedness of the Witch.

"Please," the dragons cried, shivering in the heat. "Please stop this. You'll destroy the world."

"What care have I for the world?" The Witch laughed. "The world never cared for me at all. If I want it to burn, well then, it will burn."

And the dragons had no choice. They heaved and heaved until they were nothing more than ash and embers and smoke. They heaved until the volcano burst into the sky, raining destruction across every forest, every farm, every meadow. Even the Bog was undone.

And the volcano's eruption would have destroyed everything, if it hadn't been for the brave little wizard. He walked into the volcano and—well, I'm not entirely clear what he did, but he stopped it right up, and saved the world. He died doing it, poor thing. Pity he didn't kill the Witch, but nobody's perfect. Despite everything, we must thank him for what he's done.

But the volcano never really went out. The wizard stopped it up, but it went underground. And it leaks its fury into the water pools and the mud vats and the noxious vents. It poisons the Bog. It contaminates the water. It is the reason why our children go hungry and our grandmothers wither and our crops are so often doomed to fail. It is the reason we cannot ever leave this place and there is no use trying.

But no matter. One day it will erupt again. And then we will be out of our misery.

# 30

## In Which Things Are More Difficult than Originally Planned

L una hadn't been walking for long before she was very, very lost and very, very frightened. She had her map and she could see in her mind's eye the route that she should travel, but she had already lost her way.

The shadows looked like wolves.

The trees clacked and creaked in the wind. Their branches curled like sharp claws, scratching at the sky. Bats screeched and owls hooted their replies.

The rocks creaked under her feet, and beneath that, she could feel the mountain churning, churning, churning. The ground was hot, then cold, then hot again.

Luna lost her footing in the dark and tumbled, head over feet, into a muddy ravine.

She cut her hand; she twisted her ankle; she knocked her skull against a low-hanging branch and burned her leg in a boiling spring. She was fairly certain she had blood in her hair.

"Caw," said the crow. "I told you this was a terrible idea."

"Quiet," Luna muttered. "You're worse than Fyrian."

"Caw," said the crow, but what he meant was any number of unrepeatable things.

"*Language!*" Luna admonished. "And anyway, I don't believe I like your tone."

Meanwhile, something continued happening inside Luna that she could not explain. The clicking of gears that she had felt almost her whole life was now more like the gonging of a bell. The word *magic* existed. She knew that now. But what it was and what it meant were still a mystery.

Something itched in her pocket. A small, papery something crinkled and rattled and squirmed. Luna did her best to ignore it. She had bigger problems at hand.

The forest was thick with trees and undergrowth. The shadows crowded out the light. With each step she paused and gingerly padded her foot in front of her, feeling around for solid ground. She had been walking all night, and the moon—nearly full—had vanished in the trees, taking the light with it.

*What have you gotten yourself into?* the shadows seemed to say, tutting and harrumphing.

244~

There wasn't even enough light to see the map that she had drawn. Not that a map would do her any good so far off her intended trail.

"Stuff and bother," Luna muttered, carefully taking another step. The path was tricky here—hairpin curves and needle-like rock formations. Luna could feel the vibration of the volcano under her feet. It didn't relent—not even for a moment. *Sleep*, she thought at it. *You are supposed to be sleeping.* The volcano didn't seem to know this.

"Caw," said the crow. "Forget the volcano. *You* should sleep," he meant. This was true. Lost as she was, Luna was hardly making any progress. She should stop, rest, and wait until morning.

But her grandmother was out here.

And what if she was hurt?

And what if she was sick?

And what if she didn't come back?

Luna knew that everything alive must die someday—she had seen it with her own eyes when she assisted her grandmother. People died. And while it made their loved ones sad, it didn't seem to bother the dead person one bit. They were dead, after all. They had moved on to other matters.

She once asked Glerk what happens to people when they died.

He had closed his eyes and said, "The Bog." There was a dreamy smile on his face. "The Bog, the Bog, the Bog." It was the most un-poetic thing he had ever said. Luna was impressed. But it didn't exactly answer her question.

Luna's grandmother had never spoken about the fact that she would die someday. But she clearly *would* die and likely *was dying*—this thinness, this weakness, this evasion. These were questions with one terrible answer, which her grandmother refused to give.

Luna pressed onward with an ache in her heart.

"Caw," said the crow. "Be careful."

"I *am* being careful," Luna said peevishly.

"Caw," said the crow. "Something very strange is happening to the trees."

"I have no idea what you're talking about," Luna said.

"Caw!" the crow gasped. "Watch your footing!"

"What do you think I'm trying—"

But Luna said no more. The ground rumbled, the rocks under her feet gave way, and she fell, pinwheeling into the darkness below.

# 31

## In Which a Madwoman Finds a Tree House

Flying on the backs of a flock of paper birds is less comfortable than you might imagine. And while the madwoman was accustomed to a bit of discomfort, the movement of the paper wings was having an effect on her skin. They cut her until she bled.

"Just a little bit farther," she said. She could see the place in her mind. A swamp. A series of craters. A very large tree with a door in it. A small observatory through which one might see the stars.

*She is here, she is here, she is here.* For all these years, her heart had painted the picture for her. Her child—not a figment of her imagination, but her child in the world. The picture that her heart painted was *real*. She knew it now.

Before the madwoman was born, her mother had sacrificed a baby to the Witch. A boy. Or so she was told. But she knew her mother had visions of the boy growing up. She did until she died. And the madwoman, too, could see her own dear baby—a big girl now. Black hair and black eyes and skin the color of polished amber. A jewel. Clever fingers. A skeptical gaze. The Sisters told her this was just her madness talking. And yet, she could draw a map. A map that led her to her daughter. She could feel its rightness in the thrum and heat of her bones.

"There," the madwoman breathed, pointing down.

A swamp. Just as she had seen in her mind. It was real.

Seven craters, marking the border. Just as she had seen in her mind. They were also real.

A workshop made of stones, with an observatory. Also real.

And there, next to a small garden plot and a stable and two wooden chairs seated in a flowering arbor—an enormous tree. With a door. And windows.

The madwoman felt her heart give a great leap.

*She is here, she is here, she is here.*

The birds surged upward before slowly drifting down to the ground, carrying the madwoman with them, laying her down as gently as a mother lays a baby in a bed.

*She is here.*

The madwoman scrambled to her feet. Opened her mouth. Felt her heart seize in her chest. Surely she had given her child a name. She must have.

*What child?* the Sisters used to whisper to her. *No one knows what you are talking about.*

*No one took your baby,* they told her. *You lost your baby. You put her in the woods and you lost her. Silly girl.*

*Your baby died. Don't you remember?*

*The things you invent. Your madness is getting worse.*

*Your baby was dangerous.*

*You are dangerous.*

*You never had a baby.*

*The life you remember is just a fancy of your fevered mind.*

*You have been mad forever.*

*Only your sorrow is real. Sorrow and sorrow and sorrow.*

She knew the baby was real. And the house she lived in and the husband who loved her. Who now had a new wife and a new family. A different baby.

*There never was a baby.*

*No one knows who you are.*

*No one remembers you.*

*No one misses you.*

*You don't exist.*

The Sisters were all venom and slither and hiss. Their voices crawled up her spine and wound around her neck. Their lies pulled in tight. But they were only doing as they were told. There was only one liar in the Tower, and the madwoman knew who it was.

The madwoman shook her head. "Lies," she said out loud. "She told me lies." She was a girl in love once. And a clever wife. And an expectant mother. An angry mother. A grieving mother. And her grief made her mad, yes. Of course it did. But it made her see the truth, too.

"How long has it been?" she whispered. Her spine curled and she wrapped her arms around her belly, as though holding her sorrow inside. An ineffective trick, alas. It took her years to learn better ways to thwart the Sorrow Eater.

The paper birds hovered over her head—a quiet, rustly flapping. They were awaiting orders. They would wait all day. She knew they would. She didn't know how she knew.

"Is—" Her voice cracked. It was rusty and creaky from lack of use. She cleared her throat again. "Is anyone here?"

No one answered.

She tried again.

"I do not remember my name." This was true. The truth, she decided, was the only thing she had. "But I had a name. Once. I am looking for my child. I do not remember her name, either. But she exists. My name exists, too. I lived with my daughter and my husband before everything went wrong. She was taken. She was taken by bad men. And bad women. And maybe also a witch. I am not certain about the Witch."

Still no one answered.

The madwoman looked around. The only sounds were the bubbling swamp and the rustle of paper wings. The door in the belly of the enormous tree was slightly ajar. She walked across the yard. Her feet hurt. They were bare and uncalloused. When was the last time they had touched the earth? She could hardly remember. Her cell was small. The stone was smooth. She could go from one side to the other in six short steps. When she was a little girl she ran barefoot whenever she could. But that was a thousand lifetimes ago. Perhaps it happened to someone else.

A goat began to bleat. And another. One was the color of toasted bread and the other was the color of coal. They stared at the madwoman with their large, damp eyes. They were hungry. And their udders were swollen. They needed to be milked.

She had milked a goat, she realized with a start. Long ago.

The chickens clucked in their enclosure, pressing their beaks to the willow walls, keeping them inside. They gave their wings a desperate flap.

They were also hungry.

"Who takes care of you?" the madwoman asked. "And where are they now?"

She ignored the animals' piteous cries and went through the door.

Inside was a home—neat and tidy and pleasant. Rugs on the floor. Quilts on the chairs. There were two beds pulled up to the ceiling through a clever construction of ropes and pulleys. There were dresses on hangers, and cloaks on hooks. One bed had a collection of staffs leaning against the wall just under it. There were jams and bundles of herbs and dried meats studded with spices and cracked salt. A round of cheese curing on the table. Pictures on the wall—handmade pictures on wood or paper or unrolled bark. A dragon sitting on the head of an old woman. A strange-looking monster. A mountain with a moon hovering over it, like a pendant off a neck. A tower with a black-haired woman leaning out, reaching her hand to a bird. "She is here," it said on the bottom.

Each picture was signed with a childlike script. "Luna," they said.

"*Luna,*" whispered the madwoman. "*Luna, Luna, Luna.*"

And each time she said it, she felt something inside her clicking into place. She felt her heart beat. And beat. And beat. She gasped.

"My daughter is named Luna," she whispered. She knew in her heart it was true.

The beds were cold. The hearth was cold. No shoes sat on the rug by the door. No one was here. Which meant that Luna and whoever else lived in this house were not here. They were in the woods. And there was a witch in the woods.

# 32

# In Which Luna Finds a Paper Bird.
# Several of Them, Actually.

By the time Luna regained consciousness, the sun was already high in the sky. She was lying on something very soft—so soft that she thought at first she was in her own bed. She opened her eyes and saw the sky, cut by the branches of the trees. She squinted, shivered, and pulled herself up. Took her bearings.

"Caw," breathed the crow. "Thank goodness."

First she assessed her own body. She had a scratch across her cheek, but it didn't seem particularly deep, and a lump on her head that hurt to touch. There was dried blood in her hair. Her dress was torn at the bottom and at both of her elbows. Other than that, nothing seemed particularly *broken*, which itself was fairly remarkable.

Even more remarkable, she lay atop a bloom of mushrooms that had grown to enormous size at the edge of a creek bed. Luna had never seen mushrooms so large. Or comfortable. Not only had they broken her fall, but they had prevented her from rolling directly into the creek and possibly drowning.

"Caw," said the crow. "Let's go home."

"Give us a minute," Luna said crossly. She reached into her satchel and pulled out her notebook, opening it to the map. Her home was marked. Streams and knolls and rocky slopes were marked. Dangerous places. Old towns that were now in ruins. Cliffs. Vents. Waterfalls. Geysers. Places where she could not cross. And here, at the bottom corner.

"Mushrooms," the map said.

"Mushrooms?" Luna said out loud.

"Caw," said the crow. "What are you talking about?"

The mushrooms on her map were next to a creek. It didn't lead to her route, but it lead to a place where she could safely traverse across mostly stable ground. Maybe.

"Caw," the crow whined. "*Please* let's go home."

Luna shook her head. "No," she said. "My grandmother needs me. I can feel it in my bones. And we are not leaving this wood without her."

Wincing, she staggered to her feet, replaced her notebook in her satchel, and tried her best to hike without limping.

With each step her wounds hurt a little less and her mind cleared a little more. With each step her bones felt stronger and less bruised, and even the dried blood in her hair felt less heavy and crusty and sticky. Soon, she ran her hand through her hair, and the blood was gone. The lump was gone, too. Even the scratch on her face and the tears in her dress seemed to have healed themselves.

*Odd,* thought Luna. She didn't turn around, so she didn't notice her footsteps behind her, each one now a garden blooming with flowers, each flower bobbing in the breeze, the large, lurid blooms turning their faces toward the disappearing girl.

✿

A swallow in flight is graceful, agile, and precise. It hooks, swoops, dives, twists, and beats. It is a dancer, a musician, an arrow.

Usually.

This swallow stumbled from tree to tree. No arabesques. No gathering speed. Its spotted breast lost feathers by the fistful. Its eyes were dull. It hit the trunk of an alder tree and tumbled into the arms of a pine. It lay there for a moment, catching its breath, wings spread open to the sky.

There was something it was supposed to be doing. *What was it?*

The swallow pulled itself to its feet and clutched the green tips of the pine bough. It puffed its feathers into a ball and did its best to scan the forest.

The world was fuzzy. *Had it always been fuzzy?* The swallow looked down at its wrinkled talons, narrowing its eyes.

*Have these always been my feet?* They must have been. Still, the swallow couldn't shake the vague notion that perhaps they were not. It also felt that there was somewhere it should be. Something it should be doing. Something important. It could feel its heart beating rapidly, then slowing dangerously, then speeding up again, like an earthquake.

*I'm dying,* the swallow thought, knowing for certain that it was true. *Not right this second, of course, but I do appear to be dying.* It could feel the stores of its own life force deep within itself. And those stores were starting to dwindle. *Well. No matter. I feel confident that I've had a good life. I just wish I could remember it.*

It pressed its beak tightly shut and rubbed its head with its wings, trying to force a memory. *It shouldn't be this difficult to remember who one is,* it thought. Even a fool should be able to do it. And as the swallow racked its brain, it heard a voice coming down the trail.

"My dear Fyrian," the voice said. "You have, by my last count, spent well over an hour speaking without ceasing. Indeed, I am shocked that you haven't felt the need even to draw a breath."

"I can hold my breath a long time, you know," the other voice said. "It is part of being Simply Enormous."

The first voice was silent for a moment. "Are you sure?"

Another silence. "Because such skills are never enumerated in any of the texts on dragon physiology. It is possible that someone told you so to trick you."

"Who could possibly trick me?" the second voice said, all wide eyes and breathless wonder. "No one has ever told me anything but the truth. In my whole life. Isn't that right?"

The first voice let loose a brief grumble, and silence reigned again.

The swallow knew those voices. It fluttered closer to get a better look.

The second voice flew away and returned, skidding on the back of the owner of the first voice. The first voice had many arms and a long tail and a great, broad head. It had a slow bearing to it, like an enormous sycamore tree. A tree that moved. The swallow moved closer. The great many-armed and tailed tree-creature paused. Looked around. Wrinkled its brow.

"Xan?" it said.

The swallow held very still. It knew that name. It knew that voice. *But how?* It couldn't remember.

The second voice returned.

"There are things in the woods, Glerk. I found a chimney. And a wall. And a small house. Or it was a house, but now it has a tree in it."

The first voice didn't answer right away. It swung its head very slowly from side to side. The swallow was behind a thicket of leaves. It hardly breathed.

Finally the first voice sighed. "You were perhaps seeing one of the abandoned villages. There are many on this side of the woods. After the last eruption, the people fled, and were welcomed into the Protectorate. That's where the magicians gathered them. Those who were left, anyway. I never knew what happened to them after that. They couldn't come back into the woods, of course. Too dangerous."

The creature swung its great head from side to side.

"Xan has been here," it said. "Very recently."

"Is Luna with her?" the second voice said. "That would be safer. Luna can't fly, you know. And she is not impervious to flames like Simply Enormous Dragons. That is well known."

The first voice groaned.

And, all at once, Xan knew herself.

*Glerk,* she thought. *In the woods. Away from the swamp.*

*Luna. All on her own.*

*And there was a baby. About to be left in the forest. And I have to save it, and what on earth am I doing, dilly-dallying here?*

*Great heavens. What have I done?*

And Xan, the swallow, burst from the thicket and soared over the trees, beating her ancient wings as best she could.

✻

The crow was beside himself with worry. Luna could tell.

"Caw," the crow said, and meant, "I think we should turn back."

"Caw," he said again, which Luna took to mean, "Be

careful. Also, are you aware that rock is on fire?" And so it was. Indeed, there was an entire seam of rock, curving into the damp and deeply green forest, glowing like a river of embers. Or perhaps it *was* a river of embers. Luna checked her map. "River of Embers," the map said.

"Ah," Luna said. And she tried to find a way around.

This side of the forest was far more rageful than the section that she usually traveled.

"Caw," the crow said. But Luna didn't know what it meant.

"Speak more clearly," she said.

But the crow did not. He spiraled upward, perched briefly at the topmost branch of an enormous pine. Cawed. Spiraled down. Up and down and up and down. Luna felt dizzy.

"What do you see?" she said. But the crow wouldn't say.

"Caw," the crow said, swooping back over the tops of the trees.

"What has gotten into you?" Luna asked. The crow didn't say.

The map said "Village," which should have been visible just over the next ridge. How could anyone actually live in this forest?

Luna traversed the slope, watching her footing, as the map advised.

*Her map.*

*She had made it.*

*How?*

*She had no idea.*

"Caw," the crow said. "Something coming," it meant. *What could possibly be coming?* Luna peered into the green.

She could see the village, nestled in the valley. It was a ruin. The remains of a central building and a well and the jagged foundations of several houses, like broken teeth in neat, tidy squares. Trees grew where people had once lived, and low plants.

Luna curved around the mud pot and followed the rocks into where the village used to be. The central building was a round, low tower with curved windows looking outward, like eyes. The back portion had fallen off, and the roof had caved in. But there were carvings in the rock. Luna approached it and laid her hand on the nearest panel.

Dragons. There were dragons in the rock. Big dragons, small dragons, dragons of middling size. There were people with quills in their hands and people with stars in their hands and people with birthmarks on their foreheads that looked like crescent moons. Luna pressed her fingers to her own forehead. She had the same birthmark.

There was a carving of a mountain, and a carving of a mountain with its top removed and smoke billowing outward like a cloud, and a carving of a mountain with a dragon plunging itself into the crater.

What did it mean?

"Caw," said the crow. "It's nearly here," he meant.

"Give me a minute," Luna said.

She heard a sound like rustling paper.

And a high, thin keen.

She looked up. The crow sped toward her, flying in a tight, fast twist, all black feathers and black beak and panicked cawing. It reared, flipped backward, and fluttered into her arms, nestling its head deeply into the crook of her elbow.

The sky was suddenly thick with birds of all sizes and descriptions. They massed in great murmurations, expanding and contracting and curving this way and that. They called and squawked and swirled in great clouds before descending on the ruined village, chirping and fussing and circling near.

But they weren't birds at all. They were made of paper. They pointed their eyeless faces toward the girl on the ground.

"Magic," Luna whispered. "This is what magic does."

And, for the first time, she understood.

# 33

## In Which the Witch Encounters an Old Acquaintance

When Xan was a little girl, she lived in a village in the forest. Her father, as far as she could remember, was a carver. Of spoons, primarily. Animals, too. Her mother gathered the flowers of particular climbing vines and sapped them of their essences and combined them with honey that she pulled from the wild hives in the tallest trees. She would climb to the tops, as nimble as a spider, and then send the honeycombs down in baskets on ropes for Xan to catch. Xan was not allowed to taste. In theory. She would anyway. And her mother would climb down and kiss the honey from her little-girl lips.

It was a thing she remembered with a stab in her heart.

Industrious people, her parents. Fearless. She couldn't recall their faces, but she remembered the feeling she had when she was near them. She remembered their smells of tree sap and sawdust and pollen. She remembered the curl of large fingers around her small shoulder and of her mother's breath as she rested her mouth at the top of Xan's head. And then they died. Or vanished. Or they didn't love her and they left. Xan had no idea.

The scholars said they found her in the woods all alone.

Or, one of them did. The woman with the voice like cut glass. And a heart like a tiger. She was the one who brought Xan to the castle, all those years ago.

Xan rested her wings in the hollowed-out nook of a tall tree. It would take her forever to make it to the Protectorate at this rate. What had she been *thinking*? An albatross would have been a much better choice. All she'd have had to do is lock her wings in place and let the wind do the rest.

"No matter now," she chirped in her bird-voice. "I'll make it there as best I can. Then I'll return to my Luna. I'll be there when her magic opens up. I'll show her how to use it. And who knows? Maybe I was wrong. Maybe her magic will never come. Maybe I won't die. Maybe a lot of things."

She helped herself to a portion of the ants swarming the outside of the tree, looking for something sweet. It wasn't much, but it satisfied the edges of her hunger. Puffing her feathers out for warmth, Xan closed her eyes and fell asleep.

The moon rose, heavy and round as a ripe squash, over the tops of the trees. It fell on Xan, waking her up.

"Thank you," she whispered, feeling the moonlight sink into her bones, easing her joints and soothing her pain.

"Who's there?" a voice said. "I warn you! I'm armed!"

Xan couldn't help herself. The voice sounded so frightened. So lost. And she could help. And here she was all full up with moonlight. Indeed, if she just paused a moment, she would be able to gather it in her wings and drink until she was full. She wouldn't *stay* full, of course. She was too porous. But she felt wonderful *for now*. And down below her was a figure—it moved quickly from side to side; it hunched its shoulders; it looked from left to right to left again. It was terrified. And the moonlight billowed Xan up. It made her compassionate. She fluttered out of her hiding place and circled over the figure. A young man. He screamed, loosed the stone in his hand, and hit Xan on the left wing. She fell to the ground without so much as a peep.

❉

Antain, realizing that it was not—as he had assumed—a fearsome Witch bearing down on him (possibly riding a dragon and holding a flaming staff), but was instead a tiny brown bird who probably just wanted a bit of food, felt an immediate stab of shame. As soon as the stone left his fingers, he wished he could take it back again. For all his bluster in front of the Council, he had never so much as wrung the neck of a chicken for a nice dinner. He wasn't entirely certain he *could* kill the Witch.

(*The Witch will take my son*, he admonished himself. Still. Taking a life. With each moment he felt his resolve begin to weaken.)

The bird landed right in front of his feet. It didn't make a sound. It hardly breathed. Antain thought for certain that it was dead. He swallowed a sob.

And then—a miracle!—the bird's chest rose, then fell, then rose, then fell. Its wing angled outward sickeningly. Broken. That was certain.

Antain kneeled down. "I'm sorry," he breathed. "I'm so, so sorry." He scooped up the bird in his hands. It didn't look healthy. How could it, in these cursed woods? Half the water was poisoned. The Witch. It all came back to the Witch. Curse her name forever. He brought the bird to his chest, trying to warm it from the heat of his body. "I'm so, so sorry," he said again.

The bird opened its eyes. A swallow, he could see. Ethyne loved swallows. Just thinking of her made his heart slice in half. How he missed her! How he missed their son! What he wouldn't do to see them again!

The bird gave him a hard look. It sneezed. He couldn't blame it.

"Listen, I am so sorry about your wing. And, alas, I have no skills to heal it. But my wife. Ethyne." His voice cracked saying her name. "She is clever and kind. People bring her their injured animals all the time. She can help you. I know it."

He tied the top section of his jerkin and made a small pouch, closing the bird safely inside. The bird made a warbling sound. *It's not happy with me,* he thought. And to drive the point home, the bird nipped him on his index finger when he let it linger too close. Blood bloomed on his fingertip.

A night moth fluttered into Antain's face, probably attracted by the moonlight shining on his skin. Thinking fast, he grabbed it, and offered it to the bird.

"Here," he said. "To show you that I mean no harm."

The bird gave him another hard look. And then reluctantly snatched the moth from his fingers, swallowing it in three jerking bites.

"There. You see?" He looked up at the moon, and then at his map. "Come. I just want to make it to the top of that rise. And then we can rest."

And Antain and the Witch went deeper into the wood.

❄

Sister Ignatia felt herself growing weaker by the minute. She had done her best to swallow all the sorrow she could—she couldn't believe how much sorrow hung about the town! Great, delicious clouds of it, as persistent as fog. She really had outdone herself, and she had never, she realized now, given herself the proper admiration that was her due. An entire city transformed into a veritable well of sorrow. An ever-filling goblet. All for her. No one in the history of the Seven Ages had ever before managed such a feat. There should be songs written about her. Books, at the very least.

But now, two days without access to sorrow, and she was already weak and worn. Shivery. Her wellsprings of magic depleting by the second. She would need to find that boy. And fast.

She paused and knelt beside a small stream, scanning the nearby forest for signs of life. There were fish in the stream, but fish are accustomed to their lot in life and don't experience sorrow as a general rule. There was a nest of starlings overhead, the hatchlings not two days old. She could crush the baby birds one by one, and eat the mother's sorrow—of course she could. But the sorrow of birds was not as potent as mammalian sorrow. There wasn't a mammal for miles. Sister Ignatia sighed. She gathered what she needed to build a makeshift scrying device—a bit of volcanic glass from her pocket, the bones of a recently killed rabbit, and an extra bootlace, because it was helpful to include the most useful thing on hand. And nothing is more useful than a bootlace. She couldn't build it with the same level of detail as the large mechanical scryers she had in the Tower, but she wasn't looking for very much.

She couldn't see Antain. She had an idea of where he was. She was fairly certain she could see a blur where she thought he might be, but something was blocking her view.

"Magic?" she muttered. "Surely not." All the magicians on

earth—at least everyone who knew what they were doing—had perished five hundred years earlier when the volcano erupted. Or nearly erupted. The fools! Sending her with her Seven League Boots to rescue the people in the forest villages. Oh, she certainly had. She'd gathered them all safe and sound into the Protectorate. All their endless sorrows, clouding together in one place. All according to plan.

She licked her lips. She was so *hungry*. She needed to survey her surroundings.

The Head Sister held her scrying device up to her right eye and scanned the rest of the forest. Another blur. *What is the matter with this thing?* she wondered. She tightened the knots. Still a blur. Hunger, she decided. Even basic spells are difficult when one is not operating at full strength.

Sister Ignatia eyed the starling nest.

She scanned the mountain. Then she gasped.

"No!" she shouted. She looked again. "How are you still alive, you ugly thing?"

She rubbed her eyes and looked a third time. "I thought I killed you, Glerk," she whispered. "Well. I guess I shall have to try again. Troublesome creature. You almost foiled me once, but you failed. And you shall fail again."

*First,* she thought, *a snack.* Shoving her scrying device into her pocket, Sister Ignatia climbed up to the branch with the starling nest. She reached in and grabbed a tiny, wriggling nestling. She crushed it in one fist as the horrified mother looked on. The mother sparrow's sorrow was thin. But it was enough. Sister Ignatia licked her lips and crushed another nestling.

*And now,* she thought, *I must remember where I hid those Seven League Boots.*

# 34

## In Which Luna Meets a Woman in the Wood

The paper birds roosted on branches and stones and the remains of chimneys and walls and old buildings. They made no sound outside the rustle of paper and the scritch of folds. They quieted their bodies and turned their faces toward the girl on the ground. They had no eyes. But they watched her all the same. Luna could feel it.

"Hello," she said, because she didn't know what else to say. The paper birds said nothing. The crow, on the other hand, couldn't keep himself quiet. He spiraled upward and sped into a cluster gathered on the extended arm of an ancient oak tree, shouting all the while.

"Caw, caw, caw, caw," the crow screeched.

"Hush," Luna admonished. She had her eyes on the paper birds. They tilted their heads in unison, first pointing their beaks at the girl on the ground, then following the crazed crow, then looking back at the girl.

"Caw," said the crow. "I'm frightened."

"Me, too," Luna said as she stared at the birds. They scattered, then massed again, hovering over her like a great, undulating cloud before settling back onto the branches of the oak tree.

*They know me,* Luna thought.

*How do they know me?*

*The birds, the map, the woman in my dreams. She is here, she is here, she is here.*

It was too much to think about. The world had too many things to know in it, and Luna's mind was full. She had a pain in her skull, right in the middle of her forehead.

The paper birds stared at her.

"What do you want from me?" Luna demanded. The paper birds rested on their roosts. There were too many to count. They were waiting. But for what?

"Caw," the crow said. "Who cares what they want? Paper birds are creepy."

They *were* creepy, of course. But they were also beautiful and strange. They were looking for something. They wanted to tell her something.

Luna sat down on the dirt. She kept her eye on the birds.

She let the crow nestle on her lap. She closed her eyes and took out her book and a pencil stub. Once, she had let her mind wander as she thought about the woman in her dreams. And then she had drawn a map. And the map was *correct*. Or at least it had been so far. "She is here, she is here, she is here," her map said, and Luna could only assume that it was telling the truth. But now she needed to make something else happen. She needed to know where her grandmother was.

"Caw," said the crow.

"Hush," Luna said without opening her eyes. "I'm trying to concentrate."

The paper birds watched her. She could feel them watching. Luna felt her hand move across the page. She tried to keep her mind on her grandmother's face. The touch of her hand. The smell of her skin. Luna felt worry grip her heart in its fist, and two hot tears came tumbling down, hitting the paper with a splat.

"Caw," the crow said. "Bird," it meant.

Luna opened her eyes. The crow was right. She hadn't drawn her grandmother at all. She had drawn a stupid bird. One that was sitting in a man's hand.

"Well, what on earth?" Luna grumbled, her heart sinking into her boots. How could she find her grandmother? How indeed?

"Caw," the crow said. "Tiger."

Luna scrambled to her feet, keeping her knees bent in a low crouch.

"Stay close," she whispered to the crow. She wished the birds were made of something more substantial than paper. Rock, maybe. Or sharp steel.

"Well," said a voice. "What have we here?"

"Caw," said the crow. "Tiger."

But it wasn't a tiger at all. It was a woman.

*So why do I feel so afraid?*

❋

Ethyne stood as the Grand Elder arrived, flanked by two heavily armed Sisters of the Star. She was, by all appearances, utterly unafraid. It was galling, really. The Grand Elder knitted his eyebrows in a way that he assumed was imposing. This had no effect. To make it worse, it seemed that she not only knew the two soldiers to the right and left of him but was *friends* with them as well. She brightened as she saw the ruthless soldiers arrive, and they smiled back.

"Lillienz!" she said, smiling at the soldier on his left. "And my dear, dear Mae," she said, blowing a kiss to the soldier on his right.

This was not the entrance that the Grand Elder had hoped for. He cleared his throat. The women in the room seemed not to have noticed that he was there. It was infuriating.

"Welcome, Uncle Gherland," Ethyne said with a gentle

bow. "I was just heating some water in the kettle, and I have fresh mint from the garden. Can I make you some tea?"

Grand Elder Gherland wrinkled his nose. "Most housewives, madam," he said acidly, "would not bother with herbal trifles in their garden when there are mouths to feed and neighbors to look after. Why not grow something more substantial?"

Ethyne was unruffled as she moved about the kitchen. The baby was strapped to her body with a pretty cloth, which she had embroidered herself, no doubt. Everything in the house was clever and beautified. Industrious, creative, and canny. Gherland had seen that combination before, and he did not like it. She poured hot water into two handmade cups stuffed with mint, and sweetened it with honey from her hive outside. Bees and flowers and even singing birds surrounded the house. Gherland shifted uncomfortably. He took his cup of tea and thanked his hostess, though he was certain that he would despise it. He took a sip. The tea, he realized peevishly, was the most delicious thing he had ever drunk.

"Oh, Uncle Gherland," Ethyne sighed happily, leaning into her sling to kiss the head of her baby. "Surely you know that a productive garden is a well-balanced garden. There are plants that eat the soil and plants that feed the soil. We grow more than we could ever eat, of course, and much of it is given away. As you know, your nephew is always willing to give of himself to help others."

If the mention of her husband hurt her at all, she did not

show it. The girl seemed incapable of sorrow, foolish thing. Indeed, she seemed to glow with pride. Gherland was baffled. He did his best to contain himself.

"As you know, child, the Day of Sacrifice is rapidly approaching." He expected her to grow pale at this pronouncement. He was mistaken.

"I am aware, Uncle," she said, kissing her baby again. She looked up and met his gaze, her expression so assured of her own equality with the Grand Elder that he found himself speechless in the face of such blind insolence.

"Dear Uncle," Ethyne continued gently, "why are you *here*? Of course you are welcome in my home whenever you choose to stop by, and of course my husband and I are always pleased to see you. Usually it is the Head Sister who comes to intimidate the families of the doomed children. I have been expecting her all day."

"Well," Gherland said. "The Head Sister is not available. I have come instead."

Ethyne gave the old man a piercing look. "What do you mean 'not available'? Where is Sister Ignatia?"

The Grand Elder cleared his throat. People did not question him. Indeed, people did not question *much* in the Protectorate—they were a people who accepted their lot in life, as they should. This young woman—this *child* . . . *Well,* Gherland thought. *One can only hope she will go mad like the other one did so long ago.* Locked in the Tower was far preferable to insolent questioning at family dinners, that much was certain. He cleared his throat again. "Sister Ignatia is away," he said slowly. "On business."

"What kind of business?" the girl asked with a narrowed eye.

"Her own, I suspect," Gherland replied.

Ethyne stood and approached the two soldiers. They had been trained, of course, to not make eye contact with the citizenry, and to instead gaze past them impassively. They were supposed to look as a stone looks and feel as a stone feels. This was the mark of a good soldier, and *all* of the Sisters were good soldiers. But *these* soldiers began to flush as the girl approached them. They tilted their gaze to the ground.

"*Ethyne,*" one of them whispered. "*No.*"

"Mae," Ethyne said. "Look at my face. You, too, Lillienz." Gherland's jaw fell open. He'd never seen anything like it in all his life. Ethyne was smaller than both of the soldiers. *And yet.* She seemed to tower before them both.

"Well," he sputtered. "I must object—"

Ethyne ignored him. "Does the tiger prowl?"

The soldiers were silent.

"I feel we are moving away from the subject of the conversation—" Gherland began.

Ethyne held up her hand, silencing her uncle-in-law. And he was, remarkably, *silent.* He couldn't believe it. "At night, Mae," the young woman continued. "Answer me. Does the tiger prowl?"

The soldier pressed her lips together, as though trying to force her words inside. She winced.

"What on earth could you possibly mean?" Gherland sputtered. "Tigers? You are too old for girlish games!"

"*Silence,*" Ethyne ordered. And once again, incomprehensibly, Gherland fell silent. He was astonished.

The soldier bit her lip and hesitated for a moment. She leaned in toward Ethyne. "Well, I never thought about it as you did, but yes. No padded paws stalk the hallways of the Tower. Nothing growls. Not for days. We all"—the soldier closed her eyes—"sleep easy. For the first time in years."

Ethyne wrapped her arms around the infant in his sling. The boy sighed in his dreaming. "So. Sister Ignatia is not in the Tower. She is in not in the Protectorate, or I would have heard of it. She must be in the forest. And she no doubt means to kill him," Ethyne murmured.

She walked over to Gherland. He squinted. Everything in this house was bright. Though the rest of the town was submerged in fog, this house was bathed in light. Sunlight streamed in the windows. The surfaces gleamed. Even Ethyne seemed to shine, like an enraged star.

"My dear—"

"*YOU.*" Ethyne's voice was somewhere between a bellow and a hiss.

"I mean to say," Gherland said, feeling himself crumple and burn, like paper.

"*YOU SENT MY HUSBAND INTO THE WOODS TO DIE.*" Her eyes were flames. Her hair was flame. Even her skin was on fire. Gherland felt his eyelashes begin to singe.

"What? Oh. What a silly thing to say. I mean—"

"*YOUR OWN NEPHEW.*" She spat on the ground—an uncouth gesture that seemed strangely lovely when she did it. And Gherland, for the first time in his life, felt ashamed. "*YOU SENT A MURDERER AFTER HIM. THE FIRST SON OF YOUR ONLY SISTER AND YOUR BEST FRIEND.* Oh, Uncle. *How could you?*"

"It isn't what you think, my dear. Please. Sit. We're family. Let's discuss—" But Gherland felt himself crumble inside. His soul succumbed to a thousand cracks.

She strode past him and returned to the soldiers.

"Ladies," she said. "If either of you have ever held me in any modicum of affection or respect, I must humbly ask for your assistance. I have things that I would like to accomplish before the Day of Sacrifice, which, as we all know"—she gave Gherland a poisonous look—"waits for no man." She let that hang in the air for a moment. "I think I need to visit with my former Sisters. The cat's away. And the mice shall play. And there is much that a mouse can do, after all."

"Oh Ethyne," the Sister named Mae said, linking arms with the young mother. "How I've *missed you.*" And the two women left, arm in arm, with the other soldier hesitating, glancing at the Elder, and then hurrying behind.

"I must say," the Grand Elder said, "this is highly—" He looked around. "I mean. There are rules, you know." He drew himself up and gave a haughty expression to no one at all. *"Rules."*

✵

The paper birds didn't move. The crow didn't move. Luna didn't move, either.

The woman, though, stepped quietly closer. Luna couldn't tell how old she was. One moment she looked very young. Another moment she looked impossibly old.

Luna said nothing. The woman's gaze drifted up to the birds in the branches. Her eyes narrowed.

"I've seen that trick before," she said. "Did you make them?"

She returned her gaze to Luna, who felt the woman's vision pierce her, right through the middle. She cried out in pain.

The woman gave a broad smile. "No," she said. "Not your magic."

The word, said out loud, made Luna's skull feel as though it was about to split in half. She pressed her hands to her forehead.

"Pain?" the woman said. "It's a sorrowful thing, don't you think?" There was an odd, hopeful note in her voice. Luna remained crouched on the ground.

"No," she said, her voice tight and ready, like a set spring. "Not sorrow. It's just annoying."

The woman's smile soured into a frown. She looked back

up at the paper birds. She gave them a sidelong smile. "They're lovely," she said. "Those birds, are they yours? Were they a gift?"

Luna shrugged.

The woman tilted her head to the side. "Look how they hang on you, waiting for you to speak. Still. They're not your magic."

"Nothing's my magic," Luna said. The birds behind her rustled their wings. Luna would have turned to look, but she would have to break eye contact with the stranger, and something told her she didn't want to do that. "I don't have any magic. Why would I?"

The woman laughed, and not nicely. "Oh, I wouldn't say that, you silly thing." Luna decided to hate this woman. "I'd say several things are your magic. And more things coming, if I'm not mistaken. Though it does look as though someone has attempted to hide your magic from you." She leaned forward and squinted. "Interesting. That spellwork. I recognize it. But my, my, it has been *years*."

The paper birds, as if by some signal, lifted in one great flutter of wings and roosted next to the girl. They kept their beaks faced toward the stranger, and Luna felt for sure that they had somehow become harder, sharper, and more dangerous than before. The woman gave a little start and took a step or two backward.

"Caw," said the crow. "Keep walking."

The rocks under Luna's hands began to shimmy and shudder. They seemed to shake the very air. Even the ground shook.

"I wouldn't trust them if I were you. They've been known to attack," the woman said.

Luna gave her a skeptical expression.

"Oh, you don't believe me? Well. The woman who made them is a wicked thing. And broken. She sorrowed until she could sorrow no more, and now she is quite mad." She shrugged. "And useless."

Luna didn't know why the woman angered her so. But she had to resist everything in her that told her to leap to her feet and kick the woman as hard as she could in the shins.

"Ah." The stranger gave her a wide smile. "Anger. Very nice. Useless to me, alas, but as it is so often a precursor to sorrow, I confess that I do like it." She licked her lips. "I like it quite a bit."

"I don't think we are going to be friends," Luna growled. *A weapon*, she thought. *I think I need a weapon.*

"No," the woman said. "I wouldn't think so. I am just here to collect what is mine, and I'll be on my way. I—" She paused. Held up one hand. "Wait a moment." The woman turned and walked into the ruined village. A tower stood in the center of the ruin—though it didn't look as if it would be standing much longer. There was a broad gash in its foundation on one side, like an open, surprised mouth. "They were in the Tower," the woman said, mostly to herself. "I put them there myself. I remember now." She ran to the opening and skidded on her knees across the ground. She peered into the darkness.

"Where are my boots?" the woman whispered. "Come to me, my darlings."

Luna stared. She had had a dream once, not very long ago. Surely it was a dream, wasn't it? And Fyrian had reached into a hole in a broken tower and pulled out a pair of boots. It must have been a dream, because Fyrian had been strangely large. And then he had brought the boots to her. And she had put them in a trunk.

Her trunk!

She hadn't thought about it again until this moment.

She shook her head to clear the thought away.

"WHERE ARE MY BOOTS?" the woman bellowed. Luna shrank back.

The stranger stood, her loose gown billowing about her. She raised her hands wide overhead and with a broad, swooping motion, pushed the air in front of her body. And just like that, the Tower fell. Luna tumbled onto the rocks with a yelp. The crow, terrified by the noise and dust and commotion, sprang skyward. He circled the air, cursing all the while.

"It was about to fall," Luna whispered, trying to make sense of what she had been seeing. She stared into the cloud of dust and mold and grit at the pile of rubble and the hunched figure of the robed woman holding her arms outward as though she was about to catch the sky. *No one could have that much power,* she thought. *Could they?*

"GONE!" the woman shrieked. "THEY ARE GONE!"

She turned and stalked toward the girl. With a flick of her left wrist, she bent the air in front of her, forcing Luna to her feet. The woman kept her left hand out, pinching the air with clawed fingers, keeping Luna in place from several yards away.

"I don't have them!" Luna whimpered. The woman's grip hurt. Luna felt her fear expand inside her, like a storm cloud. And as her fear grew, so did the woman's smile. Luna did her best to stay calm. "I just got here."

"But you have touched them," the woman whispered. "I can see the residue on your hands."

"No I haven't!" Luna said, thrusting her hands into her pockets. She tried to force away any memory of the dream.

"You will tell me where they are." The woman raised her right hand, and even from far away, Luna could feel the fingers on her throat. She began to choke. "You will tell me right now," the woman said.

"Go away!" Luna gasped.

And suddenly, everything moved. The birds lifted from their roost and massed behind the girl.

"Oh, you silly thing." The woman laughed. "Do you think

your silly parlor tricks can—" And the birds attacked, swirling like a cyclone. They shook the air. They made the rocks tremble. They bent the torsos of the trees.

"GET THEM OFF ME!" the woman shrieked, waving her hands. The birds cut her hands. They cut her forehead. They attacked without mercy.

Luna held her crow close to her chest and ran as fast as she could.

# 35

## In Which Glerk Smells
## Something Unpleasant

I'm itchy, Glerk," Fyrian said. "I'm itchy all over. I'm the itchiest in the world."

"How, dear boy," Glerk said heavily, "could you possibly know that?" He closed his eyes and inhaled deeply. *Where has she gone?* he wondered. *Where are you, Xan?* He felt the tendrils of worry wind around his heart, nearly squeezing it to a stop. Fyrian had perched right in between the monster's great, wide-spaced eyes, and he began scratching his backside madly. Glerk rolled his eyes. "You've never even seen the world. You might not be the itchiest."

Fyrian scratched at his tail, his belly, his neck. He scratched his ears and his skull and his long nose.

"Do dragons shed their skins?" Fyrian asked suddenly.

"What?"

"Do they shed their skins? Like snakes?" Fyrian attacked his left flank.

Glerk considered this. He searched his brain. Dragons were a solitary species. Few and far between. They were difficult to study. Even dragons, in his experience, didn't know much about dragons.

"I do not know, my friend," he said finally. "The Poet tells us,

'Each mortal beast must find its Ground—
be it forest or fen or field or fire.'

Perhaps you will know all that you wish to know when you find your Ground."

"But what is my Ground?" Fyrian asked, worrying at his skin as though he meant to scratch it right off.

"Dragons, originally, were formed in stars. Which means that your Ground is fire. Walk through fire and you will know who you are."

Fyrian considered this. "That sounds like a terrible idea," he said finally. "I don't want to walk through fire at all." He scratched his belly. "What's your Ground, Glerk?"

The swamp monster sighed. "Mine?" He sighed again. "Fen," he said. "The Bog." He pressed his upper right hand to his heart. "The Bog, the Bog, the Bog," he murmured, like a heartbeat. "It is the heart of the world. It is the womb of the world. It is the poem that made the world. I *am* the Bog, and the Bog is me."

Fyrian frowned. "No, you're not," he said. "You're Glerk. And you're my friend."

"Sometimes people are more than one thing. I am Glerk. I am your friend. I am Luna's family. I am a Poet. I am a maker. And I am the Bog. But to you, I am simply Glerk. *Your* Glerk. And I do love you very much."

And it was true. Glerk loved Fyrian. As he loved Xan. As he loved Luna. As he loved the whole world.

He inhaled again. He should have been able to catch wind of at least *one* of Xan's spells. So why couldn't he?

"Look out, Glerk," Fyrian said suddenly, swooping up and looping in front of Glerk's face, hovering in front of his nose. He pointed backward with his thumb. "That ground up there is very thin—a skin of rock with fire under it. You'll fall through as sure as anything."

Glerk wrinkled his brow. "Are you certain?" He squinted at the rock stretch ahead. Heat poured off it in waves. "It's not supposed to be burning here." But it was. This seam of rock was clearly burning. And the mountain buzzed underfoot. This had happened before, when the entire mountain had threatened to unpeel itself like an overripe Zirin bulb.

After the eruption—and the magical corking of that eruption—the volcano had never slept soundly, even in the early days. It had always been rumbly and shifty and restless. But this felt different. This was *more*. For the first time in five hundred years, Glerk was afraid.

"Fyrian, lad," the monster said. "Let us pick up our pace, shall we?" And they began tracking along the high side of the seam, looking for a safe place to cross.

The great monster looked around the forest, scanning the stretch of undergrowth, narrowing his eyes and extending his gaze as best he could. He used to be better at this sort of thing. He used to be better at many things. He inhaled deeply, as if he was trying to suck the entire mountain into his nose.

Fyrian looked at the swamp monster curiously.

"What is it, Glerk?" he said.

Glerk shook his head. "I know that smell," he said. He closed his eyes.

"Xan's smell?" Fyrian fluttered back up to his perch on the monster's head. He tried to close his eyes and sniff as well, but he ended up sneezing instead. "I love Xan's smell. I love it *so much*."

Glerk shook his head, slowly, so that Fyrian would not fall. "No," he said in a low growl. "Someone else."

❈

Sister Ignatia could, when she wanted to, run fast. Fast as a tiger. Fast as the wind. Faster than she was going now, certainly. But it wasn't the same as when she had her boots.

Those boots!

She had forgotten how much she loved them once upon a time. Back when she had curiosity and wanderlust and the inclination to go to the other side of the world and back in a single afternoon. Before the delicious and abundant sorrows of the Protectorate had fed her soul until it was indolent and sated and gloriously fat. Now, just thinking about her boots imbued her with a youthful spark. So black were those beautiful boots that they seemed to bend the light around them. And when Sister Ignatia wore them at night, she felt herself full to bursting with starlight—and, if she timed it right, moonlight as well. The boots fed right into her very bones. Their magic was a different sort than was available to her from sorrow. (But oh! How easy it was to gorge herself on sorrow!)

Now Sister Ignatia's magical stores were starting to dwindle. She had never thought to sock any away for a rainy day. It never rained in the Protectorate's marvelous fog.

*Stupid,* she chided herself. *Lazy! Well. I must simply remember how to be crafty.*

But first, she needed those boots.

She paused a moment to consult her scrying device. At first, all she saw was darkness—a tight, closed-up sort of darkness, with a single, pale, horizontal line of light cutting across. Very slowly, the line began to widen, and a pair of hands reached in.

*A box,* she thought. *They are in a box. And someone is stealing them. Again!*

"Those are not for you!" she shouted. And although there is no way the person attached to those hands could have heard her—not without magic, anyway—the fingers seemed to hesitate. They pulled back. There was even a bit of a tremble.

These hands weren't the child's, that much was certain. These were grown-up hands. But whose?

A woman's foot slid into the dark mouth of the boot. The boot sealed itself around the foot. Ignatia knew that the wearer could put the boots on and off as wanted, but there would be no removing the boots by force as long as the wearer was alive.

*Well,* she thought, *that shouldn't be a problem.*

The boots began walking toward what looked like an animal enclosure. Whoever was wearing them did not know how to use them yet. Fancy wasting a pair of Seven League Boots as though they were nothing more than work slippers! It was a crime, she thought. A scandal.

The wearer of the boots stood by the goats, and the goats sniffed at her skirts in a fawning sort of way that Sister Ignatia found utterly unattractive. Then the boots' wearer began to walk around.

"Ah!" Sister Ignatia peered more intently. "Let's see where you are, shall we?"

Sister Ignatia saw a large tree with a door in the middle. And a swamp, littered with flowers. The swamp looked familiar. She saw a steep mountainside with several jagged rims along the top—

*Great Heavens! Are those craters?*

*And there! I know that path!*

*And there! Those stones!*

Could it be that the boots had made their way back to her old castle? Or the place where the castle *had been*, anyway.

*Home*, she thought in spite of herself. That place had been her home. Perhaps it still was, after all these years. Despite the ease of life in the Protectorate, she had never again been so happy as she had been in the company of those magicians and scholars in the castle. Pity they had to die. They wouldn't have died, of course, if they had had the boots, as was the original plan. It didn't occur to them that anyone might try to steal them and run away from the danger, leaving them all behind.

And they thought they were so clever!

In the end, there had never been a magician as clever as Ignatia, and she had the entire Protectorate to prove it. Of course, she had no one left to prove it *to*, which was a pity. All she had was the boots. And now they were gone, too.

*No matter*, she told herself. *What's mine is mine. And that's everything.*

*Everything.*

And she ran up the trail toward home.

# 36

## In Which a Map Is
## Rather Useless

Luna had never run so hard or fast in her life. She ran for hours, it seemed. Days. Weeks. She had been running forever. She ran from boulder to boulder, ridge to ridge. She leaped over streams and creeks. Trees bent out of her way. She didn't stop to wonder at the ease of her footing or the length of her leaps. All she thought about was the woman with a tiger's snarl. That woman was dangerous. It was all Luna could do to keep her growing panic at bay. The crow wiggled away from the girl's grasp and soared upward, circling over her head.

"Caw," the crow called. "I don't think she's following us."

"Caw," he called again. "It's possible that I was mistaken about the paper birds."

Luna ran up the edge of a steep knoll to cast a wider view and make sure she was not being followed. There was no one. The woods were just woods. She sat down on the bare curve of the rock to open her journal and look at her map, but she had veered so far off her route, she wasn't sure if she was even *on* the map anymore. Luna sighed. "Well," she said, "I seem to have made a mess of things. We are no closer to my grandmother than when we started. And look! The sun is going down. And there is a strange lady in the woods." She swallowed. "There's something wrong with her. I can't explain it. But I don't want her coming anywhere near my grandmother. Not at all."

Luna's brain had suddenly become crowded with things she knew without knowing how she knew them. Indeed, her mind felt like a vast storage room whose locked cupboards were all at once not only unlocking but flinging themselves open and dumping their contents on the floor. And none of it was anything Luna remembered putting in those cupboards in the first place.

*She was little—she couldn't quite place how young she was, but definitely small. She was standing in the center of the clearing. Her eyes were blank. Her mouth was slack. She was pinned in place.*

Luna gasped. The memory was so clear.

*"Luna!" Fyrian had cried, crawling out of her pocket and hovering in front of her face. "Why aren't you moving?"*

*"Fyrian, dear," her grandmother had said. "Go fetch Luna a*

heartsblood flower from the far edge of the tall crater. She is play-ing a game with you, and she will only unfreeze if you bring her the flower."

"I love games!" Fyrian cried before whizzing away, whistling a jaunty tune as he flew.

Glerk appeared through the red-algaed surface of the swamp. He opened one eye, and then the other. Then he rolled both to the sky.

"More lies, Xan," he chided.

"Good ones!" Xan protested. "I lie to protect! What else can I say? I can't explain anything that's true in a way they can understand."

Glerk came lumbering out of the swamp, the dark waters shedding in great beads from the oily sheen of his darker skin. He came close to Luna's unblinking eyes. Glerk's great, damp mouth deepened into a frown. "I don't like this," he said, laying two of his hands on either side of Luna's face, and the other two hands on each of her shoulders. "This is the third time today. What hap-pened this time?"

Xan groaned. "It was my fault. I could have sworn I sensed something. Like a tiger moving through the woods, but not, you understand. Well, of course you know what I thought."

"Was it she? The Sorrow Eater?" Glerk's voice had turned into a dangerous rumble.

"No. Five hundred years I've worried. She's haunted my

dreams, and don't mistake it. But no. There was nothing. But Luna saw the scrying device."

Glerk took Luna into his arms. She went limp. He rocked back on his tail, letting the girl's weight sink into the squish of his belly. He smoothed back her hair with one hand.

"We need to tell Fyrian," he said.

"We can't!" Xan cried. "Look what happened to her when she just saw the scrying device out of the corner of her eye! She didn't get better once I took it apart—and that was a while ago now. Just imagine if Fyrian spills the beans that her grandmother is a witch! She'll go into a trance every time she sees me—every time! And she won't stop until she turns thirteen. And she'll be enmagicked and I'll be gone. Gone, Glerk! And who will take care of my baby?"

And Xan walked over and laid her cheek on Luna's cheek, and wrapped her arms around the swamp monster. Or, at least part of the way around. Glerk, after all, was very large.

"Are we hugging now?" Fyrian said, zooming back with the flower. "I love hugging." And he shot into the crook of one of Glerk's arms and insinuated himself into the fleshy folds of his body, and was, once again, the happiest dragon in the world.

Luna sat very still, her mind racing at what her own memory had revealed to her. Her own unlocked memory.

Witch.

Enmagicked.

Thirteen.

*Gone.*

Luna pressed the heels of her hands to her brow, trying to keep her head from spinning. How many times had she felt a thought simply fly away, like a bird? And now here they came, crowding back inside. Luna's thirteenth birthday was very soon. And her grandmother was sick. And weak. And some day soon, she would be gone. And Luna would be alone. And enmagicked—

*Witch.*

It was a word that she had never heard before. And yet. When she searched her memories, she found it everywhere. People called it out in the market squares when they visited the cities on the other side of the forest. People said it when they visited homes. People called it when her grandmother's assistance was needed—in a birth, maybe. Or to settle a dispute.

"My grandmother is a witch," Luna said out loud. And it was true. "And now I am a witch."

"Caw," said the crow. "So?"

She gave a narrowed eye to the crow, wrinkling her lips into a frown. "Did you know this?" she demanded.

"Caw," said the crow. "Obviously. What did you think you were? Don't you remember how we met?"

Luna looked up at the sky. "Well," she said. "I guess I didn't really think about it."

"Caw," said the crow. "Exactly. That is exactly your problem."

"A scrying device," Luna murmured.

And she could remember. Her grandmother had made them more than once. Sometimes with string. Sometimes with a raw egg. Sometimes with the sticky insides of a milkweed pod.

"It's the intention that matters," Luna said out loud, her bones buzzing as she said it. "Any good witch knows how to build a tool with what's on hand."

These weren't her words. Her grandmother had said them. Her grandmother had said them *while Luna was in the room*. But then the words flew away and she went blank. And now they were coming back again. She leaned forward and spat on the ground, making a small puddle of dusty mud. With her left hand she grabbed a handful of dried grass, growing from a crack in the rock. She dipped it into the spittle-mud and started to wind it into a complicated knot.

She didn't understand what she was doing—not really. She moved by instinct, as though trying to piece together a song she heard once and could barely recall.

"Show me my grandmother," she said as she stuck her thumb into the center of the knot and stretched it into a hole.

Luna saw nothing at first.

And then she saw a man with a heavily scarred face walking through the woods. He was frightened. He tripped on roots and twice ran into a tree. He was moving too quickly for someone who clearly didn't know where he was going. But it didn't matter, because the device obviously didn't work. She hadn't asked to see a man. She had asked to see her grandmother.

"My *grandmother*," Luna said more deliberately, in a loud voice.

The man wore a leather jerkin. Small knives hung from either side of his belt. He opened the pouch on his jerkin and crooned to something nestled inside. A small beak peeked out of the leather folds.

Luna squinted. It was a swallow. And it was old and sick. "I already drew you," she said out loud.

The swallow, as though in response, peeked its head out and looked around.

"I said, I need my *grandmother*," she almost shouted. The swallow struggled, tittered, and squawked. It looked desperate to get out.

"Not now, silly," the man in the device said. "Let's wait until we fix that wing. Then you can get out. Here. Eat this spider." And the man shoved a wriggling spider into the swallow's protesting beak.

The swallow chewed the spider, a combination of frustration and gratitude on its face.

Luna grunted with frustration.

"I'm not very good at this yet. Show me my GRAND-MOTHER," she said firmly. And the device focused clearly on the face of the bird. And the bird stared through the scrying device, right into Luna's eye. The swallow couldn't see her.

Of course it couldn't. And yet it seemed to Luna that the bird shook its head, very slowly, from side to side.

"Grandmama?" Luna whispered.

And then the device went dark.

"Come back," the girl called.

The makeshift device stayed dark. The scrying device hadn't failed at all, Luna realized with a start. Someone was blocking it.

"Oh, Grandmama," Luna whispered. "What have you done?"

# 37

# In Which the Witch Learns
# Something Shocking

*It wasn't Luna,* Xan told herself again and again and again. *My Luna is safe at home.* She told herself this until it felt true. The man shoved another spider into her mouth. Despite how repellant she found the food, she had to admit that her birdish gullet found it delicious. It was the first time she had ever actually eaten while transformed. And it would be the last time, too. The slow vanishing of her life in front of her eyes did not make her sad in and of itself. But the thought of leaving Luna...

Xan shivered. Birds do not sob. Had she been in her old-woman form, she would have sobbed. She would have sobbed all night.

"Are you all right, my friend?" the man said, his voice hushed and stricken. Xan's black, beady bird eyes did not roll as well as her human eyes rolled, and alas, the gesture was lost on him.

But Xan was being unfair. He was a nice enough young man—a bit excitable, perhaps. Overly *keen*. She'd seen the type before.

"Oh, I know you are just a bird and you cannot possibly understand me, but I have never harmed a living creature before." His voice broke. Two large tears appeared in his eyes.

*Oh!* Xan thought. *You are in pain.* And she nestled in a little bit more closely, clucking and cooing and doing her best in Bird to make him feel better. Xan was very good at making people feel better, having had five hundred years of practice. Easing sorrow. Soothing pain. A listening ear.

The young man had built a small fire and was cooking a piece of sausage he had taken from a package. If Xan had her human nose and her human taste buds, the sausage would have smelled delicious. In her birdish state, she detected no fewer than nine different spices and a hint of dried apples and crushed zirin petals. And love, too. Copious amounts of love. She had smelled it even before he opened the package. *Someone made that for him,* Xan thought. *Someone loves that boy very much. Lucky fellow.*

The sausage bubbled and hissed on the fire.

"I don't suppose you'll be wanting any?"

Xan chirped and hoped he would understand. First of all, she wouldn't dream of taking the boy's food—not while he was lost in the forest. Second of all, there was no way her bird gullet would tolerate meat. Bugs were fine. Anything else would make her vomit.

The young man took a bite, and though he smiled, more tears came pouring down his face. He looked down at the bird, and his cheeks turned bright red with embarrassment.

"Excuse me, my winged friend. You see, this sausage was made by my beloved wife." His voice choked. "Ethyne. Her name is Ethyne."

Xan chirped, hoping to encourage him to continue. This young man seemed to have so many feelings stuck inside him, he was like a pile of kindling, just waiting for that first, hot spark.

He took another bite. The sun had vanished completely and the stars had just begun to show themselves in the sky's deepening dark. He closed his eyes and took in a deep breath. Xan could feel a little rattle, deep inside the young man's chest—the precursor to loss. She chortled and cheeped and gave his arm an encouraging peck. He looked down and smiled.

"What is it about you, my friend? I feel I could tell you anything." He reached over and put another small bundle of kindling onto the fire. "Not too much," he said. "This is just to keep us warm until the moon rises. And then we must be on our way. The Day of Sacrifice waits for no man, after all. Or, at least, it hasn't so far. But we'll see, little friend. Perhaps I'll make it wait forever."

*Day of Sacrifice,* she thought. *What is he talking about?*

She gave him another quick peck. *Keep talking,* she thought.

He laughed. "My, you are a feisty thing. If Ethyne is not able to fix your wing, rest assured that we will make you a comfortable home and life for the rest of your days. Ethyne . . ." He sighed. "She is a wonder. She makes everything beautiful. Even me, and I am as ugly as they come. I loved her, you know, when we were children. But I was shy and she joined the Sisters, and then I was maimed. I had made my peace with loneliness."

He leaned back. His deeply grooved face glowed in the firelight. He wasn't ugly. But he *was* broken. And not by the scars, either. Something *else* had broken him. Xan fixed her eyes on his heart and peered inside. She saw a woman with hair writhing like snakes perched in the rafters of a house with a baby clutched to her chest.

A baby with a birthmark in the shape of a crescent moon.

Xan felt her heart go cold.

"You may not know it, my friend, but there is a witch in the woods."

*No,* thought Xan.

"And she takes our children. One every year. We have to leave the youngest baby in the circle of sycamores and never look back. If we don't, the Witch will destroy us all."

*No*, Xan thought. *No, no, no.*

*Those babies!*

Their poor mothers. Their poor fathers.

And she had loved them all—of course she had—and they had had happy lives . . . but oh! The sorrow hung over the Protectorate like a cloud. *Why didn't I see it?*

"I am here because of her. Because of my beautiful Ethyne. Because she loved me and wanted to have a family with me. But our baby is the youngest in the Protectorate. And I can't allow my child—Ethyne's child—to be taken away. Most people just carry on—what choice do they have?—but there have been those, tender souls like my Ethyne, who have gone mad with grief. And they get locked away." He paused. His body shook. Or perhaps it was Xan who was shaking. "Our boy. He's beautiful. And if the Witch takes him? It would kill Ethyne. And that would kill me."

If Xan had felt she could spare the magic, she would have transformed right then and there. Held the poor boy in her arms. She would have told him about her mistake. She would have told him about the countless children that she had carried across the woods. About how happy they were. How happy their families were.

But oh! The sorrow hanging over the Protectorate!

And oh! The tyranny of grief!

And oh! The howls of a mother driven mad by sorrow. The grief and pain that he had done nothing to stop it, even though he didn't know how. Xan could see the memory lodged in the young man's heart. She could see how it had taken root, calcified, inflamed by his own guilt and shame.

*How did this begin?* Xan asked herself. *How?*

As if to answer, she heard in the caverns of her own memories the padded footsteps of something quiet, predatory, and terrifying, coming closer and closer and closer.

*No,* she thought. *It couldn't be.* Still, she was careful to keep her own sorrow inside. She knew, better than anyone, the damage that sorrow can do when it finds its way into the wrong hands.

"In any case, my friend, I have never killed anyone before. I have never harmed any creature. But I love Ethyne. And I love Luken, my son. And I will do what is necessary to protect my family. I am telling you this, my swallow, because I don't want you to be frightened when you see me do the thing I must do. I am not a wicked man. I am a man who loves his family. And because I love them, I will kill the Witch. I will. I will kill the Witch or die trying."

# 38

## In Which the Fog Begins to Lift

As Ethyne and Mae moved through the square toward the Tower, the population of the Protectorate walked around with their hands shading their eyes. They shed their shawls and their overcoats, relishing the shine of the sun on their skin, marveling at the lack of the normal damp chill and learning how to squint now that the fog had lifted.

"Have you ever seen such a sky?" Mae marveled.

"No," Ethyne said slowly. "I haven't." The baby murmured and fussed in the bright cloth tying him to his mother's chest. Ethyne curled her arms around the warm knot of his body and kissed his forehead. He would need to be fed soon. And changed. *In a moment, love,* Ethyne thought. *Mama needs to complete a task—one that should have been completed a long time ago.*

When Ethyne was a little girl, her mother told her story after story about the Witch in the woods. Ethyne was an inquisitive child, and once she knew that her elder brother was one of the babies sacrificed, she was filled with questions. Where had he gone, really? What if she tried to find him—what then? What is the Witch made of? What does she eat? Is she lonely? Are you sure she's a lady? If it is impossible to fight that which one does not understand, then why not seek to learn? The Witch was wicked, but *how* wicked? How wicked, *exactly*?

Ethyne's constant questions had consequences. Terrible consequences. Her mother—a pale, gaunt woman, full of resignation and sorrow—began obsessively talking about the Witch. She told stories even when no one asked her to. She muttered her stories to herself while she cooked or cleaned or took the long walk with the other harvesters to the Bog.

"The Witch eats the children. Or she enslaves them. Or she sucks them dry," Ethyne's mother would say.

"The Witch prowls the woods on padded paws. She ate the heart of a sorrowing tiger long ago, and that heart still beats inside her."

"The Witch is a bird sometimes. She can fly into your bedroom at night and peck out your eyes!"

"She is as old as dust. She can cross the world in her Seven

League Boots. Mind you behave yourself, lest she snatches you out of your bed!"

Over time her stories lengthened and tangled; they wound around her body like a heavy chain, until she could not hold them up anymore. And then she died.

Or that's how Ethyne saw it, anyway.

Ethyne was sixteen at the time, and known throughout the Protectorate as a remarkably clever girl—quick hands, quick wits. When the Sisters of the Star arrived after her mother's funeral and offered her a place in their novitiate, Ethyne hesitated only for a moment. Her father was gone; her mother was gone; her older brothers (the ones not taken by the Witch) had all married and didn't come around the house that often. It was too sad. There was a boy in her class who tugged at her heart—the quiet boy in the back—but he was from one of the important families. People who owned things. There was no way that he would give her a second look. When the Sisters of the Star came, Ethyne packed her things and followed them out.

But then she noticed that in all the things she learned at the Tower—about astronomy and botany and mechanics and mathematics and vulcanology—not once was the Witch mentioned. Not once. It was as though she didn't actually exist.

And then she noticed the fact that Sister Ignatia never seemed to age.

And then she noticed the padded steps, stalking the hallway of the Tower each night.

And then she saw one of her novitiate sisters weeping over the death of her grandfather, and Sister Ignatia staring at the girl—all hunger and muscle and predatory leap.

Ethyne had spent her entire childhood carrying the heavy weight of her mother's stories about the Witch. Indeed, everyone she knew bore the same weight. Their backs bent under the burden of the Witch, and their sorrowing hearts were as heavy as stones. She joined the Sisters of the Star to seek the truth. But the truth about the Witch was nowhere to be found.

A story can tell the truth, she knew, but a story can also lie. Stories can bend and twist and obfuscate. Controlling stories is power indeed. And who would benefit most from such a power? And over time, Ethyne's eye drifted less and less toward the forest, and more toward the Tower casting its shadow over the Protectorate.

It was then that Ethyne realized that she had learned all that she needed from the Sisters of the Star, and that it was time to go. Best go before she lost her soul.

And so it was, with her soul intact, that Ethyne now returned to the Tower, still linking arms with Mae.

✣

Antain's youngest brother, Wyn, met them at the door. Of all of Antain's brothers, Wyn was Ethyne's favorite. Ethyne threw her arms around him and held him tight—and as she did so, she pressed a piece of paper into his hand.

"Can I trust you?" she whispered almost silently into his ear. "Will you help me save my family?"

Wyn said nothing. He closed his eyes and felt the voice of his sister-in-law wind around his heart like a ribbon. There was little kindness in the Tower. Ethyne was the kindest person he knew. He gave her one extra hug, just to make sure she was real.

"I believe my former Sisters are meditating, dear Wyn," Ethyne said with a smile. Wyn trembled when she said his name. No one ever called him by his name in the Tower—he was simply *boy*. He resolved right then to help Ethyne in whatever she wished. "Will you please take me to them? And while you're at it, there is something else I would ask you to do."

❉

The Sisters were assembled for their morning meditation—an hour of silence, followed by singing, followed by a quick sparring session. Ethyne and Mae entered the room just as the first notes of song began to drift down the stone hallways. The Sisters' voices stopped as Ethyne stepped into their midst. The baby gurgled and cooed. The Sisters stared with open mouths. Finally one Sister spoke.

"You," she said.

"You left us," said another.

"No one ever leaves," said a third.

"I know," Ethyne said. *"Knowledge is a terrible power indeed."* It was the unofficial motto of the Sisterhood. No one knew more than the Sisters. No one had more access to knowledge. And yet here they were. Without an inkling. She pressed her lips together. *Well*, she thought. *That changes today.*

"I left. And it wasn't easy. And I am sorry. But my dear Sisters, there is something I must tell you before I leave again." She leaned in and kissed the forehead of her son. "I must tell you a story."

✻

Wyn pressed his back against the wall next to the doorway leading into the Meditation Room.

In his hand he had a length of chain. And a padlock. The key he would press into Ethyne's hand. His heart pounded at just the thought of it. He had never broken a rule before. But Ethyne was so kind. And the Tower was so . . . *not*.

He pressed his ear against the door. Ethyne's voice rang like a bell.

"The Witch is not in the woods," she said. "The Witch is here. She formed this Sisterhood long ago. She concocted stories about another Witch, a baby-eating Witch. The Witch in this Sisterhood fed on the sorrows of the Protectorate. Our families. Our friends. Our sorrows were great, and they have made her strong. I feel that I have known this for a long time, but a cloud had settled over my heart and mind—the same cloud that has settled over every house and building and living soul in the Protectorate. That cloud of sorrow has, for years, blocked my own knowledge. But now the clouds have burned away and the sun is shining. And I can see clearly. And I think you can, too."

Wyn had a key ring on his belt. The next step in the plan.

"I don't want to take up any more of your time, so I will leave now with those who are willing. To the rest of you, I say, thank you. I treasured my time as Sister to you all."

Ethyne came striding out of the room with nine Sisters following behind. She gave Wyn a brief nod. He quickly closed the door and wound the chain around the handles in a tight knot, securing it with the lock. He pressed the key into Ethyne's hand. She wrapped her fingers around his own and gave a tender squeeze.

"The novitiate?"

"In the manuscript room. They'll be doing their copywork until suppertime. I locked the door and they have no idea they are locked in."

Ethyne nodded. "Good," she said. "I don't want to frighten them. I'll speak to them in a bit. First, let's release the prisoners. The Tower is meant to be a center for learning, not a tool of tyranny. Today the doors are opening."

"Even to the library?" Wyn said hopefully.

"Especially the library. Knowledge is powerful, but it is a terrible power when it is hoarded and hidden. Today, knowledge is for everyone." She hooked her arm in Wyn's, and they hurried through the Tower, unlocking doors.

✤

The mothers of the lost children of the Protectorate found themselves beset by visions. This had been happening for days— ever since the Head Sister had slid into the forest, though no one knew she had done so. All they knew was that the fog was lifting. And suddenly their minds saw things. Impossible things.

*Here is the baby in the arms of an old woman.*

*Here is the baby with a belly full of stars.*

*Here is the baby in the arms of a woman who is not me. A woman who calls herself Mama.*

"It's just a dream," the mothers told themselves over and over and over again. People in the Protectorate were accustomed to dreams. The fog made people sleepy, after all. They sorrowed in their dreaming and they sorrowed in their waking up. This was nothing new.

But now the fog was lifting. And these weren't just dreams. They were visions.

*Here is the baby with his new brothers and sisters. They love him. They love him so much. And he shines in their presence.*

*Here is the baby taking her first step. Look at how pleased she is! Look at how she glows!*

*Here is the baby climbing a tree.*

*Here is the baby jumping off a high rock into a deep pool in the company of cheering friends.*

*Here is the baby learning to read.*

*Here is the baby building a house.*

*Here is the baby holding the hand of her beloved and saying yes, I love you, too.*

They were so real, these visions. So clear. They felt as though they could smell the warm scent of the children's scalps, and touch those scabbed knees and hear those far-off voices. They found themselves crying out the names of their children, feeling the loss as keenly as though it had only just happened, even those to whom it had happened decades ago.

But as the clouds broke and the sky began to clear, they found themselves feeling something else, too. Something they had never felt before.

*Here is the baby holding her own sweet baby. My grandchild. Here is her knowing that no one will ever take that child away.*

Hope. They felt hope.

*Here is the baby in his circle of friends. He is laughing. He loves his life.*

Joy. They felt joy.

*Here is the baby holding hands with her husband and family and staring up at the stars. She has no idea I am her mother. She never, ever knew me.*

The mothers stopped what they were doing. They ran outside. They fell to their knees and turned their faces to the sky. The visions were just images, they told themselves. They were just dreams. They weren't real.

And yet.

*They were so, so real.*

Once upon a time, the families had submitted to the Robes and said yes to the Council and given up their babies to the Witch. They did this to save the people of the Protectorate. They did this knowing that their babies would die. Their babies were dead.

*But what if they were not?*

And the more they asked, the more they wondered. And the more they wondered, the more they hoped. And the more they hoped, the more the clouds of sorrow lifted, drifted, and burned away in the heat of a brightening sky.

❉

I don't mean to be rude, Grand Elder Gherland," wheezed Elder Raspin. He was so old. Gherland was amazed that the geezer could still stand. "But facts are facts. This is all your fault."

The gathering in front of the Tower started with just a few citizens holding signs, but quickly swelled to a crowd with banners, songs, speeches, and other atrocities. The Elders, seeing this, had retreated into the Grand Elder's great house and sealed the windows and the doors.

Now the Grand Elder sat in his favorite chair and glowered at his compatriots. "My fault?" His voice was quiet. The maids, cooks, assistant cooks, and pastry chef had all made themselves scarce, which meant there was no food to be had, and Gherland's gullet was quite empty. "*My* fault?" He let that sit for a moment. "Pray. Explain why."

Raspin began to cough and looked as though he may expire right there. Elder Guinnot attempted to continue.

"This rabble-rouser is part of your family. And there she is. Out there. Rousing the rabble."

"The rabble had already been roused before she got there," Gherland sputtered. "I paid her a visit myself, her and that doomed baby of hers. Once that baby is left in the forest, she will mourn and recover, and things will return to normal."

"Have you looked outside lately?" Elder Leibshig said. "All that . . . *sunlight*. It assaults the eye, is what. And it seems to be inflaming the populace."

"And the signs. Who on earth could be making them?" grumbled Elder Oerick. "Not my employees, I'll tell you what. They wouldn't dare. And anyway, I had the foresight to hide the ink. At least *one* of us is thinking."

"Where is Sister Ignatia?" moaned Elder Dorrit. "Of all the times for her to disappear! And why aren't the Sisters nipping this in the bud?!"

"It's that boy. He was trouble on his first Sacrifice day. We should have dispatched him then," Elder Raspin said.

"I *beg* your pardon!" the Grand Elder said.

"We all knew that the boy would be a problem sooner or later. And look. There he goes. Being a problem."

The Grand Elder sputtered. "Listen to yourselves. A bunch of grown men! And you are whining like *babies*. There is nothing at all to worry about. The rabble is roused, but it is temporary. The Head Sister is gone, but it is temporary. My nephew has proved himself to be a thorn in our collective sides, but that is temporary, too. The Road is the only safe passage. He is in danger. And he will die." The Grand Elder paused, closed his eyes, and tried to swallow his sadness deep in his chest. Hide it away. He opened his eyes and gave the Elders a steely gaze. Resolute. "And, my dear Brothers, when that happens, our life as we knew it will return, just as we left it. That is as sure as the ground under our feet."

At that, the ground beneath their feet began to shake. The Elders threw open the south windows and looked outside. Smoke curled from the highest peak on the mountain. The volcano was burning.

# 39

## In Which Glerk Tells
## Fyrian the Truth

C ome on," Luna said. The moon had not risen yet, but Luna could feel it approaching. This was nothing new. She had always felt a strange kinship with the moon, but she had never felt it as powerfully as she did right now. The moon would be full tonight. It would light up the world.

"Caw," said the crow. "I am very, very tired."

"Caw," he continued. "Also, it is nighttime and crows are not nocturnal."

"Here," Luna said, holding out the hood of her cloak. "Ride in here. I'm not tired at all."

And it was true. She felt as though her bones were transforming into light. She felt as though she would never be tired again. The crow landed on her shoulder and climbed into her hood.

When Luna was little, her grandmother taught her about magnets and compasses. She showed her that a magnet operates within a field, increasing in strength the closer one comes to its poles. Luna learned that a magnet will attract some things and ignore others. But she learned that the world is a magnet as well, and that a compass, with its tiny needle in a pool of water, will always wish to align itself with the pull of the magnetic earth. And Luna knew this and understood it, but now she felt that there was *another* magnetic field and *another* compass that her grandmother had never told her about.

Luna's heart was pulled to her grandmother's heart. Was love a compass?

Luna's mind was pulled to her grandmother's mind. Was knowledge a magnet?

And there was something else, too. This surging feeling in her bones. This clicking inside her head. This feeling as though she had an invisible gear inside her, pushing her, inch by inch, toward . . . *something.*

Her whole life, she never knew what.

*Magic,* her bones said.

❋

"Glerk," Fyrian said. "Glerk, Glerk, Glerk. I don't seem to be fitting on your back anymore. Are you shrinking?"

"No, my friend," Glerk said. "Quite the opposite. You seem to be growing."

And it was true. Fyrian was *growing*. Glerk didn't believe it at first, but with each step they took, Fyrian grew a little bit more. Not evenly. His nose enlarged like a tremendous melon at the tip of his snout. Then one eye expanded to twice the size of the other. Then his wings. Then his feet. Then one foot. Bit after bit grew, then slowed, then grew, and then slowed.

"Growing? You mean I'll be *more* enormous?" Fyrian said. "How can a dragon be *more* enormous than *Simply* Enormous?"

Glerk hesitated. "Well, you know your auntie. She always saw your *potential*, even though you weren't there quite yet. Do you see what I'm saying to you?"

"No," Fyrian said.

Glerk sighed. This was going to be tricky.

"Sometimes, being Simply Enormous actually isn't just about size."

"It isn't?" Fyrian thought about this as his left ear started to sprout and expand. "Xan never said so."

"Well, you know Xan," Glerk said, grasping a bit. "She's delicate." Glerk paused. "Size is a spectrum. Like a rainbow. On the spectrum of enormity, you were on, well, the low end. And that is completely, well . . ." He paused again. Sucked his lips. "Sometimes the truth, er, *bends*. Like light." He was floundering and he knew it.

"It does?"

"Your heart was always enormous," Glerk said. "And it always will be."

"Glerk," Fyrian said gravely. His lips had grown to the size of tree branches and hung off his jaws in a floppy mess. One of his teeth was larger than the others. And one arm was growing rapidly, before Glerk's very eyes. "Do I look strange to you? Please be honest."

He was such an earnest little thing. Odd, of course. And lacking in self-awareness. But earnest all the same. Best be earnest back, Glerk decided.

"Listen, Fyrian. I confess that I do not entirely understand your situation. And you know what? Neither did Xan. That's all right, really. You are growing. My guess is that you are on your way to being Simply Enormous like your mother. She died, Fyrian. Five hundred years ago. Most drangonlings do not stay in their babyhood for that long. Indeed, I cannot think of a single other example. But for some reason you did. Maybe Xan did it. Maybe it was because you stayed too close to where your mother died. Maybe you couldn't bear to grow. In any case, you're growing now. I had thought you would stay a Perfectly Tiny Dragon forever. But I was wrong."

"But . . ." Fyrian tripped on his growing wings, tumbling forward and falling down so hard he shook the ground. "But you're a giant, Glerk."

Glerk shook his head. "No, my friend. No, I am not. I am large, and I am old, but I am not a giant."

Fyrian's toes swelled to twice their normal size. "And Xan. And Luna."

"Also not giants. They are regular-sized. And you are so small you could fit in their pockets. Or you were."

"And now I am not."

"No, my friend. Now you are not."

"But what does that mean, Glerk?" Fyrian's eyes were wet. His tears erupted in bubbling pools and clouds of steam.

"I don't know, my dear Fyrian. What I *do* know is that I am here with you. I *do* know that the gaps in our knowledge will soon be revealed and filled in, and that's a good thing. I *do* know that you are my friend and that I will stay by your side through every transition and trial. No matter how—" Fyrian's rump suddenly doubled in size, its weight so extreme that his back legs buckled and he sat down with a tremendous crash. "Ahem. No matter how indelicate," Glerk finished.

"Thank you, Glerk," Fyrian sniffed.

Glerk held up all four of his hands and lifted his great head as high as he could, uncurling his spine and standing on his back legs at first, and then lifting his body even higher on his thick, coiled tail. His wide eyes grew even wider.

"Look!" he said, pointing down the slope of the mountain.

"What?" Fyrian asked. He could see nothing.

"There, moving down the rocky knoll. I suppose you can't see it, my friend. It's Luna. Her magic is emerging. I thought I had seen it coming off in bits and pieces, but Xan told me I was imagining things. Poor Xan. She did her best to hold on to Luna's childhood, but there's no escaping it. That girl is growing. And she won't be a girl for much longer."

Fyrian stared at Glerk, openmouthed. "She's turning into a dragon?" he said, his voice a mixture of incredulity and hope.

"What?" Glerk said. "No. Of course not! She's turning into a grown-up. And a witch. Both at the same time. And look! There she goes. I can see her magic from here. I wish you could, Fyrian. It is the most beautiful shade of blue, with a shimmer of silver lingering behind."

Fyrian was about to say something else, but he stared at the ground. He laid both his hands on the dirt. "Glerk?" he said, pressing his ear to the ground.

Glerk didn't pay attention. "And look!" he said, pointing at the next ridge over. "There is Xan. Or her magic, anyway. Oh! She's hurt. I can see it from here. She's using a spell right now, transformation by the look of it. Oh, Xan! Why would you transform in your condition! What if you can't transform back?"

"Glerk?" Fyrian said, his scales growing paler by the second.

"There's no time, Fyrian. Xan needs us. Look. Luna is moving toward the ridge where Xan is right now. If we hurry—"

"GLERK!" Fyrian said. "Will you listen? The mountain."

"Speak in complete sentences, please," Glerk said impatiently. "If we don't move quickly—"

"THE MOUNTAIN IS ON FIRE, GLERK," Fyrian roared.

Glerk rolled his eyes. "No, it's not! Well. No more than normal. Those smoke pots are just—"

"No, Glerk," Fyrian said, pulling himself to his feet. "It is. Underground. The mountain is on fire under our feet. Like before. When it erupted. My mother and I—" His voice caught, his grief erupting suddenly. "We felt it first. She went to the magicians to warn them. Glerk!" Fyrian's face nearly cracked with worry. "We need to warn Xan."

The swamp monster nodded. He felt his heart sink into his great tail. "And quickly," he agreed. "Come, dear Fyrian. We haven't a moment to lose."

❈

Doubt slithered through Xan's birdish guts.

*It's all my fault,* she fussed.

*No!* she argued. *You protected! You loved! You rescued those babies from starvation. You made happy families.*

*I should have known,* she countered. *I should have been curious. I should have done something.*

And this poor boy! How he loved his wife. How he loved his child. And look at what he was willing to sacrifice to keep them safe and happy. She wanted to hug him. She wanted to un-transform and explain everything. Except he would surely attempt to kill her before she could do so.

"Not long, my friend," the young man whispered. "The

moon will rise and we will be off. And I shall kill the Witch and we can go home. And you can see my beautiful Ethyne and my beautiful son. And we will keep you safe."

*Not likely*, Xan thought.

Once the moon rose, she would be able to capture at least a little bit of its magic. A very little. It would be like trying to carry water in a fishnet. Still. Better than nothing. She'd still have the drips. And maybe she would have enough to make this poor man go to sleep for a little bit. And maybe she could even ambulate his clothing and his boots and send him home, where he could wake up in the loving embrace of his family.

All she needed was the moon.

"Do you hear that?" the man said, springing to his feet. Xan looked around. She hadn't heard anything.

But he was right.

Something was coming.

Or someone.

"Can it be that the Witch is coming to *me*?" he asked. "Could I be that lucky?"

*Indeed*, Xan thought, with more derision than was likely fair. She gave the man a little peck through his shirt. *Imagine the Witch coming to you. Lucky duck.* She rolled her beady little bird eye.

"Look!" he said, pointing down the ridge. Xan looked. It was true. Someone was moving up the ridge. Two somethings. Xan couldn't account for what the second figure was—it didn't look like anything that she had ever seen before—but the first thing was unmistakable.

That blue glow.

That shimmer of silver.

Luna's magic. Her *magic*! Coming closer and closer and closer.

"It's the Witch!" the young man said. "I am sure of it!" And he hid behind a tangled clump of undergrowth, keeping himself very still. He trembled. He moved his knife from one hand to the other. "Don't worry, my friend," he said. "I shall make it very, very quick. The Witch will arrive. She will not see me."

He swallowed.

"And then I shall slit her throat."

# 40

## In Which There Is a
## Disagreement about Boots

"Take those off, dear," Sister Ignatia said. Her voice was cream. She was all soft steps and padded claws. "They simply do not become you."

The madwoman tipped her head. The moon was about to rise. The mountain rumbled under her feet. She stood in front of a large stone. "Don't forget," the stone said on one side. "I mean it," it said on the other.

The madwoman missed her birds. They had flown away and had not come back. Were they real to begin with? The madwoman did not know.

All she knew at the moment was that she liked these boots. She had fed the goats and the chickens, and gathered the milk and the eggs, and thanked the animals for their time. But all the while, she had felt as though the boots were feeding *her*. She couldn't explain it. The boots enlivened her, muscle and bone. She felt as light as a paper bird. She felt like she could run for a thousand miles and she wouldn't lose her breath.

Sister Ignatia took a step forward. Her lips unfurled in a thin smile. The madwoman could hear the Head Sister's tigerish growl rumbling underground. She felt her back start to sweat. She took several hurried steps backward, until her body found the standing stone. She leaned against it, and found a comfort there. She felt her boots start to buzz.

There was magic all around this place. Tiny bits and pieces. The madwoman could feel it. The Sister, she could see, felt it, too. Both women reached their nimble, clever fingers this way and that, hooking shiny bits of magic into their hands, saving it for later. The more the madwoman gathered, the clearer the path to her daughter became.

"You poor lost soul," the Head Sister said. "How far you are from home! How confused you must be! It is so lucky that I found you here, before some wild animal or roving ruffian did. This is a dangerous wood. The most dangerous in the world."

The mountain rumbled. A plume of smoke erupted from the farthest craters. The Head Sister turned pale.

"We need to leave this place," Sister Ignatia said. The madwoman felt her knees start to shake. "Look." The Sister pointed to the crater. "I've seen that before. A long time ago.

The plumes come, then the earth shakes, then the first explosions, and then the whole mountain opens its face to the sky. If we are here when that happens, we're both dead. But if you give me those boots"—she licked her lips—"then I can use the power inside them to get us both back home. Back to the Tower. Your safe, homey little Tower." She smiled again. Even her smile was terrifying.

"You are lying, Tiger's Heart," the madwoman whispered. Sister Ignatia flinched at the term. "You have no intention of carrying me back." Her hands were on the stone. The stone was making her see things. Or perhaps the boots were making her see things. She saw a group of magicians—old men and old women—betrayed by the Head Sister. Before she was the Head Sister. Before there was a Protectorate. The Head Sister was supposed to carry the magicians on her back when the volcano erupted, but she did nothing of the kind. She left them in the smoke to die.

"How do you know that name?" Sister Ignatia whispered.

"Everyone knows that name," the madwoman said. "It was in a story. About how the Witch ate a tiger's heart. They all whisper it. It's wrong, of course. You don't have a tiger's heart. You have no heart at all."

"There is no such story," Sister Ignatia said. She began to pace. She hunched her shoulders. She growled. "I started the stories in the Protectorate. *I did*. They all came from me. There is no story that I did not tell first."

"You're wrong. *The tiger walks,* the sisters said. I could hear them. They were talking about you, you know."

The Head Sister turned quite pale. "Impossible," she whispered.

"It was impossible for my child to still be alive," the madwoman said, "and yet she is. And she was here. Recently. The impossible is possible." She looked around. "I like this place," she said.

"Give me those boots."

"That's another thing. Riding a flock of paper birds is impossible, and yet I did it. I don't know where my birds are, but they'll find their way back to me. And it was impossible for me to know where my baby went, yet I have the clearest picture of where she is. Right now. And I have a pretty good idea of how to get to her. Not in my head, you see, but in my feet. These boots. They're ever so clever."

"GIVE ME MY BOOTS," the Head Sister roared. She balled her hands into two tight fists and raised them over her head. When she swept them back down, uncurling her fingers, they held four sharp knives. Without hesitating she reared back and snapped her hands forward, shooting the knife blades directly for the madwoman's heart. And they would have struck, too, if the madwoman had not spun on one heel and taken three graceful leaps to the side.

"The boots are mine," Sister Ignatia roared. "You don't even know how to use them."

The madwoman smiled. "Actually," she said, "I believe I do."

Sister Ignatia lunged at the madwoman, who took several windup steps in place before speeding away in a flash. And the Sister was alone.

A second crater began to plume. The ground shook so hard it nearly knocked Sister Ignatia to her knees. She pressed her hands against the rocky ground. It was hot. Any moment now. The eruption was almost here.

She stood. Smoothed her gown.

"Well then," she said. "If that's the way they want to play it, *fine*. I'll play, too."

And she followed the madwoman into the trembling forest.

# 41

## In Which Several Paths Converge

Luna scrambled up the steep slope toward the ridgeline. The upper edge of the moon had just begun to emerge over the lip of the horizon. She could feel a buzzing inside her, like a gear spring wound too tight and whizzing out of control. She felt herself surging, and that surge erupting wildly from her extremities. She tripped and her hands fell hard on the pebbly ground. And the pebbles began to jostle and scuttle and crawl away like bugs. Or no. They *were* bugs—antennae and hairy legs and iridescent wings. Or they became water. Or ice. The moon pushed higher over the horizon.

Her grandmother had taught Luna, when she was a little girl with scabby knees and matted hair, how a caterpillar lives, growing big and fat and sweet-tempered, until it forms a chrysalis. And inside the chrysalis, it *changes*. Its body unmakes. Every portion of itself unravels, unwinds, undoes, and re-forms into something *else*.

"What does it feel like?" Luna had asked.

"It feels like magic," her grandmother had said very slowly, her eyes narrowing.

And then Luna had gone blank. Now, in her memory, she could see that blankness—how the word *magic* flew away, like a bird. Indeed she could *see* it flying—each sound, each letter, skittering out of her ears and fluttering away. But now it came flying back. Her grandmother had tried to explain the magic to her, once upon a time. Maybe more than once. But then perhaps she had simply grown accustomed to Luna's notknowing. And now, Luna felt as though she was in a storm of memories, jumbling around inside her skull.

The caterpillar goes into the chrysalis, her grandmother had said. And then it *changes*. Its skin changes and its eyes change and its mouth changes. Its feet vanish. Every bit of itself—even its knowledge of itself—turns to mush.

"Mush?" Luna had asked, wide-eyed.

"Well," her grandmother had reassured her. "Perhaps not mush. Stuff. The stuff of stars. The stuff of light. The stuff of a planet before it is a planet. The stuff of a baby before it is born. The stuff of a seed before it is a sycamore. Everything you see is in the process of making or unmaking or dying or living. Everything is in a state of *change*."

And now, as Luna ran up the ridge, she was changing. She could feel it. Her bones and her skin and her eyes and her spirit. The machine of her body—every gear, every spring, every well-honed lever—had altered, rearranged, and clicked into place. A different place. And she was *new*.

There was a man at the top of the ridge. Luna couldn't see him, but she could feel him with her bones. She could feel her grandmother nearby. Or at least she was fairly certain it was her grandmother. She could see the grandmother-shaped impression on her own soul, but when she tried to get a sense of where her grandmother was *now*, it was blurred somehow.

"It's the Witch," she heard the man say. Luna felt her heart seize. She ran even faster, though the ridge was steep and the way was long. With each stride she increased her speed.

*Grandmama*, her heart cried out.

*Go away.* She did not hear this with her ears. She heard it in her bones.

*Turn around.*

*What are you doing here, you foolish girl?*

She was imagining it. Of course she was. And yet. Why did it seem as though the voice came from the grandmother-shaped impression in her spirit? And why did it sound *just like* Xan?

"Don't worry, my friend," Luna heard the man say. "I will make it very quick. The Witch will come. And I will slit her throat."

"GRANDMAMA!" Luna cried. "LOOK OUT."

And she heard a sound. Like the cry of a swallow. Ringing through the night.

✼

"I would suggest that we move more quickly, my friend," Glerk said, holding Fyrian by the wing and dragging him forward.

"I feel sick, Glerk," Fyrian said, falling to his knees. If he had fallen that hard earlier in the day, surely he would have cut himself. But his knees—indeed his legs and his feet and the whole of his back, and even his front paws—were now covered with a thick, leathery skin on which bright, hard scales were beginning to form.

"We do not have time for you to be sick," Glerk said, looking back. Fyrian was now as big as he was, and growing by the moment. And it was true. He was looking a bit green about the face. But maybe that was his normal color. It was impossible to say.

It was, Glerk felt, a most inconvenient time to choose to grow. But he was being unfair.

"Excuse me," Fyrian said. And he heaved himself over to a low shrub and vomited profusely. "Oh dear. I seem to have lit some things on fire."

Glerk shook his head. "If you can stamp it out, do so. But if you are right about the volcano, it won't much matter what is on fire and what is not."

Fyrian shook his head and shook his wings. He tried

flapping them a few times, but he still was not strong enough to lift off. He sniffed, a stricken look pressed onto his face. "I still can't fly."

"I think it is safe to say that is a temporary condition," Glerk said.

"How do you know?" Fyrian said. He did his best to hide the sob lurking in his voice. He did not hide it very well.

Glerk regarded his friend. The growing had slowed, but it had not stopped. At least now Fyrian seemed to be growing more evenly.

"I don't know. I can only hope for the best." Glerk curled his great, wide jaws into a grin. "And you, dear Fyrian, are one of the best I know. Come. To the top of the ridge! Let us hurry!"

And they rushed through the undergrowth and scrambled up the rocks.

※

The madwoman had never felt so good in her life. The sun was down. The moon was just starting to rise. And she was speeding through the forest. She did not like the look of the ground—too many pitfalls and boiling pots and steamy depths that might cook her alive. Instead, in the boots she ran from branch to branch as easily as a squirrel.

The Head Sister was following her. She could feel the stretch and curl of the Sister's muscles. She could feel the ripple of speed and the flash of color as she loped through the forest.

She paused for a moment on the thick branch of a tree that she could not identify. The bark was deeply furrowed, and she wondered if it ran like rivers when it rained. She peered into the gathering dark. She allowed her vision to go wide, to hook over hills and ravines and ridges, to creep over the curve of the world.

There! A flash of blue, with a shimmer of silver.

There! A glow of licheny green.

There! The young man she had hurt.

There! Some kind of monster and his pet.

The mountain rumbled. Each time it did so it was louder, more insistent. The mountain had swallowed power, and the power wanted out.

"I need my birds," the madwoman said, turning her face to the sky. She leaped forward and clung to a new branch. And another. And another. And another.

"I NEED MY BIRDS!" she called again, running from branch to branch as easily as if she was running a footrace across a grassy field. But so much faster than that.

She could feel the magic of the boots lighting up her bones. The growing moonlight seemed to increase it.

"I need my daughter," she whispered as she ran even faster, her eye fixed on the shimmer of blue.

And behind her, another whisper gathered—the beating of paper wings.

✿

The crow crawled out of the girl's hood. He arranged his fine feet on her shoulders and then snapped his shiny wings out, launching himself into the air.

"Caw," the crow called. "*Luna,*" his voice rang out.

"Caw," again. "Luna."

"Caw, caw, caw."

"Luna, Luna, Luna."

The ridge became steeper. The girl had to grab on to the spindly trunks and branches clinging to the slope to keep from falling backward. Her face was red and her breath came in gasps.

"Caw," the crow said. "I am going up ahead to see what you cannot."

He darted forward, through the shadows, onto the bare knoll at the top of the ridge, where large boulders stood like sentinels, guarding the mountains.

He saw a man. The man held a swallow. The swallow kicked and fluttered and pecked.

"Hush now, my friend!" The man spoke in soothing tones as he wrapped the swallow in a measure of cloth and bound it inside his coat.

The man crept toward one of the last boulders near the edge of the ridge.

"So," he said to the swallow, who struggled and fussed. "She has taken the form of a girl. Even a tiger can take the skin of a lamb. It doesn't change the fact that it is a tiger."

And then the man took out a knife.

"Caw!" the crow screamed. "Luna!"

"Caw!"

"Run!"

# 42

## In Which the World Is Blue
## and Silver and Silver and Blue

Luna heard the crow's warning, but she couldn't slow down. She was alive with moonlight. *Blue and silver, silver and blue,* she thought, but she did not know why. The moonlight was delicious. She gathered it on her hands and drank it again and again. Once she had started she could not stop.

And with each gulp, the scene on the ridge became clearer.

That lichen-green glow.

It was her grandmother.

The feathers.

They were somehow connected to her grandmother.

She saw the man with scars on his face. He looked familiar to her, but she couldn't place him.

There was kindness in his eyes and kindness in his spirit. His heart carried love inside it. His hand carried a knife.

✻

*Blue,* the madwoman thought as she streaked through the trees from branch to branch to branch. *Blue, blue, blue, blue.* With each loping step, the magic of the boots coursed through her body like lightning.

"And silver, too," she sang out loud. "Blue and silver, silver and blue."

Each step brought her closer to the girl. The moon was fully up now. It lit the world. The light of the moon skittered along the madwoman's bones, from the top of her head to her beautiful boots and back again.

Stride, stride, stride; leap, leap, leap; blue, blue, blue. A shimmer of silver. A dangerous baby. A protective pair of arms. A monster with wide jaws and kind eyes. A tiny dragon. A child full of moonlight.

*Luna. Luna, Luna, Luna, Luna.*

Her child.

There was a bare knoll on the top of the ridge. She raced toward it. Boulders stood like sentinels. And behind one of the boulders stood a man. A licheny green glow showed through a small spot on his jacket. Some kind of magic, the madwoman thought. The man held a knife. And just over the lip of the ridge, and nearly upon him, was the other glow—the blue glow.

The girl.

Her daughter.

Luna.

She lived.

The man lifted the knife. He fixed his eyes on the approaching girl.

"Witch!" he shouted.

"I am no Witch," the girl said. "I am a girl. My name is Luna."

"Lies!" the man said. "You are the Witch. You are thousands of years old. You have killed countless children." A shuddering breath. "And now *I* shall kill *you*."

The man leaped.

The girl leaped.

The madwoman leaped.

And the world was full of birds.

# 43

# In Which a Witch Casts Her First Spell—On Purpose This Time

A whirlwind of legs and wings and elbows and fingernails and beaks and paper. Paper birds swirled around the knoll in a spiral winding tighter and tighter and tighter.

"My eyes!" the man yelled.

"My cheek!" Luna howled.

"My boots!" a woman groaned. A woman that Luna did not know.

"Caw!" screeched the crow. "My girl! Stay away from my girl."

"Birds!" Luna gasped.

She rolled away from the tangle and scrambled to her feet. The paper birds swirled upward in a massive formation overhead before alighting in a great circle on the ground. They weren't attacking—not yet. But the way they keened their beaks forward and menacingly opened their wings made them look as though they might.

The man covered his face.

"Keep them away," he whimpered. He shook and cowered, covering his face with his hands. He dropped the knife on the ground. Luna kicked it away, and it tumbled over the edge of the ridge.

"Please," he whispered. "I've met these birds. They are terrifying. They cut me to shreds."

Luna knelt next to him. "I won't let them hurt you," she whispered. "I promise. They found me before, when I was lost in the woods. They didn't hurt me then, and I can't imagine that they will hurt you now. But no matter what, I won't let them. Do you understand me?"

The man nodded. He kept his face curled to his knees.

The paper birds cocked their heads. They did not look at Luna. They looked at the woman, sprawled on the ground.

Luna looked at her, too.

The woman wore black boots and a plain gray shift dress. Her head was shaved. She had wide, black eyes and a birthmark on her forehead in the shape of a crescent moon. Luna pressed her fingers to her own brow.

*She is here,* her heart called. *She is here, she is here, she is here.*

"She is here," the woman whispered. "She is here, she is here, she is here."

Luna had an image in her head of a woman with long black hair, writhing from her head like snakes. She looked at the woman in front of her. She tried to imagine her with hair.

"Do I know you?" Luna said.

"No one knows me," the woman said. "I have no name."

Luna frowned. "*Did* you have a name?"

The woman crouched down, hugging her knees. Her eyes darted this way and that. She was hurt, but not on her body. Luna looked closer. She was hurt in her mind. "Once," the woman said. "Once I had a name. But I do not remember it. There was a man who called me 'wife,' and there was a child who would have called me 'mother.' But that was a long time ago. I cannot tell how long. Now I am only called 'prisoner.'"

"A tower," Luna whispered, taking a step nearer. The woman had tears in her eyes. She looked at Luna and then looked away, back and forth, as though afraid to let her eyes rest on the girl for too long.

The man looked up. He drew himself to his knees. He stared at the madwoman. "It's you," he said. "You escaped."

"It's me," the madwoman said. She crawled across the rocky surface and crouched next to him. She put her hands on his face. "This is my fault," she said, running her fingers across his scars. "I'm sorry. But your life. Your life is happier now. Isn't it?"

The man's eyes swelled with tears. "No," he said. "I mean, yes. It is. But no. My wife had a baby. Our son is beautiful. But he is the youngest in the Protectorate. Like you, we must give our baby to the Witch."

He looked at the birthmark on the madwoman's forehead.

He slid his gaze to Luna. He was looking at her identical birthmark. And her identical wide, black eyes. A lump in his jacket struggled and pecked. A black beak peeked from the rim of his collar. Pecked again.

"Ouch," the man said

"I'm not a witch," Luna said, drawing up her chin. "Or, at least, I wasn't. And I never took any babies."

The crow hopped across the bare rock and leaped upward, arcing toward the girl's shoulder.

"Of course you aren't," the woman said. She still couldn't keep her eyes on Luna. She had to look away, as though Luna were a bright light. "You *are* the baby."

"What baby?"

A bird struggled its way out of the man's jacket. That lichen green glow. The bird squawked and worried and pecked.

"Please, little friend!" the man said. "Peace! Calm yourself. You have nothing to fear."

"Grandmama!" Luna whispered.

"You don't understand. I accidentally broke this swallow's wing," the man said.

Luna wasn't listening. "GRANDMAMA!" The swallow

froze. It stared at the girl with one bright eye. Her grandmother's eye. She knew it.

Inside her skull a final gear slid into place. Her skin hummed. Her bones hummed. Her mind lit with memories, each one falling like an asteroid, flashing in the dark.

The screaming woman on the ceiling.

The very old man with the very large nose.

The circle of sycamores.

The sycamore that became an old woman.

The woman with starlight on her fingers. And then something sweeter than starlight.

And somehow, Glerk was a bunny.

And her grandmother tried to teach her about spells. The texture of spells. The construction of spells. The poetry and artistry and architecture of spells. They were lessons that Luna heard and forgot, but now she remembered and understood.

She looked at the bird. The bird looked at Luna. The paper birds quieted their wings and waited.

"Grandmama," Luna said, holding up her hands. She focused all her love, all her questions, all her care, all her worry, all her frustrations, and all her sorrow on the bird on the ground. The woman who fed her. The woman who taught her to build and dream and create. The woman who didn't answer her questions—who *couldn't*. That's who she wanted to see. She felt the bones in her toes begin to buzz. Her magic and her thinking and her intention and her hope. They were all the same thing now. Their force moved through her shins. Then her hips. Then her arms. Then her fingers.

"*Show yourself*," Luna commanded.

And, in a tangle of wings and claws and arms and legs, her grandmother was there. She looked at Luna. Her eyes were rheumy and damp. They flowed with tears.

"My darling," she whispered.

And then Xan shuddered, doubled over, and collapsed onto the ground.

# 44

## In Which There Is a Change of Heart

Luna threw herself to her knees, scooping her grandmother in her arms.

And oh! How light she was. Just sticks and paper and a cold wind. Her grandmother who had been a force of nature all these years—a pillar, holding up the sky. Luna felt as though she could have picked her grandmother up and run home with her in her arms.

"Grandmama," she sobbed, laying her cheek on her grandmother's cheek. "Wake up, Grandmama. Please wake up."

Her grandmother drew in a shuddering breath.

"Your magic," the old woman said. "It's started, hasn't it?"

"Don't talk about that," Luna said, her mouth still buried in her grandmother's licheny hair. "Are you sick?"

"Not sick," her grandmother wheezed. "Dying. Something I should have done a long time ago." She coughed, shuddered, coughed again.

Luna felt a single sob wrench its way from her guts to her throat. "You're not dying, Grandmama. You can't be. I can talk to a crow. And the paper birds love me. And I think I found—well. I don't know what she is. But I remember her. From before. And there's a lady in the woods who . . . well, I don't think she's good."

"I'm not dying this second, child, but I will in good time. And that time will be soon. Now. Your magic. I can say the word and it stays, yes?" Luna nodded. "I had locked it away inside you so you wouldn't be a danger to yourself and others—because believe me, darling, you were *dangerous*—but there were consequences. And let me guess, it's coming out all up, down, and sideways, yes?" She closed her eyes and grimaced in pain.

"I don't want to talk about it, Grandmama, unless it can make you well." The girl sat up suddenly. "*Can* I make you well?"

The old woman shivered. "I'm cold," she said. "I'm so, so cold. Is the moon up?"

"Yes, Grandmama."

"Raise your hand. Let the moonlight collect on your fingers

and feed it to me. It is what I did for you, long ago, when you were a baby. When you had been left in the forest and I carried you to safety." Xan stopped and looked over to the woman with the shaved head, crouched on the ground. "I thought that your mother had abandoned you." She pressed her hand to her mouth and shook her head. "You have the same birthmark." Xan faltered. "And the same eyes."

The woman on the ground nodded. "She wasn't abandoned," she whispered. "She was taken. My baby was taken." The madwoman buried her face in her knees and covered her stubbled head with her arms. She made no more sounds.

Xan's face seemed to crack. "Yes. I see that now." She turned to Luna. "Every year, a baby was left in the woods to die in the same spot. Every year I carried that baby across the woods to a new family who would love it and keep it safe. I was wrong not to be curious. I was so wrong not to wonder. But sorrow hung over that place like a cloud. And so I left as quickly as I could."

Xan shuddered and pulled herself to her hands and knees, and slid closer to the woman on the ground. The woman didn't raise her head. Xan gingerly laid her hand on the woman's shoulder. "Can you forgive me?"

The madwoman said nothing.

"And the children in the woods. They are the Star Children?" Luna whispered.

"The Star Children." Her grandmother coughed. "They

were all like you. But then you were enmagicked. I didn't mean to, darling; it was an accident, but it couldn't be undone. And I loved you. I loved you so much. And that couldn't be undone, either. So I claimed you as my own dear grandchild. And then I started to die. And that, too, can't be undone, not for anything. Consequences. It's all consequences. I've made so many mistakes." She shivered. "I'm cold. A little moonlight, my Luna, if you wouldn't mind."

Luna reached up her hand. The weight of moonlight—sticky and sweet—gathered on her fingertips. It poured from her hands into her grandmother's mouth and shivered through her grandmother's body. The old woman's cheeks began to flush. The moonlight radiated through Luna's own skin, too, setting her bones aglow.

"The moonlight's help is only temporary," her grandmother said. "The magic runs through me like a bucket with holes in it. It's drawn toward you. Everything I have, everything I am, flows to you, my darling. This is as it should be." She turned and put her hand on Luna's face. Luna interlaced her fingers with her grandmother's and held on desperately. "Five hundred years is an awful lot. Too many. And you have a mother who loves you. Who has loved you all this time."

"My friend," the man said. He was weeping—big ugly tears down a blotchy face. He seemed harmless enough now that he didn't have that knife. Still, Luna eyed him warily. He crept forward, extending his left hand.

"That's far enough," she said coolly.

He nodded. "My friend," he said again. "My, er, once-was-a-bird friend. I . . ." He swallowed, wiped his tears and snot with the back of his sleeve. "I'm sorry if this sounds rude, but, ah . . ." His voice trailed off. Luna could stop him with a rock, though she quickly waved the thought away when a rock rolled near and started hovering menacingly.

*No hitting*, she thought at the rock with a glare. The rock fell to the ground with a dejected thud and rolled away, as though chastened.

*I'm going to have to be careful*, Luna thought.

"But, are *you* the Witch?" the man continued, his eyes pinned on Xan. "The Witch in the woods? The one who insists that we sacrifice a baby every year or she will destroy us all?"

Luna gave him a cold look. "My grandmother has never destroyed anything. She is good and kind and caring. Ask the people of the Free Cities. They know."

"*Somebody* demands a sacrifice," the man said. "It isn't her." He pointed to the woman with the shaved head and the paper birds roosting on her shoulders. "I know that much. I was with her when her baby was taken away."

"As I recall," the woman growled, "you were the one doing the taking."

And the man hung his head.

"It was you," Luna whispered. "I remember. You were only

a boy. You smelled of sawdust. And you didn't want . . ." She paused. Frowned. "You made the old men mad."

"*Yes*," the man gasped.

Her grandmother began to pull herself to her feet, and Luna hovered, trying to help. Xan waved her away.

"Enough, child. I can still stand on my own. I am not so old."

But she *was* so old. Before Luna's eyes, her grandmother aged. Xan had always been old—of course she had. But now . . . Now it was different. Now she seemed to desiccate by the moment. Her eyes were sunken and shadowed. Her skin was the color of dust. Luna gathered more moonlight on her fingers and encouraged her grandmother to drink.

Xan looked at the young man.

"We should move quickly. I was on my way to rescue yet another abandoned baby. I have been doing so for ever so long." She shivered and tried to take a single, unsteady step. Luna thought she might blow over. "There's no time for fussing, child."

Luna looped her arm around her grandmother's waist. Her crow fluttered onto her shoulder. She turned to the woman on the ground. Offered her hand.

"Will you come with us?" she said. Held her breath. Felt her heart pounding in her chest.

*The woman on the ceiling.*

*The paper birds in the tower window.*

*She is here, she is here, she is here.*

The woman on the ground lifted her gaze and found Luna's eyes. She took Luna's hand and rose to her feet. Luna felt her heart take wing. The paper birds began to flap, flutter, and lift into the air.

Luna heard the sound of footsteps approaching on the far side of the knoll before she saw it: a pair of glowing eyes. The muscled lope of a tiger. But not a tiger at all. A woman—tall, strong, and clearly magic. And her magic was sharp, and hard, and merciless. Like the curved edge of a blade. The woman who had demanded the boots. She was back.

"Hello, Sorrow Eater," Xan said.

# 45

## In Which a Simply Enormous Dragon Makes a Simply Enormous Decision

G lerk!"

"Hush, Fyrian!" Glerk said. "I'm *listening!*"

They had seen the Sorrow Eater make her way up the side of the knoll, and Glerk felt his blood go cold.

*The Sorrow Eater! After all these years!*

She looked exactly the same. What kind of tricks had she been up to?

"But Glerk!"

"But nothing! She doesn't know we're here. We shall surprise her!"

It had been so long since Glerk had last confronted an enemy. Or surprised a villain. There was a time that Glerk was

356~

very good at it. He could wield five swords at once—four hands and the prehensile tip of his tail—and was so formidable and agile and huge that his adversaries would often drop their weapons and call a truce. This was preferable for Glerk, who felt that violence, while sometimes necessary, was uncouth and uncivilized. Reason, beauty, poetry, and excellent conversation were his preferred tools for settling disputes. Glerk's spirit, in its essence, was as serene as any bog—life-giving and life-sustaining. And, quite suddenly, he missed the Bog with an intensity that nearly knocked him to his knees.

*I have been asleep. I have been lulled by my love for Xan. I am meant to be in the world—and I have not been. Not for Ages. Shame on me.*

"GLERK!"

The swamp monster looked up. Fyrian was flying. He had continued to grow and was yet again larger than when Glerk had last glanced him. Astonishingly, though, even as he became larger and larger, Fyrian had somehow regained the use of his wings and was hovering overhead, peering over the rim of the trees.

"Luna is there," he called. "And she's with that uninteresting crow. I despise that crow. Luna loves me best."

"You don't despise anyone, Fyrian," Glerk countered. "It's not in your nature."

"And Xan is there. Auntie Xan! She is sick!"

Glerk nodded. He had feared as much. Still, at least she

was in human form. It would have been worse if she had been stuck in her transformed state, unable to say good-bye. "What else do you see, my friend?"

"A lady. Two ladies. There is the lady who moves like a tiger, and a different one. She doesn't have any hair. And she loves Luna. I can see it from here. Why would *she* love Luna? *We* love Luna!"

"That is a good question. As you know, Luna is a bit of a mystery. As was Xan, ever so long ago."

"And there is a man. And a lot of birds are gathered on the ground. I think they love Luna, too. They're all staring at her. And Luna is wearing her let's-make-trouble face."

Glerk nodded his broad head. He closed one eye and then the other and hugged himself with his four thick arms. "Well then, Fyrian," he said. "I suggest that we also make some trouble. I'll take the ground if you take the air."

"But what are we to do?"

"Fyrian, you were only a tiny dragon when it happened, but that woman there, the one who is all hunger and prowl, is the reason why your mother had to go into the volcano. She is a Sorrow Eater. She spreads misery and devours sorrow; it is the worst sort of magic. She is the reason why you were raised motherless, and why so many mothers were childless. I suggest we prevent her from making more sorrow, shall we?"

Fyrian was already in flight, screaming and streaking flames across the night sky.

"Sister Ignatia?" Antain was confused. "What are you doing here?"

"She's found us," whispered the woman with the paper birds. *No*, Luna thought, *not just a woman. My mother. That woman is my mother.* She could barely make sense of it. But deep inside her, she knew it was true.

Xan turned to the young man. "You wanted to find the Witch? This is your witch, my friend. You call her Sister Igna-tia?" She gave the stranger a skeptical look. "How fancy. I knew her by a different name, though I called her the monster when I was a child. She has been living off the Protectorate's sorrow for—how long has it been? Five hundred years. My goodness. That's something for the history books, isn't it? You must be very proud of yourself."

The stranger surveyed the scene, a small smile pressed into her mouth. *Sorrow Eater*, Luna thought. *A hateful term for a hateful person.*

"Well, well, well," the Sorrow Eater said. "Little, little Xan. It's been ever so long. And the years have not been kind to you, I'm afraid. And yes, I am terribly glad to see that you are impressed with my little sorrow farm. There is so much power in sorrow. Pity that your precious Zosimos was never able to see it. Fool of a man. Dead fool now, poor fellow. As you will be soon, dear Xan. As you should have been years ago."

The woman's magic surrounded her like a whirlwind, but

Luna could see even from a distance that it was empty at its center. She, like Xan, was depleting. With no ready source of sorrow nearby, she had nothing to restore her.

Luna unhooked her arm from her grandmother and stepped forward. Threads of magic unwound from the stranger and fluttered toward Luna and her own dense magic. The woman didn't seem to notice.

"Now what's all this silliness about rescuing that baby?" the stranger said.

Antain struggled to his feet, but the madwoman put her hand on his shoulder and held him back.

"She's trying to draw out your sorrow," the madwoman murmured, closing her eyes. "Don't let her. Hope instead. Hope without ceasing."

Luna took another step. She felt a bit more of the tall woman's magic unspool and draw toward her.

"Such a curious little thing," the Sorrow Eater said. "I knew another curious girl. So long ago. So many infernal *questions*. I wasn't sad when the volcano swallowed her up."

"Except that it didn't," Xan wheezed.

"It may as well have," the stranger sneered. "Look at you. Aged. Decrepit. What have you made? Nothing! And the stories they tell about you! I'd say that it would curl your hair"— she narrowed her eyes—"but I don't think your hair could take it."

The madwoman left Antain and moved toward Luna. Her

movements were slippery and slow, as though she was moving in a dream.

"Sister Ignatia!" Antain said. "How could you? The Protectorate looks to you as a voice of reason and learning." He faltered. "My baby is facing the Robes. *My son.* And Ethyne—whom you cared for as a daughter! It will break her spirit."

Sister Ignatia flared her nostrils and her brow darkened. "Do not say that ingrate's name in my presence. After all I did for her."

"There is a part of her that is still human," the madwoman whispered in Luna's ear. She put her hand on Luna's shoulder. And something inside Luna surged. It was all she could do to keep her feet on the ground. "I have heard her, in the Tower. She walks in her sleep, mourning something that she lost. She sobs; she weeps; she growls. When she wakes, she has no memory of it. It is walled off inside her."

This, Luna knew a bit about. She turned her attention to the memories sealed inside the Sorrow Eater.

Xan hobbled forward.

"The babies didn't die, you know," the old woman said, a mischievous grin curving across her wide mouth.

The stranger scoffed. "Don't be ridiculous. Of course they did. They starved, or they died of thirst. Wild animals ate them, sooner or later. That was the *point.*"

Xan took another step forward. She peered into the tall

woman's eyes, as though looking into a long, dark tunnel in the face of a rock. She squinted. "You're wrong. You couldn't see through the fog of sorrow you created. Just as I had difficulty looking *in*, you couldn't see *out*. All these years I've been traipsing right up to your door, and you had no idea. Isn't that *funny?*"

"It's nothing of the kind," the stranger said with a deep-throated growl. "It's only ridiculous. If you came near, I would know."

"No, dear lady. You didn't. Just as you don't know what happened to the babies. Every year, I came to the edge of that sad, sad place. Every year, I carried a child with me across the forest to the Free Cities, and there I placed the child with a loving family. And to my shame, its original family sorrowed needlessly. And you fed on that sorrow. You will not feed on Antain's sorrow. Or Ethyne's. Their baby will live with his parents, and he will grow and thrive. Indeed, while you have been prowling around the forest, your little sorrow fog has already lifted. The Protectorate now knows what it is to be free."

Sister Ignatia paled. "Lies," she said, but she stumbled and struggled to right herself. "What's happening?" she gasped.

Luna narrowed her eyes. The stranger had depleted almost all but the last remnants of her magic. Luna looked deeper. And there, in the space where the Sorrow Eater's heart should have been, was a tiny sphere—hard, shiny, and cold. A pearl. Over the years, she had walled off her heart, again and again, making it smooth and bright and unfeeling. And she likely hid other things in there as well—memories, hope, love, the weight of human emotion. Luna focused, the keenness of her eye boring inward, piercing the shine of the pearl.

The Sorrow Eater pressed her hands to her head. "Someone is taking my magic. Is it you, old woman?"

"What magic?" the madwoman said, stepping next to Xan, curling her arm around the old woman to keep her upright, and giving Sister Ignatia a hard look. "I didn't see any magic." She turned to Xan. "She makes things up, you know."

"Hush, you imbecile! You have no idea what you're talking about." The stranger wobbled, as though her legs had been turned suddenly turned to dough.

"Every night when I was a girl in the castle," Xan said, "you came to feed on the sorrow that seeped under my door."

"Every night in the Tower," the madwoman said, "you went from cell to cell, looking for sorrow. And when I learned to bottle mine up, to lock it away, you would snarl and howl."

"You're lying," the Sorrow Eater croaked. But they weren't— Luna could see the awful hunger of the Sorrow Eater. She could see her—even now—desperately looking for the tiniest bit of sorrow. Anything to fill the dark void inside her. "You don't know a single thing about me."

But Luna *did*. In her mind's eye, Luna could see the pearly heart of the Sorrow Eater floating in the air between them.

It had been hidden away for so long that Luna suspected the Sorrow Eater had forgotten it was even there. She turned it around and around, looking for chinks and crevices. There was a memory here. A beloved person. A loss. A flood of hope. A pit of despair. How many feelings can one heart hold? She looked at her grandmother. At her mother. At the man protecting his family. *Infinite*, Luna thought. *The way the universe is infinite.* It is light and dark and endless motion; it is space and time, and space within space, and time within time. And she knew: *there is no limit to what the heart can carry.*

*It's awful to be cut off from your own memories*, Luna thought. *If I know anything, I know that now. Here. Let me help you.*

Luna concentrated. The pearl cracked. The Sorrow Eater's eyes went terribly wide.

"Some of us," Xan said, "choose love over power. Indeed, most of us do."

Luna pressed her attention into the crack. With a flick of her left wrist, she forced it open. And sorrow rushed out.

"Oh!" the Sorrow Eater said, pressing her hands to her chest.

"YOU!" came a voice from above.

Luna looked up and felt a scream erupt in her throat. She saw an enormous dragon hovering just overhead. It soared in a spiral, pulling closer and closer to the middle. It erupted fire into the sky. It looked familiar, somehow.

"Fyrian?"

Sister Ignatia tore at her chest. Her sorrow leaked onto the ground.

"Oh no. Oh, no, no, no." Her eyes went heavy with tears. She choked on her own sobbing.

"My *mother*," the dragon-who-looked-like-Fyrian shouted. *"My mother died and it is your fault."* The dragon dove down and skidded to a halt, sending sprays of gravel in every direction.

"My mother," the Sorrow Eater mumbled, barely noticing the enormous dragon bearing down on her. "My mother and my father and my sisters and my brothers. My village and my friends. All gone. All that was left was sorrow. Sorrow and memory and memory and sorrow."

Possibly-Fyrian grabbed the Sorrow Eater by the waist, holding her up high. She went limp, like a doll.

"I should burn you up!" the dragon said.

"FYRIAN!" Glerk was running up the mountain, moving faster than Luna had thought it was possible for him to move. "Fyrian, put her down at once. You have no idea what you're doing."

"Yes, I do," Fyrian said. "She's wicked."

"Fyrian, stop!" Luna cried, clutching at the dragon's leg.

"I miss her," Fyrian sobbed. "My *mother*. I miss her so much. This witch should pay for what she's done."

Glerk stood tall as a mountain. He was serene as a bog. He looked at Fyrian with all the love in the world. "No, Fyrian. That answer is too easy, my friend. Look deeper."

Fyrian shut his eyes. He did not put down the Sorrow Eater. Great tears poured from beneath his clenched lids and fell in steaming dollops to the ground.

Luna looked deeper, past the layers of memory wrapped around the heart-turned-pearl. What she saw astonished her. "She walled off her sorrow," Luna whispered. "She covered it up and pressed it in, tighter and tighter and tighter. And it was so hard, and heavy, and dense that it bent the light around it. It sucked everything inside. Sorrow sucking sorrow. She turned hungry for it. And the more she fed on it, the more she needed. And then she discovered that she could transform it into magic. And she learned how to increase the sorrow around her. She grew sorrow the way a farmer grows wheat and meat and milk. And she gorged herself on misery."

The Sorrow Eater sobbed. Her sorrow leaked from her eyes and her mouth and her ears. Her magic was gone. Her collected sorrow was going. Soon there would be nothing at all.

The ground shook. Great plumes of smoke poured from the crater of the volcano. Fyrian shook. "I should throw you in the volcano for what you did," he said, his voice catching in his throat. "I should eat you in one bite and never think of you again. Just as you never thought of my mother again."

"Fyrian," Xan said, holding out her arms. "My precious Fyrian. My Simply Enormous boy."

Fyrian began to cry again. He released the Sorrow Eater,

who fell in a heap on the rock. "Auntie Xan!" he whimpered. "I feel so many things!"

"Of course you do, darling." Xan beckoned the dragon to come close. She put her hands on either side of his enlarged face and kissed his tremendous nose. "You have a Simply Enormous heart. As you always have. There are things to do with our Sorrow Eater, but the volcano is not one of them. And if you ate her you would get a stomachache. So."

Luna cocked her head. The Sorrow Eater's heart was in pieces. She would not be able to repair it without magic—and now her magic was gone. Almost at once, the Sorrow Eater began to age.

The ground shook again. Fyrian looked around. "It's not just the peak. The vents are open, and the air will be bad for Luna. Everyone else, too, probably."

The woman without hair—the madwoman (*No*, Luna thought. *Not the madwoman. My mother. She is my mother.* The word made her shiver) looked down at her boots and smiled. "My boots can take us to where we need to go in no time. Send Sister Ignatia and the monster with the dragon. I'll put the rest of you on my back, and we'll run to the Protectorate. They need to be warned about the volcano."

The moon went out. The stars went out. Thick smoke covered the sky.

*My mother*, Luna thought. *This is my mother. The woman*

on the ceiling. *The hands in the window of the Tower. She is here, she is here, she is here.* Luna's heart was infinite. She climbed aboard her mother's back and laid her cheek against her mother's neck and closed her eyes tight. Luna's mother scooped up Xan as tender as could be, and instructed Antain and Luna to hang on to her shoulders, as the crow hung on to Luna.

"Be careful with Glerk," Luna called to Fyrian. The dragon held the Sorrow Eater in his hands, extended as far from his body as they could be, as though he found her repellant. The monster clung to his back, just as Fyrian had clung to Glerk for years.

"I'm always careful with Glerk," Fyrian said primly. "He's delicate."

The ground shook. It was time to go.

# 46

## In Which Several Families Are Reunited

The people of the Protectorate saw a cloud of dust and smoke speeding toward the town walls.

"The volcano!" one man cried. "The volcano has legs! And it is coming this way!"

"Don't be ridiculous," a woman countered. "Volcanoes don't have legs. It's the Witch. She's coming for us at last. Just as we knew she would."

"Does anyone else see a giant bird coming closer that kind of looks like a dragon?—though of course that's impossible. Dragons no longer exist. Right?"

The madwoman skidded to a halt at the wall, letting Antain and Luna tumble from her back. Antain wasted no time, entering the Protectorate's gates at a run. Luna stayed as the madwoman gently set Xan down on the ground and helped her to her feet.

"Are you all right?" the madwoman said. Her eyes darted this way and that, never settling on one place for very long. Her face cycled through a myriad of expressions, one after another after another. She was, Luna could see, quite mad. Or, perhaps, not mad at all, but broken. And broken things can sometimes be mended. She took her mother's hand, and hoped.

"I need to get high up," Luna said. "I need to make something that will protect the town and its people when that thing explodes." She pointed at the volcano's smoking peak with her chin, and her heart constricted a bit. Her tree house. Their garden. The chickens and the goats. Glerk's beautiful swamp. All of it would be gone in a few moments—if it wasn't already. Consequences. Everything was consequences.

The madwoman led Luna and Xan into the gates and up onto the wall.

There was magic in her mother. Luna could feel it. But it wasn't the same as Luna's magic. Luna's magic was infused in every bone, every tissue, every cell. Her mother's magic was more like a jumble of trinkets left in a basket after a long journey—bits and pieces knocking together. Still, Luna could feel her mother's magic—as well as her mother's longing and love—buzzing against her skin. It emboldened the power surging inside her, directing the swells of magic. Luna held her mother's hand a little bit tighter.

Fyrian, Glerk, and the nearly unconscious Sorrow Eater alighted next to them.

The people of the Protectorate screamed and ran from the wall, even as Antain desperately called out that they had nothing to fear. Xan looked up at the smoking peak. "There's plenty to fear," she said grimly. "It just doesn't come from us."

The ground shook.

Antain called for Ethyne.

Fyrian called for Xan.

"Caw, caw, caw," said the crow. "Luna, Luna, Luna," he meant.

Glerk called for everyone to hush a moment so he could think.

The volcano sent forth a column of fire and smoke, swallowed power un-swallowed at last.

"Can we stop it?" Luna whispered.

"No," Xan said. "It was stopped before, long ago, but that was a mistake. A good man died for nothing. A good dragon, too. Volcanoes erupt and the world changes. This is the way of things. But we can protect. I can't by myself—not anymore—and I suspect that you can't on your own. But together." She looked at Luna's mother. "Together, I think we can."

"I don't know how, Grandmama." Luna tried to surpress a

sob. There were too many things to know, and not enough time to know them. Xan took Luna's other hand. "Do you remember when you were a little girl, and I showed you how to make bubbles around the blooms of flowers, holding them inside?"

Luna nodded.

Xan smiled. "Come. Not all knowledge comes from the mind. Your body, your heart, your intuition. Sometimes memories even have minds of their own. Those bubbles we made— the flowers were safe inside. Remember? Make bubbles. Bubbles inside of bubbles. Bubbles of magic. Bubbles of ice. Bubbles of glass and iron and starlight. Bubbles of bog. The material is less consequential than the intention. Use your imagination and picture each one. Around each house, each garden, each tree, each farm. Around the whole town. Around the towns of the Free Cities. Bubbles and bubbles and bubbles. Surround. Protect. We'll use your magic, the three of us together. Close your eyes and I'll show you what to do."

With her fingers curled into the fingers of her mother and grandmother, Luna felt something in her bones—a rush of heat and light, moving from the core of the earth to the roof of the sky, back and forth and back and forth. Magic. Starlight. Moonlight. Memory. Her heart had so much love, it began pouring forth. Like a volcano.

The mountain shattered. Fire rained. Ash darkened the sky. The bubbles glowed in the heat and wobbled under the weight of wind and fire and dust. Luna held on tight.

Three weeks later, Antain hardly recognized his home. There was still *so much ash*. Stone and the remnants of broken trees littered the streets of the Protectorate. The wind carried volcanic ash and forest fire ash and ash that no one wanted to identify down the slope of the mountain and deposited it in the streets. By day, the sun barely peeked through the smoky haze, and at night the stars and moon remained invisible. Luna sent rains washing down the Protectorate and the wood and the ruined mountain, which helped to clear the air a little. Still, there was much left to be done.

People smiled hopefully, despite the mess. The Council of Elders languished in prison, and new council members were elected by popular vote. The name Gherland became a common insult. Wyn ran and maintained the library in the Tower, which welcomed all visitors. And finally, the Road opened, allowing citizens of the Protectorate, for the first time in their lives, to venture forth. Though not many did. Not at first.

In the center of these changes stood Ethyne—all reason and possibility, and a hot cup of tea, with a baby strapped to her chest. Antain held his small family close. *I shall never leave you again,* he murmured, mostly to himself. *Never, never, never.*

✧

Both Xan and the Sorrow Eater had been moved to the hospital wing of the Tower. Once people understood what Sister

Ignatia had done, there were calls for her imprisonment, but with every moment, the life that had been so extended in both women dwindled, bit by bit.

*Any day now,* Xan thought. *Any moment.* She had no fear of death. Only curiosity. She had no idea what the Sorrow Eater thought.

❉

Ethyne and Antain moved Luna and her mother into the baby's room, assuring them that Luken didn't need his own room, and anyway they couldn't bear to be parted from him even for a moment.

Ethyne transformed the room into a place of healing for both mother and daughter. Soft surfaces. Thick curtains for when the day became unbearable. Pretty flowers in jars. And paper. So much paper (though there always seemed to be more, and more and more). The madwoman took to drawing. Sometimes Luna helped. Ethyne prescribed soup and healing herbs. And rest. And endless love. She was fully prepared to provide all of it.

Meanwhile, Luna set herself to discovering her mother's name. She went door to door, asking anyone who would talk to her—which wasn't many at first. People in the Protectorate didn't love her implicitly as people in the Free Cities did. Which was a bit of a shock, to be honest.

*This will take some getting used to,* Luna thought.

After days of asking, and days of searching, she returned to her mother at suppertime, kneeling at her feet.

"Adara," she said. She pulled out her journal and showed her mother the pictures she had drawn, back before they had ever met. A woman on the ceiling. A baby in her arms. A tower with a hand extended from the windows. A child in a circle of trees. "Your name is Adara. It's all right if you don't remember it. I'll keep saying it until you do. And just as your mind went skittering in every direction trying to find me, so did my heart go wandering trying to find *you*. Look here. I even drew a map. 'She is here, she is here, she is here.'" Luna closed the journal and looked into Adara's face. "You are here, you are here, you are here. And so am I."

Adara said nothing. She let her hand drift onto Luna's hand. She curled her fingers against the girl's palm.

✻

Luna, Ethyne, and Adara went to visit the former Grand Elder in prison. Adara's hair had begun to grow. It curled around her face in big, black hooks, framing her large, black eyes.

Gherland frowned as they walked in. "I should have drowned you in the river," he said to Luna with a scowl. "Don't think I don't recognize you. I do. Each one of you insufferable children has haunted my dreams. I would see you grow and grow even when I knew you had died."

"But we didn't die," Luna said. "None of us did. Perhaps

that was what your dreams were telling you. Perhaps you should learn to listen."

"I'm not listening to you," he said.

Adara knelt down next to the old man. She laid her hand on his knee. "The new council has said that you can be pardoned as soon as you are willing to apologize."

"Then I shall rot in here," the former Grand Elder huffed. "Apologize? The very idea!"

"Whether you apologize or not is irrelevant," Ethyne said kindly. "I forgive you, Uncle. With my whole heart. As does my husband. When you apologize, however, you may begin healing *yourself*. It is not for us. It is for you. I recommend it."

"I would like to see my nephew," Gherland said, a tiny crack in his imperious voice. "Please. Tell him to come and see me. I long to see his dear face."

"Are you going to apologize?" Ethyne asked.

"*Never*," Gherland spat.

"That is a pity," Ethyne said. "Good-bye, Uncle."

And they left without another word.

The Grand Elder maintained his position. He remained in prison for the rest of his days. Eventually, people stopped visiting, and they stopped mentioning him—even in jest. And in time, they forgot about him altogether.

✺

Fyrian continued to grow. Each day he flew across the forest and reported back what he had seen. "The lake is gone, filled with ash. And the workshop is gone. And Xan's house. And the swamp. The Free Cities are still there, though. They were unharmed."

Riding on Fyrian's back, Luna visited each one of the Free Cities in turn. While the residents were happy to see Luna, they were shocked not to see Xan, and, at the news of her ill health, the Free Cities grieved as one. They weren't so sure about the dragon, but when they saw how gentle he was with the children, they relaxed a bit.

Luna told them the story of a town that was under the control of a terrible Witch, who held them prisoner under a cloud of sorrow. She told them about the children. About the terrible Day of Sacrifice. About the other Witch, who found the children in the forest and brought them to safety, not knowing what horrors had delivered them into this predicament in the first place.

"Oh!" cried the citizens of the Free Cities. "Oh, oh, oh!"

And the families of the Star Children held the hands of their sons and daughters a little more tightly.

"I was taken from my mother," Luna explained. "Like you, I was brought to a family who loved me and whom I love. I cannot stop loving that family, and I don't want to. I can only allow my love to increase." She smiled. "I love the grandmother who raised me. I love the mother I lost. My love is boundless. My heart is infinite. And my joy expands and expands. You'll see."

In town after town, she said the same thing. And then she climbed onto Fyrian's back and returned to her grandmother.

✻

Glerk refused to leave Xan's side. His skin grew cracked and itchy without the daily wash of his beloved swamp water. Every day, he looked longingly at the Bog. Luna asked the former Sisters—friends of Ethyne's—to please keep buckets at the ready to douse him when he needed it, but well water just wasn't the same. Eventually, Xan told him to stop being such a silly and walk down to the Bog for a daily bath.

"I can't stand the thought of you suffering, dearest," Xan whispered, her withered hands on the great beast's face. "Plus—and don't take this the wrong way—but you stink." She took a rattling breath. "And I love you."

Glerk laid his hands on her face. "When you're ready, Xan, my darling, darling Xan, you may come with me. Into the Bog."

✻

As Xan's health began to fail more rapidly, Luna informed her mother and her hosts that she would be sleeping in the Tower.

"My grandmother needs me," she said. "And I need to be near my grandmother."

Adara's eyes filled with tears when Luna said it. Luna took her hand. "My love isn't divided," she said. "It is multiplied." And she kissed her mother and returned to her grandmother, curling up next to her night after night.

�֍

The day the first wave of Star Children returned to the Protectorate, the former Sisters threw open the windows of the hospital.

The Sorrow Eater by now looked as old as dust. Her skin crinkled over her bones like old paper. Her eyes were sightless and hollow. "Close the window," she rasped. "I can't bear to hear it."

"Leave it open," Xan whispered. "I can't bear not to."

Xan, too, was a dry husk. She hardly breathed. *Any moment now,* Luna thought as she sat by Xan's side, holding her tiny hand, as light as feathers.

The Sisters left the windows open wide. Cries of joy wafted into the room. The Sorrow Eater cried out in pain. Xan sighed with happiness. Luna gently squeezed her hand.

"I love you, Grandmama."

"I know, darling," Xan wheezed. "I love . . ."

And she drifted away, loving everything.

# 47

# In Which Glerk Goes on a Journey, and Leaves a Poem Behind

Later that night, the room was quiet and utterly still. Fyrian had ceased his howling at the foot of the Tower and had gone to sob and sleep in the garden; Luna had returned to the open arms of her mother, and those of Antain and Ethyne—another odd, beloved family for an odd, beloved girl. Perhaps she would sleep in the room with her mother. Perhaps she would curl up outside with her dragon and her crow. Perhaps her world was larger than it was before—as it is for children when they are no longer children. Things had become as they should be, Glerk thought. He pressed his four hands to his heart for a moment, then slipped into the shadows and returned to Xan's side.

It was time to go. And he was ready.

Her eyes were closed. Her mouth was open. She did not breathe. She was dust and stalk and stillness. The stuff of Xan was there, but the spark was not.

There was no moon, but the stars were bright. Brighter than normal. Glerk gathered the light in his hands. He wound the strands together, weaving them into a bright, shimmering quilt. He wrapped them around the old woman and lifted her to his chest.

She opened her eyes.

"Why, Glerk," she said. She looked around. The room was quiet, except for the creaking of frogs. It was cold, except for the heat of mud underneath. It was dark, except for the shine of the sun on the reeds, and the shimmer of the Bog under the sky.

"Where are we?" she asked.

She was an old woman. She was a girl. She was somewhere in between. She was all of those things at once.

Glerk smiled. "In the beginning, there was the Bog. And the Bog covered the world and the Bog was the world and the world was the Bog."

Xan sighed. "I know this story."

"But the Bog was lonely. It wanted a world. It wanted eyes with which to see the world. It wanted a strong back with which to carry itself from place to place. It wanted legs to walk and hands to touch and a mouth that could sing. And so the Bog was a Beast and the Beast was the Bog. And then the Beast sang the world into being. And the world and the Beast and the Bog were all of one substance, and they were all bound by infinite love."

"Are you taking me to the Bog, Glerk?" Xan asked. She pulled herself from his embrace and stood on her own two feet.

"It's all the same. Don't you see? The Beast, the Bog, the Poem, the Poet, the world. They all love you. They've loved you this whole time. Will you come with me?"

And Xan took Glerk's hand, and they turned their faces toward the endless Bog, and began walking. They didn't look back.

☼

The next day, Luna and her mother made the long walk to the Tower, up the stairs, and to that small room to gather the last of Xan's things, and to prepare her body for her last journey to the ground. Adara wound her arm around Luna's shoulder, an antidote to sorrow. Luna stepped out of her mother's protective embrace, grabbing Adara's hand instead. And together they opened the door.

The former Sisters were waiting for them in the empty room. "We don't know what happened," they said, their eyes bright with tears. The bed was empty, and cold. There was no sign of Xan anywhere.

Luna felt her heart go numb. She looked at her mother, who had the same eyes. The same mark on the brow. *There is no love without loss*, she thought. *My mother knows this. Now I know it, too.* Her mother gave her hand a tender squeeze and pressed her lips against the girl's black hair. Luna sat on the bed, but she did not cry. Instead, her hand drifted to the bed, where she found a piece of paper tucked just under the pillow.

> "*The heart is built of starlight*
> *And time.*
> *A pinprick of longing lost in the dark.*
> *An unbroken chord linking the Infinite to the Infinite.*
> *My heart wishes upon your heart and the wish is granted.*
> *Meanwhile the world spins.*
> *Meanwhile the universe expands.*
> *Meanwhile the mystery of love reveals itself,*
> *again and again, in the mystery of you.*
> *I have gone.*
> *I will return.*
> *Glerk*"

Luna dried her eyes and folded the poem into the shape of a swallow. It sat motionless in her hand. She went outside, leaving her mother behind. The sun was just beginning to rise. The sky was pink and orange and dark blue. Somewhere, a monster and a witch wandered the world. And it was good, she decided. It was very, very good.

The wings of the paper swallow began to shiver. They

opened. They beat. The swallow tilted its head toward the girl.

"It's all right," she said. Her throat hurt. Her chest hurt. Love hurt. So why was she happy? "The world is good. Go see it."

And the bird leaped into the sky and flew away.

# 48

## In Which a Final Story Is Told

*Yes.*

*There is a witch in the woods.*

*Well, of course there is a witch. She came round the house just yesterday. You've seen her, I've seen her, we've all seen her.*

*Well, of course she doesn't just advertise her witchiness. It would be rude. What a thing to say!*

*She turned magic when she was just a baby. Another witch, an ancient witch, filled her to bursting with more power than she knew what to do with. And the magic flowed and flowed from the old witch into the new, the way water flows down the mountain. That's what happens when a witch claims someone as her own—someone to be protected above all else. The magic flows and flows until there is no more left to give.*

That's how our Witch claimed us. The whole Protectorate. We are hers and she is ours. Her magic blesses us and all that we see. It blesses the farms and the orchards and the gardens. It blesses the Bog and the Forest and even the Volcano. It blesses us all equally. This is why the people of the Protectorate are healthy and hale and shining. This is why our children are rosy-cheeked and clever. This is why we have happiness in abundance.

Once upon a time, the Witch received a poem from the Beast of the Bog. Perhaps it was the poem that made the world. Perhaps it was the poem that will end it. Perhaps it is something else entirely. All I know is that the Witch keeps it safe in a locket under her cloak. She belongs to us, but one day her magic will fade and she will wander back into the Bog and we won't have a witch anymore. Only stories. Perhaps she will find the Beast. Or become the Beast. Or become the Bog. Or become a Poem. Or become the world. They are all the same thing, you know.

‿The End‿

*For the first time ever in print: Kelly Barnhill's story about Xan's girlhood and her first encounter with magic . . .*

# In Which a Lost Girl Discovers Bees

The girl lay on the table in the central workshop dreaming of bees again.

Or still.

Perhaps she had always been dreaming of bees.

"I told you this was a bad idea," a man said from . . . *somewhere.* His voice set off a flood of murmurs. Or they sounded like murmurs. Perhaps they were more bees.

In her dream, the bees landed on her body—great, soft, swarming masses of them, all pollen and summer and sting. They gathered on her hands and face. They covered her skin. She wasn't afraid. Why should she be? They were just bees.

*Bees,* she thought, delighting at the swarm in her dream. *Bees, bees, bees.*

"Did she say something?" the man from somewhere said.

Other voices murmured in response.

Perhaps they were other people.

The girl hoped they were bees.

"She's speaking," one voice said.

"No," said another. "She's listening."

*Blossom*, her dream voice said. *Petal.*

The voices gasped.

*Honey and stamen. Leaf and root.* Each word, once sounded, gave her a thrill. She had only just learned them. She had known them all her life. Both things were true. She was missing something. Something important. And the missing of it gave her an ache in her chest.

"She is sorrowing," someone said. A hungry voice.

"Step back," the man said with a growl. "And anyway, she's not sorrowing, and she's not speaking neither. She's singing. Don't you dolts know a song when you hear it?"

The murmurs grew louder.

Was she sorrowing? The girl didn't know. She wasn't sure what that meant. Was she singing? She had no idea.

She didn't know her name. She didn't know anything outside what her dreams taught her. And then . . .

She looked around. Blinked.

"She's awake," a man said, his spyglasses falling from their braces on his face.

"She's alive," a woman said, furiously scribbling notes on a stack of papers.

The girl pulled her knees to her chest. She didn't know where she was or who these people were. She missed her dream. She also missed . . . something else. Something she couldn't remember. The loss of the bees and the tree was so real, so *immediate*, that she felt her heart splinter in her chest.

"Come back," she choked. Her mouth was dry. Her lips had begun to crack. How long had she been sleeping?

"How she sorrows," said a woman at the back, her face hidden by shadow. The girl could see only the way the woman paced along the wall, back and forth, like an animal in a cage.

The room was crowded with men and women in strange clothes and an odd assortment of tools. One man wore metal extensions on the fingers of his left hand, each ending in a bright point. Tiny baubles hung in another man's silver mustache, catching the light each time he spoke, sparkling like stars. A small woman moved about on mechanical legs that made her the tallest in the room. The legs creaked each time she walked. A woman with green skin had a third eye positioned right below her throat.

And then that woman in the back, separate from everyone else in the room, pacing.

The girl stared at the adults. The adults stared at the girl. And, like a sudden storm, the questions began.

"Tell us, in detail, how you feel."

"Any pain? Any pain anywhere?"

"What taste do you have in your mouth right now? Is it animal, vegetable, or mineral?

"Exactly how sad *are* you? Can you express it in numbers?"

"Earthquake or wave? Your magic, I mean. When it arrived. Please be specific."

"Have you been able to effect transformations in your dreams? Will you tell us when you can?"

"Any current murderous tendencies? Toward anyone specific, or in general?"

The questions came thick and fast without any explanation or context. No one was kind. The girl closed her eyes.

The strange adults with their strange tools continued to pester, so the girl drew herself into a tight knot, laying her forehead on her knees and gripping her ankles, and she let out a long, high scream.

The table beneath her shattered, sending stony shards scattering, cutting skin and dumping ink and careening into open eyes. The commotion and hullabaloo and panicked coming and going would have delighted the girl had she been watching it from afar.

And then she felt a sharp knock on the back of her head and saw a brief flash of light, followed by nothing at all.

❄

Zosimos, an ancient wizard in the group of magicians (trapped, he felt, in a sea of nincompoops), couldn't stand this persistent nonsense for another second.

"*Enough*," he bellowed. Using a combination of a few swift kicks, two well-aimed spells, and enough foul language to make even the saltiest among them blush, he cleared the room of witches and magicians and wizards and scholars within a few moments of the table's explosion.

No one was happy with him. But that wasn't particularly unusual.

"I say!"

"Manners!"

"This is for science, you old fool. *Science!*"

He refused to dignify their protestations with a response.

*Science!* he thought. *You idiots have no idea what that means.* He stomped his foot against the granite floor, causing it to ripple like water, knocking the last of the magicians to their knees and carrying them in wave after wave into the hall. The door slammed behind them.

The old castle groaned, and Zosimos could hear the crackle of spidery fissures along the pillars and beams. "Sorry, old thing," he whispered, directing a spell for healing at the foundations. A temporary salve, alas, but it was better than nothing.

Zosimos looked down at the tangle of arms and legs and patchwork clothing and long braids sprawled over the rubble on the ground. Magic, too. So much magic.

*Poor child. She never asked for any of this.*

She would have to be moved, the wizard knew. Away from the magicians and their incessant meddling. For now, anyway. The question was *how.*

Zosimos eyed her warily.

The girl had obliterated a table made from a block of the densest stone in the world. Was it the squeeze of her eyelids that had caused the explosion? Or the note of her scream? Magic manifests differently depending on who touches it, and even more differently in the rare cases of full bodily enmagickment like this. The changes inflicted on her were irrevocable. She was enmagicked forever.

He took care before picking her up.

"Come now, little thing," he said, first fitting a leather apron reinforced with lead over his clothing and then sliding his hands into iron gloves. Even then he winced when he curled his arms under her back and hefted her to his chest.

*They shouldn't have done this to her. They should have asked me first.* Such things were supposedly only possible with babies. Half-grown children required a process that Zozimos did not want to think about. The descriptions alone turned his stomach.

It was a miracle that it had worked. It was a miracle that she hadn't died.

Bodily enmagickment was a rare thing, only attempted once in a generation or more. Zosimos had never met anyone else enmagicked as he was, and he had assumed he was the only one in the world. And perhaps he had been. Until now.

"Bunch of irresponsible dunderheads," he muttered as he gingerly made his way through a gap in the wall that only he could see, down the hidden stairs, into the labyrinth of cellars, and along the bottom corridor that opened out to an underground stream. The stream poured out of a little cave in a heavily wooded area on the western slopes, a good ways away from the castle itself. No one else knew about the gap, or the stairs, or the corridor, or the stream, or the cave. They belonged to Zosimos alone.

The girl was heavy—heavier than she looked. "Blasted *magic*," the wizard grumbled.

"Is that you, old friend?" a rumbly voice said from a short way down the mountain. Four heavy paws shifted on the stony slope. A tremendous tail uncurled into the green, and a magnificent pair of jaws widened in a yawn.

"Ennyn," Zosimos said. The scales on the enormous dragon's back gleamed brightly, illuminating the wood. At least the day was cloudy. On bright days, it was difficult to look at the tremendous creature head on.

"With humility and grace," Zosimos huffed. He had difficulty remembering the words. "Aaaannnd," he struggled under the weight of the girl. His arms began to shake. "Oh, bother." There was a particular pattern of gestures and phrases with which one was to greet a dragon: eye contact followed by eye aversion, a bow, a clasp of hands, and a salute. Zozimos had counted Ennyn among his few friends for nearly a century now, but he did not take that friendship for granted. Dragons are sensitive, after all, and self-conscious. Respect matters.

"Forgive me." His breath changed from gasps to painful wheezing. "For putting my manners aside." He crinkled his face to divert the rivulets of sweat from his eyes. "This one is heavy."

The dragon inclined her head. The trees bent as she pushed

forward. She raised one glittering eyebrow. And then her eyes went suddenly wide.

"They didn't," she breathed.

"They did," Zosimos sighed.

"She hasn't been—" Ennyn whispered. "Is she . . . like you?"

"Alas. She has been. And she is. I was not consulted, obviously." He stumbled toward a grassy hollow and gently lowered the girl to the ground. He sank back on his haunches. *Troublesome thing*, he thought. *Already so troublesome.*

Underneath the dragon's broad belly, an egg the size of a small basket sat on a soft pile of feathers and moss. It wriggled and smoked and vibrated. Zosimos knew better than to look too closely at a dragon's egg.

"Not hatched yet, is he?" Zosimos asked politely, keeping his eyes on the mother.

"Not yet. Soon. I will tell him when it is time."

The girl rolled onto her side, murmuring in her sleep.

"Any mishaps yet?" the mother dragon asked.

Zosimos shrugged. "Just an explosion." He creased his brow. "Could have been worse. In any case, she managed to spook the lot of them. It bought me some time."

The great dragon inclined her head even further, until her massive jaws were nearly touching the girl. She closed her eyes and inhaled deeply. The girl did not stir.

"Honey," the dragon said. "Pollen and wax. Were her parents bee keepers?"

"Unknown," Zosimos sighed.

"Well." The mother dragon pulled her haunches under the shimmering curve of her torso and uncurled her long neck until the top of her head was nearly level with the trees. She tilted her skull to one side, and then the other, cracking her spine. Then she leaned on her forearms, tilting forward and thrusting her face into the magician's.

Even though he knew Ennyn was his friend, Zosimos felt his knees begin to shake.

"She isn't staying here." Ennyn's voice was quieter than one would expect from a creature so large. But even in its quiet, it shook the mountain and sparked a tremble in the old wizard's bones.

"Oh, but she is," Zosimos said, hoping he sounded braver than he felt. "She doesn't have anywhere else to go. Not yet, anyway."

"And what about the baby?" Ennyn said, her eyes narrowing to two bright slits.

"I can't imagine that any spell—no matter how volatile—could possibly penetrate dragon shell. The girl must stay here, away from the magicians, while I try to understand the best way to help her. In the meantime, you must do what you can to find out her name. Try to help her remember. Also—" He gave the massive dragon a skeptical stare. "Do try not to frighten her, will you? She's delicate."

❧

On the morning of her first day in the dragon's lair, the girl opened her eyes, saw the enormous creature looming above her, saw the intolerable brightness of the monster's scales, saw the merciless sheen on the razor sharp edges of each terrible tooth, screamed—and fainted.

"Oh dear," Ennyn muttered. Because Ennyn was a very good mother—or she hoped she would be some day—she found a bit of moss and put it under the girl to give her something soft to lie upon. With the freshly plucked down from the nine geese that she had eaten for lunch, she made a nest around the girl to keep her warm. She pulled a honeycomb from a nearby hive, mixed it with fresh spring water, and dripped it, little by little, into the girl's mouth.

The second morning the girl woke and saw that the dragon was not only looming over her with those massive jaws but apparently stroking her with the padded undersides of those cruelly tipped claws. The creature opened its mouth; the girl screamed again and was once again struck unconscious with fright.

"Bother," the dragon said. But, because it couldn't be helped, she continued to care for the child as before.

On the morning of the third day, the dragon was ready. She crouched a little ways away from the girl, and tried to make herself as small as could be. The girl opened her eyes, stretched, looked around a bit, and—

"Wait!" Ennyn said before the girl could scream. "I'm not going to hurt you."

The girl pressed her lips together. She wrinkled her brow. She looked as though she was trying to remember something. Finally, she spoke.

"M-monster," the girl said, her lips shaking as she formed the word.

"Truly I am not. I am a friend."

Large tears appeared in the girl's eyes.

"M-mother," she managed, her lips tripping on the sounds.

"Alas. You are missing yours. But I am a mother—or I soon will be. And I will take care of you."

This was too much, Ennyn realized, for the girl had begun to cry—huge tears bubbling out of her eyes and falling in gushes to the ground. And before the dragon could comfort the child, the tears had soaked the moss, causing it to enlarge upon itself until it was the size and shape and structure of a small house, with an open door and shutters on the windows. Moreover, each feather touched by a tear became a toddling gosling, stumbling and tumbling through the grass looking for bugs.

The girl was so shocked she could hardly speak.

"How—" she began, her voice tumbling over the simplest words. "How did that happen?"

The dragon cleared her throat. "Right," she said. "Listen, you should probably sit down. Oh. I see that you are. There is this small side matter to discuss, regarding your magic."

And, patiently, tenderly, the dragon explained things to the girl. The great, sinewy bulk of her crept slowly toward the shaking child, curled a wing around those tiny shoulders, and, eventually, scooped her close, holding her tight and protecting her from harm.

Back in the castle, the other magicians had worked themselves into a frenzy.

"It isn't that we wanted to lie to you, old friend," Lady Tenyik said after cornering Zosimos in the archive room. "It's just that we knew that you'd tell us not to do it."

The old wizard paused a moment to glare at her. Then he gathered the documents he needed into a large leather portfolio and hurried out of the room.

"What on *earth* have you done with her, you ridiculous old man," the Estimable Fitz fumed as he followed the old wizard through the corridors of the oldest library. Though Zosimos outaged the Estimable Fitz by several centuries, the young magician had trouble keeping up with the elder wizard. He stumbled and huffed and kept having to readjust his spyglasses as they hurried past stack after stack. Every once in a while, Zosimos would spy a book that interested him and, with a flick of his left wrist, magick it off the shelf and onto the growing tower of books that floated and bobbed behind them like an oddly shaped balloon.

"I am talking to you, wizard. I will not tolerate this perpetual ignoring!" the magician said, gesticulating widely until he knocked his hand hard against a wall.

Zosimos continued to ignore him, keeping his own eyes on the ancient spines in the long rows of bookshelves and muttering to himself—often in languages that the magician did not know. Volume after volume skittered from shelf to floating stack.

"You bury yourself in books, but here we have a living, breathing specimen that we may—"

Swifter than the Estimable Fitz would have thought possible, Zosimos turned on his heel, knocked the magician's spyglass off his face with the heel of one hand, and grabbed him by the throat with the other. Using the force of his body (and some magic, too) Zosimos pinned the younger man against the bookshelf.

"Well," the Estimable Fitz gasped. "There is no call for—"

"If you ever call that child a specimen again, you'll get worse than this," the old man said. "She has a name."

"Yes, but I do not know what it is," the magician said. He gave the wizard a narrowed look. "Do you?"

"She has a name," the wizard repeated, letting the magician fall to the ground. "And it doesn't belong to you." He motioned for the stack of books to follow him as he exited through the back door.

Lady Ignit was waiting for him there. She was a good head and shoulders taller than the wizard, and her curved gait made him think of a tiger when it prowls. She was all muscle and hunger and predatory pounce.

"She belongs to me," Lady Ignit said, her voice so low it was almost a whisper. "I found her. I saved her. She is mine now. That is the way of things."

"And then you put her in harm's way. Or perhaps you, dear lady, *are* the harm. In any case the magic binding you to her was disrupted. She belongs to no one. Only herself." He hoped this was true.

Lady Ignit showed her teeth. "You can't keep me from her. You know you can't. The cord that binds me to her is stronger than your paltry magic."

"That's where you're wrong," Zosimos said, skirting from her grasp and hurrying down the hall.

He checked over his shoulder. Again. And again. She wasn't following him. He was sure of it.

✵

The girl still did not know her name.

Strangely, this didn't seem to bother her.

The old man had come and gone for two weeks. Ennyn explained that he was kind. The girl wasn't so sure. He was cranky. He liked to bark orders too much. And fuss at her for not learning. And not knowing. How could she learn and how could she know? The world she came from was all a muddle. Her few memories were fuzzy and barbed—they hurt if she grasped too tightly.

"Surely you must have *some* recollection," Zosimos said. He kept looking over his shoulder. "Were you named for a bird, for example? Are you Heron or Crow or Wren? Are you Feather or Claw?"

"No," said the girl.

"Are you Ocean or Meadow or Glen?"

"I don't think so," the girl said.

"Useless," the wizard said. And the mother dragon scooped her up again and cradled her in her great wings.

"Enough," the dragon said.

"You're coddling her," the wizard fumed. "Do you realize what we're up against?"

"Do you realize that you're a cranky old toad?" For a creature of her size, Ennyn had surprisingly dexterous talons. She picked delicate blossoms from a flowering tree nearby, weaving the petals into the girl's dark braids.

"If she doesn't know her own name, then one of those idiots will name her. Harness her or drain her or bore her to death with their insufferable presentations. They are making it up as they go along."

"Last I checked," the dragon said mildly, "so are we." She uncurled her neck to its full extension and lifted her head to the sky. All those fine movements had given her a crick in her shoulder. "You don't know that anything bad will happen. Perhaps *she* will drain *them*. Did you think of that?"

The egg on the bed of moss gave a little shiver and a shake. The mother dragon scooped the egg in her other wing, and held both girl and egg close to her chest.

"Of course I thought of that," Zosimos snapped. "I think of everything." And it was true: he had no idea what would happen. That was just the trouble. How could he protect her from things that he didn't understand?

*I want to protect her*, the wizard noticed himself thinking. *More than anything in the world.*

Zosimos jumped. "Did you hear that?"

"I heard nothing," the dragon said, laying her neck around

the girl in a hoop, and offering her cheek as a large, warm surface for the child to lean upon.

"Someone knows," Zosimos muttered. "Someone's been following me. I can feel it."

"I felt nothing," the dragon said.

But the girl did. There was something in the forest—a dark, prowly something. Like a wolf. Or perhaps a tiger. The girl kept one hand on the dragon's neck and stretched the other toward Zosimos.

"I'll try harder," the girl whispered.

But it was no use. Other than the tree and the blossoms and the bees in her dream—other than the vague faces of the man and woman she assumed must be her parents—whoever she was and wherever she was from were nothing more than a formless darkness in her mind. And she could not penetrate it. She climbed out of the protective embrace of the dragon's wing and onto the ground. She held out her hand to the wizard and closed her eyes.

A tulip, large and lurid, grew from the center of her palm. She smiled at the old wizard. "You see? I'm learning."

"*Very good*, child!" the dragon enthused. "Very clever!"

"Am I supposed to be impressed with this?" the wizard fumed. "None of this matters."

"Don't you like my flower?" the girl asked.

"No," Zosimos said. "Do you have a name?"

"But I worked so hard on it," the girl said, pretending to be crestfallen, but Zosimos could see it was a sham. *Plucky little thing*, he thought, trying not to be pleased.

"The flower is irrelevant. The only thing that matters—" But Zosimos didn't finish his sentence.

The magicians emerged from the curtain of green. They looked at the girl. There was hunger in their faces.

✣

Bees, the girl thought. *Bees, bees, bees.* Though she didn't know why.

Her mind jumbled.

She had memories that she couldn't remember and knowledge that she didn't know. She'd had a name once. She'd had a house and a family and parents once. They slipped in and out of her knowing—a glint here, a corner there, and here an edge, but never all at once.

She had magic now, but her name was nowhere to be found. She'd never imagined she'd miss it.

Despite the girl's annoyance at the magician, she understood what he meant. There was a power in a name, in the possession of one's own name. Just as the word *bees* was powerful and the word *tree* was powerful, her name would be powerful, too. She could own herself outright.

The magicians picked their way through the forest. Only one moved with any kind of nimble grace—the rest stumbled as though they hadn't walked outside in years. The girl watched them come.

"There she is," said the magician with the metal leg extensions. "There in the flowers. Isn't she lovely?"

*Flowers*, the girl thought. And the flowers enlarged themselves. They lifted her from the ground. The dragon began to hiss, but the magicians didn't notice. Instead they smiled, raised their hands, and began to clap, delicately, at her. They were quite pleased. Well, most of them were.

"Well done!" said the man with spyglasses attached to his face.

"Marvelous!" said the woman with green skin and a third eye below her throat.

"You are ever so much more advanced than we would have thought," said the man with jewels in his mustache. "I am sorry that we frightened you before. You have so much to teach us. You don't even have to do a thing. I'm fairly certain our experiments won't hurt a bit. You are a very special child. Do you know that?"

The dragon couldn't stand another second of this. She lowered her head, extended her neck, and uncurled her wrath between the girl and the magicians.

"Away," she snarled. "All of you."

Dragons, of course, are mostly immune to magic, but they are not immune to rocks hurled by magic. The tall magician with the predatory walk stepped forward. The girl felt a great wave of sorrow crash over her. *I don't like that woman*, she thought. And the more sorrow she felt, the more the magician began to smile.

"Move along, all of you," Zosimos said. "The child is not for you, and she's not for your experiments, neither. You can stuff your scholarship in a sack and drown it in the river for all I care. The child belongs to herself."

"She'd have died if I hadn't saved her. She was drowning in a sea of sorrow," the tall woman said. "She already belongs to me."

"The day I take your words as anything resembling the truth, Lady Ignit, is the day I eat my cloak for supper."

Lady Ignit rolled back her shoulders. She smiled as boulders launched themselves into the air and hovered just overhead. Trees, too.

"Move back, dragon. You do not want us as enemies. There will be much sorrowing if you are dead."

The magicians edged away from Lady Ignit, alarm on their faces.

"Well," huffed the magician with the mustache "I say."

"This is a bit much, dear lady," said the man with the metal points on his hand.

"This is not what we agreed," said the woman with the third eye. "Dragons are rare. It is a sin to harm one." She turned to the old wizard. "Zosimos. Please. There is no need for any of this."

If the girl could have done so, she would have named herself already. But she couldn't. Just as she couldn't speak the names of things until the time was right. Just as all words were gone from her—until they *weren't*. She looked at the tall woman.

"Bees," she said. "Bees, bees, bees, *bees*."

And just like that, the woman was bees. Or bees were the woman. A woman-shaped swarm hovering in the midst of everything. Arms of bees touched a face of bees. A mouth of bees opened into a buzzy scream.

The magicians gasped.

"Take it back," they shouted at her. "Take it back."

"I don't know how," the girl cried.

She tumbled off her enlarged flower and fell hard on the ground, cutting her hands and knees. Panic burned her throat. "I don't know what to do," she said, clutching the wizard's long cloak the way she once had clutched her mother's skirts. "Give me a name," the girl pleaded. "If I have a name, I'll know what to do."

The old wizard tilted his head. He could leave Lady Ignit in this state. Of course he could. The bees remained in their woman-shape, a mask of terror pressed upon its face.

Zosimos closed his eyes.

*Bees,* the girl thought. *Bees, bees.* She couldn't stop. The flowers became bees. The stones became bees. The baubles in the mustache of Master Ulf. And then his entire mustache. And then his hands.

Zosimos had buried what was left of his family eons ago. Before any of these magicians were born. Before even Ennyn was born. Ever since he made his way to the castle, through wave after wave of scholars and mages and magicians and hangers-on, he had been separate. A codger among codgers. A grump among grumps. If he named her she would be—

He could hardly bear to think of the word.

Master Ulf screamed as his arms became bees. Then his shoulders, then his chest.

"Xanthippe," Zosimos said. "Your name is Xanthippe. But I shall call you Xan."

It was his sister's name.

His sister was troublesome, too. Belovedly troublesome. He hadn't thought of her for centuries. Now the memory of her nearly broke him in half.

"Xanthippe," he said again. "I claim you, child. I am responsible for you. You are as family to me as my first family was. Now. Try hard, dear. Your magic is beholden to you, not you to it. Tell it what you want it to do."

The girl was not entirely sure if she wanted the cranky old wizard as family, but she knew what he said was true. Her name was Xan. She felt it in her bones. Just as *bee* belonged to bees and *tree* belonged to trees, so *Xan* belonged utterly to her. The magic in her bones and her skin and her blood and hair and eyes all moved in the same rhythm. *Xan-thip-pe, Xan-thip-pe, Xan-thip-pe*. Like a heartbeat. She saw the bees. The bees that were the tall woman. The bees that were flowers. The bees that were stones. The bees that were the hands and the shoulders and the mustache of Master Ulf. And she knew what to do.

She raised one hand. And then the other.

There was magic all around her. And it harmonized with the magic in her bones. She felt herself draw it inward, with her own strange gravity. It was dizzying, this magic. Satisfying, too, taking that which was wrong and making it right.

The bees hummed, the old man sighed, and the woman who had been transformed howled in shock and relief and rage.

Though how much rage, the girl did not know. Not for a long time.

✿

Though Zosimos remained wary of his colleagues' motives, Xan was quick to forgive. She grew to trust Master Ulf and Magister Lynia and the Estimable Fitz, and seek their knowledge and research and company, though she never was able to warm to any one of them. And this was only partially her fault.

Xan could not forgive herself for what she had accidentally done to Lady Ignit. And Lady Ignit, for her part, could not forgive the girl for being the one to reverse the spell. The woman had saved the girl, so a favor had been owed. And then the girl saved the woman, fulfilling the debt. Xan now owed Lady Ignit nothing, and Lady Ignit couldn't forgive her for it.

"There," Zosimos had said at the time. "Now you're even." The woman spat in his face.

There are some people, Xan decided, who will never be your friend. And that was that.

✿

Sometimes at night, when Xan's dreams were particularly heartbreaking, she would wake up convinced that something waited outside her door. A hungry something.

"Sorrow is dangerous," she told herself. It was a thing she knew was true, though she couldn't say why.

One night she woke to a strange dream. She realized with no small amount of relief that there was no sorrow anywhere to be found in the dream—but it was unsettling all the same. And curious. There were birds. And poetry. And a dragon so small it fit in her pocket. And a creature in a swamp.

She was about to call out for Ennyn but thought better of it when she heard the dragon nearby, speaking in low tones to Zosimos. Xan pricked up her ears.

"Are you sure?" the dragon said.

"Quite." The wizard sighed. He sat down. His joints cracked and creaked as he bent. Had they always done that?

"How much time?"

"Unknown. This sort of thing isn't well covered in the literature. It was warned against for a reason. All this magic. And she'll have to learn how to use it on her own. I just hope I have enough time to teach her a little bit. I just hope she'll have the sense to listen. I just hope she'll be ready."

"And then she'll grow up," the dragon said, a great weight in her voice. "As they do. Is anyone ever ready for that?"

Xan waited and waited for Zosimos to answer. He didn't. He said nothing; the dragon said nothing. Xan pulled her knees to her chest, listening to the silence between wizard and dragon, silence as big as a mountain, or the ocean, or the sky. She laid her cheek on her knees as the wind pushed through the trees, swirling past the rumbling sky and the bright flashes in the clouds promising rain.